SAINT RICHARD PARKER

SAINT RICHARD PARKER

His search for love and enlightenment across India, Singapore, Thailand, Malaysia, and Indonesia

MERLIN FRANCO

First published in the United States in 2023 by Merlin Franco
Copyright © Merlin Franco 2023
All rights reserved.

This book is a work of fiction and, except in the case of historical fact, any resemblance to actual persons, living or dead, is purely coincidental.

Part I

For the Love of Cows

Chapter 1

"Latha, is the chairman here yet?" I breathe into the receiver.

"Hey, Parker, if I hear this question one more time, you are not meeting Mr. Sajeev. Grow up. Show some patience, pal," the chairman's personal secretary replies, brandishing her power.

"Sorry, sorry . . . just that . . . you know, this could be the biggest scoop for our newspaper. I promise we will beat—"

"The *Democracy TV* team, by tomorrow, right?" Latha interrupts. "I have heard this ten times today. Good luck with that. But remember, people wait for weeks to meet the chairman. You don't even have an official appointment with him."

Latha is right. Mr. Sajeev Chandrasekhar, our busy chairman, wears many hats. He is a politician, a businessman, a journalist, and a movie producer.

I apologize, put the receiver on its cradle, and blow warm air into my hands. Outside the glass panels of the *Indian Republic*, New Delhi's September is pumping heat and dust. Inside, it's freezing, as always.

It has been six months since Malaysia Airlines MH370 disappeared, four months since our supreme leader became the prime minister of India, and one month since my self-published nonfiction *For the Love of Cows* went on preorder. The year 2014 will soon be history, but its annals will see one more major event etched into it—the rise of Richard Parker, the greatest investigative journalist, businessman, and writer India has ever produced.

You are witnessing history in the making.

I look at the lower end of my computer monitor—11:00 a.m., it says. The window for getting my piece into tomorrow's daily edition is closing fast. I take an icy breath and order my thighs to stop shaking. It doesn't help.

I pull open the drawer and fish out the laminated newspaper clipping from 2006—my first column in the *Indian Republic* espousing cows in small-scale organic farms. This lucky piece has been my everyday anxiety buster, the piece that catapulted me onto the buddy list of our cow-loving nationalists. Since then, my column has appealed to the greener pastures of their hearts, where fat cows prowl, unlike their real-world counterparts peeling movie posters from dirty public walls.

My hands are itching to let go of the article and reach out to the intercom. I restrain them and pass my glance around the plywood walls of my cubicle, appreciating my milestone articles on cow dung and cow urine, attached with yellowing cellophane tape. At the left end hangs the yellow windcheater I bought in Manali. *I need to find prime space for my masterpiece roaring out tomorrow!*

"Heard you are meeting the chairman?" The nosy nose of Mr. Malhotra pops above the four-and-a-half-feet-high partition. I see five of his crooked fingers tapping on the divider. The other stunted arm in his short figure must be busy with the usual crotch scratching. Meet our editor in chief, the king of multitasking.

Mr. Malhotra wouldn't appreciate me going over his head. *So what?* My middle finger debates whether to flip or not to flip.

"Yes, sir, we are publishing the biggest scoop of this millennium tomorrow!" I watch the light in his eyes flicker and die. Wish I could kill it again.

"Do you want to run it by me once? My experience could be of help." He is shameless.

I give him my coldest stare. "Thanks, but I'm fine."

He drums his fingers for a while more, then disappears.

There goes my beloved boss, who tries to get my contract terminated at every annual board meeting. His case? I can't be a journalist at the *Indian Republic* and the CEO of Cow 'n' Roots, my traditional health-care company, at the same time. Conflict of interest, my foot! He earns his peanuts only because of my stories.

Mr. Malhotra very well knows that I'm here writing the series on cows at the invitation of the chairman himself. But that doesn't stop him from trying. To show my appreciation for his hard work and bald head, I finger-comb my curly hair every time I am in his office. And whenever he hits a slump, I also mail him vibrant renderings of web traffic to my articles.

I have written pieces about the gold content in cow pee and the antinuclear capacity of cow dung, all supported by cooked-up research published by my imaginary tax-free university in Andorra. You see, having an undergraduate degree in zoology and a postgraduate diploma in journalism has its perks. With every article that has seen the light, the popularity of the *Indian Republic* and the profits of Cow 'n' Roots have seen a corresponding rise.

You might question my methods. But hey, it's called *emotional intelligence*—writing that connects with readers and makes them feel good. Without my column on cows and its popularity among our nationalists, Mr. Sajeev would have shut down the *Indian Republic* the day his *Democracy TV* shot into the limelight. Malhotra's pedantic journalism is no match for *Newstime*, the high-pitched reality show of Pranab Gossain, the chairman's pet anchor.

My salary is peanuts, too, a nut less than Mr. Malhotra's. But I don't care because my major income is from Cow 'n' Roots. We sell cow urine "From Grass-Fed Country Cows"—at twice the price of milk. That is an unbeatable 300 percent profit margin. We also sell pure, sun-dried organic cow dung that emits oxygen while burning.

My editor, blessed be his soul, is killing himself next week when *Time* magazine arrives to interview me about the recipe for my success. *Time* wants to know how a South Indian who doesn't speak Hindi could make it big in the north. If Mr. Malhotra survives that, he is burning the week after when my book releases. It wouldn't stop there. His charred fossil would be annihilated in 2021, when I fly into space, like all saviors of the modern world.

Cow 'n' Roots is lean and mean, with everything outsourced, except the profit. We don't own cows and bottle nothing ourselves. We only connect the consumer with the products. Yes, I am a celebrity businessman from the southernmost tip of mainland India who mushroomed overnight on cow dung from the north.

But what is business without challenges?

Lately, we haven't been able to fulfill our orders, and the backlog has piled up. My journalistic instinct smelled something fishy, and I went undercover for a scoop. The stench of cow dung and methane numbed my senses. Yet the resultant report is sensational. Inside my file folder skulks the Medusa I unearthed—the vast nexus of politicians-turned-businessmen who purchase cows from distressed farmers for low prices and export their meat to the Middle East after obtaining Islamic halal certification.

The intercom rings. It's Latha. "The chairman has agreed to meet you, but three minutes, just three minutes, OK?"

I spring up. Fifteen seconds is all I need to get him hooked on my scoop.

I pick up my file folder, pull back the chair, and step out of my cubicle. Nine brainless heads sit stiffly in their chairs, staring at me. One of them, Mr. Malhotra's, will rise and follow me to the big boss's office for the shock of his life. *Burn!*

I knock thrice on the frosted glass door, then push it open when I hear the chairman say, "Come in."

Mr. Sajeev is focused on some file in his hand. A step behind him stands Latha. In this avatar, she is a symbol of total humility, unlike the one that spoke over the phone.

I wait in silence, ignoring my shadowing editor.

"Yes, Parker. Latha says you have something important to discuss. Something you haven't even discussed with your editor?" The chairman speaks with his eyes still locked on his file.

I swallow saliva, tuck in my tummy, and take a deep breath. "I have an explosive story, sir. With your permission, may I present it?"

"Explosive? Oh . . . Oh . . ." He places the file on the table and passes a glance at me and my editor. "Interesting. Let me hear what it is."

Sweat rains from my face and neck, despite the freezing air-conditioning. I steady myself and drain the train of words pent up in my head. "I have the company's name, sir. It's the Lahm Brothers. I have a list of some of the politician-cum-investors. I couldn't zero in on the kingpin. But if we get the story out there, we can flush him out, sir." I finish and wipe the sweat off my face with my handkerchief.

Mr. Sajeev strokes his beard, nods, and sweeps his glance in a semicircle from me to Malhotra to Latha.

"May I?" I stretch out the file in my hand.

He doesn't take it. Instead, he cups his hands behind his head and rocks his chair, eyes fixed on me.

Seconds tick past like hours. I await his lips to part and spill the magical words.

He drifts his eyes farther beyond me to Mr. Malhotra and asks, "Malhotraji, do we have any information about this kingpin?"

Mr. Malhotra chuckles, like he does before every annual board meeting, and replies, "Yes, sir, we do."

My jaw drops. So, this simpleton knows more than what we think he knows? I wait for him to spill the beans. But he stops talking, as if he has relayed the baton to the chairman.

"Malhotraji, looks like this has lived past its shelf life," Mr. Sajeev says, then gestures his fingers toward the door.

I rub my forehead. I can't say what that gesticulation meant. Did he just send Mr. Malhotra away, or did he ask him to fetch something? And *shelf life*?

The chairman picks up his file and continues where he left off. I look at Latha, wondering if she knows what's happening. But she lowers her gaze and avoids me.

We hear Mr. Malhotra's knocks on the door.

"Yes . . ." Mr. Sajeev lets him in.

Mr. Malhotra marches in, followed by two security guards twice his size. Sweat streams flood my armpits. I alternate my glances between the five faces.

The two security guards step forward and take position beside me in no time.

"I am the kingpin you are looking for, Parker." Mr. Sajeev returns his file to Latha. "I own the Lahm Brothers. I own everything here, including you. You got a problem with that?"

"What?" My file slips out of my grasp and spreads out like a wilted flower.

"Know where your salary comes from, Parker? Certainly not from the dying print journalism." He points his finger at me. "You are late to the party, too late. Everyone else in my company knows we export beef, man. Had you known that, you wouldn't be the stupid Richard Parker." He gesticulates toward the security guards.

Four heavy arms land on my shoulders and pull me down. In the next few seconds, my jeans-clad bottom is dragged on the tiled floor, the buckle of my heel strap screeching on the tiles. I see the false ceilings of the chairman's office and the common offices whoosh above, including the cobwebs that the lazy housekeeper forgot to clear. The scene pauses before the elevator. Digging my heels on the floor, I try to free myself from their clutches, but it only strengthens their grip on my aching arms.

Ding, ding.

The elevator door must have opened. I am lifted to my feet and dragged once again, this time into the elevator.

After a deep plunge and another dragging session, I am flung over the pavement.

New Delhi's warm September air strikes me. I plant my elbows on the dusty pavement and thrust my body upward to rise.

My yellow windcheater, the first of my belongings, comes flying through the air and lands on my face.

Chapter 2

The *Indian Republic*, September 25, 2014

New Delhi: A disgruntled employee went on a rampage at the *Indian Republic* yesterday after being fired for misappropriation of funds and indiscipline.

Eyewitnesses recollected that Richard Parker, a forty-two-year-old journalist, abused his boss and attacked nine of his colleagues with a machete after he was caught siphoning funds and indulging in cow abuse.

The chairman of the *Indian Republic* group, Sajeev Chandrasekhar, has granted a rupees one lakh ex gratia to each of the injured employees. The police have received multiple complaints and are investigating the matter.

Chapter 3

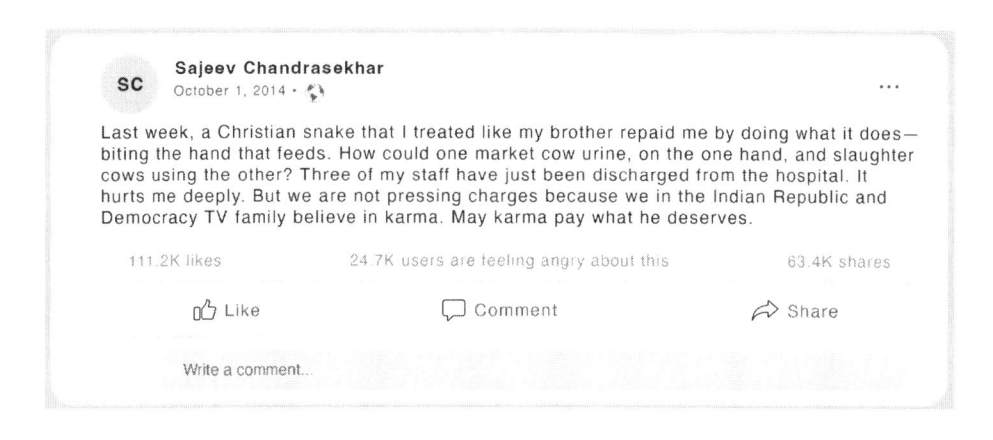

> **Sajeev Chandrasekhar**
> SC October 1, 2014 ·
>
> Last week, a Christian snake that I treated like my brother repaid me by doing what it does—biting the hand that feeds. How could one market cow urine, on the one hand, and slaughter cows using the other? Three of my staff have just been discharged from the hospital. It hurts me deeply. But we are not pressing charges because we in the Indian Republic and Democracy TV family believe in karma. May karma pay what he deserves.
>
> 111.2K likes 24.7K users are feeling angry about this 63.4K shares
>
> 👍 Like 💬 Comment ➤ Share
>
> Write a comment...

"Rice-bag convert! What else do you expect from descendants of traitors who accepted the white man's religion for a bag of rice?"

"I can't find tickets to India from Hawaii now. If not, I would have gone there and lynched him myself."

"Tulsi, give me his location, no? I can get him skinned alive in 24 hours."

"He has sisters or daughters? Somebody post their address and location, please."

"Presstitutes are worse than prostitutes. These fake journalists will even sell their mother."

"Why are you crying, Chairman sir? Who asked you to give the job to a Christian? If you employ a Christian, Muslim, or lower-caste Shudra, you will cry, cry, and cry only."

"Enough of this drama, bro. We all know the Brotherhood brokered peace between you both, in return for dissolving his company and donating all its wealth to Kendram, its nonprofit."

"Get out of this page, you secular pig. Go to Pakistan."

PART II

Richard Parker in Little Lotus Pond

Chapter 4

"Eleven dollars and forty-five cents?"

I read it again. And again. And again. That's all I have received in royalties so far. It has been more than a month since my book was published, but the sales chart has remained static, oblivious to the ticking clock.

I hit the sign-out button on the self-publishing portal and release a deep sigh. My dream of a writing career thus evaporates along with water vapor, germs, and air.

You know my story. Even the sand grains on the rocky seashores of Kanyakumari, also known as Cape Comorin, and the coconut fruits on the west coast of India know my story.

Let's recollect the facts you know so far: one, I'm currently jobless; two, I was once a successful businessman; three, coconuts are indeed fruits.

Mr. Sajeev destroyed my career. But it was his words that hurt me the most.

"Everyone else in my company knows we export beef, man. Had you known that, you wouldn't be the stupid Richard Parker." They ring like tinnitus in my ears.

I was lynched online by India's hi-tech troll army. They would have lynched me in real life, too, if I had not retreated to Kuttithamaraikulam, my native village.

Kuttithamaraikulam, or "Little Lotus Pond," lies hidden at the far end of the Western Ghats, shielded by a fold of hills from civilization and cancer-inducing cell phone signals. Little Lotus Pond gets its name from the many lotus ponds fed by muddy runoff from the hills. The only silver lining of being born in this dingy little village is that it offers me a haven right now. This place is a paradox: it's a backward shit heap with no cell phone signal and thus no WhatsApp. But we have broadband cables at home and jobless aunties on the main street who spread misinformation faster than radio waves. If you are about to puke, stop! This Podunk is not worth that retch. I shouldn't even be talking about it early in the morning. The place is like one big soggy pit that could rub off its bad luck the moment we utter its name.

I've lost six kilograms in the last month from all parts of my body except my handsome belly. Wrinkles have begun to appear below my eyes, and my curly hair, which could have turned gray in proper salt-and-pepper style, is graying in odd patches.

My wounded heart would have died the day I returned to Little Lotus Pond but for the healing touch of Pujya Sri Swami Gurushankar, or Guruji. His YouTube channel has shown me the path to regaining my honor—resurrection through moksha, the enlightenment.

But . . .

Doesn't matter how hard I try—that nanosecond when the doors of heaven open to liberate me from worldly desires and the cycles of misfortune to bestow wisdom and courage continues to elude me. Mark my words, it is just a matter of time before it happens, and I will rise as Richard Parker, the wise. Until then, I must grab all opportunities before me for enlightenment, including my meditative baths in the pond.

I shut down the computer, pick up my toiletries, and trudge to the pond.

Here I am, ready for my morning dip in the biggest of all the ponds, fondly called the mother pond by locals who haven't seen a proper swimming pool with clear blue water. It has become a routine for me to log on to the self-publishing site every morning to check my royalties and then proceed to the pond to let it gracefully swallow my grief alongside the buffaloes on the other ghat. I have nothing to do during the day other than masticating the bland food prepared by Susheela—the helper—and counting the number of times the bald crow caws from my jackfruit tree. Dips in the pond are always before sunrise for three reasons: one, the water is warmer than the air above; two, there is little chance of me being spotted by another lowly human from the village; three, I don't have to worry if the towel remains wrapped around my waist every time I surface. These morning dips aren't mere baths, either. They are routines of deep meditation I have developed through lived experience—my way of cutting off the dirty world above and connecting to the goddess of the waters.

I pinch my nose and take another dip in the dark waters, breathing out bubbles and listening to them bursting over the surface. The brief spell of silence between the bursting of the last bubble and my appearance at the surface, gasping for breath, is precious. I crave this heavenly feeling, for I know that one day, one of these moments might bring me to enlightenment.

The last bubble for the day bursts overhead, and I prepare to savor the serenity and soak up the light, as usual.

A strange voice rends the silence. I hear it calling from beyond the realm of the water world. "Paaark . . . ," the voice repeats, and my inner ears pick it up clearly. Of course, I'm sure it's my name; the "er" in *Parker* is silent at times, as the primary school bullies taught me. I surface, presenting my torso to the world above, leaving my naked privates to the water world below, as my towel has slipped to my ankles.

Two black buffaloes peer at me from the bund. *"Maaaaaaa,"* one of them bellows, and the other follows as if it's a symphony. They don't sound like *parker*, *paaaarker*, or *paaark*. It's clear my name is being called from elsewhere. I look up to see if the heavens have opened their morning gates. But there's nothing except the first signs of the sun god beginning his routine.

"Maaaa," the buffaloes bellow again.

Stupid beasts! I shrug my shoulders and spit water in their direction. They stand unfazed.

I turn around and face eastward for sun salutations.

"Helloo . . ."

I hear the voice again; this time, it's clearer. Could it be the water goddess? I scan the pond all the way to the other ghat but see nothing.

"Um . . ."

I still can't pinpoint where it's coming from. I turn around to look at the buffaloes again. There is no way they could have spoken.

"Excuse me . . ."

The voice rings once more. My eyes drift to the ground beyond the buffaloes, and I spot the silhouette of a wiry figure. In the *Who's Who* of Little Lotus Pond, there is only one possible match for this lowlife—Isakki.

Don't waste precious time wondering why I failed to spot her in the first instance; not even the gods themselves could spot the creature they sculpted out of the darkest night. If you eavesdrop in the marketplace or on the public bus, you will hear frustrated young men referring to this musteline life-form as "the witch in jeans." "Bitch in jeans" is the name I've given her. They fear her; I loathe her.

"My buffaloes want to bathe." She breaks the silence, training her wicked eyes on my torso. I'm sure she can't see my precious nakedness hidden in the water, but her bold stare and the sheer tenor of her voice rub Styrofoam on my underbelly. I wouldn't be Parker if I failed to return the favor by rubbing some chilies on her perky bosom.

"The cattle ghat is on the other side," I say, grabbing the opportunity to be the first guy to outsmart her.

"I see. Why are you on this side, then?" she asks with a straight face.

Stay calm, Richard Parker, I tell myself. I can't let my newly found inner peace be disturbed by the evilest of hearts. I kneel in the water, search for my towel, find it, and wrap it around my waist. Believe me, I do all this while she and her two buffaloes stand there, watching without a hint of shame.

I climb the slippery steps carefully, pick my clothes up from underneath the coconut tree, and start walking. Behind me, the water splashes thrice. The devil in me wants to turn back and see if she is half-naked in the water, but my hyperintelligent brain flashes back to restrain me. *No, Parker, no,* it says as I remember the man who once made that mistake. I hold my head straight and walk away, thanking Christ for not leading me into temptation and delivering me from evil.

You may think that I made an unfortunate decision. Make no mistake. Crazy Lucas, who was packed off to the asylum in Kerala, used to be a brilliant guy. Things changed when he learned about Isakki's naked bathing sessions behind her home on full-moon nights. The drunken balladeers of Little Lotus Pond had warned about the curse, but Lucas ignored it. Lucas dared to sneak onto the white pegmatite hillock behind her home and gleefully watched her naked body shining under the moonlight. The permanent glee on his face now serves as a lesson for every man in the village. Isakki might bathe naked on other nights, too, but you couldn't tell her apart from the dark night. It's beyond me to comprehend why someone would risk everything to see that inglorious sight. Pay me a billion rupees, and I still wouldn't do that. Not even in my sleep.

A familiar confusion creeps in as I walk through the banana farm. Was it Christ who saved me or one of the 330 million Hindu gods? I abandoned Christ the night I saw Father Cornelius sneaking out of the house of Shanta, the widow. It was an unforgivable crime for three reasons: one, it's forbidden for a celibate priest; two, she is the prettiest lady in the entire village; three, she never looked into my eyes, even once. Eventually, I discovered various other reasons, including child abuse, to justify my hatred for the Church and God. But Guruji brought my faith back, and I've now learned to live in harmony with all the gods. In my heart, I thank Guruji one more time for bringing me back to faith, fortified with blessings from all the gods.

I return home, toss my clothes in the bucket for Susheela to wash, and swig the watery milk tea she has left in the flask. When I'm done, I dump the glass in the sink and tune into Guruji's YouTube channel for my prebreakfast dose of wisdom.

Today's sermon is about "staying detached," says a red ticker running at the bottom of the frame. "Stay detached," Guruji exhorts in his charismatic style. I can simply sit and look into his mesmerizing eyes, even if his mouth doesn't utter a single word. His eyes ooze truckloads of energy—such is the power of rigorous meditation. I wish my eyes could be as powerful as his. *Will I be able to seduce Shanta then?* I quell the old thought and remind myself that I should renounce worldly desires and use the power of meditation only for constructive purposes.

Guruji's sermon repeatedly warns of the consequences of using energy for unconstructive purposes. "If all Indians meditate, focusing their energy on evil Pakistan, we could reduce the country to ashes in a second," he says, while also reminding us that if we use it for selfish goals, the same energy will burn one's alimentary canal from the mouth to the rectum. I wouldn't want that. Memories of accidentally tasting the bird's eye chili chutney Susheela made for her family still linger in my muscles. Don't ask me what muscles these are. All you need to know is that I consider this newfound energy precious, and I'm keen on concentrating on it in a responsible way.

"Saint Nicholas of Flüe left his wife and became a hermit to attain enlightenment," Guruji continues. I like the secular nature of his teachings. He doesn't hate any religion and borrows good thoughts from all of them. "His abstinence made him powerful enough to prevent a bloody civil war. Buddha, our beloved teacher, left his wife, renouncing all the worldly pleasures and royalty, and that's how he remains in our hearts even today. Even our own supreme leader, the prime minister, sacrificed his conjugal relationship with his wife and deserted her overnight to serve this great nation." Guruji goes on to explain the importance of abstinence and celibacy to liberate oneself and achieve our goal. Tears roll from his eyes, and he chokes on his words repeatedly. His ex-wife, now the chief nun of his ashram, brings him a glass of lemon water energized under the morning sun.

The day's video penetrates my rib cage, touches my heart, and leaves instructions for enlightenment. Three things become clearer to me: one, I must give up all my wealth, especially what I have earned by selling cow urine; two, sexual desires are unholy distractions that prevent us from conserving energy; three, I cannot attain moksha, the enlightenment, without renouncing my wife. The last point is crucial, as it guarantees my passage into sainthood.

Saint Richard Parker. I like the ring of that!

I sit on the floor facing east, legs folded into *padmasana*—the tried-and-tested lotus pose—and meditate on Guruji's sermon, ruminating on the three takeaway points for today. That's when I remember I'm still a bachelor and have no wife to renounce.

Chapter 5

I gnaw the lump of dough that Susheela has undercooked, wondering how her darling husband, Thankamoni, and their litter survive on her food. In his YouTube channel, the president of the Hindu Brotherhood, the secret society that runs the Indian government from the shadows, is reiterating the ethos of Indian culture.

My admiration for the Brotherhood has only grown since the day they brokered the truce between me and the chairman, in return for dissolving my company and donating all its wealth to the New Delhi branch of Kendram, their flagship nonprofit.

"*Vasudeva kutumbakam*," he says, stroking his walrus mustache. "This must be the bond that unites all Indians. We may eat differently, dress differently, and even worship different gods, but we are one family united under the umbrella of Hinduism. Thus, any person who is born in India is a Hindu."

I nod in agreement. The influence of Hinduism is all over the church and our lives beyond its stone walls: We wear saris and dhotis to church, light traditional lamps, apply sandalwood paste on our foreheads, and choose auspicious days to schedule important events. Our girls sport the round dots resembling Hollywood laser-sight spots on their foreheads, and every Christian in the south celebrates Diwali with the same fervor as any Hindu.

I turn down the volume and meditate on the sermon. My mind questions the fucked-up life I lived until I found Hindu spirituality and realized the importance of renunciation and suffering. It's an entirely new world, like the beautiful rosy dawn at the tip of Kanyakumari, if you ignore the wild crowd. I pray to the gods to help me find the path to enlightenment.

A few cycles of breathing later, a strange light ignites my brain. I realize three points: one, I don't have to leave my wife to be a bachelor because I'm already a bachelor; two, inside the Western attire and baptized forehead, I'm a Hindu; three, as a bachelor, I should seek guidance from a bachelor god.

The image of South India's bachelor god, Ayyappa, appears in my vision. My inner eyes see the Dravidian god seated over the dreaded tigress of Sabarimala, deep inside the thick forests of the Western Ghats. He drops his mighty bow and stretches out his arm, inviting me to make the arduous trek in the wilderness. Moses, Jesus, Muhammad—they all found enlightenment in the wilderness. *How did I miss that?*

I kneel and stretch my hands like coconut fronds, exuding tears of joy. When the tears stop, I bow and kiss Bhoomadevi, the earth goddess, as a sense of safety cocoons me. It's time to take my body to the lotus feet of Lord Ayyappa, for my soul has already reached the banks of the holy river Pampa.

I dash out, leaving the doors of my home open for the first time. I run along the footpath lined by barbed wire and halt before the palmyra palm. There, I pause for five seconds, letting my overworked lungs take in some air, then turn to the right, forking downhill into the farmland. A band of gamblers shuffles their cards in the coconut grove, as usual, oblivious to the turning point in the destiny of Little Lotus Pond. I ignore them and run into the banana farm, where banana stems rot after sacrificing their lives. The slippery path traversing the fallowing paddy field conspires to slow me down. But I beat it hands down and arrive sweating and panting at the doorstep of Gurusaamy.

Nobody knows the actual name of Little Lotus Pond's spiritual mentor. All we know is that Gurusaamy quit teaching in the Maldives and headed home when Lord Ayyappa's calling came. Since then, he has led the annual pilgrimage to Sabarimala as the head guru, better known as the Gurusaamy.

"Gurusaaaaamieeeee," I call before the open doors of his house. As with most houses in the village, an unlocked door doesn't guarantee a human inside. But something in me senses he is here.

"Yes, my son?" He startles me from behind.

I turn around to look at the wise elder caressing his silky gray beard. I'm pretty sure he wasn't there three seconds ago.

"I'm taking you this time," he says, presenting that serene smile below his powerful eyes. My heart craves to kneel and cry aloud. My legs weaken, and my knees tremble; the earth goddess pulls me toward her. I tumble down on his doorstep made of reclaimed bricks.

"How . . . how do you know?" I stammer, fighting hard to rein in my tears.

He bends and touches my forehead. "I know nothing, my son. But he knows everything." He points west in the direction of Sabarimala. The child in me bursts into tears while Gurusaamy sits next to me, patting my back, helping me vent my heart's pain.

As the wise men say, the key to happiness is to have a heart as pure as a child's—a heart that sees the world as a child sees, a heart that smiles and cries like a child. For such a heart will also sleep like a child. I cry until I fall asleep happily under the watchful eyes of the 330 million gods plus Christ.

Preparing for the Sabarimala pilgrimage is no easy feat. One must first undertake the prerequisite fifty-one-day fast, abstaining from meat and worldly pleasures. The program looks tailor-made for me, as if Lord Ayyappa is trying to help me tame my mind.

Fasting begins in the month of *vrischikam*, according to the Malayalam calendar, and *karthikai*, according to the Tamil calendar. Everywhere else, the period has been trimmed to forty-one days. But in Gurusaamy's books, there's no room for compromises. If you get the urge to box him into a rigid square, you might as well stop now. Outside of this fifty-one-day window, Gurusaamy is the most liberal soul you will find in Little Lotus Pond. You will see him in the church and in the *nizhal thangal*—the shanty where some of the ignorant people of Little Lotus Pond worship a mirror. When Kadher Bhai was alive, you would even see Gurusaamy at Sufi prayers. Well, to be fair, you will find the entire village at Sunday Mass, and on Fridays, you will find the same heads swaying before Gurusaamy's temple. That's one of the many stinking traits of the lowlifes of Little Lotus Pond: they flock toward music and food. But Gurusaamy is different from the crowd. He isn't here for the food but for his love for the people. And that's why I revere him.

The fasting period falls in mid-November of the Gregorian calendar. Eight of us have enrolled for this year's pilgrimage. We grow beards, shed our earthly names and assume the title of *saamy*, bathe before dawn, wear only black or blue dhotis, eat vegetarian food, and apply sandalwood paste on our bodies. Walking barefoot to the tiny temple behind Gurusaamy's rammed-earth house for morning prayers amps up our spiritual experience. We thus spend our mornings renewing our vows to end thoughts of violence and cleanse our hearts of lust.

I work hard to avoid those recurring dreams where gorgeous virgins belly dance in shiny costumes. They have been my entertainment avenue, with the widow Shanta making the occasional cameo. To be honest, those dreams weren't always pleasant, as Isakki often slithered in, waking me up sweating and fighting for breath.

Guruswamy leads the daily prayers. He hardly speaks, but every word he utters packs power. I ask him how to get rid of the virgin maidens from my head. I don't tell him about Shanta.

"Don't fight your thoughts. Accept and follow them," he says.

It seems absurd, as embracing them means violating the spirit of abstinence. But it makes sense, as the maidens eventually fade into the background beyond green meadows, just like in Bollywood movies. I soon forget how an early-morning erection felt. No, it's not because of the early-morning dip in the pond. Do not suspect vegetarian food, either, because vegetarians and vegans do reproduce, and it would be gross to assume that their contempt for humans and love for animals comes from a lack of libido. There can only be one reason—meditation.

Money becomes as precious as dirt, too. When Thankamoni, Susheela's husband and my lessee, comes to renew the lease of the banana farm, I shake hands with him without the usual haggling. "Give me whatever you can when you harvest," I say, watching his eyes widen like the Indian Ocean. Two years ago, when the hurricane destroyed his banana crop, I extracted every penny scribbled in the lease. Now, if the profit from my land is his, so are the losses.

Many consider it trendy to do a crash-fasting course of just seven or nine days. You can tell them apart when Lord Ayyappa sends them tumbling down the temple stairs. Yes, there's no shortcut to his blessings. The other *saamis* are in awe of my passion and devotion. Gurusaamy doesn't utter a word, though I am sure he notices it.

The Tamil month of *markazhi* arrives, and it is time for *azhi puja*—the last ritual at Gurusaamy's temple before we commence our pilgrimage. After the morning bath, I wrap my lower half in the customary black dhoti. I offer greetings to my deceased parents and ancestors, ask God to show me a sign, and step out of my home. A southern birdwing flaps its beautiful yellow wings and dances above my doorstep before flying westward. The butterfly is native to South India, just like Lord Ayyappa. I look skyward and thank Lord Ayyappa for the sign.

Oh, Lord Ayyappa
Ayyappa, oh, Lord

I chant, letting my bare feet relish the sandy footpath wet from last night's rain. This means I will soon need to balance myself on the wet clay path leading downhill after the palmyra palm. A palmyra and a cloggy narrow path are all that remain between me and my quest. But my autonomous legs brake before the palmyra palm, and I find myself staring at two pairs of eyes stuck to the heads of Isakki's buffaloes. I look around for their mistress. She isn't to be seen, but I can hear her Enfield Bullet thundering from afar. I can see that the sorceress on the motorcycle has sent her beasts alone to cast a bad omen.

"Oh, Lord Ayyappa!" I chant. I can't retreat, as that would bring bad luck. I can't cross the buffaloes, either, for their bloodshot eyes remain glued on me. The beasts jiggle their heads in unison and chime their ominous bells. I sense the battle cry. A drop of impure water seeps into my boxers, and I tighten my sphincters to stall the flood.

"*Saamy sharanam. Ayyappa sharanam.*" I surrender myself to Lord Ayyappa and pull closer to the palmyra tree that's as dark as the buffaloes that are as dark as their mistress. Breathing slowly, I hold my position until they stroll past me. I look up to thank Lord Ayyappa.

"Ritchie..."

A coarse voice breaks my thanksgiving prayer. I open my eyes and look at the man in the red dhoti before me. Ask me another day, and thou shall hear a hundred adjectives describing him. For each bad memory he has gifted me, I have entered an adjective.

Oh, Lord, why are you testing me? I ask Lord Ayyappa in my heart.

"Ritchie . . ." he calls again.

I haven't heard anybody addressing me by my birth name in the entire fifty-one days.

"Saamy . . ." I correct him.

"I'm sorry." He plasters a fake smile on his lips and pulls it to one side, pretending to apologize. "Where are you going?"

Even a mongrel in this filthy village would know it's inappropriate to pose such a question to someone who has set out on a voyage. The right way is to ask, "Traveling far?"

"Sabarimala. Today is the *azhi puja*," I mutter. He surprises me by nodding and stepping aside to let me pass.

I walk a few steps downhill and look back. He has disappeared.

Murugan was named after our Tamil god. But he knows no gods, no empathy, no humanity. He is the mastermind behind the labor unrest that shut down the brick kilns. The poor laborers, I heard, are desperately hunting for new jobs. He has always been a shady character. In my preteen days, I used to take eggs to an old chap at the cool-drink kiosk. The old man was an underappreciated artist who made ducks, swans, and kittens out of eggshells. I was happily growing my collection of figures until Murugan, a teenager back then, caught me returning with a tortoise figure. I remember every frame of that scene.

"Are you that stupid, Ritchie?" he asked with his hands on his barrel hips, like any normal bully. "Can't you see he sucks out the raw egg for free on the pretext of making you these ugly figures?"

Murugan didn't know three things: one, he ended the dollops of happiness those eggshell figures gave me; two, he destroyed a hobby that could have entered my name in the *Limca Book of Records*; three, I paid the artist five rupees for each eggshell figure he made me.

Chapter 6

Only six of us arrive at Gurusaamy's temple for the *azhi puja*, as the other two had ejaculated out of fasting. Their temptations were stiffer than their quest for spirituality.

"Five more will join us, including a foreigner," Gurusaamy says after offering prayers. That will make us twelve, including Gurusaamy but excluding the van driver.

We balance the offertory cloth pouch with the two ghee-laden coconuts on our heads and convoy behind Gurusaamy to the meeting spot under the banyan tree. The driver is busy smearing adulterated sandalwood paste over the van while the torn speakers inside do their bit to enhance the holy atmosphere:

Oh, Lord Ayyappa
We surrender to thee . . .

My mind fast-forwards and plays the next song in the playlist:

Stones and thorns
They caress our feet
Oh, Lord Ayyappa,
Ayyappa, our Lord . . .

"Don't forget to bring *laddoo* for your brother-in-law," the wife of a *saamy* opens her doughnut-shaped mouth and yells from across the road, reminding him to bring the famous sweet ball prasad. Oh boy, her sound waves will have reached Sabarimala by now.

"Papa, I want three *laddoos*," shrieks a larva with a liter of coconut oil on his scalp, screwing his finger into his slimy nose. The curd rice I had for breakfast churns inside my belly, and I struggle not to puke.

I divert my attention to the shops on the main street and the *nizhal thangal*—the temple for followers of Ayya Vaikundar—that's partly visible. On the temple veranda, you can usually see Gurusaamy and the *panividaiyalar*, the chief servant—another bearded guy with saffron headgear who officiates silly rituals before a mirror. They would engage in animated discussions with Murugan, pretending to solve the world's problems while struggling to tame their gray beards. The group has two more members, the parish priest and Isakki, whom you won't see there. Together, they complete the bunch of contraries—a Catholic priest, a Gurusaamy, a Communist, a *panividaiyalar*, and a witch. While the other four are notorious, Gurusaamy stands out like a calm rock that wouldn't budge a millimeter in integrity. Someday, I will ask Gurusaamy how he sees himself in the group.

Strange are the ways of the world. I sigh.

We board the van one by one as the crowd cheers. I offload the offertory pouch and place it on the luggage rack. Gurusaamy tells me that the foreigner *saamy* is a veteran. My mind replays the stories of foreigners who embraced Hinduism. Search for Hinduism on YouTube, and you will see white sahibs and madams sing "Hare Rama, Hare Krishna." In my mind, I hatch a plan to take a leaf or two out of his book.

Oh, Lord Ayyappa . . .
Ayyappa, oh, Lord . . .

Gurusaamy leads the prayers, and we follow as the driver starts the engine.

The journey to Sabarimala is complex: one, the road is winding and loopy; two, we stop before several temples on the way to seek blessings; three, the final holy stop before reaching Lord Ayyappa will be the Dargah of Vavar Saamy—the Muslim saint who shares a special bond with Lord Ayyappa. That's how religion works in India: we all are Indians beneath the skin, as the president of the Hindu

Brotherhood says. I take a deep breath of the Indian air inside the van, enriched with sandalwood and ghee. I try to take another deep breath and realize I can't until I've exhaled the previous breath.

We drive past Kendram, the Brotherhood's flagship nonprofit, which has now inherited my company's wealth, and make our first holy stop before Goddess Bhagawathi at the tri-sea junction of Kanyakumari. The sea is rough, so we are forced to forego the boat ride to the Swami Vivekananda memorial built on the sea to commemorate the Hindu monk from eastern India. A group of *saamis* waves to us from the parking lot. I count five of them, but no signs of the sahib *saamy*. Gurusaamy lists their names as we alight, balancing the coconut pouches on our heads. Since it's our first meeting, he introduces them by their earthly names with the *saamy* suffix: Gopal Saamy, Ganesh Saamy, Ramesh Saamy, Thirumal Saamy, and Aroonan Saamy. We greet each other with a one-armed hug because our other arms are busy balancing the offertory pouches on our heads. We all look the same and smell the same—of ghee.

"Aroonan Saamy is from Kuala Lumpur," Gurusaamy says.

I look at the *saamy*. He is no white sahib, but the sandalwood pattern on his forehead and the faded blue Ayyappa bag hanging from his shoulders proclaim his veteran status. Gurusaamy reads aloud the earthly names of the Indian *saamis*. I wait to hear my embarrassing name "Richard Parker Saamy." Instead, I hear Gurusaamy call aloud, "RP Saamy." I bow my head. I don't ask Gurusaamy why he abbreviated my name, for I know there's a reason behind his every action. Besides, "RP Saamy" sounds good.

I turn toward the foreigner *saamy*, hoping to hear his story. What follows is a plethora of inquisitive queries from him and a long narrative from me. I spin my otherwise dull life into a spiritual odyssey. Evil forces such as Shanta, Isakki, Murugan, and the chief servant priest are duly excluded.

"But Saamy, it's rare to see Christian *saamis* these days. Most Christians don't even touch the prasad we bring them from the Lord's temple," Thirumal Saamy exclaims. I wonder what the big deal is about accepting a prasad as my salivary glands reminisce about all the *laddoos* they had moistened.

"My Ayyappa receives everybody. He has only one religion, and that's humanity," Gurusaamy responds on my behalf. I like the way he does that without blaming people for the stupidity of evangelical Christianity.

Our first holy stop is fruitful as we behold the goddess and her nose stud. The legend is that the light from her nose stud has safely brought home many lost seafarers in ancient times. You must see the nose stud at least once to believe in it. Beautiful, powerful, and serene, it shines on her divine face.

When we resume, I move my bottom to the seat beside the foreigner *saamy* and switch roles. He introduces himself as Aroonan A/p Kisnan, meaning Aroonan, son of Kisnan. Aroonan Saamy winds out his exciting story as our van cruises toward Thiruvananthapuram, the capital of Kerala state. A truck carrying Kerala's biomedical waste for dumping in Kanyakumari's wetlands crosses in front of us, and the fake sandalwood paste fails to neutralize the odor.

Aroonan's father had wanted to name him Arunan, but Malaysia's sons of the soil dominating the bureaucracy had other plans. They stretched it to *Aroonan*, the same way they contorted *Krishnan*—the romantic name his grandfather chose for his father. Kisnan lived and died with that name, just as Aroonan would. My heart aches for his father, though I think a Communist born to another Communist deserves it. Kisnan's father survived by inciting the plantation workers—a legacy that young Kisnan continued after his father's mysterious death. Fortunately, by the time Aroonan was born, communism was uprooted from Malaysian soil, and Aroonan qualified for Malaysian citizenship, albeit with 80 percent fewer rights than the sons of the soil.

Aroonan was thankful for the opportunities Malaysia provided him. He couldn't forget them even if he wanted to, as politicians reminded him how generous the country was toward aliens like him. Meanwhile, his grateful heart had also traced his roots to Tanjavur in central Tamil Nadu.

Life was routine for Aroonan until Lord Ayyappa's call arrived in the form of a *laddoo* through his neighbor. It was perfect timing for three reasons: one, at eighteen, Aroonan was already slipping into hooliganism like his Tamil peers, risking execution; two, black country chickens in his neighborhood began disappearing, only to surface headless in male vitality-enhancing rituals; three, had the *laddoo* found him a day later, the mold inside would have turned it velvety black. He has been visiting Sabarimala regularly since then.

Soon after his first pilgrimage to the celibate god, Aroonan found love and married young at twenty-one. Things weren't rosy as he struggled to provide for his family. He wouldn't have found money to travel to Sabarimala, either, but for the blessings of Lord Ayyappa. Every week, Aroonan spent at least a quarter of his earnings on Malaysia's famous lotto that dangled prosperity before the alien citizens. His luck with the raffle followed the regular pattern—he won it only toward the end of September, just in time to book tickets to India. He knew it was Lord Ayyappa's way of reaching out to him.

Aroonan inspires the dormant buds in my heart. Indeed, nothing can stop you from visiting Sabarimala when the calling comes.

I lean back, close my eyes, and reflect on my spiritual journey. Mine wasn't as tedious as his, but the pattern is obvious: my calling also came at a challenging point in my life. I touch the rosary made of *rudraksha* beads hanging around my neck since the first day of the fast and thank the bachelor god for finding me.

One and a half hours after crossing the Tamil Nadu–Kerala border, our van enters the chaotic parking lot of the Lord Padmanabhaswamy temple for our second holy stop. Khaki-clad policemen push us through security screening to ensure that our offertory coconuts contain ghee, not nitroglycerine. I, otherwise annoyed by long queues, am super patient today.

"Identity card, please," the guard asks.

I hand over my driving license.

"Richard Parker," he reads aloud.

I look around, embarrassed. My fellow *saamis* are as cool as the ghee in their offertory coconuts, but three onlookers close to the guard appear amused. Gurusaamy doesn't bat an eyelid. I know the bystanders will soon approach me to inquire about my journey. My heart jumps in glee. I prepare to narrate my story for the umpteenth time.

"Are you a Christian?" the stoutest of the onlookers asks, tightening his lower garment, a faded orange lungi.

"Yes, Saamy, kind of," I respond, tracing the grooves of my rosary.

He exchanges looks with the two not-so-stout guys flanking him, and before my brain can figure out what's happening, I find myself on the ground. In my vertical frame of vision, I see the two coconuts rolling out of my offertory pouch, spilling dashes of yellow ghee. The queue scatters as devotees run in all directions.

"Can't you rice-bag converts leave our temples alone? Why the fuck do you want to pollute them?" asks the stout guy before lunging at me.

Luckily, a guard bounces his enormous belly and restrains him. Gurusaamy steps forward and lifts me up. I balance myself and adjust the dhoti on my waist while Gurusaamy wipes the mud off my face. The guard is now busy on a mission of pacification. The stout guy pumps his fist and spits out some cuss words while his accomplice shouts into his cell phone. Gurusaamy places himself between the guard and me.

"Never raise your hand against the Lord's son," Gurusaamy tells the stout guy.

"Saamy, if you don't shut your mouth, you will fall next. And there's no guarantee you will get up again!" he sneers, stretching his neck like an ostrich to present his face.

The guy behind him waves his phone and screams in ecstasy, "Lenin, they have given the green signal. You go ahead—I shall live stream it on Facebook."

The stout guy pushes the guard aside, cocks his head like Jean-Claude Van Damme, and inches toward me. Gurusaamy tries to stop him but gets pushed aside.

My mind regains clarity and takes stock. Lenin! That name makes it clear. Every Indian knows how Kerala's Communists colonized the governing committees of temples and churches. They haven't even spared the hospitals. I recollect our supreme leader's sermons about his battle to retrieve temples from the "red bugs." Hologram versions of Murugan and Isakki's buffaloes appear swiftly before me. The omens were right. This has been foretold.

I must do something before he attacks again. But he springs forward and grasps my collar, the rosary pressing against my neck.

The queue is now back in order, and coconut-laden heads pop out to debate whether it's divine justice or just another lynching episode.

Three more guards arrive and join the other guard in pleading with Lenin to let me go. I hold still, anxious that the slightest movement will tighten the noose around my neck. Lenin loosens his grip and steps back—or rather, is pulled back. Another commotion arises, and I see three men in khaki shorts and white shirts running toward us. I recognize their uniform—brothers from the Brotherhood. *Anybody born in India is a Hindu.* The golden words of the Brotherhood ring in my ears. My mind assures me that the Brotherhood will appreciate me. The only question now is if I can resume the pilgrimage. Perhaps there will be a rectification ritual, and I can adorn the offertory coconuts again. Luckily, the rosary still hangs intact around my neck.

Lenin approaches the three men, grasps their hands, and leads them away. The guy filming with the cell phone points it alternatively at Lenin and me as if he's some illicit son of Roger Deakins. The brothers are all pumped up, ready to beat Lenin, just as he deserves. Gurusaamy touches my bare back in reassurance.

But things take an awkward twist. The three men turn toward me instead, led by Lenin.

"Do you see the board there?" Lenin points.

I swivel my head in the direction of his hand and spot the blue board stuck to a pillar: No entry for non-Hindus.

I swallow the two drops of liquid under my tongue and stammer. "I am—I am an Indian. We all are Hindus, and . . ."

The sentence stays incomplete as I am pinned to the ground again. Kicks and punches land on my back as the voices of Gurusaamy and the guards drown in the chaos.

"Rice-bag convert!"

"Beat him to a pulp!"

"Kill the bugger!"

"Long live Mother India . . ."

A bare foot brushes my ear.

My mind repeats the last phrase while my mouth picks up some dust. *Long live Mother India*—that's the classic slogan of the Brotherhood and not the Communists. It strikes me that the brothers from the Brotherhood aren't my brothers anymore.

I'm still on the floor, but a miracle happens; the kicks don't land on me anymore. I tilt my head and look at the tent-shaped gap between me and the warring humans above. The stout guy's lower garment has disappeared, and he is in his old boxers, his arms reaching for the guard's crotch. A pair of legs under khaki shorts land empty kicks in the air. Two arms wring the neck of a body that threatens to fall over me at any moment.

"*Aiyoh*, my balls!"

"My neck . . . my neck!"

"I can't breathe!"

Muffled voices rain over me. I fix my hands on the ground, assume a semi-*bhujangasana*—the half-cobra pose—and survey the dusty ground through the space between Lenin's legs. Gurusaamy's face appears. *Come out,* he mouths and helps me crawl out of the melee. Above me, the tussle continues.

"Run, son, run!" Gurusaamy coughs and pushes me toward the entrance.

"But, Gurusaamy, the coconuts." I point at the coconuts on the ground.

"Save your head now. We can think about them next year. Run, now!"

He's right. I lift my left leg to grab the tip of my dhoti and fold it at my knees. When I have tightened it at my waist, I retreat a few steps and turn around to break the queue and take flight. "Run, Saamy, run!" I hear somebody cheering from the line.

I run along the autorickshaws parked by the roadside. Two arms stretch out from the last autorickshaw and grab me by my dhoti. "Why are you running, Saamy?"

"They . . . they are . . ." I pant as my eyes zoom in on the words above his windshield. *Lal Salaam*, it says—the red salute!

I look at him, speculating whether he is a friend or foe. But my mind warns me this is not the time for thoughts.

I shove that commie back into his three-wheeled coop and resume my run.

Chapter 7

Sunbeams streak through the coconut trees, hauling me out of my slough of despondence. Soon, Gurusaamy arrives with the blessings of Lord Ayyappa packaged in sweet *laddoos*. He is out of the pilgrimage mode—the black dhoti has changed to the lungi, and the shirt is back on his torso. He is not officially a head guru until the next pilgrimage season. But for Little Lotus Pond, he will always be the Gurusaamy.

"You will come with me next time," he reiterates with his arm on my back. I nod as the prasad releases molecules of ghee, sugar, and happiness on my tongue. He watches me relish the *laddoos*, and when I'm done, he opens the topic like a dad talking to his son.

"Have you ever thought of finding a life partner, Ritchie?"

"Life partner?" I divert my senses from the *laddoo* in my mouth to his face. "I used to, Saamy. But I am now focusing on taming my mind and renouncing worldly pleasures. The fasting period helped me there. But . . . but the pilgrimage was a setback."

He strokes my back and smiles. "Not everyone should renounce conjugal life to achieve moksha, Ritchie. What worked for me might not work for you. As I've mentioned before, I feel your search would be fruitful if you could embrace your desires rather than fighting them."

I rub my forehead.

"I leave you with one keyword, Ritchie. *Tantra*! You might want to read about it. There's a reason why feminine energy exists in this world." Gurusaamy hugs me and leaves.

I don't know how it happens. Call it the will of gods. Gurusaamy has always been there for me, like he can sense my mood from his home. I list *tantra* for future reading. Don't ask me when this *future* will arrive. Attaining moksha without relinquishing worldly desires sounds like unlearning everything I have learned until now. I decide to take it slow.

I turn on YouTube. "Spirituality is a journey," says Guruji. "Those who back off will never reach the destination." He lists the meditation courses his ashrams run.

The spiritual warrior in me awakens, shrugs off the battle wounds, and marches to Guruji's ashram in Thiruvananthapuram the very next day for a half-day basic course in mindfulness.

We sit in circles; sing devotional songs; sway our heads; and dance to ecstatic music. A damsel in a yellow frock floats around, as if she were sent by Gurusaamy to teach my first lesson, and I work hard to stay focused.

"Congratulations, dear knights in spirituality, you are chosen for the next-level course. Your devotion has reached the ears of Guruji on his way to New York in his private jet," says the instructor at noon before ending the session.

I pick up the pamphlet flaunting the picture of a white sahib in a lotus pose, or *padmashana*, with the mighty Himalayas in the backdrop. *Twelve days of intense spiritual awakening in Rishikesh,* it reads.

A caterpillar pupates in my heart, readying itself to spread its wings above the fresh flowers of the Himalayan spring.

I turn to the last page. *Pay only $4,999 US dollars, and liberate your soul.*

To faint or not to faint: a Shakespearean dilemma beckons me. I lean against the lime-washed wall and close my eyes.

"Namaste *ji*." A honey-laden voice rescues me. I open my eyes and look at the lady in yellow. I pinch my arm to assure myself that she's indeed talking to me. *Never knew my lesson in unlearning renunciation would arrive this fast!*

"Namaste," I reply.

"I am Chandini." She sets free the butterfly in her eyes.

"RP Saamy, from Kanyakumari." I introduce myself by my pseudonym and extend my hand. She doesn't take it. Instead, she bows with folded hands. I pull back my arm.

"Kanyakumari! Lucky you to be from the land of Swami Vivekananda, the greatest Hindu monk of the nineteenth century!" she exclaims like a child with a clap of her hands. I struggle to keep my eyes fixed on her face as Kamadev, the god of lust, lures them downward. She explains how much she loved Vivekananda and how his teachings influenced her life. I learn three things: one, pencil-slim waists are strong enough to support big endowments; two, you never know when luck will find you; three, the Christian-majority Kanyakumari in South India is now the land of a Hindu monk from eastern India, simply because the Hindu Brotherhood built a monument for him in the district. I occupy my mind with point one. The shrewd journalist in me pulls out his lens and spots the visual cues: the batting eyelids, how she peers into my eyes, the way she pulls her shawl across her bosom. But this is only a hypothesis until I confirm it.

"You always come here?"

"Rarely, as I'm busy with social work."

"Ah, social work! How cool. I'm a social worker, too." I pick up her lead and bake an instant nonprofit. "My organization has been working for the street children of Kanyakumari since 2000," I tell her.

"Oh . . . kids . . . ," she mutters, and I spot the light draining from her eyes.

What went wrong with my fictional nonprofit? Would planting trees have been a better choice? Old-age home, perhaps?

"There are so many organizations to care for humans. It's the animals, Saamy . . . the poor animals!" she says.

I notice the light returning to her eyes. "Oh yes, the wildlife . . . damn! We are losing them fast . . . climate, deforestation, fragmentation of forests, human greed. Oh man, what a relevant theme!" I applaud.

"Oh no, Saamy. You've got me wrong again. There are so many working for the tigers. It's the stray dogs and cows. Who cares for them?"

My enthusiasm tanks, but my hormones don't. For a moment, images of stray dogs mobbing Isakki as she feeds them in her backyard come to my mind. My mind draws a quick comparison between the two—one an angel, the other a witch.

"Of course, the dogs . . . the stray dogs! They protect female joggers and prevent plague by exterminating city rats; they are even vegetarian." I regain form and blurt out the scientific facts I stole from India's leading ecologist, Meneka Gandhi, who has a master's degree in German language.

"Oh my God! I've found you!"

She puts her hands together and jumps again. "What clarity of thought. You know what? I have been looking for a man like you all my life. Thank God!"

She then closes her eyes, tilts her head upward for a moment, and utters those precious words: "Together, we can work wonders!"

I pinch myself again. Here is a goddess knocking at the doors of my forty-two-year-old heart. She's still jumping for joy while my eyes follow everything bouncing along. What dogs? I'm willing to tend dinosaurs for her.

She halts her bout of happiness, steps closer, and unleashes the laser in her eyes to torment me.

"Can I hug you?" she asks.

I pinch myself for the third time. *Is this the same lady who refused to shake hands with me moments ago?*

"Please . . ." I stretch out my arms.

Chapter 8

First hugs and first kisses are special. *My first hug has arrived, and soon will my first kiss, too,* I tell my mind, which is partying on cloud nine. The spiritual quest has subsided; the constant fight against carnal pleasures has bid adieu. Yet, my mind brimmeth with joy. I now appreciate the true meaning of Gurusaamy's words—the warmth and comfort of feminine energy and its capacity to make us achieve the impossible.

Chandini means "moonlight" in Hindi. I admire her parents, who found such a befitting name for her bright, round face. Over the humongous mountains does the moon rise!

Chandini's rented one-bedroom apartment is in a posh locality close to the beach. She invites me to stay with her, and I readily settle on her couch. We can see the beach from our windows—she from her bedroom window and me from the living room. We share the kitchen and the food, and one day, we will share the bedroom, too.

Chandini soon becomes the synonym for my happiness. The more I please her, the more she smiles. The more she smiles, the happier I am. I work harder to keep the cycle alive at all costs, even when it involves doling out a thousand lies a day, most of them devoted to covering up or providing continuity to the previous ones. My couch comes with its perks, such as the opportunity to see her in a bikini in the pool below. She, of course, knows that I'll be watching, so she makes a point of waving at me often.

We jaywalk through erratic traffic, laugh in the middle of the road, ignore the traffic signals, wet our feet in the blue waters caressing the golden sands of Kovalam, pose for photographs at the tourist village, and haggle with the hawkers of Chalai market over fresh tomatoes. She does the talking and I do the watching, especially when she bends down to haggle. When she slips on the stairs to the apartment, I leap forward to catch the flower God has plucked for me.

"Sorry," she says, excusing herself from my arms.

"No worries," I mumble, hoping history repeats itself.

The fear of being lynched evaporates gradually, partly because of my confidence in the beard I've grown as a disguise and partly because of the courage she infuses. I'm happy to die today as long as I get to kiss her before my end.

"You know the specialty of this apartment?" she asks one evening while flattening chapatis.

"No," I reply. I would have said the same even if I had known the answer.

"It is free from the anti-nationals. Can't imagine how hard it would have been for my friends to find an apartment free of Communist rats." She wipes the sweat off her forehead with the back of her hand.

My hands itch to reach out and dab her sweat.

"This place is a bit more expensive than I thought, but it keeps those cheap bastards away. Simple psychology." She winks. "They prefer the shanties and the slums. Made for each other!"

She laughs. I join in.

"Your friends did a good job," I say.

"Oh, but it isn't all rosy." She sighs, shaking her head. "You remember that sick lady on the fifth floor? They are Communists—the only Communist family in this building."

I remember the frail lady who keeps her door perpetually open. I don't like her prying gaze, either. But we must both endure it, as Chandini is determined to take the stairs, and I must follow her, lugging my belly.

We pass our time this way in each other's company. It has been just a month since my failed pilgrimage. I am lucky to be alive. It's like the gods had other beautiful plans for me. Now I know Chandini is their plan. Chandini has graced my life with so much happiness that I hardly recall the temple brawl these days.

There has been a timely power cut. Chandini and I are before the living room window, watching the moon in her full glory. *Is the moon goddess reaching out to her twin?* I admire both the moons—one within my reach and one beyond.

"I have a dream," she says, still looking at the moon. "Thiruvananthapuram is a soulless city, Saamy. This is not how cities should be. This place is dead. I want to breathe life into it."

She compares it with her hometown, where streets brim with life: the cows that roam the roads and expressways with equable gait, the street dogs that howl happily in the middle of the night; they were all part of her village life.

"In Thiruvananthapuram, you only see people. Goddamn people, people, everywhere on the streets. It's disgusting. This city needs a strong animal component."

When she turns toward me, I spot the light in her eyes.

"Saamy . . ."

"Yes?"

She takes my hand and cradles it. "Will you stand with me?"

Why wouldn't I? This is what I've been waiting for. I would sit, stand, and roll with her anytime.

"I'm here, always, for you. Anything you do, you can count on me," I say, suppressing the glee in my eyes.

"Thanks. Thanks, thanks," she says gracefully and steps closer. A glowing ball of energy lights me up as her rosy lips rub over mine and part ways. My heart is moonstruck, and my legs are spellbound; her roasted-wheat-flavored breath is inside my nostrils. My heart beats faster, craving for more, and I reach out.

"No. This is enough for today, my dear *kallu*."

Kallu! That's a new entrant in my lexicon. I know not its meaning, but it sounds so musical.

Kallu . . . Kallu . . . Richard Parker Kallu—it sounds heavenly. Oh wait, she only knows my pseudonym. RP Saamy Kallu it is!

"Sleep tight, and be a good boy, Saamy," she says, running her finger from my forehead, over my nose, down to my lips. "Wonderful moments are yet to come," she says and retreats into her room.

Sleep turns elusive. That taste of her silky soft lips and warm breath . . . they were mine just for a microsecond, but I still feel them on my lips.

We visit celebrities on Chandini's list. Coincidentally, they all are linked to the Brotherhood in one way or another. I stay low profile so that nobody asks for my name or where I came from. Luckily, the aura of Chandini is so entrancing that even the celibate brothers from the Brotherhood are oblivious to me standing behind her. Our idea—or rather, her idea—is to set up a series of *goshalas*, or cow shelters, and dog shelters in the city, all manned by people from the Brotherhood. We will set up a proxy nonprofit to conceal the Brotherhood's link to it. I learn how the Brotherhood works. They run eight hundred nonprofits, including the Kendram, with varying objectives. One speaks about secular India rooted in the secular stream of Hindu philosophy, whereas another preaches the need to exterminate all non-Hindus. One speaks about the need to practice Islam and Christianity as per the Indian ethos, whereas another chants about the importance of being an Aryan Hindu. It's too much for me to handle, and I rub my forehead repeatedly in search of clarity.

Chandini is a doer, a lady with a powerful will to do anything her mind dictates. In a way, she reminds me of Isakki—but an adorable version of her.

The cow shelters are the first to be set up. We manage to rescue cows brought in across the border from Tamil Nadu for slaughtering. Incidentally, negotiating their release wasn't difficult, as the cattle smuggler himself is a Brotherhood sympathizer. We just had to pay. I mean, she had to pay the demanded sum, and bingo, the cows were free. Chandini selects a vacant land close to Kovalam Beach, and we erect two thatched-roof shelters. The next day, the Brotherhood loans us three young volunteers to tend the cows. It is smoother than we expected.

The first thing she does after returning to the apartment is to remove the shawl from her *churidar*—the North Indian pajamas and fling it over the pedestal fan. Hands stretched out, she swirls in the living room, letting her endowments recite sonnets.

"Saamy..." She stops and flicks her finger. It's her love language—the sign she deploys to summon me when she's in a good mood. The grocery bags slip down from my arms, and I dash toward her.

She wraps her arms around me and rubs her nose against mine. Her warm breath flows over my mustache, caressing every cell on the way, while my chest revels in the softness of her bosom.

"You are my lucky charm, Saamy. My *kallu*. It's all possible only because of you."

The warmth of her breath intensifies.

Kiss me . . . kiss me . . . My heart screams from the parched desert.

She flicks her hair, letting the silky brown aphrodisiac glide over my face, and winks. "I'm taking you to heaven, Saamy. Just a few more days, a few more dreams to accomplish."

She buries her face in my neck and kisses me there.

Parker, don't let the moment slip, my mind says. I cradle her face in my hands and lift it.

"No, not now." She wriggles out like a veteran eel.

"Your time will come." She winks, picks up her shawl from the floor, and runs to her room.

I sink into the couch, sweating profusely, trying to figure out what happened. I hear the door being latched firmly.

Could I have kissed her if I had tried harder? Maybe I should have hugged her and unhooked her bra? My thoughts keep me awake like nails under my back. Her gentle snore rises like a song behind the latched door and vibrates every particle of the night. I would choose it anytime over a Beethoven symphony.

Chandini pulls all her strings, and we go around meeting people, selling heartwarming stories of compassion. Funds flow freely, and we draw up plans for more cow shelters. In the evenings, she teases me a little further. It's her way of celebrating milestones. I long for nights that never end.

It is one fine evening, two hours past sunset. We are preparing to visit the cow shelters after a busy day. I am yet to see her regular teasing, a change of routine. *Maybe she will get excited and kiss me at the cow shelter!*

"Saamy." She bursts out of her bedroom with tearful eyes, biting the back of her hand.

"Yes, Chandini?" I hold out my arms.

She stops short and hands over her phone instead. "Your people . . . your people . . ." She sobs.

The three young volunteers deputed by the Brotherhood had sold the cows overnight to some beef vendor, and the cow shelters have vanished without a trace, along with my dreams. Drops of tears gather beneath my eyes.

She maintains silence for one whole day. That's how she recharges her battery. The next day, she emerges even more determined—but with a change in plans.

"We are shelving the plans for cow shelters now. Let's focus on stray dogs first."

That makes sense for three reasons: one, every setback reduces my chances of winning her; two, stray dogs are aplenty in Kerala; three, Keralites do not eat dogs.

Finding volunteers for dog shelters turns out to be a piece of cake.

"Tell me, what motivates you to join us?" she asks the first lady. I like the emphasis on the "join us" part. We are together in this, now and forever.

"There is so much animal cruelty. This isn't India. Everybody in my university eats one animal or another. This is disgusting, and I need to do something," the lady replies with clenched fists and a red face. I wipe the sweat off my forehead.

"This is the spirit we are looking for," Chandini tells the young lady.

She lays out the rules and dog-care tasks, which include vaccinations, regular washes, grooming, and feeding vegetarian food. Vegetarian food is essential because dogs are genetically vegetarians, and it's a Christian conspiracy to turn them nonvegetarian. Besides, she has read a research article in the *Indian Cow and Happiness Journal* that proves dogs fed on yogurt run faster, have a higher IQ, and do not mate, despite retaining their balls.

I sit there admiring her in action. Her facial expressions are impressive, exuding confidence, power, and charm in the proper proportions. Occasionally, my glance slips down when she leans forward to scribble something on the notepad. But it's not the same stealthy look I used before. This time, I look at her with confidence. She loves my attention, too. I know this from the way she pulls her shawl across her bosom to hook my eyes.

A lady is not a pet to own. Neither is she to be treated like a trophy. But love is amazing; the sense of belongingness at the borderline of ownership it brings—that's a fantastic feeling. I have waited forty-two years for this angel, and it was worth every second! She is a delight to hold, a delight to talk to, a delight to spend time with, and a delight to watch. And she's mine!

"What do you say, Saamy?" Chandini finishes interviewing and asks, catching my smile. I like the tone of her voice. It's like a faithful Indian woman asking for her husband's opinion.

"Let's go ahead. She's the kind of start we need. Exactly the person we were thinking of," I tell Chandini, emphasizing the last part of the sentence. That should give the young lady an impression of my relationship with Chandini and preempt any possibility of falling in love with me. I want to signal to her I'm taken.

More people get grilled by Chandini. In the end, we finalize a gender-balanced team of three young girls and three boys—all born into vegetarian families. That's great because their chances of turning into dog-eaters are rare.

Two dog shelters replace our cow shelters. Thatched roof, netted sides, plenty of water from the well of a brother's farm. The rescuers, whom Chandini pays on a per-dog basis, bring in thirty dogs. But we had to return five of them when their owners turned up at the shelter, ready to beat us up. Apparently, the rescuers stole them from families. Chandini is disappointed, but her spirit remains as strong as before. I look at the remaining dogs. Some are skinny, but some look super healthy. We can't rule out the chances of more dog owners turning up with cricket bats. That's a danger because cricket bats always swing toward balls. I decide to stay away from the dog shelter for a few days until things settle.

My hopes of seeing Chandini excited in the evenings come crashing down. I hope she will invite me to her room every time she pops up at her door, but she's asking for either the accounts ledger or the list of people to approach for donations, and so on.

Things do not get better as three healthy white dogs go missing from the shelter. Chandini thus learns about the mafia kidnapping photogenic dogs. These gangs rent out dogs to wannabe brides cuddling dogs in well-lit studios. Such photographs are a strategic way of impressing prospective grooms of Indian origin from the DWSA—also known as the Dog Worshipping States of America.

Thus, brushing and grooming the dogs disappear from the to-do list for the volunteers. The decision to put up a large signboard saying CHANDINI'S DOGGIES also gets shelved.

Gloom rules over my love life until hope arrives in the form of Payal, Chandini's bestie. Their fathers were besties, and so were their mothers, I learn. Even the lower-caste women from Gujarat serving their families are besties. In addition, their families have a long-standing relationship with the Brotherhood, traceable back to when Veer Savarkar, a Brotherhood guru, apologized to the British, offering his unconditional loyalty to Her Majesty's government. That was such a proud moment for India's nationalistic Brotherhood and Payal's grandparents.

Payal announces that she's in Kerala for a mission. "I'm a feminist with an Indian ethos, and I'm here to break the patriarchy in a manner that conforms to our great Indian culture," she says with a fist in the air.

Her organization is at the forefront of offering arms training to Indian spinsters, educating upper-caste Indian women on body language—how to tell from a guy's demeanor if he is a lower-caste Shudra, Muslim, or Christian and how not to fall in love with them and so on. She is a fan of girl power. Once, a lady asked for her help because her husband was always quarreling at home. Payal spoke to them and discovered that it was the lady who was causing trouble by responding to her husband's taunts. After eighteen hours of counseling, the couple regained their marital happiness. She doesn't respond to her husband's insults anymore, and all her arrogance causing trouble in the family is gone. The last thing Payal heard from them is that the lady has given up her teaching job, as she had realized it's more important to bring up kids than earn money. Payal is a true feminist, just not the Western type.

So, what brings Payal to Kerala?

I am worried she might smoke the Richard Parker out of RP Saamy.

"I realized the patriarchy denies women opportunities to visit Sabarimala," she says.

Payal believes women can also enter the temple and venerate the celibate god. The Brotherhood is ready to help her in all forms, from providing legal support to illegal security guards who look, talk, and walk like thugs, terrifying my fragile heart.

I don't know Payal. The thought of the Brotherhood plus Payal churns the vegetarian lunch in my belly. Chandini is in the equation, too, but my heart assures me that my angel means only good and will not mirror Payal.

But Chandini leaps in joy, kicking over my pail of hope.

"You know, Saamy? We have been planning for this occasion for such a long time." She holds my arms and hops around in circles. We dropped Payal off at the airport and are now back at the apartment.

"Do you know Payal wanted to stay with us overnight?"

"No, did she?"

"Yes, I discouraged her, and she understands." Chandini winks while continuing to hop, her head swaying in the air.

Why would she turn her closest friend away? I don't understand.

"You still don't understand?" She pulls herself toward me. "Oh, my *kallu, mere pyare kallu*, today is our day. It's going to be just you and me." She rubs her pointed nose against mine and enacts her favorite tormenting routine. My mind tells me I shouldn't let this moment slip again. I wrap my hands beneath hers and pull her close.

"Oh no . . . not now, my *kallu*." She puts her finger on my lips and pushes my face away. "It's not an auspicious time." She points to the wall clock.

Three in the afternoon.

It makes no sense to me. In fact, nothing makes sense anymore. All I want is her. I leap forward.

"No." She backs off and runs to her room. But before shutting the door, she stops and turns back. "Tonight, it's just me, my *kallu*, and the crescent moon."

I'm back on the couch, quivering and feverish. A headache is creaking in my head while the pinnacle of my emotions stands erect.

We shower together. Well, she in her bathroom and me in the guest one. I tap on the wall and yell, imagining her perfect body under the shower.

"Chandini, want some help?"

"No thanks, boy. You can't handle the heat. Trust me."

That makes sense because I—my mind and body—have gone out of control.

When the sun dips into the Arabian Sea, she drives us to the temple.

"I'm opting for a silent conversation with God," I lie and crawl into an alley to avoid another temple incident.

"We will have a light dinner tonight. No onion," she says, placing a sandalwood mark on my forehead when she finds me waiting for her outside later.

"I'm fine even if we don't have dinner." I beam in joy.

On the way back, she stops at the men's hair salon.

"Why here?"

"Your beard, your hair. We're getting *kallu* groomed."

A truck full of acid overturns in my stomach. I play around with words to convince her not to. She doesn't budge, and I surrender as all men do.

The hairstylist stares at my denuded face. "You look so familiar, sir. I have seen you on TV."

"No way," Chandini interrupts. "RP Saamy doesn't appear on television. He is just a village boy."

I roll my eyes.

"My handsome village boy." She touches my shaved cheek when we return to her car.

"Thanks." I take her forearm and kiss it. Two pink flowers bloom on her cheeks. I congratulate myself for accomplishing level one.

She drives around the city instead of driving straight to the apartment, often looking at her watch. I know what she is checking for—the auspicious time.

"I want you in the moonlight, Saamy." She bites her blushing lips.

"Me too . . ." I say, touching her hand that's on the gear stick.

"The union of male and female under the moonlight releases tons of energy. All my previous partners loved it. They say my naked body looks gorgeous under the moonlight, especially the faint light of the auspicious crescent moon," she says and points her middle finger at the motorcycle guy who almost lost his life to her wheels.

Partners? Oh, she isn't a virgin, after all?

"How about you? Do you like it in the moonlight?"

"Oh yes, yes, it's amazing. You will shine like an angel," I blurt. I don't tell her I'm a virgin.

We take the elevator and dash into the apartment.

"I'm yours." She hugs me from behind. We forget to turn on the light. A dreamy light, not that of the moon but from the light pollution, sets up the stage for our union. The crescent moon is too faint. But who cares?

I draw her toward me and hug her.

She takes my arm, leads me to her room, and pulls the curtains to let the light in.

"Come." She lies on the bed strewn with rose petals. My eyes go wide, wondering how she sneaked the roses in.

"I like it this way," she says with a petal on her lips.

I pull off my T-shirt and throw myself over her like a starving bull.

"Gently . . . gently, *kallu*. I'm yours." She guides my face toward hers. "It's such a beautiful moment, Saamy," she whispers beneath my ear.

"We should have done this a long time ago. If only the cow smugglers hadn't ruined it!" I murmur, aiming for her lips.

"Wait . . ." She puts her hand on my advancing face and stops me. "I have a question."

"Yes, please . . ."

"Do you eat beef?"

"Beef . . . well . . . er . . . not anymore."

She pushes me aside and sits on the edge of the bed. Her face reddens, and her lips tremble. "You . . . you mean you ate it before?"

"Well, yes, before I turned spiritual." My temperature drops.

"Yuck! Payal warned me about that. I should have been more careful." She clenches her jaw, springs up, and points to the door. "You should go."

"Go?" I stand up. "Hey, babe, I don't eat beef anymore. I'm willing to do anything for us. Trust me, please."

"There is no us!" She switches on the light, picks up my T-shirt, and throws it at me. "You need to get out of my house. Now!"

"Chandini . . ."

"What part of the 'get out' don't you understand, you fucking *kallu*?" she screams. "Get out of my fucking house, now. If not, I'll call the cops and book you for attempted rape."

"No, please don't." I pull the T-shirt over my head and walk out of her room.

"Here . . ." My bag slides over the floor and hits me from behind. I unzip it and stuff my clothes in.

"Don't show me your fucking face again. You don't want to see the other side of Chandini."

I hear her door slamming.

Chapter 9

Fate stomps me back to Little Lotus Pond. I recollect the fond memories, the dreams, the hopes, and the goose bumps Chandini gave me. Like a hot-air balloon, I flew high in the sky with my fly full of hope until she punctured it. My sore heart hankers for her bosom until I search online for the meaning of *kallu*.

Kallu: A derogatory term equivalent to the N-word, used to refer to people of dark complexion.

Origin: Hindi

I have three reasons to end my longing for her: one, *kallu* doesn't mean "honey," "sandwich," or "apple of my eye," as I had imagined; two, she could have inherited genes for color blindness; three, my fly is back to its dejected self.

But my life can't end like this. Hindu spirituality, with its paradoxical dogmas of renunciation and embracing desires, hasn't helped me so far. Maybe it's time for the prodigal son to return to his roots in Christ. And I respond to the old Belgian church bell that sounds inviting after two long decades.

It's déjà vu at the church; only the tin roof has rusted, letting light beams seep through. The stone walls are still strong, like they would outlast Christianity itself. Father Cornelius's sermon is bland, though, with no spiritual content. The padre calls for leading a simple life in honor of Christ, who was born in a manger. The lad next to me, whom I have never seen before, whispers in my ear that the priest is alluding to the people's demand for a majestic cathedral. Simon, the contractor, has been at the forefront of the campaign. I take an instant stand, favoring Simon for three reasons: one, Simon is a pious Christian who returned to serve the village after his construction company in Chennai went bust; two, unlike Father Cornelius, he did not have an illicit affair with the widow Shanta; three, at last, Little Lotus Pond will have something to be proud of.

The council secretary wipes the sheen off his bald head with a torn kerchief and announces a seven-day spiritual retreat at Saint Thomas Ashram in Ernakulam. My mind flies to the coconut-lined shores of an imaginary lake, sensing three opportunities: one, a chance to strengthen my relationship with Christ; two, an opportunity to forget Chandini forever; three, a venue to meet some cool Keralite girls.

People pass strange looks at me as I exit the church. Even the old guy who fixes bicycles is curious about my church visit. "Nothing special," I scoff and hurry, offering nobody a chance to repeat the question.

I dial the ashram in Ernakulam soon after reaching home and reserve a slot at the dorm for Monday, February 23.

I arrive at the ashram on Sunday evening itself, after a seven-hour commute by bus and train.

It's a spiritual retreat with a difference. The discourse centers on Communion and self-preparation to receive the body and blood of Christ.

"My child," Father Sebastian calls out to the faithful from his teakwood podium. "Your heart is the farm where the body of Christ will be sown. It will grow into a tree from which birds fly, disseminating new seeds for Christ. But we should have our hearts cleansed first to receive Christ."

The reverend narrates the stories of bad luck and agony that befell those who received Christ without repenting their sins. My excitement for receiving Christ dies because I am yet to take Confirmation.

So, what am I to do without Christ in my body?

Well, I can at least admire his creations. I turn to the right half of the auditorium, reserved for women. They forbid even married couples to stay or sit together for the retreat period. There's no way I can tell from the female faces whether they are married. So, I focus on the Mass again. Hours later, my mind flashes the sign that a pure heart is enough to accept Communion.

The sermons are an ordeal. The priests want us to suffer at least a nanoliter of Christ's pain on the cross. The auditorium is a large shed with iron pillars and tin-roof sheets. If you ignore the few thousand people sitting in perfect silence, it's just an oven in a shed's guise. I regret my graduation from the tiny tin shed in Little Lotus Pond to a bigger one.

George Varghese, the soul next to me, turns out to be a friendly one, however. He inquires if I'm an SC.

"Partly, yes," I say to make him happy. The truth is that most people in Little Lotus Pond don't know their caste. I could be a scheduled caste—SC, a Shudra of the lower strata—or maybe from a privileged caste. I will never know because my parents never wrote it down on my caste certificate. Honestly, I didn't expect to make instant friends for being a scheduled caste person. A marginalized identity isn't something one would be proud of. But Keralites are progressive souls.

"Brother Richard Parker, may I ask if you are married?"

"No, unfortunately. Time to find a girl is a luxury in my tight work schedule," I brag.

"Would you like to meet my sister?" he asks with zero hesitation.

The heavens open before me.

I knew it! It was a message from God. If not, why would I be in church after two decades, and why would the announcement for this spiritual retreat come? It must be God's will!

"Yes, of course!" I say, concealing my emotions.

"Lunchtime, I will introduce her," he whispers, activating the countdown in my head.

After lunch, we walk to one of the smaller tin sheds where the womenfolk lodge. He texts his wife to bring his sister along. That's how Annamma glided into my life. If you put her next to Chandini, you would mistake them for twins, except that Annamma has a pointed chin that makes her face a perfect heart shape. It's love at first sight for both of us.

George and his wife bloom with happiness; they'd joined the retreat to pray for a partner for their thirty-five-year-old goddess. George encourages us to exchange numbers, though I tell him that once I return to Little Lotus Pond, they can only reach me on my landline.

For the next three days, we steal precious time to meet between the sessions or talk over the phone in hushed tones under smelly blankets. We shift our seats closer to the aisle. We are now nearer, separated only by a narrow walkway and some archaic norms.

Sarah, George's wife, receives an intimation that her father is unwell. And they leave the retreat midway on Thursday.

"The Lord has answered our prayers," says George before leaving.

I agree.

At ten o'clock in the evening, after the postdinner sermon, Annamma and I decide to meet in the alley behind the audio shed.

The path between the audio shed and the boundary wall is narrow. Annamma has no trouble walking through it. I scrape my belly on the wall a few times, though. When she is close, she runs straight into my arms.

"I can't believe this." Her words mix with my heartbeat.

"Me either."

"There aren't many SCs in Tamil Nadu, right? You are a rarity, a specialty made for me." She presses her face farther into my chest.

"We have many SC people in Tamil Nadu, but you wouldn't know. That's how the world works; the marginalized are invisible." I sigh, patting her back. I'm sure that passage straight out of my journalism course impressed her.

"Marginalized?" Her grip loosens, and she looks up. "Aren't you partly Syrian Catholic?"

"Oh no, there's little chance for—"

"Oh God, what have I done?" Annamma's sobs rise. Before I can convince her, the bald head of the audio operator appears between us. The sound of her sobbing is too strong to be confined to the narrow space.

He escorts us to a junior priest, who must have bathed in coconut oil instead of water. Annamma doesn't want to see me anymore, for I had conspired to adulterate her lineage. I explain why she should reconsider her decision: one, though we have known each other for a short period, we have a lot in common; two, it was God's decision that we should meet in his house; three, I'm willing to convert to Syrian Catholicism. But after scratching his armpit with the tip of his pen for the tenth time, the priest presses it against the corner of his mouth and rules that it isn't in Annamma's interests. One, there are tons of cultural incompatibilities between a part-scheduled caste SC and a Syrian Catholic

SC; two, I have sinned by accepting Communion without the sacrament of Confirmation; three, a person can become a Syrian Catholic only by birth.

And the priest's word is the law.

Annamma leaves on Friday morning. My bruised heart stops me from dialing her number. But Christ reaches out to me through the morning sermon on forgiveness. The priest drives us through high-pitched singing and catharsis. I almost faint, but fortunately, I don't. I forgive Annamma in my heart and congratulate myself for that. Father Sebastian makes us recollect every face that has hurt us in the past and teaches us the art of forgiving by giving them imaginary hugs. I send hugs to Annamma, the junior priest who counseled us, Chandini, Murugan, and Isakki.

I wake up on the faux-leather dorm bed on Saturday with a single thought. *If I can forgive Chandini, why can't she forgive me?* I should meet her and explain my newfound love for vegetarian food. Indeed, the gold-hearted lady will accept me.

Sunday is to be spent fasting until the evening, when the confirmed shall receive the final Communion of the retreat. I take the bus in the afternoon, skipping the last session. But I ensure my fellowship is intact by reciting Hail Mary and maintaining the fast.

My watch reads 7:00 p.m. when the red Kerala Transport Corporation bus, with the two-elephant symbol stuck to its belly, drops me at the Thiruvananthapuram bus station.

Another forty minutes tick by, and I'm at the apartment, enveloped in darkness except for a few battery-powered lights.

The elevator is asleep, and the impact of the whole day of fasting shows up as tremors in my knees. Lugging my bag, I make my way up the stairs, using my cell phone torch to light the way. I don't even turn to look at the Communist couple's apartment. But I notice her shadow waving over the stairs, projected by some dying candle. When I reach the sixth floor, my legs are shaking. It's darker now; my blood sugar falls, and my eyes don't cooperate. I walk to her door, only to find an oversize lock with a note stuck over it.

> *I have moved out. For any information, contact the vegetarian club of Thiruvananthapuram. Love, C.*

I have seen enough Bollywood movies to understand what has just happened and what is supposed to happen from now on: one, the heartbroken heroine can't live in the same city as her love and decides to return home; two, the hero arrives just a few minutes after she leaves and rushes . . . rushes . . . rushes to the airport; three—

"*Mone . . . mone . . . son . . . son . . .*"

I open my eyes, sensing wet, frail fingers on my face.

"Are you OK, son?"

I look up. It's the Communist lady. The lights are bright; the power is back on.

"I found you lying down."

"Oh, I was fasting." I fake a smile and try to get up but can't. It's the first time I've skipped meals for a whole day.

"Take this candy." She unwraps the molten candy in her hand and gives it to me. "Both me and comrade are diabetics. We carry candies always."

The sugar rushes into my blood.

"It's dinnertime for us. Nothing fancy, but we would love your company."

Any other time, I would have refused, but not tonight. I'm hungry and hanging on the edge of another blackout. Besides, I don't want to disrespect the elderly lady who dragged herself to the sixth floor to check on me. She walks ahead, supporting herself on her cane, and I follow.

She'd noticed me struggle up the stairs but didn't see me return. Knowing that Chandini had vacated four days ago, she came up to check if things were all right. Guilt bugs me for making her walk up and down the stairs.

Comrade Latha and her husband Sudhakaran Nair thus enter my life.

"You could have ended up with a stroke, you know?" Comrade Sudhakaran says shakily, sitting on his bed in the living room corner. I pull a chair from the dining table, honoring his request to take a seat while Comrade Latha excuses herself to the kitchen.

"She insists on cooking for us. My son offered to get a maid, but she doesn't want one. I wish I could assist her . . . like in the good old days." He sighs. I watch him speak with long pauses between sentences to recoup his energy.

Both were teachers and members of the Communist Party. The injuries caused by their union's agitations have worsened the troubles of old age. They have a son in Ernakulam who visits once a week. He is a Communist Party member, too. Pictures of Shiva, Krishna, and Rama on the walls illustrate their religiosity. I turn my head to the adjacent wall where Fidel, Che, and some other dodgy figures show their grim faces.

"You look surprised." He reads my emotions through his black-rimmed glasses. "There is no contradiction. We are Communists; we are spiritual. A god who loves the downtrodden and lives among them is a Communist," he says with a laugh.

It's so profound that I don't know how to reply. Comrade explains the deep meaning of socialism and the various shades of red. I struggle to keep my hand away from my forehead.

Dinner is rice gruel cooked with mung beans, served with chutney. The chutney is bland. But it still tastes good. I wipe the tears from my eyes.

"Spicy?" she asks.

"No, no. It's just right," I reply.

"She left four days ago," Comrade Sudhakaran says, pointing a finger to the ceiling.

"Hmmm . . ."

"The security guard says that her American visa arrived."

I didn't see that coming. So much for nationalism.

"That apartment belongs to the Brotherhood. It's the same story year after year. North Indians arriving to foment some spiritual revolution in the south and vanishing as soon as their American visa comes. In a way, that's a lucky apartment," Comrade Latha says, lighting up laughter in their faces.

"Will she be coming back?"

"Of course. They always do." She stops giggling and continues, "They return twenty-five years later to find matching same-caste horoscopes for their children."

Chapter 10

The dark clouds part on my way back to the bus station, replicating a Bollywood pathos scene. The plot twist is that her flight left days ago, and my autorickshaw is going in the opposite direction.

"Sir, you look so tired. Do you want me to stop for dinner?" That's the autorickshaw driver exhibiting his manners.

We stop before another tin shed for toddy and cassava tubers sautéed with curry leaves. Oh, I should also mention the spicy beef roast, my revenge on Chandini.

For the first time ever, I bond with an autorickshaw driver. I tell him about my life story so far, including my search for enlightenment. When I'm done, he offers a panacea: to meet an astrologer who could show me the path. The noble soul offers me three options: one, traditional horoscope reader; two, palmistry; three, a tarot picked out by a parrot. I pick palmistry. When we are back in his chariot, he pulls out a card from his dashboard, which is just a dent in the metal frame.

"*Amme* Bhagvathy, Goddess Bhagvathy, show him the way," he prays and hands the card over. The address points to a remote locality in Parassala, between the Kanyakumari and Thiruvananthapuram districts. With that, my spiritual pendulum swings back to Hinduism.

"He charges just two thousand five hundred rupees," he says.

I thank him for giving me directions. But the toddy in his belly does its mean act, and he forgets the route to the bus station. I still tip him generously when we finish our impromptu city tour. Thus ends our two-hour journey, which was supposed to be forty minutes.

It's too late in the night to return to Little Lotus Pond. I can find buses for Nagercoil, but finding the 1½ route bus thereafter for my village is impossible. Not that they are frequent during the day. So, I rent a room and roll all night in the company of mosquitoes.

After an *idli-vadai* breakfast, I set out to Parassala. *Idli*, the steam-cooked South Indian rice cake, and *vadai*, the fried Indian doughnuts made of lentil flour, are the odd food couple. The fried *vadai* is an antithesis to the healthy *idlis*. But together with the tomato and coconut chutneys, they can lift one's spirit.

The astrologer's hometown is on the way back to Little Lotus Pond. I tell myself it's just a pit stop. Another autorickshaw drops me before a wooden signboard with the name MOHANAN PANICKER scribbled over an arrow mark. I trek through a rubber farm and then descend across a creek to arrive at a traditional, tiled house. I thank God it's not tin-roofed, as life has shunted me enough through multiple tin-roof buildings.

A dozen heads turn in my direction from the veranda. They hold trays with betel leaves, nuts, and lemons in their hands. I ask the gray-haired gentleman with a bulging purse tucked under his armpit when his turn is. "No idea." He flips his hands and lets the purse slip down to the floor. A lady in the group spots my empty hands and gives me a betel leaf with half a betel nut on it. "He won't meet you if you don't present this at his altar," she whispers in a husky tone, as if she's some long-lost twin of Adele, giving me an unsolicited tip. "Remember, only he speaks. You can't ask him questions unless he permits."

I'm the thirteenth person in line to walk in through the small door to his living room—a symbolic representation of the blessed life I've been living.

I place the betel leaf, the nut, and five five-hundred-rupee bills on the wooden plank before him and secure a nod of acknowledgment.

"*Namaskaram*," I greet him in Malayalam, his mother tongue.

"No, no talking, please. Show me your writing hand."

I stretch out my right hand.

He takes it and hovers a giant magnifying glass over my palm with the fervor of a treasure hunter. "All the way from the south, from the southern tip to this sacred space."

That is indeed an accurate location of Little Lotus Pond. I watch the lines on his forehead climb up and down as his glass hovers over my hand.

"Lucky palm," he exclaims, almost giving me a heart attack. "To the east lies your destiny, your moksha, the enlightenment. Your luck line runs all the way to your wrist. You were born lucky; luck shall beckon you in every path you take, and you will make a lot of friends from across the seven seas and mountains. You will find answers to unanswered questions, eat food nobody else has eaten, and see things nobody else has seen."

My eyes widen. I know I'm destined for great things. But this is monumental!

"The paths. The paths you take are important. Never look back; never anticipate," he continues.

"How do I find the path?" I scratch my forehead. "I would appreciate some clarity on whether this is the path of renouncing worldly pleasures or embracing them."

"Shhh . . ." He puts a finger over his lips. "Extra questions, two thousand rupees."

I pull out four more five-hundred-rupee bills and place them before him.

"Just follow the signs. The signs shall take you through the right path. You will travel to the east, retracing the footsteps of your ancestors and great kings, conquering the hearts of many women along the way."

Many women! *So, Chandini and Annamma were just teasers!* That explains why those relationships didn't materialize.

He peers into my eyes and then swings back to my palm.

"The Venus, ah, the Venus. My Goddess, I haven't seen a fleshy one like this in so many years!" He shakes his head in disbelief. "The horizontal lines and the crescent moon here. You are Prince Charming. No girl can resist your charm. But it's all about the path you choose. To the east lies your destiny. Go forth and claim it!"

"But, sir—"

"Two thousand rupees."

I pull out another two thousand rupees.

Go ahead, he signals.

"These girls . . ." I rub my forehead. "Ummm . . . are they virgins?"

"Of course they are." He smiles. "It's not me saying this. I'm just the reader, the translator."

He continues reading the lines and then translates them.

"But there are points you have to remember." He taps my hand. "To sail to the east and claim your destiny, you need a firm base, a launchpad. Your spiritual self should be the launchpad. Listen to your inner self. Take help from teachers and embrace spontaneity. Remember, your path has been laid out. All you need to do is trust, put your right foot forward, and you will find enlightenment, your destiny."

He places my hand on the wooden plank and withdraws his.

I wait, hoping he will say more. All I get is another plain smile, and I realize it is time. I stand up, and we both bow to each other.

I can't stop admiring myself. The poor lady who told me not to speak did not know that the ex-journalist Richard Parker could squeeze out a hundred answers if he wanted to. Holding my head high, I walk, banging my head against the low doorframe. I realize the following: One, my destiny is in the East. I don't belong here; I was born for greatness. Two, I must find my teacher, my spiritual guru. Three, I need to find some medicated oil for my forehead.

Chapter 11

I buy a 50 mL bottle of Siddha oil from a kiosk at the Nagercoil bus stand before boarding the bus to Little Lotus Pond, which I'm destined to leave.

The first thing I do is run to Gurusaamy to seek advice. I narrate the palmist's prophecy, including the virgin girls. To my surprise, he isn't thrilled.

"I don't believe in foreseeing the future, son. I trust in God and walk the path before me. Worrying about the future will only stop me from appreciating the moment, this moment," he says and puts his hand on my shoulder. We are sitting on his doorstep.

My excitement sinks, and the wise man senses that.

"Ritchie..."

"Hmm?" I sigh, staring at the hibiscus plants lining the edge of his courtyard. They are in full bloom. I have never seen so many flowers on a hibiscus plant.

"I've known you since the day you were born, Ritchie. And I don't need an astrologer to tell me the greatness in you. You are special. The beauty of Little Lotus Pond is its soul that lives in all of us. But to realize that—and to discover love—you need to travel more. The astrologer is right there."

I wish he had skipped the Little Lotus Pond part. I broach the topic of the teacher. He lists all the great spiritual teachers of modern India and summarizes their teachings.

Narayana Guru
Ayya Vaikundar

Tagore
Gandhi
Jiddu Krishnamurthi
Chandra Mohan Jain

They all sound good, except for Ayya Vaikundar. Mud temples with open doors and people queuing before the mirror to see themselves, as if the ones on their dressing tables weren't enough. It's no wonder that the head count inside is diminishing. People say that most of his temples, also known as *nizhal thangals*, also known as shanties, are deserted. Ayya has nothing to offer me.

The rest are all great philosophers, too, but they'd appeal more to people who are about to buy their first walking stick. Only one guru stands out—someone who has something to offer for every age: Chandra Mohan Jain.

You will love Chandra Mohan Jain if you appreciate Eastern spiritual traditions. If you have read the Kama Sutra, he will appeal to you. If your brain analyzes the act's physical, psychological, and spiritual themes while your partner desperately looks forward to climaxing, chances are you are a follower of his philosophy. Just that you won't recognize him by the name Chandra Mohan Jain but as Osho or Bhagwan Rajneesh. However, since they have trademarked Osho, I shall refer to him as Bhagwan.

Gurusaamy smiles when I tell him which teacher I chose.

"You knew I would choose him. Didn't you?" I ask.

"There's no better teacher than him to learn the sexually liberating, tantric way to enlightenment, Ritchie. He is the teacher you are looking for. Stick to him," Gurusaamy advises with the same smile.

The wise elder knew I would choose him but wanted me to make the choice! I wonder what else he knows but wants me to discover myself.

"For those who choose the worldly way, tantra works wonders, Ritchie. It helps us transform our desires into divine experiences. Imagine sexuality as the gateway to moksha rather than a hindrance." He looks up to the roof eave and smiles repeatedly, as if he is recollecting or imagining something. "Tantra is about cultivating ecstasy and the awe for Shakti—the raw feminine energy that drives the world. When the male force Shiva and the feminine

Shakti unite in unrestrained love, freedom is born. Freedom from ignorance, fear, hatred, bigotry, patriarchy, and misogyny." He stops with that and slips into silence.

Everything he says is new to me. But something about it sounds so familiar, like a passive knowledge I had always known before. *I want this liberation, this boundless love!*

I prepare my inner self for the voyage ahead. Every morning, I read the books I had borrowed from Gurusaamy before my bath in the pond with Isakki. Well, to be precise, with Isakki's buffaloes, as I have never seen Isakki bathing in the pond. That's why I'm still sane. Sometimes I wonder how it is for her to live a cursed life. Young, dark, and wicked, feared and loathed by everyone. She dropped out from the five-year traditional Siddha medicine course to care for her dying father, yet she goes around practicing traditional medicine as a quack. Bhagwan teaches not to be judgmental, so I leave my thoughts on Isakki there and move on, only to come back again and again.

The key to being a lover is to have an open heart, the teacher says. He is always there to set my mind right. I could never love a person like Isakki, but I can't fill my heart with hatred for her, either. My morning ritual undergoes a transition. I now begin with Bhagwan, a toothbrush, towels, soap, drinking water, a comb, coconut oil, the pond, and Isakki's buffaloes.

The color of my lungi and shirts transforms from black to orange, the hue of love prophesied by Bhagwan. People do stare, but I care not. A young man with polished nails stops me at a garment shop in Nagercoil to ask if I am gay. I smile and say no, only to see the disappointment on his face. "No hard feelings." I open my arms and give him an unexpected hug.

"Oh, so you are gay!" His eyes widen in surprise.

"No . . . No . . . please don't mistake me." I back off as I can sense his manhood hardening. I am happy for him, though, for he has found his sexuality, whereas I am just beginning to discover mine—a discovery through Bhagwan, the friend, the guide, the philosopher, and the guru.

Because happiness is impossible without renouncing my past, I must forget Chandini and move ahead. I must renounce Annamma, too, and it isn't as difficult as I would have imagined before embracing Bhagwan's ways. The revelation that I'm destined to meet many virgins from the East and the promise of limitless love they hold in their bosoms gives me strength, fortitude, and tenacity—and the wisdom to know that all three are synonyms.

Tamil New Year is fast approaching, but my signs are yet to arrive. Bhagwan doesn't believe in signs or opportunities. He advises to jump, to play with the idea of jumping. He wasn't a serious man. For him, life was full of playfulness. For me, jumping isn't easy. One, I have become accustomed to looking for signs from above; two, I must prepare my inner self more; three, entering a country without a visa is a punishable offense.

I mark Singapore and Malaysia as the first two countries I will fly to, hoping the signs point to Malaysia, Aroonan Saamy's country, first. Both Singapore and Malaysia require prior visas because they do not consider my "Indianness" as automatic eligibility for entry. The sign will come along with the visas in the New Year, I know.

In my mother tongue, Tamil, there is a proverb that translates as "The birth of *thai* will open the gates." *Thai* is the first month of the actual Tamil year, which coincides with the first week of January in the Gregorian calendar. But for unknown reasons, we Tamils celebrate Tamil New Year's Eve in April, or *Chithirai*. Thus, we are the only ethnic group in the world that knows when the first month of the year is but celebrates it three months later. The belief that the New Year will bring good fortune is supposed to apply to January only, but we brilliant people expect good fortune to arrive three months later.

Until the sign comes, I will use the opportunity to prepare my inner self. Bhagwan says that forsaking knowledge is the key to enlightenment, the essential quality that defines a mystic. A mystic renounces his self-proclaimed knowledge in order to gain new information. I erase my slate clean, ready to gain fresh wisdom in my voyage.

You might be wondering if Bhagwan wants me to be an idiot. No, Bhagwan wants me to drop all my preformed notions and knowledge, but he also wants me to stay alert. Being mindful and alert is the key to becoming a conscious being, free from society's conditioning. Society loves executives in neat dresses and ties, ready to execute orders without question. An alert person questions everything. He is the watcher, the observer who develops a bird's-eye view of society. That's what society detests. This also explains why we consider mystics lunatics for defying society. The human mind cannot be automated; automation is for automobiles, like the ninety-six Rolls-Royces that Bhagwan owned. I'm not a Rolls-Royce with an engine invented to perform predetermined actions. I'm Parker the Great, destined to achieve greatness in the East.

Dropping my preformed knowledge becomes easier with practice. I vow not to gain an understanding of the lands I travel to before my voyage. Instead, I shall travel with playfulness, following the signs to choose my destinations and learning from every soul I meet. These humans shall be my libraries.

I pledge to drop my journalistic inquisitiveness. I drop my past; I drop my expectations; I drop my ego, maturing into a mystic ready for his quest. Human ego is like the shadow that scares the cat. The cat keeps running away from it until it reconciles itself with their inseparability. The shadow is scary if you pay attention, but it becomes nothing the moment we drop our fears.

Bhagwan says one doesn't have to meditate in the lotus pose. I unlearn meditation in the lotus pose and learn to meditate anywhere—while walking, bathing, or sitting idle on the pond bund. I learn to dissociate my actions and thoughts. The world is out to fool me, to discourage me from the greatness I'm destined to become. But I can meditate anywhere if I'm alert to the world's designs.

"Parker, are you alert?" I often call out to the me in me, then reply, "Yes, sir, I am alert."

"Don't let the world fool you, Parker," I remind myself.

"Yes, sir, I won't let the world fool me," I reply.

I repeat this exercise many times a day to stay alert. The more I become alert, the easier it is to meditate. I meditate fourteen hours a day—two hours out of bed and twelve hours in bed. The mortals call it sleeping, but the enlightened are awake. It's just the body that sleeps.

"Parker, are you awake?" I call out to myself on the embankment separating the mother pond and the banana field.

"Yes, sir," a chorus responds. I turn around to see a bunch of half-clad kids, the kind that every Westerner would love to pose with for their Instagram.

"Yes, sir, you are alert." They giggle and run away.

"That's crazy Lucas version two," one of them shouts.

I realize I am a mystic. The time has come.

Chapter 12

We just finished celebrating Tamil New Year's Eve.

I'm in my bright-orange robe, sidestepping the hundreds of elbows at Kanyakumari temple, when a text from Mercy, my cousin in Singapore, pops up. The title deed of her ancestral land is ready, and she asks me if I can collect it from her mother and courier it to her.

My sign has just arrived!

I'm flying to Singapore soon. Shall bring it, I answer.

She is excited, and so am I. Then she remembers that she and her husband are traveling to Hawaii for a two-month vacation. But her apartment is available for me to use, and I can collect the key from her friend.

My travel agent calls me the next day to confirm my travel dates. I order flexible tickets to and from Singapore for early May. The return ticket is just for visa reasons, and depending upon where the forces take me, I can change the destination, he says.

It is done.

My journey starts with 416,200.92 rupees in my personal bank account. Since this figure casts aspersions on the strength of Indian rupees, I shall quote it in US dollars. It's $6,564 plus the $11.45 in my self-publishing account. Technically, I can't access the $11.45 because it is below the portal's cutoff limit for payment release. Nevertheless, it belongs to me.

The prophecy has been revealed: Moksha, my destiny, awaits me in the East. My path to enlightenment guarantees girls, friends, luck, prosperity, fame, and wisdom. I have always known that I am destined to be great. But it never occurred to me that my greatness would be revealed in the East. No wonder I have been having a hard time in India.

While I'm grateful for the prophecy, I wish the astrologer had given more details. The oracle doesn't specify what I will become—*a sexually liberated tantric or an austere, self-disciplined yogi?* I should resolve this before my voyage.

If my female Shaktis come first, then my enlightenment is through tantra and sexuality, when our energies rise through our axes like serpents and unite. If enlightenment comes before my girls, it must be through the ascetic spiritual route, with sexuality coming later. It could happen anytime, anywhere in the East, through an act of kindness, like when I rescue the daughter of a Cambodian millionaire, who then bequeaths his fortune to us. Or when an indigenous community such as the Hmong of Vietnam recognizes me and names me as their chieftain.

Enlightenment through spirituality versus sexuality is a chicken-and-egg situation. But I'm not bothered about what comes first—as long as I have both the chicken and the egg. All I have to do is to keep my eyes open for the signs and surrender my humble self to the moment. I am the learner, the seeker, the traveler. A disciple should not constrain himself with artificial boundaries of knowledge. Nor can he be immune to the power of space and time, spirit and matter, until he develops the mastery to transcend them. I must be open to all possibilities.

The oracle says whatever I touch in the East will turn into gold. But spirituality is all about staying grounded. My spiritual quest is limited by the 416,200.92 rupees in my bank. If spirituality is my path to moksha, then I will lose all my money on the voyage, only to gain manifold after enlightenment. Bhagwan says that running after money will never bring happiness, and finding true happiness is to touch the center of one's soul. I can have all the money in this world and still be unhappy. Likewise, I can have no money and still be happy. Happiness is just a state of mind. I choose to be happy. But a wise man always has backup plans!

I might lose money, yet not go bankrupt, as I have leased out my farmlands. Thankamoni, my banana lessee, will have the money ready soon after the harvest. After enlightenment, I shall return with my Shaktis to collect the lessee fee, sell the house and the farmlands, and donate the proceeds to my ashrams. Remember, an ascetic might be a pauper, but he has ashrams where love, happiness, and prosperity overflow. I just can't wait to sell my properties and end my relationship with this crappy village.

After delineating the philosophical underpinnings of my quest, I slip into my evening meditation routine.

When I wake up from my overnight spell of deep meditation, my brain hands me a one-hundred-watt idea: to convert my adventures into an inspiring novel. The bumper proceeds from it could add to my ashram fund. When I return as the enlightened, I shall submit my manuscript to Oxtail Publishing, the sister company of the *Indian Republic* I worked with. Unlike the newspaper and *Democracy TV*, which were minting money, Oxtail Publishing lived on peanuts doled out by Mr. Sajeev.

Mr. Sajeev and all his employees hate me. But this will be my way of winning them over. Help their publishing business hit an all-time high, and they will regret branding me as stupid and kicking me out. I cannot hate them because that's not what Bhagwan teaches me.

Guruji's morning sermon is now live on YouTube. His talk today is about the rise of India, Indians, and Indian spirituality on the global stage. White Westerners who have lost their peace to capitalism flock to India to eat, pray, and love while Indians rise through the hierarchies of Silicon Valley to find comfort at the top. In the East, Southeast Asia is rediscovering its Hindu and Buddhist past and welcoming Indians with open arms. Malaysian and Singaporean Indians are loved and respected in their countries for the glory they have brought. Thailand and Indonesia issue visas on arrivals for Indians, just because they love to see Brown people on their land.

The recent rise of Indians cannot be a coincidence. *The gods have prepared the ground for the enlightened!* I close my eyes and offer thanks to the gods for preparing the East for my arrival.

I shave my beard and get a haircut. Susheela folds my orange robes and stuffs them into Mom's steel trunks. I don't need them anymore. They were symbolic, and I'm now ready for the future in the East. My attire reverts to the pants and shirts the British impressed upon us.

It has been just a few minutes since the birth of Monday, May 4, 2015. I'm rolling on my bed, tormented by the full moon sneaking in through the transom window. My body struggles, but my spirit is awake. It picks up the familiar rustle in the bushes and the faint notes of the so-called song composed of mumbo jumbo. I know what happens next. My mind readies me for the high-pitch sound.

A-ooooooo!

A-ooooooo!

The howl rises from the bushes, and I spring to my feet. I run to the door, unbolt it, and step into the courtyard. At the entrance to the courtyard, I see him. He sits on his butt, eyes fixed on my door. His coat is so dark that you'd never see him on a new-moon night—a trait that he shares with his guardian, Isakki.

He spots me and stops howling.

I bend down to pick up an imaginary stone and throw it in the dog's direction. He squeals and bolts away. This has been a familiar drill since I returned to Little Lotus Ditch as a failed entrepreneur. Every full moon, I lose sleep. It's always Anonymous's howl tearing into the night, followed by Isakki's trumpet, as though they are in some orchestra. A being worth no name, I call him Anonymous—just a beating heart on four legs. Somebody must put an end to these two creatures because I'm sick of going sleepless every full-moon night. But then, a glowworm butt lights up in my heart; this is ending soon. I smile and roll and smile and roll until Nidra Devi, the sleep goddess, embraces me.

In the morning, I wake up without the usual tiredness, pull water from the well, and wash in its warmth. I kneel before the pictures of my parents, take their blessings, and open my wheeled duffel to take stock of what Susheela has packed.

A pair of sports shoes for the adventure, three pairs of socks, two cargo shorts, a pair of faded jeans, three T-shirts, a pair of formal trousers and shirts, and toiletries. It looks perfect to me. I stuff my laptop, chargers, and journal into the daypack. The duffel has oversize wheels compared to the normal ones. I picked it because it makes it easy for me to drag it along the footpath, avoiding the funny gazes on the main street.

A part of the prophecy is that I will taste food I haven't tasted before. I walk around with my hands knotted behind me to fit this food list into my voyage. After three rounds of walks, Richard Parker's buccal list is born, alluding to the food entering our buccal cavities, also known as the mouth. You might wonder why I chose jargon instead of an easy term such as *oral list*. Simple, it's because I don't want my list to be popular among hookers for a mouthful of reasons!

For mortals' sake, I define the buccal list as "a list of food a person has never tried before but wants to taste during their lifetime." You might wonder how I could accomplish this without prior research on my destinations and their delicacies. Let me tell you, as a trendsetter, I will fill my list as I encounter those deserving dishes. My followers, however, shall do their homework and set up their lists in advance.

The cereals Susheela left in the fridge struggle to pass the gate in my throat, and I console it by chanting, *"One last time."* I drop the dishes in the sink for Susheela. She should have something to do. I have already paid her the salary for the whole of May.

I call up my bank and inform them of my travel. The lady assures me in her fake American accent that their ATM card works throughout East Asia, for a fee. At ten, I wear my daypack, pick up my duffel bag, lock the door, put on my sandals, and walk to the footpath. I turn back to look at the house. A thought comes into my mind: *Should I sell it off? Or save it for the people of this village as a museum in my honor?*

I shrug and put my right foot forward.

Part III

The Voyage to Southeast Asia

Chapter 13

My voyage begins!

My SilkAir flight, Singapore Airlines' low-cost sibling departing from Thiruvananthapuram, comes furnished with blue seats and silky-haired hostesses. I grace the window seat my agent had chosen. The middle seat is empty.

The flight reaches cruising altitude, and the guy in the aisle seat gets up to open the luggage compartment. "Sir, please, the seat-belt sign is still on." A hostess comes running.

"It's OK, sister. I just want to change to a lungi."

"Please, sir, you must sit now," she pleads.

He pretends not to hear her and pulls out a lungi from his bag, then slips it up to his waist with ease. The hostess returns to her seat, shaking her head in disbelief, the seat-belt sign still on. My fellow passenger takes his seat with a proud smile. Next in line is the guy in the seat ahead, followed by the guy in the other row. Soon, I lose count of all the proud Indian men shedding their colonial legacies and donning the traditional lungi midair. I'm the only man left in pants. The seat-belt sign goes off. I sigh, regretting that I forgot to pack my lungi.

I close my eyes and take a deep breath. But the flight shudders, interrupting my meditation.

Tat-tat-tat . . .

I shut my eyes and brace myself, with my forehead kissing my knees, just as the pretty hostess instructed during the safety briefing. My heart is halfway down the racetrack. This can't be. I can't die while my destiny awaits.

The shudders stop just as abruptly as they began, and I lift my head. Everything seems normal. And then it resumes. I repeat the drill. The seat could be ripped out of the plane anytime, tossing me midair. We are all dying!

I tilt my head to see how my co-passengers react. My heart loses steam; everybody else appears normal.

"OK, *va*?" The guy in the aisle strokes my back.

"Yes, yes." I lift my head. Everything is calm.

He leans across and whispers, "Don't worry, liquor will be here soon. And you won't feel a thing." He winks.

I smile. The shuddering returns, and this time I notice the feet pedaling the rear end of my armrest. I turn back and peep through the seat gap and spot a baby boomer with his leg resting next to my waist.

"Sir, please . . ." I tap on his foot to signal.

He retracts his foot, leans forward, and stuffs his flat nose and mouth between the two seats. "Take a walk to the toilet. There might be some seats vacant. Make yourself comfortable there."

My hand itches to reach out and pull his nose, Tom and Jerry style. But a voice in my head halts me for three reasons: one, his nose is flat as a chapati; two, making him Tom would render me a Jerry; three, they might handcuff me on arrival for midair violence.

The foot reappears on the armrest, and the pedaling continues. I take a deep breath and whisper to myself, "Richard Parker, are you alert?"

There is no reply. I abandon the attempt and stare out through the window.

Meals arrive. For the first time, I eat Indian meals that thou shall find nowhere in India. "Sir, drink for you?" the hostess asks.

I like the plastic smile on her tired face. The journey has just begun!

"Just apple juice." I point to the carton. I'm intoxicated enough from the thought of arriving in my grand future soon and want no alcohol in my blood.

"Beer for me," the guy in the aisle seat says, holding a beer cup. "My lucky cup! I carry this every time I fly." He winks after the hostess leaves, pushing her service trolley.

The shuddering of my seat turns into gentle rocking. I realize I won't be able to sleep as the agent had promised, and the window seat was just meant for me to look out for flying yogis.

Four hours later, the air hostess announces our descent. I widen my eyes and look at the yellow specks of light adorning my promised land beneath the clouds.

Our aluminum bird lands on the lit-up tarmac of Changi. I disembark and somnambulate to the immigration queue.

"Do you carry any prohibited items, sir?" the officer asks when my turn comes.

"No, sir. No compressed gases, corrosives, explosives, flammable materials, or poisons." I shake off drowsiness and present my proactive side.

He does a face-palm. "I mean, any chewing gum, any rubber bands?"

"No, sir."

I proceed to the carousel.

"We shouldn't fly on this damn route again. I'm sick of this!" a flight attendant from our plane swears to her colleague as they pass by. Racists!

My male co-passengers have inserted themselves back into their pants and now stand around the carousel like soldiers in some weird military drill.

A loud yawn escapes me.

"Kumar!" I hear somebody yelling, but I ignore it because I'm not Kumar.

"Kumar . . ." the voice rings again, this time next to my ear; I turn back with a start. A petite lady in a pink fur coat, holding a pink shoulder bag and a hard-shell spinner suitcase with kitty stickers stuck all over, flicks her dyed-brown hair and smiles at me.

"Oh, Kumar . . . I found you. I'm so happy." She drops the suitcase and hugs me tightly while I stand perplexed, wondering who this lucky bastard Kumar is.

"It would have been easier if you had a paging board with my name, you know? Anyway, I'm so happy you are here to take me to your master." She relaxes her hug.

I gently remove her puny hands from my shoulders. "Sorry, miss. I'm not Kumar. I think you are mistaken."

"Hey . . . you, *ah* . . . no joking?" Her eyes roll. She pulls out an iPad from her handbag and swipes to show me the photograph of a pale-looking man in an unbuttoned yellow shirt, white pants, and sunglasses seated on a red chair. Thick gold chains adorn his hairless torso while his arms haul multiple bracelets. I like the long chain with a red ruby sitting on his belly.

"Who is he?" I point to the image.

"Jackson. Jackson Sung. My man, your boss."

"I'm sorry . . . I—"

"Hey, no joking, *ah*!" She interrupts and pokes a finger at my tummy. "You no know him, *ah*? Look, who is this?" She zooms out of the earlier frame to reveal a dark man with a big mustache standing behind Jackson. He must be his bodyguard, I guess.

"Who is he?"

"Hey, no joking. It's you! It's you, Kumar."

I pull the iPad closer, and her hands come, too, as she doesn't want to let go of the tablet. I scrutinize the bodyguard. He doesn't show any resemblance to the great Richard Parker. I look at her—straight brown hair, perfectly tattooed eyebrows above sparkling brown eyes. I can't believe such a person could be so unbalanced. My heart fills with sympathy. But I must get rid of her. I can't be late for my destiny. Time and fate wait for none!

"Look here, young lady—"

"No . . . no, please. Say nothing. Take me to your boss. He will be excited to see Rachel."

"Rachel?" My eyes expand their geographical area. Something in me tells me I have known her, like we had sailed together through some significant moment in history. It's like destiny trying to reach out to me from beyond a great wall.

"Yes, Rachel Voo from China."

China!

I spot the sign. She's from a parallel universe that is about to save humanity from chaos and absurdity! Surely, there must be a reason why the gods have put her in my path. I shouldn't let this moment slip by.

"You are from China?"

"No, I mean Chinatown in Manhattan."

My excitement holds steady. Chinatowns are not China, but they are mini-planets by themselves.

I go down on one knee, put my hand to my chest, and pledge to help her in finding her fiancé.

Just as quickly as I get excited at the thought of creating a significant moment in history, I realize there's a problem. I don't know who Jackson is or where he lives. I don't know what Singapore looks like beyond the glass panels of the airport.

Rachel met Jackson, her long-distance fiancé, on Instagram. She tells me she's an American, and he is a well-known Singaporean. Jackson's Instagram is replete with photographs of him posing in front of his pricey sports cars or surfing in some blue waters. His cult status and charisma impressed the go-getter Rachel straightaway. It was love at first message, for both. Rachel owned an employment agency in Manhattan, bringing laborers from Fujian Province in China and matching them with employers. But with restaurants and other businesses driven out to Brooklyn and her rat holes running underneath the fences separating Mexico and San Diego sealed, her business collapsed. She could have leased other tunnels, but the Mexican cartels had leased them all to Indian, Filipino, and Vietnamese mules.

Rachel was contemplating a career change when Jackson entered her life in twenty-four-carat style. But twenty-six days after falling in love and ten days after a modern e-betrothal, the connection went cold, and there were no social media updates. No more pictures of cars, beaches, and the pork-rib *bak kut teh*. She downloaded all his photographs and bought a one-way ticket to Singapore, her new home. Her favorite picture of him is the one on the red antique chair, with a man provisionally identified as Kumar standing behind.

Rachel believes I'm that Kumar. I convince her we are not the same and don't look alike, without giving her any opportunities to kick me off history. It isn't hard; Rachel soon spots many more Kumars around. Tears of disbelief dampen her eyes, and I can see she's about to bid me goodbye. But I can't let that happen.

"Rachel, we are going to find him. I will help you," I promise, taking her hand in mine.

"Thank you." She leaps in joy and hugs me.

Should I repeat the promise? I wonder.

This is my first time in Singapore, and I must find Jackson—the golden needle in the haystack.

"Don't worry. He rich, famous man. Everyone in Singapore know him."

That isn't inspiring. Nevertheless, I'm sticking to her. You may wonder why. Apart from the prophecy that has put Rachel in my path, there's something special about us Indian men. We date only betrothed women. Our Bollywood heroes always help heroines on their epic voyages through green meadows and daisy fields in the Himalayas to unite with their love. That love turns out to be a married man, a womanizer, or a drunkard, and our hero proves his true love, thus winning her hand.

The story has always been the same; just the songs, stunts, and title credits change. As a true Indian, I wouldn't jinx it.

Rachel doesn't have a place to stay, but I do. She has a sweetheart to look for, and I don't. But Rachel doesn't know the climax; I do. I invite her to stay with me. The rumor in my family is that Cousin Mercy struck gold in Singapore and lives in a posh apartment worth a crore rupee. Rachel agrees to join me, but she won't take the MRT via Tanah Merah, as Cousin Mercy had advised.

"Back home in China, only poor people do trains," Rachel insists.

"China?"

"I mean Chinatown in Manhattan."

"Oh, OK." I nod.

A man in a black-and-white suit approaches us. I rapidly assess him and conclude that he is an enforcement officer.

"Good morning. Would you be interested in a place to stay?" he asks.

"Oh, thanks. We already have one."

He isn't prepared to take no for an answer. "I can get you rental properties for a cheap price. You are lucky that we just set up our booth." He points to a corner where two people are busy unfolding a blue canopy and rods.

"Hmm." I scratch my chin. "Do you know how I can get to Clementi without using the MRT?"

His facial expression changes from warm to rigid. "Oh, I see. You want me to be your data broker!"

My brain sifts through its corpus in vain. *Data broker* is a new term. But I can't give up, especially before Rachel. *Be alert!* I remember Bhagwan's mantra.

"Oh no . . . You look like a helpful soul. I don't want to give you sleepless nights. If you don't help us, this will keep replaying in your mind the whole night." I smile.

But his expression only freezes further. "Ah. Now you are guilt-tripping me!"

He stuns me even more. *Data broker* and *guilt-tripping* are both complex words I have never heard before.

Take route number 1½ bus from Nagercoil to Kanyakumari, and alight at the obscure bus stop next to the banyan tree. Ask for the house of Gurusaamy, Isakki, Shanta, Lucas, or the late Khader Bhai, and people will walk you to their homes. They wouldn't accuse you of seeking an unpaid data broker.

"Ahem . . . In Singapore, everything has a price. We are hardworking people." He cinches his tie. "I'm willing to trade information, but what am I getting in return?"

I tell him I'm a writer in search of stories.

"Marvelous! Can I shadow you in your writing? Just send me the link to your cloud docs, and I can keep abreast of your work. You won't even know I'm reading it. I have always wanted to be a rich and successful writer," he says, eyes wide open. "Besides, it's also fair we trade information."

I remember the $11.45 in my self-publishing account. I have no option but to apologize for wasting his valuable time. He finally allows us to go without sharing his valuable data.

We decide to hail an app taxi. Rachel and I both buy SIM cards. I install the taxi app as directed by the flashing billboard that shows a lady with long legs for unknown reasons.

Six more minutes for the taxi to follow the maze on my cell phone screen. I look at the intriguing doll sitting on the spinner suitcase next to me. I inquire about her journey so far.

"It was long flight. Twenty hours and fifty minutes via Taipei. I had a terrible experience, you know?" Rachel was updating her travel progress on social media every time she found free Wi-Fi, hoping that Jackson would see it when he surfaced. When the flight from Taipei landed, she tried to take a selfie with the open cockpit door behind her. The pilot, a white man, slammed the door and rebuffed her. "It hurt me a lot." Two tears appear in her eyes.

"I'm sorry, Rachel."

"It's OK."

She pulls a mirror from her pink handbag. I watch her remove her eyelashes and place them carefully in a tiny box before wiping the tears. I thank the gods for sliding her into my life. Throughout my college days, girls were the majority in my classes. But I have never seen one stylish enough to sport extra eyelashes.

"Back home in China . . ." she starts.

"China?"

"I mean, in Manhattan, white people are minority. But we treat them well. But . . ." Tears descend again.

The taxi arrives, and we take the rear seat. She is silent, like a philosopher lost in deep thought.

"Rachel." I reach out and touch her arm. "Back there, when I asked you about the journey so far, I was inquiring about your life, what motivates you every day."

"Oh . . . that." She sighs and opens her handbag again to pull out a purple-colored book.

"Open it, Kumar."

I open it to the first page.

> *China is a sleeping giant*
> *Let her sleep, for*
> *when she wakes*
> *she will move the world*
> —Napoleon Bonaparte

"But, Rachel—"

"No, Kumar, no," she interrupts. "Please don't ask anything."

I set the question aside for another occasion.

Chapter 14

I text Cousin Mercy's friend. She keeps her word by appearing at the door before us. She hands over the key, wishes us a happy honeymoon, and leaves, consuming just forty seconds of the Singaporean clock. I notice the glint of naughtiness in her eyes.

I take a step closer to the door.

"Wait!" Rachel stops me. I follow her instruction like a humble lamb. She sidesteps me, moves closer to the door, and puts her ear on the door as if she wants to eavesdrop.

"It's empty," I tell her.

"Shh." She puts a finger to her lips, demanding silence. She holds still, with her ears fused to the door. "Got goats inside . . ."

"Goats? My cousin doesn't have goats."

"Not goats, ghosts . . . spirits. We tell them we are coming." She knocks thrice and steps back. "Can open . . ." I learn something new.

Cousin Mercy's apartment is on the twenty-fifth floor of a forty-two-floor high-rise. What was supposed to serve as the luxurious backdrop of this chapter turns out to be a cramped 505.904-square-foot space with walls that have miraculous self-heating properties despite the donkeywork of the air conditioners. We decide not to use the lone bedroom as a courtesy toward my cousin and her husband. We settle on the L-shaped couch, with Rachel on its east wing and me on the northern one. It reminds me of the sofa at Chandini's place, but unlike Chandini, Rachel isn't in the bedroom.

My eyes scan the cramped yet well-maintained apartment inspired by high-tax-imposed minimalism. Being a tiny country of just 728 square kilometers, there isn't enough room for spacious housing. The government is contemplating whether to build the next residential area under the earth or above the Singapore Strait. While they work it out, Singaporeans got together and resolved not to procreate. Mercy and her husband were among them. Though she has left her motherland, she has ensured her genes stay pure by marrying a Singaporean Indian. I point at the laminated picture of Mercy and her husband on top of the fridge and give Rachel an idea of her. Behind it stands another image of them with an interracial couple. The guy looks Indian, and the girl looks Caucasian. I have no clue who they could be.

Mercy has left sticky notes on the dining table.

> *There are vegetables in the fridge and rice in the bucket. Please feel free to cook.*
> *Please water the potted plants on the balcony.*
> *Water is expensive; please make frugal use of it.*

My mind replays our childhood days. Most of our childhood games were on water—the ponds, irrigation ducts, or the brown puddles with tadpoles that we mistook for fish. The ponds in Little Lotus Pond always brim with water. Even when the rest of the state reels under summer, we never face drought, as the perennial springs from the foothills of the Western Ghats keep our ponds filled.

We take frugal showers and cook fish-skin-flavored instant noodles. Mercy's taste has transformed, as evidenced by her stash of instant noodles. Dried fish skin, salted egg, chicken feet, bird's nest—all exotic flavors to me but dear to Rachel. Rachel pulls out chopsticks from her bag and eats with ease. I watch her long fingers handle the chopsticks like wands conjuring magic from the soupy ocean while I struggle to stop the noodles from falling from my fork.

"Yummy!" says Rachel.

"Hmm . . . ," I reply.

I'm still struggling to swallow it. Not even a day has passed, and I already miss curry. So, when Rachel is busy researching localities to visit, I walk to the provision store and purchase curry noodle packets. Mercy's friend, who brought us the smart key, is also there for errands, and I strike up a conversation. Sadly, she doesn't know who Jackson Sung is. But she's sure he's a distant relative of hers, as all rich Singaporean Chinese are related to each other. That's why they refer to every other rich man or woman they meet as uncle and aunt. I ask her if she lives on the same floor as Mercy.

"My culture doesn't allow me to live on the middle floor," she says.

"I don't eat curry," says Rachel in a muffled tone, seeing me place the noodles on the table. She has a mask covering her nostrils and mouth. She says she sensed poisonous fumes. The chivalrous detective in me sniffs around and discovers that some neighbor is frying fish in authentic Indian style.

We make a pact: fish skin or salted egg noodles for her and curry noodles for me. It's a heavenly lock-and-key match. If I could win Rachel's heart, we could go to the fish market daily. In the evenings, while Rachel relishes the skin, I would have the meat! The signs are everywhere. Like God had planned this long before our birth.

Rachel lists probable localities where Jackson's mansion could be. We are ready for the investigation, armed with all three essential items required: one, pictures of Jackson, including details of his embellishments; two, pictures of his red bungalow house(s); three, two sharp minds like Sherlock Holmes and Dr. Watson. We have difficulty agreeing on who between us is Sherlock, and I cede the title to her. Rachel presents a valid point. Investigation requires research, and for that, one must do online searches. Remember the oracle? I'm to go with the flow, as Dr. Watson would have. I can't do an online search, but like Holmes, Rachel does.

Rachel's online research brings up thirty-nine areas where classic good-class bungalows (GCBs) are located. Nassim, Ladyhill, Rochalie, Bishopsgate, Chatsworth, Cluny Road, Tanglin Road, Swettenham Road, Holland Road, Bukit Timah Road, and so on. We begin from Swettenham Road because it appears eighth on her list and hence is lucky.

Our taxi driver turns out to be super patient, making things easier. At one point, I start worrying that he might mistake us for burglars scouting for targets. I explain our mission to him.

"She is madly in love, and I'm just trying to help her. Please don't mistake us for burglars or antisocial elements."

"*Haiyoh*, you people, ah? Not at all. No, *lah*. Where got bad people look like that?" He giggles.

I look at his badge displaying *Lim Kim Kuan*. My heart leaps for joy at finding a cabbie as good as us, and I thank him, addressing him by his name.

"Just call me Kewin," he says, confusing me.

I learn something new. Authentic Singaporeans have dual names—a native name for community circles and an English name for *atas*, elite circles. *Kewin Kuan* is the anglicized name for *Lim Kim Kuan*.

Kewin does his best to help us, but unfortunately, our whole-day mission yields zero results.

We hire Kewin's cab for the next day's investigation, too. Again, our search yields zero results. None of the bungalows resembles those in the pictures. On the third day, we go sightseeing to refresh our minds. Rachel insists we split the bill because it isn't part of her mission. She is happy to fund the other trips; Jackson will refund her later.

Her skillful makeup application masks the toll this manhunt has taken on her. But I can read her like a crystal ball. She craves some tasty food, something traditional. "I want crocodile tail soup," she says. We can't deny her that, not at this moment when comfort is all she needs.

Kewin takes us to the classy South Bridge Road. "*Atas* people go there," he says.

Rachel is at home in Chinatown, under the comfort of her pink umbrella. "The weather is too hot," she complains, adjusting her pink fur coat. I don the role of her official photographer every time she poses before a Peranakan structure. From her sanctum, Goddess Sri Mariamman pings an invitation straight to my heart. But Rachel's advice is to go alone later, as she is allergic to spices.

"Sandalwood!" I try to correct her.

Rachel finds her crocodile tail soup while Kewin and I sip chrysanthemum tea. "Crocodile soup full of collagen, very good for skin," she says through slurps.

I learn the secret behind crocodiles' flawless skin.

A white man with a sharp nose gulps coffee at the table opposite us, eyes fixed on Rachel. He notices me noticing him and approaches us.

"Hello, we have met before." He stretches out his hand toward Rachel. Rachel's face turns red, and she stands up, pushing back her chair.

"You hurt me. I don't want to meet you. Go away!" she screams. The gentleman backs off, apologizing repeatedly.

I learn from Rachel that he is the pilot from her flight.

"I will ask my Jackson to buy that airplane," she says with barrels of determination. I agree.

We pay for the soup and drinks and leave. I look back at the man, who is back at his table, his eyes following us. The thought that I'm luckier than a pilot to have a chance at winning Rachel's hand lights fireworks in my mind.

We stop before a familiar-looking big red building.

"I found it. It's my Jackson's house!" Rachel throws her pink umbrella in the air and clasps her hands. "Look at that. It's beautiful, stupefying all my senses with its pomp and splendor."

"Shh . . . respect." Kewin points to the signboard. "That one, *ah*, Buddha tooth relic temple."

The me in me is confused at the unexpected turn of events. Seconds after discovering Jackson's home, we learn it's a temple. In addition, the sudden poshness in Rachel's English has also begun weighing on me. She just sounded like a Lady Shakespeare.

Rachel's eyes moisten. "But it's the same building in my Jackson's photo."

Yes. I recollect the caption on the screenshot Rachel had shown me. "My little home," it said.

Rachel starts sobbing even before she can remove the eyelashes. We are now forced to cut short the trip and return to the apartment.

"Kumar, do you think my Jackson could have built that?" she asks with swollen eyes. She has removed the eyelashes.

"No idea," I reply.

"Kumar, do you think Jackson could buy that for me?"

My gut is drying, and she refuses to eat the salted-egg-flavored noodles I made for her. I must cheer her up, or else I won't be able to eat my curry noodles, for manner's sake.

"Don't worry, we will find him." I put my arm on her shoulders. It is time to give her a prelude to what is coming. "Well, you don't have to worry even if we don't find him. I'm here for you. We can get married and live happily like this." I point to the interracial couple in the picture above the fridge.

"This?" She frowns and wriggles away from me. "This is no good, Kumar. Relationships should have cultural compatibility. Same culture, no problem."

"Why do you say so?"

"White man eat burger." She cups her left hand as if she were holding a burger. "Indian eat curry rice." She stretches out her tongue and inserts her hand into her mouth, pretending to swallow it. "Please don't mistake me. We are open-minded. Back home in China, we marry white men. No problem; white man culture and Chinese culture same-same."

"Ahem . . . I beg to disagree." I field my IQ to impress her. "Indians eat *idli*; Chinese eat *bau*. It's indeed a perfect match!"

"Hmm . . ." She looks down, scratches her chin for a moment, and sighs. "OK, let me explain. There are many type of humans. Look here." She steeples her hands and puts her chin on top of it. "On top is white man. White man culture, very good." She slides her chin down to her wrist. "Second comes Yellow man culture. Yellow also good." She lifts her head and serves me a pitiful glance. "Sorry to tell you, Kumar. Other species comes only below."

"Species?" My eyes pop out.

"No, no . . . no. I mean, culture . . . culture." She crosses her arms and tightens her lips. When she opens them again, pearls of wisdom roll out. "Kumar, Yellow mix white, become white. White mix Black, become Black. Yellow mix Black, still become Black."

A labyrinth of thoughts forms in my mind. It takes seconds for me to realize that it's my traumatized mindscape.

I decide to shelve the topic for a while. The next day, when Kewin picks us up, we are clueless as to where to go. That's when it strikes me. We never showed him the photographs. A billionaire like Jackson wouldn't need a cab, but what if the cabbie knows his home? Perhaps he knows a maid there? Or runs errands for them? I suggest the idea to Rachel. She isn't convinced. But I decide to take a chance. Kewin glances at Jackson's picture and bursts into laughter. I look at Rachel, and she looks at me.

"*Haiya*, you people looking for him for what, *sia*?" He continues laughing.

"Do you know him, Kewin? Would you take us to him?" Rachel asks.

"Sure, *lah*, *aiyoh*, he is Master Jackson. I know him since young *loh*. His place *sibei shiok* one. Me and my friends always bring clients for him."

I look at Rachel. *I told you!*

"They big family, *ah*?" Rachel seeks reaffirmation.

"*Yalor, yalor.*" He hands the phone back. "Their clan famous people in Singapore. Got three sisters: Alice Stu, Abigail Stu, and Audrey Stu. Then *hor* they married three powerful cousins from the Sing, Sang, and Sung clans. Their family so strong, like grab Singapore *lampa*."

"*Lampa?*"

"Crotch . . . crotch." He chortles, pretending to squeeze two softballs in his hands.

I knew Jackson was a rich man. But I didn't think he would also be so powerful. They hold Singapore by its crotch—that means that he has deep political connections! Here I am, sitting next to Singapore's future most powerful woman. A giant merry-go-round turns in my stomach.

"Very powerful." The words spring out of my mouth.

"*Yalor*, you know Master Jackson is one *ah-beng*, a gangster?"

The puffed-up image of Jackson in my heart expands further. I take a sneak look at Rachel. Her eyeballs have sunk into some dreamland.

I must get back into the picture.

"Gangster? Oh . . . he must have plenty of injuries," I say, highlighting the not-so-rosy part of gangster life. You see, no woman would marry a goon who had hurt his balls in brawls.

"Injury? No, *lah*." He laughs. "Master no fight, he make Indians fight. Master, he only boss of secret society. He work from office."

My weapon fizzles. And before I can fire another, Rachel wades in.

"Knew it!" She clasps her hands. "My Jackson is one classy person. I want to meet him now, like, really now."

Robert steps on the brake and shifts the automatic gear stick to D.

"Stop, stop!" Rachel calls. "I need to bring my stuff."

All chances for a Bollywood ending where our energies unite are disappearing before me.

"Why don't we just check first? We could come back and take your stuff later," I suggest, attempting to buy time.

"No, Kumar. It's him. I have my responsibilities. He has been working day and night, and he needs a break. I should shoulder some responsibilities. He working alone. Not nice."

So, we return to the apartment and pack Rachel's stuff. There isn't much to pack; her stuff is still in her spinner suitcase. She has kept its contents a guarded secret, opening the lid just a little to pull out those pink dresses.

I am going to be alone in the apartment starting tonight! I don't even want to think of it.

Kewin holds the door open for Rachel. When she is in, he looks at me like he has read my mood. "You don' worry, *ah*. I bring China rich girlfriend for you. Very pretty. No need pay now. Can pay on delivery."

I decline his kind offer and pull myself next to Rachel.

"Kumar," Rachel calls. She has slid against the seat with her eyes closed. I can see that she's back in her dreamy heaven.

The cab jumps forward.

"Yes, Rachel?"

"I have lots of dreams, Kumar. Our businesses, our little bungalows in Singapore, our children, our wedding," she murmurs.

Everything on her list is in reverse order.

She opens her eyes and looks at me. "Will you attend my wedding, Kumar?"

"Yes, I will. It would be a privilege to be your best man," I assure her. In my head, rehearsals for a nuptial where Jackson fails to show up begin.

She shuts her eyes, slides into her dreams, and begins mumbling. "My wedding. It will be in a lush green paddy field surrounding a little pond where lotuses bloom and ducks swim. There will be goats in one corner and cows in another. Birds will chirp from the branches of trees whose green apples swing in the gentle breeze."

Tears of joy blossom in my eyes. I know such a locality, and I see a man who can gift her such a wedding.

"Rachel." I take her arm. "Come with me, Rachel. Let's go to my village. It has many little lotus ponds, goats, unroasted ducks, cows, and even buffaloes. There are no green apples but ripe, fibrous mangoes and a hundred colored bananas. We can live happily thereafter, like the Bush family, the Obama family, and the Addams family."

"Huh?" She pulls back her arm. "I no want village. My wedding in Singapore."
"Singapore? I don't think we have paddy fields here in Singapore, Rachel."
"Right, Kumar. We don't have. Where there's nothing, create something."
I like her philosophy. It sounds more like a mantra. But questions remain.
"Where in Singapore would you create a paddy field, Rachel?" I ask.
"In the church."
"Church?" My heart skips a beat.
"Yes, Kumar. In the church. And I want you to be there for us."

The lower half of my stomach churns, demanding a gentle rub from me. Christ being born in a manger is indeed a romantic concept. Do I want to see a church turning into a cattle shed? Not even in my tin-roofed church.

She shuts her eyes again. A brief lull follows. When she opens them, I spot a strange emotion. Her soft hands land on mine. I know this is when she tells me she'll miss me in her life, and had she not known Jackson first, she would have loved me.

"My wedding won't happen without you, Kumar."
My mind is at the edge of my seat. *Say it, Rachel.*
"You grow big mustache, Kumar. I buy you big turban, long shirt, and long staff. You stand at church gate and receive guests."

I want to say something but can't find words. I turn my head away from her and stare out.

"Please, Kumar, this is our Singapore culture, and we've decided it already."

I have no words. My ECG graph plummets close to nonexistence.

The taxi turns left onto Geylang from Guillemard Road. It skips the finely laid streets with traditional landed houses, slows down, and halts before a shop with the sign 88 KTV and Body Spa. My mind recalls the well-known fact that crazy-rich Singaporeans live in landed houses, not apartments.

"This one from the Sung clan," Kewin says, unlocking the doors.

I look at the traditional two-story shop lot with the name 88 KTV stuck to it. A Frog Leg Soup Restaurant flanks it on the left, and a Body Spa to the right. A handful of women in short skirts and sleeveless tops are at the entrance. It's just 10:30 a.m., and to have such classy women before the KTV only vouches for its popularity and class.

Rachel alights and surveys the area with pride in her eyes. Kewin retrieves the spinner suitcase from the boot. I hand over her pink handbag. The ladies in the corridor spot us and huddle, discussing something in a hush-hush tone. Four fingers point at Rachel, and cell phones take her picture. They all begin texting on their phones. By the speed at which their thumbs move, I can tell they have broadcasted hundreds of messages.

Kewin pushes the KTV door. "Get in," he says, holding it open for Rachel.

Rachel walks in like a princess, and I follow.

"*Waseh*, Mama . . . you *sibei heng*. See who I bring, *nah*," Kewin says, gazing at the wooden cashier's counter. I see no soul behind the counter and wonder whom he is talking to. All I see is a golden cat with one arm swinging, a bowl with tiny bamboo plants, and a small board that reads MONEY MONEY COME COME.

"*Lai Mama* . . . your grandson's girlfriend. Come from America, *leh*," Kewin speaks again. We still hear no response.

I survey the room. Red cushioned sofas and paintings of landscapes with cherry blossoms. In the center sits a tea table with a quaint kettle and a few glasses.

Rachel is fidgeting with the strap of her handbag. She is nervous. So am I. So is Kewin.

"My gran'son *dun wan* Amelican," a frail voice says from behind the counter. Kewin sinks to his knees and rests his fat bum on his heels. He signals us to do the same. We follow.

A hundred-year-old woman with silver hair and wrinkles of experience steps out. I lift my head to steal a proper glance. Rachel and Kewin have their foreheads kissing the wooden floor.

"Get up."

We rise.

"Where got luck?" She surveys Rachel from toe to head, shoulder to shoulder, navel to neck. "My gran'son *mai* Amelican. You canno come. You canno see him!" She points at the door through which we have just come.

"Mama, please let me see my Jackson. I have traveled thousands of miles to see my love. My heart and soul belong to him." Rachel kneels and kisses her wrinkled arm.

Mama pulls back her arm. "You Amelican. No Chinese. You no know Chinese culture. You no know how I make this business so *atas*." She points to the wooden roof, and it begins creaking like magic.

Put your hands up . . . oh oh, ah ah

I hear a lady singing. Not a bad singer. But perhaps asthmatic, as she gasps for breath.

Ah . . . oh . . . ah . . . mhhh

It isn't easy to sing while wheezing. I appreciate her passion for singing, despite the difficulty.

"I tell you *har*, this house use sweat, and bed build one *hor*."

I'm confused if Mama meant *blood* or *bed*.

"Famous people come here: China, *ang moh*, Lindian," she continues. "Everyone come, everyone happy, make business good."

She then touches Rachel's forehead as if in a curse. "You no understand, catch no ball. Go back, dun *kacau* my business."

"Mama—"

"Dun talk," Mama interrupts her.

I look at Rachel. She is still on her knees, her spinner suitcase behind and her handbag to the side. I know the hardships she has gone through for love's sake. *What will she do now?* Kewin is back on his feet, but I can see his trembling knees.

Rachel looks up. I spot no tears in her eyes. Instead, I see beams of confidence, as if she has anticipated this. She leans back while still on her knees, drags the suitcase closer, and opens it.

"Chopsticks." She pulls out a pair of chopsticks and places it at Mama's feet.

"*Budai.*" Out comes a golden laughing Buddha. Rachel holds it with utmost care, like it's a newborn, and places it next to the chopsticks. I look at the mama. She isn't impressed.

"Sarong." She pulls out a pinkish lungi. "My girls will wear this to sarong parties when they grow up."

Not a wrinkle moves on Mama's face. My heart paints pity over Rachel as her weapons fizzle out one after the other.

But Rachel is unfazed. She takes a deep breath, tilts her body sideways, and as if she is pulling the mythical *dao* sword, she retrieves a puffy pink cloth and places it before the old lady. "Sponge-padded bra," she says in the same poised tone. "Where there's nothing, create something."

I learn the true meaning of her mantra.

Mama's facial expressions change. Her tears find their way through the wrinkle channels as she eyeballs the sponge-padded bra. She wipes the tears, bends down, and touches Rachel's shoulders.

"You, my child, O, my God-sent child. This family wan you. You the right person for Jackson!"

She hugs Rachel, and Rachel hugs her back. Copious tears flow in their eyes, in mine, and in Kewin's.

"Bring Jackson here!" Mama orders Kewin, and he darts to the stairs like an obedient servant. The women are still hugging and crying in happiness.

Footsteps thump down the wooden staircase, and Jackson descends. Since Mama is still hugging Rachel, he has no option but to join them. Kewin and I witness the happy ending. When the group hug ends, Mama takes Rachel's hand and places a bunch of keys.

"*Haiya*, time for me retire, *lah*. Now you boss *liao*. You make this place *hoseh* an' *atas*, OK?"

Rachel bows and takes the keys. "I will do everything to uphold the reputation of this house, Mama."

"I tell you one thing, *ah*, never stop the music." Mama points to the squeaking ceiling. "You no mistake that I so *ya ya*. January 1992, George Bush Senior come Singapore, got music in this KTV. November 2009, when Obama come Singapore, there still got music in this KTV. One day, a super *atas* man will become the president of United States an' make Amelica white again. He come *lai*, an' that one our golden moment in history. But . . . but you canno let him grope our women." She raises her finger to make a point and continues, "Not like that, not for free. Here, no money, no honey."

"*Haiyo*, Mamasan . . ." The door swings open, and a group of men with black faux-leather bags tucked under their armpits walks in. I spot many others in the corridor, where a commotion has brewed. The faces of the ladies who were texting in the corridor are visible near the jamb, but their bodies remain hidden.

"You got new package coming, *ah*? Can reserve, oh?" the guy at the front of the group asks, showing her the images on his cell phone.

"Why you talk cock? Package, you head, *lah*! My gran'son already chop, oh. She my mooncake, my darling." Mama's voice rises as she speaks.

"Oh, Mama, why you so *kiasu*? Relax, *lah*. We pay good price, *lo*!" He takes out his wallet.

"You get out, *kanina*."

Her voice is frail but determined, with the tone and tenor of the matriarch elephant that senses danger to her herd. The group retreats and makes themselves scarce behind the door.

The music stops on the floor above, and the asthmatic singer is now in pain; I can hear her moaning.

Rachel gives me a parting hug.

"Goodbye, Kumar." She holds my arm and places a business card of the house in my hand.

"Eighteen percent flat discount," it says. I see her moving into her new role with ease and my destiny shifting further away.

The apartment is empty. Not that Rachel was the talkative type, but she had a certain aura. Had we clicked, we could have consummated our union on the next full-moon night and achieved moksha through sexuality. I roll on the couch, staring at the vacant one opposite me. I take a long time to fall asleep. But my sleep doesn't last long, as my cell phone tears into my slumber.

Rachel calling.

Why would she call me at midnight? Is she missing me, too? Is the prophecy being fulfilled? Thoughts flash by.

"Kumar, I am going back!" Her voice trembles. My sleep evaporates as I stand, wondering what could have gone wrong.

She narrates the events amid sniveling and sobbing. Rachel was born in 1988, the year of the Dragon. Jackson was born in 1985, the year of the Ox.

"Dragon and Ox cannot be in love. Dragon eat Ox. We no match," she explains.

She has even bought a return ticket for the next flight through Taipei, via the same airlines.

I meet her at the airport to see her off. She has the same determination and confidence that I saw in her eyes when she pulled out the chopsticks before the mamasan.

"Come to Little Lotus Pond, Rachel." I give a final try, for the sake of the prophecy. "We can write our love story and sell a million copies. We can go back to China—I mean Chinatown in Manhattan—for holidays every year. I can also get you a lavish wedding right in a paddy field, with cows and buffaloes. We will shower each other with limitless love and revel in eternal happiness."

"No, Kumar, no. Our cultures not same-same." She breaks my heart.

We hug and pour tears on each other's shoulders. My heart sinks, knowing that we won't be meeting again. Rachel opens her handbag and pulls out that purple book. "It's for you, Kumar. I won't need it anymore." She hands it over.

I open it to the first page.

> *China is a sleeping giant*
> *Let her sleep, for*
> *when she wakes*
> *she will move the world*
>   *—Napoleon Bonaparte*

"But Rachel—"

"No, Kumar, no. Please don't stop me. I must go," she says and walks away with the spinner suitcase trailing behind.

China is a sleeping giant.

I read it again. And the unasked question bugs me once again.

But why Singapore?

I sit down on the steel tubing running parallel to the departure area's glass walls and flip the pages. The young girls opposite me have their eyes fixed on a cell phone screen. Must be a soccer match or a fashion show. One of them looks up at me and says something to the others. They all fix their eyes on me. I turn back to see if there are some celebrities behind me. All I can see is the glass panel. They march toward me.

"Your friend, your friend." One of them hands over her phone. I look at it. In an ongoing live stream on Facebook, Rachel is hugging a white man in a pilot's uniform. I recognize him by his sharp nose. It's the pilot who rebuked Rachel. He proposed to her at the security gate, the girls explain.

"Oh my God! Lovely couple. Me so happy for them."

"*Walao*, she so lucky, got *ang moh*!"

"Made for each other."

"I want one, oh. Can bring him *chionging* every day."

"*Yalo, yalo.* Maybe he got brother."

I walk back, shaking my head. It is clear the loves of my life are awaiting me elsewhere.

"*Thampi*," a voice in chaste Tamil halts me. My legs stop; I spot a man in orange robes and a long beard smiling at me.

"She's calling you." He hands over a pamphlet.

Ten-day tantric retreat in Thailand, organized by Happiness Yoga. I read it over and over again.

Tantra comes looking for me!

Chapter 15

The SilkAir flight lands in Koh Samui and pulls over next to a cargo plane basking under the Thailand sun. I disembark and walk over to the arrivals, accepting the ground staff's warm *sawadee khap* greeting.

The airport is more of a resort, with little chalet-like buildings and coconut trees. I withdraw Thai baht from an ATM, decline a printed receipt, and save a tree. Someday, an atheist will disrupt my sermon, accusing me of constructing my ashrams in wildlife corridors. The tree I saved will collapse over him and repay its debt.

For three hundred Thai baht, I buy a SIM card with bountiful internet. I will now have to find a shared taxi to Maenam Pier, then a ferry from there on to Thong Sala—as stated in the mysterious monk's pamphlet. Finding a taxi operator offering shared ride combos with a ferry ticket isn't difficult. But finding a taxi is—because there isn't one! After I've been walking around and around the parking bay, a lady spots me and comes running.

"You go to Koh Pha-Ngan, sir?" she asks, pointing at the yellow, pink, and white bills in my hand.

"Yes, to Thong Sala."

She ushers me to her vehicle. I learn something new—a taxi in Thailand can be a pickup converted into a passenger vehicle—*songthaew* is the name. Most of them are tangible manifestations of psychedelic visions. Mine just comes in white, pure white. I'm offered a seat in the rear deck, next to a box full of durians, to add some flavor to the trip. We wait for a few more people to join and then set out—me; my white *farang* co-passengers; the driver, who is always on the phone; and the durians.

At the pier, I transfer to the ferry. The thirty-minute ferry ride to Thong Sala is as smooth as the stewardess's blushed-up cheeks.

"If you put your luggage inside, please take it with you. If you left it outside, you can collect it from the pier," she announces our arrival.

I had transferred 400 euros in advance, taking a considerable load off my bank account. Accommodation charges are extra, to be paid in person. The mission is to find cheaper accommodation close to Happiness Yoga.

"*Kob-khun krab*," I read out from the pamphlet to the *songthaew* driver. He takes me up and down the undulating roads for ten minutes and drops me at the tile-roofed ashram, standing on a neatly mowed lawn like the cherry on a green velvet cake.

I have seen pictures of Happiness Yoga on Guru Shivpremananda's Instagram account. He humbled me by following me back almost instantly. That was a sign. I now look forward to taking a leaf out of his book, with or without his permission. Because every disciple of Bhagwan is a signboard on the path to my destiny.

Our paths and mission are similar. We both found our calling to spread love through Bhagwan. But he has found his destination while I'm still searching. The seeker in me has questions lined up for the guru. For instance, how did a weed-smoking van Dijk from the Netherlands metamorphose into Guru Shivpremananda?

"Namaste." I put my hands together at the reception.

"Namaste," she replies, getting up from her seat and stretching her neck, curious to know if somebody else was with me. I look back; a mongrel is scratching his belly on the lawn.

"I'm here for the tantric retreat." I tell her about the prophecy and the signs that led me here.

She flips the pages of the register so fast. "I'm sorry, sir, but we are running full. The workshop is exclusively for registered participants."

I show her the screenshot of the registration I had made.

"Richard Parker?" She makes a capital *O* with her lipsticked mouth.

"Yes."

"Has he come?"

"Who?"

"Richard Parker?"

"I am Richard Parker." I control my irritation.

"Oh . . . please wait here, sir." She takes the ledger and disappears behind the white curtain with frangipanis embossed all over.

I sit on the lumbar bench. Ten minutes tick past, and she is yet to appear. Brass bells chime, and the sound of *kirtans* soon fills the air. My heart hankers to get in.

Another *songthaew* arrives, and a tall, pale-faced guy in black boots, pants pulled above the navel, and a tucked-in shirt steps out. *A fellow Indian, but from the north, or a Pakistani,* I guess.

"Woof!" the mongrel that didn't even notice me runs to him like he is his long-lost relative. He sidesteps it and walks in, filling the lobby with a mustard-oil scent.

"Hello," I greet. He pretends not to notice and sits on the bench opposite me.

The lady reappears. "I'm sorry, sir. Because of certain policy constraints, we cannot admit you."

"What?" I spring to my feet. "This is unfair. I have flown all the way from Singapore for this!" I thump on her desk.

"Relax, buddy. They deserve the right to deny admissions." It's the stranger. His strong accent strikes me in my face, especially the way he pronounced *deserve* as *dejerve*. He steps closer, unfolds the pamphlet, and puts it on the desk before me.

"Let me read it for you. The organizers reserve the right to deny access or entry to the workshops or any related events at any time if they feel that the presence of the candidate would vitiate the safety and well-being of others."

"Excuse me, do I know you? I'm talking to the lady here."

"I'm trying to help." He shakes his head and looks at her. "Maybe you can sort this out later at your mutual convenience. Could you please check me in?"

"May I know your name, sir?" She turns her attention toward him like I did not exist.

"Sharma, Ranjit Sharma." He drums his fingers on the desk, looking at me with pity.

She turns the pages of the ledger while I rewind my memory to figure out what went wrong. *Does the Brotherhood's overseas wing run the retreat? Is there an international blacklist for cow offenders like me? Was the wise man in the orange robe playing a prank on me?*

"I'm sorry, sir, you have been denied entry, too," she says with the same polite tone she used on me.

"This is impossible! I have traveled from Gorakhpur in Uttar Pradesh, ignoring the tantra retreats in the Himalayas. You can't deny entry to me!" He thumps on the desk exactly as I did a few moments ago.

I smile. A beautiful sense of peace has replaced the anger and disappointment in me.

She takes the pamphlet he had read to me and drags her finger over it. "The organizers reserve the right to deny access or entry to the workshops or any related events at any time if they feel that the presence of the candidate would vitiate the safety and well-being of others."

"Can I talk to the guru, please?" I intervene to remind her of my presence.

She looks at me like I just committed blasphemy. "Sorry, sir. You cannot meet him without an appointment. He is in the session already. If you want an appointment, I can book one for you. But the next one will be eleven days from now."

"Oh."

I think about it. I could harness my Indian democratic spirit and do a sit-in. That might have some effect. But why? I came here for something precious that had been promised to me. The romantic idea of Koh Pha-Ngan as a sacred space disappears, and the promise of limitless love now appears as solid as ether.

I close my eyes and take a deep breath, listening to my heart. *Leave the island*, it says. I shouldn't be in a place that doesn't want me. She books another colorful taxi for me and assures me of a refund of the registration fee.

"Hey, bro." Sharma waves from across the tiny lobby. "Are you a South Indian?" I notice the scorn on his face.

"Yes. I am. I'm a son of the south."

"May I know your good name?"

"Richard Parker." It wasn't me but the receptionist who responded.

Sharma breaks into laughter. "Rice-bag convert!" He laughs again. "You guys should stay in the south and eat the rotten rice the missionaries have left behind. Why do you follow us everywhere? Look what you have done. I would have been in if it weren't for you."

I look at him. Bhagwan's teachings call upon us to ignore idiots. I, his disciple, am alert. The world can't betray my peace. But I must point out his ignorance. Ignorance is not bliss.

The *songthaew* arrives, and I get up. "Bye, Ranjit Sharma. Are you flying back to Uttar Pradesh?"

"I might."

"Enjoy sipping cow urine . . . and, *ah*, take care not to step on cow dung on your roads." I smile and walk out. I imagine his expression staring at my back. It feels good.

The first thing I do on the *songthaew* to Thong Sala is to look for the guru on my Instagram followers list. Shivpremanand69 does not appear anywhere. He has unfollowed me. So, I unfollow him, too. Two minutes later, the app buzzes. He follows me again. I follow him back. Ten seconds later, my followers count drops back to 199 from 200. I find his profile and unfollow him again. He keeps me company until I reach the pier.

I buy a ticket to Koh Samui. I also book a flight ticket to Bangkok—the city of love.

Chapter 16

Once in Bangkok, I lose the excitement of *songthaew*. Like the *Agaricus* mushrooming after the monsoon in the coconut groves of Little Lotus Pond, the colorful pickup taxis are everywhere. Everything in Bangkok is multicolored, occurring in contrasting pairs. It doesn't take much time to figure out how the whites became a minority in the West; they are all in Bangkok with girls half their age and size.

I check into a budget hotel in Soi Sukhumvit 11. The receptionist inquires about the purpose of my visit. I blurt out that I'm a writer, sending her eyebrows up and down like catamarans.

The first thing I do after checking in is to install Tinder and set up a profile. I never used it in India, to avoid honey traps. I would have used it in Singapore, except for Rachel and the spring blossoms she'd brought into my mind. But life must move on.

I swipe right until I hit the quota threshold. Tinder swipes in Thailand come with a caution: objects in the profile may not be of the same sex as they appear. I have read plenty of jokes on the internet; so have you. One thing we must appreciate: Thailand has given its people the freedom to explore the boundaries of gender. Back home in India, a transgender person has only two occupations: to beg or to steal. Their wealthy families abandon them the moment they notice their fluid gender. They then flock to their community, which welcomes them with open hearts. Mission tantra at Koh Pha-Ngan might have failed, but I'm thankful to the orange-robed monk for leading me to the city of love. Maybe Bangkok is the missing tab of the puzzle, and Pha-Ngan was just a pit stop.

My heart craves an intense tantra session. I have heard that some of Bangkok's famous spas also offer tantric massage sessions. As the saying goes, something is better than nothing! But how can I find a spa without an online search? After multiple deep breaths and closed-eyed contemplations, I relax the rule of going with the flow. Online searches are permitted henceforth on rare occasions that guarantee enlightenment.

I shortlist three spas and settle for Passionate Spa. They offer tantric massage sessions that will awaken the senses. Although every other spa promises the same, I choose this one for a particular claim: "We accept every nationality; we are not worried if you are a Westerner or Asian." A cheap spa in Bangkok has a better sense of diversity than self-proclaimed gurus charging hundreds of euros to spread love. The plan is to go for a massage this evening and then join some day tour tomorrow.

I walk to the lobby and browse through their tour brochures. The package with temples and the floating market appeal to me. I pay 1400 baht.

"The van come seven oh cock. Please have breakfast quick-quick and be ready," the receptionist reminds me.

I take a tuk-tuk to Passionate Spa. Since it isn't an app tuk-tuk, I must feed the address into my cell phone map. In my excitement, I had forgotten to recharge my phone. Three streets before the spa, the battery enters the meditative state. That's a sign. I ask the driver to drop me there and begin walking, using the map I have memorized.

"Hello . . . want massage?"

"Bubble bath!"

"Nuri Gel . . ."

"Fish bowl?"

"Happy ending, sir?"

I ignore them because the tantric in me knows what he wants. Ignoring such calls is not without its pains, however. The last one I avoided calls out from behind. "I know you, Indian. Indian like boom-boom! You can boom-boom me. You want, sir?" I walk fast to escape further embarrassment. In front of me are four men dressed in formal attire, complete with office bags and boots. One of them wears a black suit and has a file in hand. It doesn't take much to identify my compatriots. As the famous saying back in Little Lotus Pond goes, *a snake knows its legs*. They must be on the way to attend interviews. It's half past eight, and I wonder what kind of firm would invite them for an evening interview.

I am ashamed. Here I am in Bangkok, rubbernecking in half pants and an orange T-shirt, looking for a cheap tantric massage to heal my wounds. And walking ahead of me are middle-aged Indians hunting for jobs. I put myself in their black boots. Ridiculed for being unemployed in their hometown and setting out to strange lands to find whatever job comes up! I admire them.

"Boom-boom, sir. All fair girls," a lady in a blue T-shirt and black shorts calls out to them from a corridor. All four stop in perfect synchrony, turn in the direction of the lady, and walk in one after the other.

My admiration vanishes without a trace.

Passionate Spa is just fifty meters from where my admiration ended. It looks like every other spa I have avoided on the way.

"You want massage?" one of the ladies in the corridor asks. They are all dressed in pink tees and black skirts.

"I . . . I . . . tantra . . . ," I stammer, swallowing saliva.

"Yes, yes. Come in, sir. Our tantric massage very good." She steps forward and takes my arms. I follow her like a child on the first day of kindergarten or a sacrificial lamb—whichever you wish to imagine.

"Which one you want, sir?" she says, pointing to the giggling girls. My inner thighs receive the first drops of sweat.

"You don't have tantric? Tantra . . . tantra." I open my arms and join my thumb and forefinger to form the chin mudra.

The girls burst into laughter. They line up on the bench and point fingers at each other, signaling, *Take her*.

My sweat glands work overtime. *Richard Parker, are you alert?* I ping. There's no response. *Should I go back? Was it a mistake?* I hesitate, but the lady who brought me in is alert. Before I can take off, she thrusts me, and I land in the embrace of an angel in pink. My hands grasp her thin waist, and my face is between her bosoms. She lifts my head and kisses me below my ears.

"Four thousand baht, sir, pay now," the mamasan calls from the counter.

I pull out my wallet. I pay. I follow her.

She is young, charming, and attractive, her dental braces enhancing her smile. She has braces!

My mind alerts me to the possibility of ending up in a Thai jail for pedophilia, one of the worst crimes of our time. I try to guess her age but can't because I should be looking at her identity card, not her sexy bottom swaying ahead of me on the stairs.

The room isn't lit in red. There's no burning lamp, no smell of sandalwood or incense. A king-size bed with blue sheets contradicts the pink walls. On one corner stands a clear glass shower enclosure. "Tantra, tantra." I remind her of my mission.

"Here have tantra, sir. No worry, no worry," she says in Tinglish. She holds her identity card before my eyes, and I read her age as twenty-seven.

"My name Cupid," she says, giggling. "Work part time."

Cupid. I love the name. It's romantic, but not as much as Shivpremanand69.

"Are we lighting incense?" I ask.

"Thai use incense for prayers only," she replies.

I insist on lighting incense to transform the ambience into a meditative one. She instead is keen on stripping me nude and sending me to the shower. I tire of fending off her arms, which are aiming for my undies, and we come to a compromise—I'm to shower while she fetches the incense sticks. I bolt the door and get my mortal body into the warm shower.

When I'm done with my express shower, I hear the knock on the door. I open the door. She stands with her hands on her hips, wondering what's happening. I tell her I had to lock the door because the shower enclosure is transparent. She laughs and stretches out her hand to show the three incense sticks nestled between her fingers. She sets them on the corner table next to a bottle that reads *Thai aromatic oil* and lights them. A jasmine-smoke aroma graces the room.

"Please sit here. I go shower first."

I sit in the lotus pose and close my eyes. Behind me, I hear the shower. I focus on my breath because the shower sound is too distracting. The goal is to transcend into a spiritual state before she joins me.

After a few breaths, I realize she is in the shower, and the shower enclosure is transparent, and I'm just sitting there with my back to her.

I jump out of bed. Behind the enclosure, frosted by the vapors, is Cupid, her hourglass body moving like a lotus swaying in the morning drizzle. I haven't seen a naked female before, except in wet dreams. My throat is dry, and I sweat once more.

The door opens, and the vapors emerge first, followed by her. Her naughty eyes fixate on my waist while the towel in her hands pats the remaining droplets on her body. I look down and realize that my towel had deserted me long back, and I'm in nirvana. She giggles as though her second name is Gigglepid. I pick up my towel and wrap it around my waist with a nice tent at the center. Not knowing where to look, I turn semicircle and face the wall.

"You ready?"

"I'm ready anytime. Let me know when you are ready, too," I say, still facing the wall, where a happy lizard has appeared.

Her arm is around my waist, and her breath is behind my ears. Three seconds later, I feel the hard bed beneath my back and the soft Cupid over me. "Tantra, tantra," I say, stopping her.

"This is tantra already, sir."

"No, no! Tantra. Tantric massage." I join my thumb and forefinger, shut my eyes, and inhale-exhale.

"Oh! You want hand job?" Her hands slide down to my hardening part.

"No! No!" I stop her. I explain to her in simple English about tantra, who Bhagwan was, and how to attain moksha. She sits with her face cradled on her hands across her naked bosom. I bet she has never heard about achieving orgasm through the mere union of souls. Nobody has ever told her that making love is a spiritual act.

"Kiss is not about suckling each other's lips. It begins with the gentle brushing of lips. But according to the Kama Sutra, there are thirty different ways to kiss, you know?"

Her eyes widen. "Nice, sir. But . . . but here no kiss." She puts her index finger on her lips. "Here, everything safety. No kiss, no AIDS," she continues, spotting the disappointment in my eyes. "But here can." She flips her hair and points to her bosom.

I look at the ceiling, pondering how to explain. I realize three things: one, I want a tantric massage, but I don't want to be nude; two, I want the union of masculine and feminine powers, and I've got a hooker with whom I don't want to have sex; three, I'm confused and don't know what I want.

I explain the union of male and female powers and the path to moksha.

"I no need moksha," she protests.

"Yes, you do." I explain the beauty of moksha, the eternal bliss.

"Oh . . . I understand." She laughs. "It's like, you tip me a lot, sir. I go shopping. Shopping make me happy. Shopping make me bliss."

I sigh. We stop discussing and hug each other.

"Breathe with me . . ." I whisper in her ear.

She obliges, and we breathe in unison until I hear her snore vibrating over my shoulders.

I lay her down on the bed and rest next to her, listening to our breathing streams. Sometimes we sync; sometimes we don't. Sometimes it's a treble and sometimes bass. My mind digs into all the books of Bhagwan I have read for anything he said about breathing. I don't remember any. If he were still alive, I would ask the teacher about deciphering the music in a lady's breath cycle. Or maybe I should decode it myself. After all, he is my master.

I press my ear against her bare back and listen to the rise and fall of her breath. Between our two streams of breath, I hear a third one—a faint one like that of a child. *Is she pregnant?*

The sound grows in intensity, and it's more like a grumble now. But I can hear three hearts beating.

Richard Parker, I hear a voice say.

I withdraw from her and look around. My eyes confirm there's just the two of us while my mind chides me for not buying a talisman from the astrologer.

I put my ears back against her soft skin and hug her. She wriggles a bit, takes my arm, puts it over her bosom to bring us to the spoon-sutra position, and slips back into sleep. My blood would have boiled but for the mysterious voice, which is louder now.

Richard Parker, my son. Do you hear me?

Yes, I do.

My mind returns the call without waiting for my permission.

I'm glad to hear that, my son. It's going to be a long journey together, and communication is important.

Huh? May I know who this is?

You know me. I have watched you sleep, seen your tears, and listened to your heartbeat. You called for me.

Me? Call for you? I don't know you.

Don't worry, you will get to know me. Do you see the pure soul within your arm's reach?

I bend my neck and send my eyes down the contours of her back, to the curvy world beneath.

Yes, I do.

Are you alert?

Yes, I am.

Why aren't you having a quickie, then?

Her cell phone sounds an alarm, and she wakes up. The voice disappears, but I pick up the clue in the quickie gibe. *Was that Bhagwan himself speaking to me?* I pinch myself. He could have chosen any among his thousands of postmenopause followers. But he has chosen me! The muscles around my hair follicles tighten, and my hairs stand erect.

Thus ends my tantric session with a wholehearted embrace and deep breath. The incense has died long back, leaving a weird smell behind. The lizard on the wall has also disappeared.

I tip her and take a tuk-tuk back to my hotel, with Bhagwan's voice in me.

"How is Bangkok, sir?" the driver asks after our brief introduction. His name tag reads *A-wut*. I notice there's no Ting in his English.

"Amazing. Thai women, beautiful. Thai women, great hospitality," I explain in simple English.

"Oh yes, sir. You Indian?"

"Yes!" I gift him the rare pleasure of meeting an Indian. We all know how much influence India had on Southeast Asia. I look at him with pride in my eyes.

"We get plenty of Indian tourists," he says, looking at my image in his rearview mirror. "All male tourists, looking for sex."

He is looking at the mirror more than the road. I notice.

"Oh no, A-wut. Sorry to know that. I'm not here for sex. I wanted a tantric massage. It's so spiritual, you know?"

"Really, sir?" A-wut is surprised.

"Yes." I simplify tantra for him. You never know—he could be my first disciple.

"The last passenger I picked up was also an Indian. He also said the same." He pauses the conversation to overtake a truck and continues, "Every year, a million Indian tourists visit Thailand. Together with Chinese and Australian tourists, they fuel prostitution and women trafficking," he says, still looking at the mirror.

My heart picks up the tone and tenor of his voice, its ideology, and analyzes it. All this happens in split seconds.

When my analysis is done, I ask if he is a Communist.

"No, sir, I'm a Socialist," he says.

I learn something new: one can be a Socialist without being a Communist.

Chapter 17

I wake up early with a clear head. It wasn't difficult to sleep because I was confused enough. Bhagwan says confusing the mind prevents it from boarding thought trains and tricks it into sleep. Like the wise fisher in muddy waters, a saint stirs his mind to achieve clarity. Setbacks are part of the spiritual journey, and my job is to keep going, following the signs.

I ask the server what's for breakfast, and he replies, "*jokee*," without batting his eyelids and proceeds to serve the Chinese tourists. That's the Tinglish version of *joke*, I'm sure. I look at the multiple reflections of me in the mirroring wall panels. Nowhere close to a joker; I'm handsome as usual.

"Wow, *jokee's* yummy," a tourist exclaims, and I take a telescopic look at her bowl.

Thai people have a great sense of humor. That's why they named their favorite breakfast dish *joke*. It's an overcooked rice porridge served with egg and minced pork. I close my eyes and savor the first spoon. Pure delicacy! I add it to my buccal list.

I can't eat breakfast alone because that would look weird in the modern world. So, I put my cell phone on the table, and like any normal human, I bifurcate my attention between the *joke* and the cell phone. After five minutes, I figure out that Tinder is as delicious as joke and shift my focus toward it.

You have zero matches.

A traveler should never give up until he reaches his destination. I swipe right on every profile that looks like a lady. I respect ladyboys, although I just don't understand why Tinder doesn't allocate them a third gender. As I swipe, I learn something new. Thai women love porn and boast about it in their screen names. I swipe left on a few porns and realize I don't have many profiles left to swipe right. So, I swipe right on porns, too. Bhagwan would have agreed that it's a form of meditation. My thumb is the only part moving until a familiar face flaunting her braces pops up.

> Cupid
> Age 27
> 18 km away
> *I want a Farang husband. If you looking for hookup, swipe left!*

As I'm not looking for a hookup, I swipe right.

"I sit here, OK?"

I put my phone face down on the table and look up. It's a pretty lady in a flowery frock and hat, reading from her cell phone. She is probably using translation software. No, I don't ask her if her name is Rachel. I don't ask her for her name at all.

"Yes, please." I nod and look around at the empty seats. My alert mind rings the alarm, reminding me that ladyboys aren't a part of the prophecy.

She gets a bowl of *joke*, too. An awkward silence prevails. I try to break it.

"Oh . . . you from Bangkok?"

"*Mai chai*, Thai. Chiang Mai," she replies. I can understand that without the translating software.

"You?"

"India."

She types something into her cell phone and reads with astonishment. "A country where soups don't have lemongrass." She types again and reads. "Why you hate lemongrass, *la*?"

"No, no. We love lemongrass. We have it in our soaps and mosquito repellents."

She shakes her head in disbelief. I wonder if she understood the sarcasm. But the word *soap* should have been obvious. We immerse our attention in our *jokes* and bid polite, well-mannered goodbyes once we are done. I pat myself on the back for not wasting time on a character that is not a part of the oracle.

After breakfast, I wait in the lobby for my day-tour operator. I have fifteen days in Thailand before the visa on arrival expires. I'll have to leave the country even if the sign doesn't come by then. But fifteen days is enough to go bankrupt if I'm not prudent with my expenses. I'll have to stick to public transport and sour street food from tomorrow onward.

The van that's supposed to pick me up at 7:00 arrives at 7:30. That's thirty minutes earlier by Indian standards and thirty-one minutes late by Singaporean practice. The white *farang* tourists occupy the front seats, displaying the privilege they get in Asia. I walk to the rear and take the window seat.

"Wait, *gorn*. Have one more tourist," the tour operator says, tucking his black faux-leather bag under his armpit. The "lady" in the hat pops up in the lobby and hurries toward us. I wriggle my bum on my seat. There is only one seat left, which is beside me.

"Hi again." I grin as she sits next to me.

The long, winding road to Damnoen Saduak, twisting through the hinterlands, is a romantic scene. It's picture-perfect, with a pretty lass napping on my shoulder. Except that it isn't a lass at all. I sigh.

The operator drops us at the corner of the floating market. "You walk one hour, later come back here," he says.

The group disperses, and I stroll through the rows of shops selling souvenirs, T-shirts, and hats on the embankment. The hat reminds me of her, and I wonder where she went. She could be anywhere. It's her country, after all. I turn around to see what she might be up to and spot her following me, tracing my steps one after the other as if she is my effing shadow.

"I join you, yes?" she asks.

"Hmm . . . OK. Why not?" I can make use of a translator if needed. That way, she can contribute to my mission and not be a distraction.

We get to a kiosk, and I pick a *khanom buang*, the Thai crepe with white cream at the center, garnished with silky egg-yolk threads. I take a bite, punching my incisors through the crispy crepe and into the cream filling. Sugar molecules escape and grace the tip of my tongue. A spring of sweetness jets out from underneath my tongue, and the crepe enters my buccal list.

She buys nothing. "Very sweet, no healthy," she says.

I chuckle.

We spend the remaining fifteen minutes at a café, savoring coffee and crepe in the company of the now-familiar awkward silence.

She types on her phone. I know another question is coming.

"What are you doing this evening? Can we go out for dinner?"

"What?" The snack slips from my hand.

"Dinner . . . dinner. You, me, go eat together."

"I know. I know the meaning of *dinner*. But I'm busy." I shake my head.

"Oh . . . solly," she says and bows her head.

I sigh in relief.

We embark the same boat, too. It's tough to avoid looking at the beauty sitting on the seat before me. Our longboat cleaves through the inches of spaces between boats, scraping a couple of them. We stop before souvenir shops where vendors sit with their feet immersed in water. I buy nothing. The fumy atmosphere makes us smell like diesel; people scream to be heard amid the roar of the engines. She now has a surgical mask covering her nose and mouth. I wish the ordeal would end soon.

"Many tourist. Not good *loey*," she says, reading my mind, pointing out where the problem lies.

"Yes." I nod.

"We tourist, too." She chortles.

I sit tight-lipped.

We stop at the Karen village on the way back to the city. "Long-neck tribe, Karen people, very cute, very innocent. Can take photo," the guide shouts. We all reciprocate with a "yay" in chorus. It's another once-in-a-lifetime opportunity. I hope to take Instagrammable pictures with the long-necked girls; that should get me at least another ten followers. She refuses to join us and remains in the van. After paying three hundred baht as an entrance fee, I walk into the circular courtyard lined with shops, where long-necked girls crochet when they aren't posing with tourists. I zero in on a young girl and an old lady for my photographs. A wrinkled face held up by the brass neck rings is the perfect shot I want, but the poor camera on my cell phone doesn't help much. I remind myself to invest in a good camera when this novel becomes a bestseller. Time flies so fast at the Karen village that I must forgo the elephant safari in the adjacent park.

"You missed the opportunity," I say, showing her the photographs on my cell phone. It would have been a bonus to have her posing next to the wrinkled lady; that contrast would be an instant hit.

"Me no go there *ar*," she says, staring out the window.

"Why? You no like culture?"

"Culture what?" She frightens my gentle soul. "Thai people no monkeys. People go free. People no good in zoo," she adds with tearful eyes.

I am silent. A million-dollar question arises in my mind: *What is she doing on this trip if she enjoys nothing?*

She has a point. But then, the people who set up this village also have a point. I rub my forehead, and a familiar question pops up: *Could she be a Communist?* She doesn't look anywhere close to the dirty commies back home. In subtle makeup and well dressed, she is elegant and beautiful. Even with that sad face, she could beat a beauty pageant winner hands down.

Don't let the world fool you, Bhagwan reminds me.

True. The last thing I want is to invest in an entrance that will never open.

I delete the photographs I took with the Karen people. Somehow I feel better.

"You go elephant safari?" I ask her.

"Elephant wild. Wild animal go free in jungle. Elephant safari no good," she says, anger replacing the sadness in her tone.

Then why are you here on this trip? I want to ask, but something in my heart stops me.

The van starts, and she swaps seats with a big white guy in the front. Thankfully, he doesn't nap on my shoulder.

When we reach the hotel, she steps out of the van and darts to the stairs. I wish she would turn back and say goodbye. But she doesn't.

I don't want a ladyboy, but I can't help wishing "she" would turn around, run toward me, and ask me again for dinner. I sit on the lobby couch next to the empty tour desk with pamphlets strewn all over. The receptionists are giggling, passing frequent glances at me. They are having a good time at my cost. But if that gives them happiness, why not? That's a zen moment.

I look up and close my eyes. A question comes into my mind: *Am I bisexual?*

The giggles repeat, and I open my eyes to look at the receptionists. They stop and pretend to work.

I pick up my bag and walk to the elevator. I know there will be another morning, and I'm going to meet her again for another *joke*.

The morning arrives, and so does my bowl of *joke*. But she isn't there.

After breakfast, I walk to the lobby. The ladies who giggled at me last evening are still on their shift.

"Sawadee khap."

"Sawadee khap."

"I'm looking for the . . ." I struggle for the right word to describe "her."

"She left early morning, sir," one of them says.

"Oh . . ." I spot the sympathy on their faces. "You mean the one with the hat? You know, the—"

"Yes, sir," she interrupts and turns toward the magazines on the desk behind her.

"This lady?" She spreads three magazines on the desk.

"Yes, yes. It's her."

"Khun Nita," they titter. "She famous model girl in Thailand, sir."

"Oh, you have ladyboy models, too?"

"She lady, sir. No ladyboy!"

"Oh . . ."

They look at each other and cackle. I can't understand their conversation anymore, but I figure out they are having fun again.

I look at the cover pictures on all three magazines.

"She very good lady. My boss friend. Always stay this hotel."

"Mhmm."

"She is a vet, take care of stray animals. Free surgery. Have animal shelter. Have two bookshop in Chiang Mai. She help poor people, too, sir. Thai love her very much."

I shake my head. *Why would she ask me out for dinner?*

They read my mind. "She curious about you. We say you writer. She like write. Have many good writer friends. We tell her go picnic with you."

"Really?" It weighs on me that I just missed an opportunity the gods sent my way.

"She always stay this hotel. But first time go picnic."

"For you," the other lady adds.

My tear glands get ready for work. "Can I take the magazines?"

"No, sir. Can read there." She points to the couch. "But return, please."

The magazines are in Thai, so I can't determine what they say about her. One has her featured in the middle pages in multiple avatars—a mechanic in one, a doctor in another. A nurse, a high school girl, a mother cradling her infant; she fits into every frame. There are even two pictures of her as a village girl. She is on a boat plucking lotus flowers in one and tending to buffaloes in the other. I close the magazine and sigh like the kid at the Friday market who dropped his candy into the sewer.

The two hotelier ladies are busy with their job, attending to a new group of Chinese tourists. I shut my eyes and take a deep breath. Disappointments of this sort aren't easy to handle.

Give her a hug, says Bhagwan.

I try imagining her. She is there with her buffaloes, and she is dark, dark as her buffaloes. I open my eyes and look around. The magazines are now in the hands of the tourists. I home in on the magazine I want and pounce on it, startling the middle-aged, bespectacled man. "Sorry, sorry, urgent," I apologize, then turn the pages and glance at the picture of her as a mechanic holding a wrench. The eyes, the chin, the sharp nose, and the fiery look. It's Isakki! A pale-faced version of Isakki. I flip pages to the picture of her with the buffaloes. I only see Isakki. Put them side by side and give them the same skin tone; you won't tell the difference!

I hand over the magazine to the bespectacled man, who is blabbering at me.

"Terribly sorry," I apologize again and walk back to my room.

Chapter 18

The chaotic traffic outside my window stirs up memories of Chennai. I pull the curtain and sink back into the mattress. The flat-screen TV loops the hotel's advertisement with annoying background music. Wide-angle visuals of the warm-toned rooms appear and fade into a dark screen announcing "Today's events."

> Kizomba Bangkok festival
> Thai Lily Hall
> Second floor

The screen dims, and the image of a Black man holding a petite white lady appears with a catchy phrase.

> Ignite your passion, share the love
> Just like in Angola

My brain digs into the rules of my voyage and finds the recent amendment to the online search clause. I feed the keywords *kizomba* and *Angola* into my cell phone and hit the return key. The three significant findings of my research are as follows: one, kizomba is a sensual Angolan dance; two, it's derived from *semba*, an energetic dance; three, it's a partner dance where men embrace round-bottomed ladies and sway in ecstasy.

It's a sign, a compensation sent by Thai gods for the lost chance with Nita!

I look up videos. They all feature African hulks embracing haute ladies, caressing the small of their backs. For every stroke, the bottoms curl up and down, cranking up my perspiration. I imagine myself holding a damsel. The babes, the bosoms, the bottoms—it's a tantalizing package. They aren't Nitas, but I have to make up for the loss.

The timepiece next to the bed blinks 8:49 a.m. I present my side view to the dressing table mirror and look at the future dancer in the reflection. My tummy may not be flat, but it has its charm. I'm muscular. OK, fine, not muscular. But too many muscles are ugly. I lift my arms to curl my biceps, but a dead-fish stench strikes me. I run to the bathroom to take my second bath of the morning.

I pay ninety-nine dollars to register myself and pick up the yellow wristband. People are hugging and laughing on the dance floor. Everybody seems to know each other. There are three rooms, one each for salsa, bachata, and kizomba. I walk to the kizomba room.

Two dudes lift their legs in the center of the kizomba floor. They remind me of the precopulatory acrobatics of the roosters back in Little Lotus Pond. The ladies on the chairs lined against the walls outnumber the men. I sit next to a lady of unknown ethnicity who is strapping on her dancing shoes.

Be brave, Richard Parker. The world is yours, Bhagwan encourages.

"Can I help you?" I generate some words.

She looks up without lifting her hands off her shoes. "I'm fine. Thanks." She smiles.

"The straps can be stubborn."

"It's not the straps. Look at this." She crosses her leg and lifts it, pointing to a scratch. "Got this during the preparty last night. I can't imagine walking around with a scar. Hope it disappears soon." She rubs the scar and then looks at my feet.

"You are new to dancing!" Her eyes widen.

"Yes, yes. That was a smart guess," I compliment. I know girls fall for compliments.

"No biggie. But . . . those shoes." She points to my feet. "Oh, boy. You don't wear them on the dance floor."

I look at my feet, hers, and those of the two acrobats, still busy with their stretches. One of them has soft-soled leather shoes, and the other has only socks on. If I weren't on a tight budget, I would have bought a pair of shoes for him.

"Ladies and gentlemen..."

I look at the Black man walking to the floor. He isn't muscular like those in the YouTube videos. But who cares? What matters is I get to hold the girls. I rub my hands.

"We're going to warm up with Afro-Kuduro. Line up behind me," he says, and we follow.

Music flows, filling the room with vibrant beats. But it drums away my hopes of holding the girls because Afro-Kuduro isn't a partner dance. After an hour of jumping, clapping, and hoo-ha, we are back in our chairs, sweating and smelling. Even though the number of dancers has increased, ladies still outnumber men.

Ten minutes later, the announcement for kizomba comes. Another Black instructor appears, with a blonde trailing him. Whoever designed her must have been an antique hourglass maker.

"I'm Armando, and this is my gorgeous partner Zoe, from Hungary," the man says. "Let's form a circle and sit down," the announcement continues.

How are we going to dance by sitting in a circle? I wonder.

"Tell me what you think about kizomba," he asks. Nobody has an answer.

I raise my hand. "A sensual dance where men and women are in a close embrace."

I look around, expecting some applause. But there's none.

Armando waits for a while and continues without acknowledging me. "You think kizomba is a booty dance? It is not. Let me tell you its origins. Trust me, it ain't any fun." He reads our faces. "Kizomba is an Angolan dance that was not born in Angola," he begins.

I learn that *kizomba* means "party" in the Kimbundu language. Following its independence from Portugal in 1975, Angola plunged into a twenty-six-year civil war that claimed half a million lives. The war in their homeland anguished the Cabo Verdean and Angolan musicians living in the Netherlands and Portugal. They vented their pain through kizomba music, taking inspiration from zouk, konpa, and other Angolan genres. Meanwhile, kizomba as a dance form developed from semba, which means "belly to belly."

"We enjoy kizomba. But let's not forget the underlying pain," Armando finishes.

Am I in the wrong place? I rub my forehead. But my moment of doubtfulness doesn't last for long. After all, I'm not here by chance. Everything has been foretold, and I'm just following the sign sent my way.

"Ta-da. It's kizomba time. Stand up, my princes and princesses." Armando gifts bonus blushes to the ladies. "Leaders to my left, followers to my right." He stretches his arms sideward.

I walk to his left, following the other men. There are a couple of ladies, too, on the leaders' side. We leaders are to follow Armando while the followers take their cue from the damsel.

"We begin with half tempo." He points to his hips. "Stand straight, shift your weight to the left leg, and drop your weight. Nice and easy."

That's pretty cool and easy to do. The next move is side to side, where we step left, drop weight to the left hip, and step back to the right.

"The third basic figure is the *marka*. You walk three steps forward, mark your fourth step without shifting weight, and return." He demonstrates, and we follow. I fight my motor skills to stop at the fourth step and then move the same leg back without shifting weight.

"Awesome, we are pros now, aren't we?" He claps. "Let's form a circle. Leaders, face your left shoulders toward the center," Armando instructs, taking the center of the circle.

I expected to struggle, but it has been smooth so far.

"Followers, you may now position yourself before a leader. If you can't find a leader, place yourself between two couples, and your turn will come when the partners rotate."

I rub my hands again and look at the followers. *Who is that lucky lady? The blonde? The one with dyed-red hair? Or the sexy Black girl with curly hair?*

The ladies seem to take forever to walk. Snail walkers!

The red-haired girl, the blonde in the crowd, and the sexy Black goddess walk past me as if I'm invisible. I'm the last to pair: with a white lady one foot taller than me.

"Introduce yourself and look into each other's eye for a moment," Armando says, reminding me of tantra. *The sign did not lie!* I arch my neck and look up into her eyes. That turns out to be a painful exercise, and I give up. Armando explains the sequence of steps. I ready myself for my maiden dance, staring into the cleavage of my partner while she gazes at the couple behind me.

"Here we go, six... seven... eight," Armando chants, leading us into half tempo. Eight counts killed; we step sideward and return.

Time for the third basic move, and any hesitation in me has vanished. I put my left foot forward, but my follower doesn't move.

"You are supposed to move," I whisper into her cleavage.

"Of course, I would love to, but would you please release my foot?" she bends down and whispers.

I look at my left foot, which has conquered her right. That's how I ended up dancing in socks, just like the acrobatic professional whom we met before.

Dancing in socks ensures I injure no other lady. But my left foot takes the brunt of the red-haired lady's heels. I retreat to my room to fish out a first-aid plaster from my toiletry bag. The session is over by the time I return, but I survive the afternoon's intermediate-level classes. We end the day's workshops at 5:00 p.m.

Around 9:00 p.m., I arrive for my first social dance party, wearing a fresh pair of dancing shoes I had just purchased. I walk around the crowded floor, where people dance, their shadows flipping from one wall to another under the multicolored roof-mounted lights. There are many new faces—the partygoers who only attend the evening parties. I approach a few and ask for a dance. They all point to some random dude on the dance floor. "I'm actually in the queue, waiting for him," is the standard response. The tall Russian lady from the morning session is the only one dancing with me. We dance two numbers with the meager steps I have learned.

When we hug and part, she says, "I'm thirsty. Do you want to walk over to the bar and get a drink?"

I'm thirsty, too, and lime juice would be great. We walk to the desk vending overpriced drinks and snacks. She orders vodka for both of us. I think of asking for lime juice but decide otherwise as a matter of respect.

"Svetlana." She leans forward and hugs me.

"Richard Parker." I stroke her bare back.

We pull up two plastic stools and sit in a corner beside cartons of food and drinks. I give her an idea of Little Lotus Pond and my epic voyage, skipping the writer part. Our conversation drifts to worldviews and relationships, ignoring the curious looks from others. She proves her conversation skills by keeping it going. I love her sense of humor because she ends every joke by leaning over and hugging me. Once, she rubs her nose against mine.

"Hello, people . . ."

I turn to see a gorgeous lady in a green, flowing dress. That would have been an unwelcome interruption on any other day. But I make an exception, considering her beautiful smile and the dress that makes her stand out.

"I'm Mariyam," she introduces herself.

Svetlana reciprocates and then turns toward me. "This is Richard Parker."

"Richard Parker? Oh my God! The famous Richard Parker?" Her eyes widen.

I don't know what to say; I didn't expect my fame to reach the dance floor that fast.

"God, I watched your movie. Was mind-blown!"

I realize that she's got the person wrong. "Which movie?"

"*Life of Pi*," she says, chuckling.

I don't laugh. Svetlana doesn't, either. I watched the movie twice. Not that popular in India, but those who watched it never asked if I was the tiger.

Mariyam realizes the joke didn't go well. "Sorry, just kidding. I'm so jetlagged. Just landed from Perth."

Svetlana pulls out another stool for her to sit on and says, "Jeez . . . You flew from Australia for the festival?"

"No, no. I'm on the way home to Malaysia. Just thought of attending the festival en route."

I'm thankful for that decision because I sense a spark.

Svetlana introduces more of herself, and I repeat my story you are now familiar with.

"I'm a Malaysian, settled in Perth," Mariyam says. She shares her long, sad story of how she ended up in Perth.

"I must go now. Need to dance to lighten up my heart." She sighs and gets up. I want to ask her for a dance, but Svetlana's arm weighs on my shoulders.

"Sad story!" Svetlana shakes her head, sipping the last drop of vodka in her plastic glass. It's standard practice not to serve drinks in glasses during dance festivals; broken glass is detrimental to dancing feet. Svetlana gives me an account of Mariyam's community. "An indigenous community from Malaysia who live in constant fear of their country being taken over by Chinese and Indians. Many have fled to Australia and the United States, fearing the apocalypse. It's heart-wrenching to hear their stories."

I sense the darkening mood. I am sorry for the pain her people go through because of Indians. "You seem to know a lot about them."

She rolls her eyes. "I used to live in Kuala Lumpur, where we hear many such stories."

"I understand. It isn't easy being a minority." I exude compassion.

"Minority? Jeez, no. They are the majority."

I rub my forehead.

"Have you been to Kuala Lumpur?" She leans over and rescues me from perplexity.

"No . . . not yet."

"Oh, you should visit Kuala Lumpur. I love Bukit Bintang and its dance bars. They would make you a pro in a week."

She drops the sign just like that! I note it down in my head.

"I think I'm done. Listen, would you like to go somewhere quiet where we could sit down and talk? Maybe to my room or yours? I would love to hear more about this magical Little Lotus Pond," Svetlana asks.

"Some other time, please. I think I'm going to call it a day," I reply. She already knows everything she should be knowing about Little Lotus Pond.

I hug her and walk to my room.

I book my tickets to Malaysia. The plan is to leave Thailand on the third day of the festival. I don't feel like attending the finale.

Svetlana doesn't talk to me much after that evening, and I don't know why. As for Mariyam, I spot her only once, hanging on the shoulder of an instructor. She is never on the dance floor. I watch people walk in solo for the party and return to their rooms in pairs.

Why didn't it happen to me? What could have gone wrong?

Maybe Kuala Lumpur is the answer.

I see Svetlana on the balcony, blowing circles of white smoke into the air, and thank her for the Kuala Lumpur tip.

"You're welcome," she says and turns away.

Chapter 19

Did you know? There are three major milestones in human evolution. One, the discovery of fire; two, the invention of the wheel; three, the creation of budget airlines. I and the epic novel in your hands owe a lot to the third.

"Do you have a visa for Malaysia, sir?" the ground staff in a red dress inquires, looking at my passport and ticket.

"Yes, a multiple-entry visa." I take my passport back from her and flip to the visa page. I'm not telling her I paid the agent thrice the usual cost. Boasting isn't typical of an apprentice saint.

"Would you like to buy our special package, sir? It gives added privileges for just four hundred baht," Ms. Red Dress asks me with a sudden upshift in tone.

"Privileges?" I am excited now. "May I know what they are?"

"You get a red doormat to step onto the plane, a warm seat, a sandwich, a 49.5 mL water bottle, and three complimentary smiles from our specially trained flight crew."

I can board without a red carpet, and why pay for extra smiles when many girls await me in Kuala Lumpur? The warm seat is tantalizing, though. Perhaps it's their code name for a business-class seat!

"May I know what a warm seat is?"

"Warm seat comes with a red cover and two inches of extra leg space, sir."

I shake my head. Privilege has a different meaning in airline parlance. "That's quite tempting, but you know, I am letting it pass," I decline.

Her expression backshifts to a frown.

Deciding not to pay for the special seat turns out to be a squeezy mistake—they sandwich me between two oversize passengers. Yet I don't regret my decision. I have stood up for my principles and for my bank balance, even if it means having my elbows tucked in for the entire flight.

I sneak a look at the guy in the window seat—pale face and tiny eyes. On the aisle is another man with curly hair, a big beard, a big belly, and a dark complexion. I'm sure he's South Indian. But I'm not in the mood for a snub. So I wait for a sign. My sign arrives in the form of prebooked cup noodles. Mr. Aisle pulls off the lid and slurps the MSG-laden soup.

That brings to mind Isakki's buffaloes drinking from the pond. That's the sign!

"Are you an Indian, sir?" I ask him.

"No." He stares at me with a strand of noodle hanging from his mouth. "I bet you are."

"Yes, yes. How did you guess?"

"The curly hair, big beard, and big belly," he sniggers.

"Huh." I look at my tummy. It's beyond average size, but not as big as his. But a confrontation is not in my interest. So, I smile. "I bet that soup is tasty."

"Of course it is. Look here." He points at the microscopic letters on the sticker. *Buatan Malaysia*, I read.

"Product of Malaysia. Not your village, you *ooran*." He rolls the noodles on the flimsy white fork and pushes them into his mouth. I now remember Isakki's buffaloes jumping into the pond.

"*Ooran?*"

"Yes, you speak Tamil? *Oor. Oor* as in village. That's how we Malaysian Indians identify you darlings."

Ooran sounds good. It's good to know Malaysian Indians refer to us *ooran* to affirm our authenticity.

"So, when are you joining?" he asks.

"Join? Join what?"

"A restaurant. Your gateway to heaven." He drains the soup into his mouth, slurps it, and continues, "Arrive as cooks and waiters, learn the local language, seduce a local girl, impregnate her, and buy a permanent residency. Isn't that the standard recipe?"

My heart foresees where this conversation heads, so I don't reply. I think of Isakki's buffaloes again. I remember them standing still, except for their moving jaws, on a rainy afternoon. Lightning can't frighten them, nor does thunder stall their constant munching. They turn into my inspiration for the rest of the journey. The thought of reclaiming my armrests never arises again, even when my hands, tucked in between my thighs, sweat.

We land on the tarmac, and I am tempted to walk across to the unpaved area, bow down, and kiss the Malaysian soil, my promised land, in classic Indian style.

This is the post-9/11 world, my son. You want to be my first disciple to be shot dead?

Bhagwan whispers in time and saves my 4.99 liters of blood from splattering on the runway. So I perform an imaginary kiss and another imaginary namaste.

I follow the arrow pointing toward immigration and position myself at the tail end of the long queue. Before me are tired faces, mumbling and sighing. Somewhere in the line is a toddler making his presence heard with his wail. Fifteen minutes in, the line remains still. I pray to the gods that my bag stays on the carousel. I spot a man, definitely another South Asian, getting slapped by the immigration officer. Two other officers in blue arrive quickly and whisk him away. The queue resumes inching forward.

I hand over my passport, boarding pass, and return ticket to the officer in blue and instinctively cover my cheek. He stamps on a fresh page and hands it back. You could describe it as straightforward, a cakewalk, or like the morning breeze in Little Lotus Pond.

I retrieve my baggage, sigh in relief, and walk to the door with the sign KELUAR above it. No, I don't speak Malay yet, but the running-man symbol below *keluar* is universal.

Near the exit are three men dressed in blue, isolating Brown and Black people for baggage screening. The three white men before me pass through without any hurdles. When my turn comes, I slip the bags into the X-ray machine and smile at the officer.

"You from India, *ka*?"

"Yes, yes. I'm an Indian, sir . . . an *ooran*," I say, beating my drum.

"Any dangerous item in bag?"

"No, sir. No bombs, no knives, no acids, no rubber bands, no chewing gum."

He face-palms. "I mean hazardous goods like books on human rights, democracy, free media, or pluralism?"

"No . . . no . . . Not at all," I assure him. "We Indians do not get along well with democracy, secularism, and pluralism these days."

"Good." He nods in appreciation and signals me to go.

A question still prods me. "Can I ask you something, sir?"

He nods again.

"Do you stop only Brown and Black people for random checks?"

"Of course not. We are not racists." He grins. "We also stop Chinese."

I learn something new.

Malaysia had a dual-screening policy back in 2015. Malaysian Customs would randomly inspect our physical luggage at the airport, and the pubs would screen our emotional and financial baggage later at Bukit Bintang. I intend to stroll into Bukit Bintang later because that's where the kizomba bar is located. But before that, I must check into a backpacker hostel at Jalan Alor.

I book an app taxi for Jalan Alor. Indeed, taking the bus would save some money. But I opt for the taxi because one of these bookings could put me in Aroonan Saamy's taxi. Besides, I want to get oriented with the city in comfort before stripping down to the proper budget version of me.

I have switched over to dorms for two reasons: my budget and the fact that mixed dormitories are the best way to pick up traveling chicks from the Wild West and realize my path.

Finding the hostel is as easy as navigating a maze blindfolded. After circling a deserted Jalan Alor thrice, I find the hostel right before my eyes, but with a different name. It simply changes its name on the board every year without reflecting it on the booking app. Thankfully, my app-taxi driver has the mind to look it up online. Don't ask me why I didn't.

The receptionist wipes her wet hands on her apron and takes my passport. I guess she also doubles as the hostel chef.

"You booked for mixed dorm, sir?"

"Yes."

"Unfortunately, it's full, sir. We can give you a bed in the men's dorm."

"But—" I am about to alert her to the negative online reviews when Bhagwan calls out from his bunk bed in my heart.

Don't, Parker, don't. Everything that happens is for good. The wise man makes the best out of opportunities that come his way.

"No worries, I shall take that," I reply to her, then pick up the key to my locker.

The first thing I do after occupying my bed is to open Tinder and swipe. My routine swiping process has earned a name. No, it's not called "madman's rush" but "swiping meditation." When I hit the end of the quota, I close my eyes and recollect all the pretty faces. I massage my right thumb, stretch my arms, arch my back, and lie down for ten minutes for all the good energy to spread.

Ting, ting . . . Tinder beckons me.

> You have a match!
> Su
> Age 32
> 8 km away
> *—nothing here to look for, meh—*

I swipe through her pictures. Definitely Chinese.
Chinese eat bau.
White man eats burger.
Indian man eats rice.

Rachel's pearls of wisdom echo in my head, and I decide to save some text messages. The unwritten rule in Tinder for men is: thou shall not unmatch, for it's the lady's job to do so. I turn off the Wi-Fi, slide the phone back into my pocket, and step out of the dorm.

The street has metamorphosed from nearly empty to one full of round tables and chairs. One could easily mistake it for a festival.

"Lulian!" a few Chinese tourists scream as they home in on a durian vendor. The vendor must be so popular, they know her name!

I turn toward Changkat Bukit Bintang, negotiating through the tourists and hawkers. Three girls with makeup caked on their faces block my way. Black miniskirts and white shirts with long files in hand—I scan them from head to toe and identify them as university students seeking wisdom.

My moment has arrived! *Yes, it's me you are looking for,* the pumping organ beneath my sternum wants to tell them.

The girl in the center opens her file and stretches it before me.

"Sir ... massage?"

I realize it's not my moment. I excuse myself and try to walk away when one of them catches my arm. "Sir, we got every massage. Back massage, foot massage, cuckoo massage, happy ending, sir, later you feel very relaxed, oh."

Richard Parker! Bhagwan reaches out to me. *Don't let the ladies fool you. Stay alert.*

I stand stiff, staring into their eyes. "Sorry, not interested. I'm happy without it," I say, ending the conversation, and turn away.

"I know you no happy. Later you come back. Number 33 ... ask for number 33," she yells from behind.

I hasten my walk. A few other masseuses try their luck, too, but I quickly learn the rule. *Thou shalt not make eye contact, for the moment has not cometh yet.*

"Sir, nice Indian food," a man calls.

Of course, I know, because that's what I have been eating all my life. I continue walking until I find a restaurant that boasts authentic Malaysian food. I scan the alluring menu: *mee mamak, mee hoon goreng, nasi lemak, ayam penyet.*

"*Apa minum?*" the waitress asks.

"*Minum?*"

"Drink." She gestures.

"Later," I say, surprised. In Kanyakumari, we drink liquids only after food. It's the opposite in Malaysia. Here, they serve us drinks, half fill our stomachs, and then bring the food.

I choose the *mee hoon goreng,* thin fried rice noodles, for its pinkish color.

I walk to the washbasin because it's universal manners. But in the excitement of *mee hoon goreng,* I forget to turn off the tap. The housekeeper shouts to draw my attention.

"*Keling ... keling ... ayer ... tutup!*"

I sprint to the tap and turn it off. "Sorry," I apologize to the elderly woman.

"*Keling.*" She shakes her head. The intelligent man in me figures out that either *keling* or *ayer* means "water." *Tutup* means "to close" because she gesticulated that.

Once we step out of Little Lotus Pond, water becomes precious! I appreciate the way she cares about the environment. I apologize again.

"Lots of *keling* waste. I'm sorry."

"No, you! You *keling* waste water."

I look around, ashamed of my deed. While I expect other faces around the tables to be angry at me, my eyes catch them laughing instead.

"You from India, *ka*?" a man holding a large cup of brown drink in his hand—which I later discover to be Malaysia's national drink, MILO—asks me.

"Yes, yes."

"Oh, you *keling*!" He laughs, shaking his belly.

I learn something new. *Keling* means "Indian."

Richard Parker *keling*—that sounds good! *It has a nice ring to it, too.* I twist and retwist it over my tongue, along with the *mee hoon goreng* that's now on my buccal list.

My love for language doesn't go down well with Bhagwan.

You need only two languages, your mother tongue, Tamil, and English. A common language unites people; multiple languages create barriers, he chides me.

For once, I pretend not to listen because I know three languages: Tamil, Malayalam, and English, and it has been a blessing. Had I known Hindi, I would have spotted the *kallu* taunt from Chandini right when it began.

Let me tell you a story, like all saints in the making do. The great king Shenbaga Pandiyan from the erstwhile Pandya kingdom of Tamil Nadu developed an intellectual curiosity regarding the scent of women's hair. He was curious to discover if the long curly locks in his kingdom had a natural aroma. Pandiyan proclaimed that anybody who answered his question would receive a thousand gold coins as a reward. Dharumi, a poor chap, thought the prize money would solve all his financial woes. So, he prayed to Lord Shiva to help him. The mighty Shiva, moved by his plight and plea, granted him a poem arguing that women's hair had a natural aroma. Yet when the king was about to remunerate Dharumi, the great Tamil saint Nakkirar arose and questioned him. For him, the locks of women carried the scent of the pomades they applied and the flowers they adorned. They had no natural aroma to them. Nakkirar stood his ground and refused to budge, even when Shiva himself appeared in person. As a Tamilian with such a heritage, I must refute Bhagwan when he is wrong.

I keep my ears open to the soundscape—in the restaurant, on my way back, and in the dorm—collecting words. *Nama, saya, anda, makan, ayer, minum, lelaki, perumpuan, tandas, awas, keling* . . . the list has grown in just a couple of hours.

The hostel's lobby is now a fruit stall, and the desk has moved into a tiny corner where two white men with tattooed arms are inquiring about the availability of beds. Looks like I have cool company at the dorm!

I return to my bunk bed and connect to the Wi-Fi.

Su has sent a message: How are you, mister?

I ignore that. A Chinese lady texting an Indian, that's the first indication of a scam.

> You have a new match!
> Rose
> Age 24
> 11 km away

I can't guess her ethnicity, but she looks genuine, like she is the Shakti who could make a difference in my mission. I think of a pickup line because "How are you?" doesn't do justice to such a beauty.

I wish you were a rose in my garden, I type.

I can be one. The reply is quicker than I expected. You buy me good wine.

Why wouldn't I? Having wine with a Malaysian rose is the best way to begin.

My pleasure, I type.

No pleasure, only drinks. Pleasure cost extra.

I unmatch. Because the rule on unmatching only applies to genuine ladies. I must find a way to filter these Tinder rattlers. After three hundred seconds of intense brainstorming, I edit my profile:

> What's green, has long thighs, and sings in the rain? Answer me if we match.

I put down the phone and look around. Mine is the only bunk that's occupied, and under the dim lights, the dorm looks haunted.

Thankfully, more guests arrive, and soon this place is turning lively.

Jayden and Stijin introduce themselves as travelers from Amsterdam. Their Dutch English accent tests my comprehension skills. Syncing syllables with their hand and lip movements, I stay in the conversation. They stand one and a half feet taller than me and walk with their tattooed biceps rubbing against each other. No, they aren't from the progressive LGBT community; they are buddies who grew up in the same locality, went to the same Coffee Academy, and work in the same café. The two baristas have been backpacking through Southeast Asia. After Malaysia, they head to Bali to meet the legendary shaman.

Shaman! Is that a sign? Perhaps he could fast-track me to enlightenment?

Stijin says he is the most popular shaman in Indonesia and America. I ask for his name. Ketupat, says Stijin. Or something like that. Doesn't matter—popular shamans are easy to find. Just ask around for the wise man, and people will lead you to him.

We vibe well because Stijin also writes gourmet columns for a magazine in his hometown. In a way, he is a journalist, too, but one still in business. I show them pictures of Little Lotus Pond, making them instantly choose India for their next backpacking adventure. I offer tips and local connections but stop shy of hosting them. That's because my new home awaits me here in the East. *Why make a promise I can't keep?*

There's another reason for our instant rapport. They are devotees of Lord Krishna, also influenced by Bhagwan's teachings. But I keep Bhagwan's voice inside me a secret.

When I return from the shower, an idol of Lord Krishna has sprung up in the aisle between our bunks. Jayden is tuning his ukulele while Stijin caresses his *bansuri*, the Indian bamboo flute, as if it's his baby.

Come, join us, they gesture.

Stijin blows life into his six-hole flute, and Jayden sings.

Jai jai shri Radhe . . .

I shut my eyes and sway to the melody. A few more *bhajans*, and it's time to wrap Lord Krishna in his silk cloth and send him to sleep. I admire the way Stijin handles the idol gently. Perhaps these angels were sent by the gods to accompany me until my moment of enlightenment. I ask them if I may travel with them in Malaysia; it can't be for long, as my visa is only for a month.

"Why not? That would be amazing, brother!" Jayden affirms my hunch. "But we aren't staying here long. Tomorrow morning, we're moving to our hostess's place."

"Hostess?" I wonder. If it's a paying guest service, I could join them.

"Yes, we found a host through CouchSurfing. Here . . ." Jayden taps on his smartphone and shows me a message:

Hey Jayden and Stijin,

Welcome to Malaysia. Have you found a host yet? If not, I can give you beds and a kitchen where we can cook together. I have a personal wine cellar and an excellent collection of beers. In the evenings, we can relax on my balcony, sharing stories and drinks. I am a superb listener, open-minded and nonjudgmental. I have hosted people from a diverse background—Italian, American, British, Romanian, and Greek. You can read their reviews. I am amid changing jobs, so I have a month free, and I can drive you around. Let me know if this appeals to you. Hugs, Sandra.

"Is it expensive?"

"Not at all! It's free, bro. It's CouchSurfing!"

That's the first time I've heard of it. They explain to me how it works.

The mood in the dorm turns sober. I will miss this fellowship.

"Hey, brother, I have an idea." Stijin comes closer and puts his arm on my shoulder. "Why don't you set up a profile and send Sandra a request? If she accepts, we could share her apartment."

A spark ignites in me. I download the app and set up a profile using my Facebook profile. Stijin tutors me on how to compose a catchy request message. Nurtured on Indian English for forty-two years, my brain continues its struggle with his Dutch English lingo. But then, great passages materialize when brilliant minds work together!

Dear Sandra,

I am a traveler from India, here in Malaysia for a two-week visit. My hometown, Little Lotus Pond, is in the foothills of the mighty Western Ghats. I have so many stories to share about my village and the journey that brings me to Malaysia. I have been fortunate to meet inspiring personalities from Singapore and Thailand during my travels and hope to continue with that luck in Malaysia as well. As a newbie to CouchSurfing, I am yet to accrue any reviews. However, I am sure we could create some amazing moments. I am also a beer lover, so we could hunt for good draught beers in the city.

I hit the send button. Stijin gives me a thumbs-up.
Another beautiful evening. The music flows again, and Mr. Loh, the hostel owner, and Grace, the master chef and receptionist, join us to sing Scott McKenzie's "San Francisco."
The melodies lull me to sleep.
The first thing I do in the morning is to check my CouchSurfing inbox.
Sandra Ooi has declined your request.

> Hey there!
>
> I have been extremely busy these days, and sorry I can't host you this time. I hope you will find another suitable host. In case you cannot find one, I suggest you look around Jalan Alor for good hostels. They are damn cheap, too. Good luck with your journey. Sandra.
>
> PS: It is not polite to ask your hostess to go out barhopping. No sensible lady would do that.

Disappointing, but Sandra doesn't surprise me. A corner of my heart was ready for this message. I tell Jayden and Stijin that she hasn't replied yet. Why would I spoil their stay with Sandra?
Sandra arrives to pick Jayden and Stijin up after breakfast. I hug the gentlemen goodbye and shake hands with Sandra. Fortunately, she doesn't recognize me.
I have a new app to play with now. Back on CouchSurfing, I browse for profiles within 25 km and find three Malaysian Indians. Divendra, Naren, and Ambika. The first two are men; the last is a female, a round-faced lady with a big round *pottu*—a red dot on the forehead. I send them the same message, minus the beer part.

I am an ooran from India, here in Malaysia for a two-week visit. My hometown, Little Lotus Pond, is in the foothills of the mighty Western Ghats. I have so many stories to share about my hometown, which is an authentic Tamil village, and the journey that brings me to Malaysia. I have been fortunate to meet inspiring personalities from Singapore and Thailand during my travels and hope to continue with that luck in Malaysia as well. As a newbie to CouchSurfing, I am yet to accrue any reviews. However, I am sure we could create some amazing moments.

None of them have responded until today.

I make three decisions: one, someday, I will have my own cottage with a beautiful garden around it; two, my doors will be open to everyone, regardless of skin color; three, I will go active on CouchSurfing, and together, we will create beautiful memories.

I only have to figure out where in the East that cottage will be.

Chapter 20

My brain prods me to write. But the dorm reeks of emptiness. Grace suggests I visit the iconic Petronas Towers.

The twin towers are indeed marvels of modern architecture. But I spend more time in the park beside them. It's hot and humid, but the trees and lawn fill my heart.

When I return to the hostel in the evening, a guitar is audible despite the cacophony of the market street. I spear through the crowd, hoping to see Jayden and Stijin, but it's somebody else. I say hello to the Western man in a sleeveless top and puny tattooed biceps who is conjuring music.

Smith introduces himself as a global citizen. He is a proud bartender in Shoreditch. But his English doesn't sound British enough to the proud colonial subject in me. The expert mixologist makes drinks throughout the night and hits the sack early in the morning with earbuds pinned to his ears. Smith is popular among the minority whites for his cocktails and for his mocktails among the Pakistanis who make up East London's majority. This means I have found a spirit guru who can teach me the nuances of mixology.

It's an odd coincidence. First, we had two baristas—and now a bartender. If I stay long enough, there will be a chef, a butcher, and a farmer coming through to complete the chain.

We discuss music, or rather, he speaks, and I listen. My knowledge of music genres and musicians is grossly inadequate for any conversation. The topic then changes to travel expenses. I ask him if he is CouchSurfing, too, and he replies in the negative. He is happy with the hostel. I guess he isn't as budget constrained as Jayden and Stijin.

"Can I sing for you?" Smith surprises me. Back home, we refer to it as offering someone two *laddoos*, the Indian sweet balls.

"I would love that." I sit before him on the floor between the bunk beds while his fingers romance the chords.

I take a complete minute to realize it's a Malay song.

"Did you like it?"

"That was exceptional. Thank you so much for that." I clap my hands. "I couldn't understand the words, but I feel the emotions packed into them."

"Oh, you don't speak Malay?"

"No, no. Remember, I'm not from here."

"Oh, yes. I have been rehearsing that song for a while. That was *Janji Manis Mu* by Aishah. One of the greatest hits of the '90s."

He places the guitar on the bed, stands up, stretches out his arms, shuts his eyes, and sways to the left and then to the right, reminding me of kizomba.

"Thanks for the feedback, Richard Parker. That makes me happy," he says, eyes still shut and body swaying. I note the pride on his face—the pride that every musician should have.

It's time for my swiping meditation. The only message I have is from my lone match, Su.

> A big green frog in Little Lotus Pond

She has given the correct answer for the filter prompt I left on my profile. But how did she know the name of my little village? I message her back.

> No biggie. Your profile picture, lah. Got one before a milestone.

She's right. One of my Tinder photos is from Facebook, where I stand next to a milestone that reads LITTLE LOTUS POND, 0 KM. I took that selfie as a metaphor to show that I was back at ground zero, hurt, bruised, and broke.

We text. I reproduce the description of Little Lotus Pond that I recited to Stijin, Jayden, and Smith. I also tell her I'm a writer.

> Would you write about me? I want to be in your novel.

If you can meet me for dinner tomorrow, why not?

I ask for her phone number. She refuses. She wants to be the mysterious lady in my novel. But she suggests meeting for a late coffee at 6:00 p.m. tomorrow. She chooses the venue—a café at Jalan Mesui—and offers to pick me up. It serves authentic local coffee, she says. Local or exotic, it won't make a difference to my taste buds. I'm a proud South Indian with tea in my veins, arteries, and kidneys.

I walk to the pickup point thirty minutes early, as I don't want to make my first Tinder date wait. I make use of the time to do some girl-watching.

"Sir, I know you come back."

I turn in the sound's direction. It's the same masseuse.

"Want happy ending, sir? That one so nice, sir."

No, I don't take that as a sign. I excuse myself and cross the lane to continue girl-watching.

I am here . . . Su texts.

I spot Su on the other side of the lane, wearing a red-and-white soccer T-shirt and shorts. She had walked past me to the exact meeting point. I wave my hand in the air and call out, "Su Su . . . Su Su . . ."

I hear the massage girls cackling. I ignore them.

"Su . . . Su!" I call again.

Su zeroes in on me, face-palms, and runs across to me.

"Huh, Richard Parker!"

I wonder what went wrong and look around. The massage girls, the fruit vendor, and the bubble blower are all laughing at me.

"Come faster; let's go before you embarrass me more!" Su leads me to a narrow lane.

"Where's your car?" I ask to break the silence. She points to a red sports coupe parked between two mini-trucks.

"Oh my—Nissan Fairlady!" I don't hold back my excitement.

"Yes. You follow me, *ya*?" The door locks release with two buzzes.

"Follow you?" I can't believe she drives a Fairlady slow enough for me to follow. I stand still, wondering what to do.

"You can look and admire it later, Richard Parker. Now, follow me."

I bow my head. "I'm sorry . . . I don't think I can run behind a car, especially not a Fairlady!"

"*Haiya*, Richard Parker!" She face-palms again. "You're in Kuala Lumpur now, you know? Here, *follow me* means 'get into the car.'"

"Oh!" I laugh.

"You need to learn Manglish, Parker," Su says.

I learn something new. Manglish is the Malaysian form of English. It's superior to Singlish when you're in Malaysia and inferior when you're in Singapore. It's known for its love for Malay, Cantonese, Tamil, Mandarin, and Hokkien. Occasionally, there are English terms, too. It's different from Indian English, which is spoken with a punchy tone, or British English, which is an endangered language in London. A key distinction between Manglish and Singlish is Manglish's recognition of Tamil words. Singlish denies the existence of inferior Tamil words.

"Richard Parker, when you hear someone say *lah*, then you know he's a Malaysian."

I note that point. Our discussions turn to the car. Contrary to my presumption, it's not her car but that of a long-standing client who leaves it with her every time he travels to Hong Kong. By the time he returns, his car shines like quartz and smells like new leather, plus Su's perfume.

"In this country, I'm the only woman car detailer, *lah*," she announces.

"Awesome, *lah*," I reply.

Learn her story; take a leaf out of her book, Bhagwan says, bugging me. *Seize every opportunity to learn, son.*

"I really, really love cars!" Su narrates her story. Her parents wanted her to become a banker; her boyfriend, since sweet sixteen, wanted her to become a real estate agent. But she loves cars. She broke off from her boyfriend, set up her car-detailing enterprise, and began dating again.

"Is he Chinese, too?" I ask, trying to hide my disappointment.

"I don't want to say. We broke up for one year. He goes backpacking. Later, when he comes back, then only we decide, *lo*," she says, pulling out a brown cigar with her free hand and lighting it up. The cigar packet has no branding, I notice. We are still crawling in the traffic.

"Parker, you smoke or not?"

"No, I don't."

"Good, *lah*." She winks. "Then you have three choices. You become a passive smoker today, open the window, or jump out of the car. You choose."

She doesn't know it's the gods who choose for me. But the three choices, and the way she put them forward, show the same wavelength we are cruising on, or you could say, crawling on.

Maybe she is a mind reader? I rub my forehead.

"These are very good-quality Swiss cigars. Davidoff Exquisitos. But you see, Parker, they come in boxes. So, it's extra task for me to transfer them into small, driver-friendly packets. I'm very busy, you know?" she says when we reach the restaurant. She orders three coffees and pulls out two phones from her bag. I watch her texting on both phones at the same time.

"Yes, I'm ambidextrous," she says, still focused on the dual-channel texting. "No, I'm not a coffee freak. The third coffee is for my friend."

I scan around to see whom she is referring to.

"He will arrive in two minutes." She is still ambi-texting.

"Oh." I sigh. My hopes for a date get smashed.

"Don't worry. He will be here very fast one," she continues, reading my mind.

A tall Chinese gentleman joins us.

"This is my friend, Jeffrey." Su introduces us.

They discuss a Porsche 911, 1985 model. That's the only thing I can make out, as the rest of the conversation is in Chinese. Su takes quick notes on her phone.

Jeffrey rises to leave.

"See you later, tailgater." Su shakes his hand firmly. When he vanishes beyond the glass door, she says, "Here, everybody likes tailgating. In your hometown, do you people like tailgating?"

The projector in my head rewinds ultra-high-definition images of vehicles with barely a few centimeters between them.

"No, *lah*, we don't tailgate. We call it driving."

She raises her eyebrows and returns to the track. "Four hundred and fifty thousand ringgit. *Wah*, I can get forty thousand ringgit!" She flicks her thumb.

"Wow, I didn't know detailing would cost that much."

"*Haiya*, Parker." She pulls out a cigar and puts it to her lips.

"Sorry, ma'am. Smokers' corner is over there," the server reminds her.

"I know, I know. I only holding a cigar. Not smoking." She turns toward me. "See, Parker, I'm also a car agent. I help to sell classic cars. The friend wants to sell his car. I help him. He gives me ten percent commission."

"Nice friends to have," I say. If an Indian friend of mine sold my car, I would get him a cup of chai.

"*Haiya*, Parker. He's not my friend. I only met him not long ago. It's just a business word. Somebody wants to sell his car. Then I will call them my friend."

"You are a lady of multiple skills."

"OK, thanks, Parker. You know what, the guy who said that last time wanted to sleep with me." She winks and returns to ambi-texting.

"Oh no . . . no, no. That was genuine. I never met someone who can handle two phones simultaneously." I point to the phones in her hands.

"I'm a woman who has many skills. Look at this." She holds both her phones up high for me to see. "You know what it means?"

I look at them like a cruciverbalist. "You're the only ambidextrous female car detailer in Malaysia who is also a classic car agent."

"No, *lah*, this one Blackberry." She shakes the black phone with a worn-out keypad. "This one iPhone, you know. So, what do you think?"

"You're an ambidextrous lady who owns a Blackberry and iPhone?"

"*Aduh* . . . No, no, no. This means I can be modern and classic together!" She winks for the hundredth time.

"Ah, yes . . . and a soccer fan, too." I point to her T-shirt.

"*Walao*! This is not a soccer T-shirt. This is my company uniform." She rolls her eyes. "OK, OK, stop talking about me. Tell me more about you and your Little Lotus Pond." She lays the phones on the table and returns the cigar to her lips.

"It's a beautiful village at the tail end of the Western Ghats," I begin. I describe life in the little village, losing my parents, the tin-roofed church, the shanty where shirtless men worship the mirror, the palmyra tappers whose songs wake us up, the banana fields encroaching into the rice fields. Her eyes widen when I tell her about the witch in jeans who seduces men with her piercing gaze, that enigma who heals the sick but also brings down the wrath of the gods. I recount the gossip about her nude baths on full-moon nights and how the young men who ogle at that ignominious view turn crazy. I end with my love for Christ, my devotion to

Lord Ayyappa, and my journey to the East in search of salvation. Not all things can be said. My love for cows, my failed business, Chandini, and the oracle and his predictions on the virgins remain private.

"Hmmm . . . very interesting, *wo*." She taps the tip of her cigar on the table. "So, Parker, come tell me. Where does the soothsayer come in?"

"Soothsayer?" My jaw drops.

"Yes. There must be one. You know, a granny with a parrot, a tarot card picker, a palm reader. Someone who tells you to travel to the East to find your fortune."

"Oh no, there was none." I rub my forehead.

"You sure or not?"

"Well, there was one. Not exactly an oracle, but kind of." I'm forced to tell this mind reader everything the astrologer said.

"Good boy. Next time don't lie to me anymore. I tell you, there's a soothsayer behind every successful traveler." She leans forward, touches my arm, presses it, and says with narrowed eyes, "Now tell me, Mr. Richard Parker, why you leave Isakki?"

"Isakki? Leave her?"

"Yes, your crush. The woman who has piercing eyes, sharp-sharp nose with a pearl stud, and dangerous curves."

"I didn't. She is not my crush. My nemesis, my bête noire, the witch of Little Lotus Pond."

"It's OK, Parker." She pats my arm. "I totally understand. I understand your little crush on her. Can see that in your eyes, you know. Your eyes become so wide when you talk about her. In fact, you only talk about her and not your village story."

I look into her eyes. "Oh, Su Su, I'm afraid you are wrong."

"Well, time will tell. And please stop calling me Su Su. My name is Su. Su is my name. Just Su, one word, understand?" She thumps on the table.

I'm not sure if she is furious or just feigning.

"But what's wrong with Su Su? Su . . . Su Su . . . it's the same."

"*Su Su* means 'milk' in Bahasa Melayu, Mr. Parker. It also refers to breasts."

"Oh, sorry, I didn't know that!" My eyes drift down her neck.

"Now stop staring at my boobs. You are not getting them."

I bite my tongue. "Sorry . . . I didn't mean to."

We split the bill 35:65, as Su insists that she will pay for Jeffrey.

"My boss says you play shares," the server says, picking up the faux-leather pad with the money.

"Yes, I do," she says and looks at me. I get the meaning of that. It means, "Please add share market to my skills, along with car detailing and brokering." The server seeks some quick tips on investment.

"Simple! Su's motto is to invest in small companies instead of big ones. In one year, the small ones can double their profit. Big ones only show little growth, not a good one."

He notes the point and looks at me. Su introduces me as her friend.

"Nice meeting you, Mr. Parker. You not from here, right?"

I look at Su and remember her language point.

Parker, this is the occasion; grab it by its horns. Go for it! Bhagwan appears.

I take the empty coffee cup, roll it between my hands, and take a deep breath. "I'm a *keling*," I say and watch their eyes widen while their mouths draw O shapes.

"Parker!" Su pushes her chair back and stands up. "Do you know how serious it is when you say that?"

"Of course I do. I picked up some cool terms. I think I will pick up the language in a week." I try not to sound boastful.

"Parker!" Su's voice rings loudly, attracting attention from other tables. "*Keling* is a derogatory term used to denote people of South Asian origin. It's not a Tan Sri title."

I put the coffee cup down.

She pulls her chair closer to mine and sits while the server excuses himself. The unlit cigar on the table has twisted into a weird shape because of the constant thumping.

"Let me tell you some history." Su details the story behind *keling*. I open my ears, eyes, and mouth and memorize every word she speaks.

Keling, sometimes pronounced as *cling*, could have originated from *Kalinga*, a historical kingdom of India. It's like the Malay term *barat* referring to the West, where Bharat, also known as India, is located. It was common in the pre-Islamic Malay kingdoms to refer to the inhabitants of Kalinga as *keling*. That was when India was at its glorious peak—much before the Moghuls—and later, the British—plundered her. India's spices and riches were used to prop up Her

Majesty's queendom, and in return, they bequeathed India with multiple famines, including the notorious first Bengal famine of 1765. By 1901, all that remained in India were famished souls wheezing inside skin-cloaked skeletons. Some of these skeletons were packed into ships and unloaded on the shores of Malaya to work in rubber plantations. The Japanese who invaded Malaysia during the Second World War found the dark-skinned skeletons easy toothpicks to build the Siam–Burma Railway, which the dark tourism industry lovingly calls the Death Railway. They crushed over 150,000 Tamil skeletons beneath those rails. When the war ended with the nuking of Japan, the remaining skeletons returned to the rubber plantations as bonded slaves. Just when flesh began forming under the dark skins, the plantation industry collapsed, throwing the workers into the Malayan streets to compete with street dogs for food. *Keling* became their name.

I take a while to process and condense the story. It's clear the word has a notorious context. But if it's derogatory, why would people use it? I raise the question.

"It's so complicated, you know. We should be a peaceful and harmonious country, but our politicians keep reminding us of our racial differences. For example, we have full-page newspaper ads screaming intellectual questions like '*Apa lagi Cina mahu,*' meaning 'What more do the Chinese want?'"

The zing in her conversation has disappeared, and we return to the car. I recall Aroonan Saamy's story in silence. It's like destiny is trying to say something to me. I rub my forehead hard but can't comprehend the message. The traffic has thinned down. I stare through the window as the Fairlady cruises. To change the mood, I inquire about the secret behind Malaysia's successful city planning and the neatly laid-out roads.

"You see, Parker. It's all about zoning. Not like your cities. We have separate zones, like residential, commercial, and agricultural. In fact, we divide the entire country into two zones: the development zone, called *semenanjung*, in the west, which got all the infrastructure development, and the East Malaysian zone of Sabah and Sarawak, where funds come from. Think of the east zone as a bank you never have to repay."

"Really? Don't you have people living there? Don't they need the money?"

"We got people there. But very innocent and generous, *lah*. We convince them to take only five percent and give us ninety-five percent. Not just that, Parker. They also put on nice costumes and dance for us when we visit them for ecotourism. In return, we send them pictures of Petronas Towers and Birkin bags. Sometimes we also recruit their school toppers as nurses and technicians."

I note the sign. My mission can't be complete without meeting such noble people. But a question pops up. "What if they have a change of heart one day? You know bad things always happen."

"No worries, there. That day, they will be the minorities in their homeland."

I rub my forehead.

"Let me help you." She chuckles. "We bring illegal immigrants and settle them there. *Walao*, the majority natives become the minority. Here in West Malaysia, we bring Bangladeshis and give them voter rights. You know, majority remains majority that way. It's called demographic engineering, boy."

That sounds like Morse code to me. I am still confused.

She changes course and inquires about my stay at the hostel. I tell her about the musclemen and the pattern: the muscles, the tattoos, and the music.

"I see. Do you want to stay with me? I have bought a new condominium; soon I will move out. Have packed most of my stuff. But the beds and mattresses belong to my landlord. Actually, if you don't mind the big cartons and bundles lying everywhere, you can use them."

That sounds like a good idea. There's a lot to learn from this lady. Not a sweet-talker, but there's a charm in her bluntness.

Su offers to pick me up from the hostel the next day after work. She drops me off at the other end of the lane, near a disabled man summoning spiders out of black metallic wires. I watch the weird little creatures taking shape and buy a spider for myself for fifteen ringgits. Holding it in my stretched-out arm, I step back into the busy lane. The wire creature wriggles as if it's alive. I put it on my left hand and press on its egg-shaped bum. The abdomen wriggles. I repeat it.

"Lulian!" a voice rings, and two Chinese tourists run past me, pushing me aside. In my struggle to maintain balance, I let the spider fly. It lands on top of a giant red lobster in the center of a round table. "Yee!" the people around the table scream.

"It is not real. I'm sorry," I explain to the lady standing with wide eyes and arms on her chest. I apologize again and retrieve the spider from the lobster's head.

"See, it's not real." I place the saucy spider in my hand and press it. It wriggles its butt, and the lady screams again.

"Go away!"

"Sorry."

I walk away, congratulating myself for not getting beaten up. That's a Bollywood moment for me. Such miraculous moments ought to come with thunderous background songs. Mine was Aishah's *Janji Manis Mu* rising from the sides of the lane.

I take two steps forward and look at the busker next to the durian stall of Ms. Lulian. It's Smith in his blue shorts and sleeveless top. A bucket half filled with blue-green ringgit notes sits before him. My hostel mate is not a backpacker but a begpacker who begs to fund his travel! He is singing his heart out with his tattooed arm on the guitar and eyes closed. I look at the crowd surrounding him—women of all ages and me, the lone male spectator.

"Oh . . . handsome, Oh . . ." a lady in a floral skirt and matching top exclaims. I shake my head, affirming my learning takeaway: all white men are attractive. She then turns toward the durian stall and orders "two yummy Lulians." I identify her as a progressive LGBT human, a connoisseur of body fluids. But the shop owner points at her durians and asks, "Yellow or white?" I learn something else, too: *Lulian* is the Chinesized name for durian fruit.

With Mr. Metal Spider, my new companion, in hand, I reach the hostel. He loses his sauce flavor after a mini-bath, but he is still my friend—a buddy with a wriggling bum.

I pour the day's experiences into my laptop before going to bed. Today's date with Su was the first Tinder date of my life. I think we began in a romantic way, but now I sense no physical attraction between us. *Why?* Whatever destiny has in store for us, I'm grateful that Su has offered to host me despite knowing me for only a few minutes.

Today has also shown me the most important lesson of this mission: I can't run away from being a *kallu*. It's my wendigo, my berserker, constantly getting introduced as a benevolent friend, shape-shifting into the absolute beast as I get to know it. *Kallu, keling*—the names change, and so does the geography. But the meaning doesn't.

Chapter 21

Su turns up, as promised, in her regular soccer uniform.

"This is our uniform this year. Every year, design same, only the color change." She preempts the question in my mind. We are in her own metallic-green car, a Proton Saga, 1985 model. "This is the very first batch. You know, they are the Malaysian avatars of the Mitsubishi Lancer," she says, filling me in.

Given her love for classic cars, it would only be a surprise if she owned a new model. Besides, as a car detailer, she gets to drive the most expensive cars for free, anyway.

"I like your love for classic cars. You are so unique, Su." I reach out to stroke her shoulder.

"Parker, OK, I need to tell you two things." She puts a brown cigar in her mouth and continues without lighting it. "First thing first, your compliments are not getting you into my pants."

"Pants?" I look at her shorts.

"OK, half pants, *lah*!"

She continues, "Number two: I'm doing business, 'kay? Waste money to buy new car is no smart. You see, I drive a new car out of the showroom, it straightaway drops twenty percent from its original value. This one, in 2012, I used seven thousand ringgit to buy this Saga. Today, I sell it, I can get seven thousand ringgits back. No loss, only profit because I already use it for my business."

That makes sense to me. I saw glimpses of this business acumen at the café last night, too.

"Well, I now see how you made money to buy an apartment."

"Huh. Apartment, what?" She throws the cigar into the black hole in the dashboard. "*Walau*, Parker, this is a condo, condominium."

I rub my forehead, trying to figure out the difference.

"You see, apartment, right, it's so old already, *lo*. Modern generation likes condominium more. My condo got swimming pool, sauna, and gym. Even got nursery. Later I send my kids there."

"Oh, you have kids?"

"No, *lah*. I mean later when I have them."

"Oh, I see."

Su's apartment stands tall in Taman Sri Sinar, a middle-class locality in Segambut. It's supposed to be a twenty-minute ride, but the traffic at Jalan Alor delays us by another twenty minutes.

Parker, unleash the tiger in you, Bhagwan advises.

I had decided that even before stepping into her car.

"Cool. I'm going to share the apartment with Richard Parker, the tiger," Su says, reversing the Proton Saga into her garage, next to a Mahindra Scorpio.

Shh, Parker. Don't even think about anything. This soul can read you, Bhagwan advises.

I agree.

"Don't worry, Su. I don't bite." I laugh.

"Of course, *lah*. I know you won't. You can see this, right?" She points to her soccer-style T-shirt. "I kick balls, including tiger balls."

I divert my glance to my bags.

We walk to her apartment.

"Surprise, *leh*, it has elevator!" she teases, punching her finger into the keypad.

A sign written in Malay with a staircase symbol catches my eye. "Translate this, please," I ask.

She tilts her head and takes a look. "If a fire breaks out, blame the Chinese and Indians."

My brain stacks up images of Jackie Chan and Shah Rukh Khan burning the streets.

"Richard Parker, welcome to my penthouse. You are my last guest here, you know?" she says as the elevator opens to the twelfth floor.

Hum tum . . .

A manly voice floats into my head, accompanied by guitar notes. I didn't expect a Hindi song, and an oldie at that, here in Kuala Lumpur. Then I remember the Mahindra Scorpio in the garage. Perhaps the owner of that Indian car is also an Indian.

"That's Professor Halim. Very funny guy."

"Your neighbor is Indian. That's cool. Sounds pluralistic."

"It's a pluralistic country. Also, he is Malaysian. Can talk to him tomorrow. You will love him. You both are very funny, *lo*." She giggles, more like a fake giggle.

We are before her door now. And she is still on that pseudo-giggle, passing glances at me. She thinks I am some simpleton. Poor thing doesn't know the weapons this saint in the making has in stock. I draw the first one out.

Putting my ear to her door, I signal, *Wait*, and I knock thrice.

"*Oi*, Parker. Nobody is inside, *lo*."

"Shh . . ." I put a finger on my lips. "There are spirits inside. We must alert them."

In my heart, I thank Rachel for that weapon.

Su puts her hands on her hip and presents a stumped look. I wink.

"*Walao*, Parker, this is so stupid. Why you so superstitious? I really can't believe it. You know what, I really don't have time for this nonsense thing. Faster, give me the key, *lah*."

"Well, you know, it's a Chinese tradition."

"Parker, it's not tradition. It's a Chinese superstition. You no need to teach me this, OK?"

I dig into my quiver for any other magical arrows that might work.

"Give me the key, *lah*!" She stomps on the worn-out ceramic floor.

I hand it over to her. No, I don't concede defeat, as I still have many other weapons left.

Su pushes the door open, and we walk in. I look around at sealed cartons and furniture swathed in cling wrap. It smells fresh, like a garden, because beyond the packages lies the couch, surrounded by potted plants of uniform height.

"They are my pet figs, you know? Yes, Mr. Parker, come meet my other side business."

"Gardening? Indoor gardening?" My eyes widen.

"No, *lah*." She puts her bag on the coffee table and walks to the first pot. Petting the tip of the shoot, she says, "This is my next big business. These are special hybrids; in two years, it is fruiting. There's a very big market for dried fig fruits in Malaysia, very good business."

The only two fig trees I know are the sacred fig and the banyan. They take decades to grow, and the fruits are only eaten by birds and bats.

"I know you don't believe it. But *hor*, remember!" She points to her forehead. "I won't do anything without a good plan."

"Can see that." I thrust my tongue out.

"Parker, treat this like your own home." She points to the two sofas between the fig garden and the cartons.

I put my bags down and familiarize myself. The walls are all blank. Whatever adorned them before must have gone into the boxes. I recline on the stained-fabric sofa, and Su takes the sofa opposite me.

"I will rent a farm and plant hundreds of figs there," she says, lighting a cigar. Then she looks at me and stands up, as though she just remembered something. "Wait, wait, let me open the window first; I don't want you to die from the smoke."

"Thanks for being considerate." I smile.

"Don't expect this always." She makes a fish face before returning to the seat.

"I continue," she resumes after blowing a ring of smoke. "In two years, they fruit. And then I will dry them and sell them to supermarkets. I will put the money I earn back on the farm. In five years, I can have my own farm and grow thousands of figs. *Walau!* Imagine, in five years, I will have an established business!"

I rub my forehead. That story sounds familiar. I've heard it before.

Su gives me a bed. But the bedspread is packed already, so she peels off the tape from a carton to retrieve one for me.

I sleep well, though I dream of being in a jungle, maybe because of the fig plants.

In the morning, we have Maggi noodles and MILO. Su drops me at Bukit Bintang on her way to work. I spend the day hopping from mall to mall. When I return to her apartment in the evening, the fig plants have vanished, and Su sits in a cloud of smoke. "One person offered me good price, so I sold them. You know, the fig market is not so good now."

"Oh . . . they don't have a market, so you sold them off?"

"That's not what I mean, *lo*."

"OK, I stand corrected. You win!"

"Good boy. You can sit down now." She points at the sofa.

I follow the order.

"Later, I'll meet an Indian businessman. We'll eat dinner with him."

I rub my forehead and look at the space vacated by the fig plants.

"Are we bringing jack tree saplings later?" I ask.

"Ha ha! You so funny." She blows a ring of smoke. "You think I don't know that you doubt about my business thing? Too early, son. Tonight, we meet an Indian guy. He is doing vintage Ambassador cars business. For your information, he wants my company to detail them, *lo*."

I'm sure that will turn out like the fig business because we just got rid of the rusty Ambassador cars off the Indian roads. I wonder who the brilliant man is. But Su is adamant. According to her, since the vehicle is off the road, its value will increase year after year.

"You don't know the value of your car, *ah*? Got so many people love Ambassador."

Su explains her plan on the way to the meeting. She chose an Indian vegetarian restaurant because her new partner is a born vegetarian. Her business acumen is back on track again. I'm the trust winner, the invisible mediator here. I won't be able to contribute anything, but my mere presence will foster trust. That's important in interracial business meetings. I remember my former chairman hired Chinese damsels as facilitators whenever he negotiated deals in Shanghai.

Rahul has an impressive plan for the number of Ambassador cars likely to come to him for car detailing. "It's all in the big data harvested from social media," he says, and I watch him explain. If the deal takes off, Su could make close to ten thousand US dollars per month in profit.

In between explanations, he excuses himself to take a call.

"See, Parker. This guy is so handsome. Look at his broad shoulders . . . *Walao*."

"Focus on the deal, Su," I remind her. I see nothing special about him. A foot taller than me, pale skin, meatless chin, and a nose that looks like a bridge. And above all, the way he pronounces *Ambassador—Ambajador*!

"How long are you here for, Mr. Rahul? I want to bring you around Kuala Lumpur," she gushes like I don't exist. Rahul grabs that offer. Just when I sense the third-wheel vibe, Rahul's rotis and *mattar masala* arrive. He pinches off a roti's rim and dips it into the pea curry. But instead of putting it into his mouth, he throws it on his plate and springs up.

"Waittterrr!" he screams.

The young man who served us comes running. He looks like he's from some old town in central Tamil Nadu—a fellow *ooran*.

"I thought this is Indian vegetarian hotel. But you put onion." He points to the peas. "Don't you know, in my caste, we don't eat onion?"

I notice a few onion pieces there. The server apologizes and offers to get him a fresh one without onion.

"How can I trust you, idiot? Do you know who I am?" he asks, beating his chest. "If this was India, I would have skinned you alive!"

"Parker, come, let's go." Su rises.

"It's OK, Miss Su; I got this. I can handle him," he tells Su.

"No, it's not OK for me. Not interested in doing business with you anymore."

Su apologizes to the server and settles the bill with a fifty-ringgit tip while Rahul stands baffled.

"I prefer to die of hunger," Su says later, another unlit cigar on her lips. We are in a Japanese restaurant. Su has just ordered salmon sashimi. She helped me pick *uramaki* from the menu.

"*Fuyoh*, it's so nice." She takes the first bite of pink salmon. I scrunch my eyes and swallow whatever just entered my grieving mouth.

"Parker, how do you feel?"

"Amazing, just like driving on Indian roads," I reply as the *uramaki* in my gut tries to return through the path by which it entered.

"Like driving an Ambassador?" She chuckles.

"No." I shake my head. "More like driving an Ambajador."

We both laugh.

Chapter 22

It's evening.

We are on Su's little balcony with beers in our hands. The sky is visible, but not the stars or the moon, as the human-made lights obscure them. We talk and drink and talk. Occasionally, she flicks her lighter to breathe life into her cigars. But as usual, there are more unlit cigars in the skull-shaped ashtray than burned stumps.

"Parker, where do you plan to travel later?" Su asks with smoke in her mouth and beer in her eyes.

I rub my forehead because I have no plan at hand. The only strategy is to spot the signs, follow them, and heed Bhagwan's advice whenever he speaks.

"You think that one is Aladdin's lamp?" Su points at my forehead. Our chairs have moved closer, and I can now smell the cigar breath. "I always see you rubbing it, but no genie comes out."

"No, not at all. I rub my forehead whenever I think. But I know an Aladdin's lamp." I stick my tongue out.

"Really? Tell me, *lah*." She leans toward me and squints.

"Here . . ." I pick the cigar packet from the tea table, draw out a cigar, and place it in my mouth. "I do this whenever I think. Just to pretend that I'm a badass lady, you know . . ."

"Why stop? Light it. Can see the genie." She flicks her lighter and shuts it off.

"I don't want to corrupt you."

"Thank you for your kind consideration."

"You're welcome, Mr. Parker," she says, sending a circle of smoke into the air. "You know, I can give you a suggestion."

I sit up.

"Why not go to Sarawak? It's totally different from West Malaysia. You should go there to visit."

I note the sign. But I don't want to leave. The company, the conversations, they're all so good, like I've known her for a long time. *Is it time to leave? Does she want me to leave?* I rub my forehead.

"Please don't, Parker. The lamp is going to wear out." She chuckles. "I know what's going on inside that lamp."

She kills the cigar and looks at me. "On the first of June, I'll be moving out. You can fly over to Sarawak. We fix a date and time, and then you fly back here. I'll meet you at the airport, and then we go to Bali."

"Yay." I pump my fist in the air. "Let's do it." She stretches out her arm, and we bump fists.

"OK, Parker, here is the trick." She gets up and walks to the end of the balcony. Turning back, she says, "You don't have my number, right? This means if you don't show up at the airport, we won't see each other forever. And we can only use Tinder to chat, you know. For your information, Tinder profiles always go missing. So, even if I lose my profile, I will still wait for you at the airport that day, as we planned."

I agree. She would change her heart and give me her number soon, I know. Women make a big fuss at the beginning to show they are hard to get, but eventually, they mellow.

Su does not go to work the next day. She will be overseeing the interior furnishing in her new condominium. I offer to help.

"Remember, if you show up at the airport, then only you can see my condominium, understand?" She smothers my chances of discovering her new residence.

After she leaves for work, I drop by Professor Halim's house. The plan in my head is to say hi and dash off somewhere into the city, but the hi and the chats stretch until lunch. His wife fills the table with ethnic Malay dishes: fried fish, beef rendang, and stir-fried *kangkong*, along with fried banana fritters for dessert. Banana fritters were my mom's favorite teatime snacks.

"You see, *ah*, Parker. Su is so choosy with food. She says she's a healthy eater. But she smokes a lot. For me, she's a paradox. I think I'm seeing happiness in her eyes after a long time, long after her she broke up with her ex." She smiles.

I see where she is going with this. "Yes, yes. She's so happy about moving into her new house," I say, wiping my hands.

Mrs. Halim giggles. "You think it's the house? She's like my daughter. I know her well. You should know her, too."

"Parker, did you see my car?" Professor Halim changes the subject. The car is something I want to discuss with him, too. *Why would a Malaysian professor, earning well, settle for an Indian car?*

"Most of my teachers were Indians. They kindled my passion for literature. When I was thirty, I was among a contingent of Malaysian academics sent to the University of Madras for a course. That was a life-changer for all of us. In the evenings, we strolled along Marina Beach, nibbling street food sprinkled with fine sand from the breeze." He laughs. "That car symbolizes my relationship with India," he says, removing his glasses and wiping them on the hem of his black tunic. "I can't believe how that university lost its stature." He sighs.

Professor hospitalized after getting hurt by a falling ceiling fan. I remember reading the newspaper story sometime back. I had walked through the school's dark corridors during my journalistic days. It doesn't feel like a university anymore. Appointments of vice-chancellors are not based on qualification but political patronage, which has extracted its toll.

I drop the idea of going out after that. My stomach is full, and my head is heavy.

"*Walao*, you look like a dead man, *wo*," Su says, switching on the lights when she returns. I open my eyes and get up from the couch. We make chrysanthemum tea and share the day's happenings. "The guys are too slow, *lah*. I think the condo is half-furnished." She updates me on the furnishing work and looks at me.

"Your turn. Why? You see a ghost? Why you look dead?"

I tell her the history behind Professor Halim's car.

"Why is your education system walking backward, *lo*?"

"It's a funny scenario, Su." I explain the relationship between teachers and Indian democracy. Good teachers produce excellent leaders. When India matured as a democracy, the relationship came full circle. Corrupt politicians appointed poor teachers, and those teachers sank Indian education. Our schools now produce substandard politicians.

Su is on the couch, listening with crossed legs and hands folded behind her head.

"OK, I know it already. Mr. Parker is guilty."

I look at her. *Was she even listening to what I said?*

"A Malaysian professor misses his past connection with the Indian education, and an Indian feels guilty because he left his own country that nurtured him."

"Huh. Where did that come from?" I ask, cradling the cup of tea in my hand. "Your inference has to come from data, which in this case is the story I narrated."

She smiles. "You know what, words are just one small part of the conversation. It's not everything."

She picks up her empty cup and walks to the sink. She turns the tap on and yells, "Parker boy, I can read your mind clear, like on piece of paper, 'kay?"

Mind reader! She confirms my suspicion.

When Su goes to shower, I sit down to write. Words flow from my fingertips to the laptop screen, washing away the heavy feeling.

"*Wah*, good, *wo*, you're alive again, my boy," Su says, back from the bathroom. Wrapped in a white towel, she's wielding a hair dryer.

"Yes, I was writing, and it feels good."

"Oh, I see. This means you will finish your book in this apartment?"

No, that's not my plan. It won't be conclusive if I end it before I find my destiny. Instead, I have another idea; something else suddenly occurs in my mind.

"I want to learn Italian, Su. Do you know an Italian teacher?"

"Italian? *Walao*, you want to learn Italian in Malaysia, *ah*?"

"Of course, all writers on spiritual quests learn Italian. It's a romantic language, they say."

"Of course, Mr. Parker. *Braccia rubate allágricoltura.*"

"You speak Italian!"

"Got one friend Italian." She winks. "By the way, the meaning of the expression is that Mr. Parker should stop writing and do farming." She raises two fingers and waves the peace sign.

"Yes, fig farming."

Chapter 23

My routine shifts gear from a spiritual traveler to a detailer's apprentice. On the first day, I go overboard at the garage, sniff paint dust, and cough nonstop. Su cooks me apple, pear, and pork rib soup to prevent my lungs from bursting. On the second day, she stations me inside the office and says, "Parker boy, you sure belong to the air-conditioned room. I don't want you cough and disturb my sleep again."

She tasks me with managing her social media handles and reminding her to eat and drink on time.

You know that she's hardworking. But she can also be an annoying hypocrite. The other day we went to the Western café for breakfast. *"Fork in left hand and knife in your right,"* she said, teaching me dining etiquette. I spent ten minutes slicing a chicken chop that I would have otherwise picked apart in two minutes with my hands.

When we went to a Chinese restaurant for lunch, I tried to impress her with a fork in my left hand and a spoon in my right.

"You use chopsticks to eat noodles," she said, enjoying watching me wrestle with the noodle monster. Ten minutes later, she said, "Why so difficult . . . doing something you cannot do? You can just use a simple fork, you know?" And she put the fork in my right hand.

The other day, we had an Indian banana leaf meal for a late lunch. As I was ready to dig my fork and spoon into the rice, she said, "Parker boy, you use hand, right hand, to eat Indian food."

Sometimes I wonder if I'm a little mouse she keeps around for amusement. I'll have to get even with her to restore the balance of forces in the universe.

"Su, I have an excellent opportunity for you to showcase your English proficiency." I hand over the rolled newspaper to her. She's in the garage, bantering with the detailing staff over tea.

She puts the teacup on the table and takes the newspaper from me as if it's a time bomb.

"Bad idea. Did you say showcase?"

"Yes."

"Not my cup of tea."

"No, you'd love it. It's an excellent opportunity." I tempt her again.

"Excellent opportunity? That one sounds like a scam." She returns the newspaper. "Can read it for me?"

I open the tabloid and turn to the page I bookmarked.

> *Is your English perfect? Then you could be the dubbing artist we are looking for.*

I read the ad put out by Malaysia's leading animation firm.

The detailers swallow their tea and chortle. Su puts her cigar back in her mouth and nods, but she doesn't reply. I revel in my taste of victory.

In the evening, when we are about to close, she takes my phone and inquires about my progress on Tinder.

"Parker boy, let me help you set up your profile. Guarantee you can get ten matches tomorrow, very *syok* one."

With those golden words, she installs the shrine of guilt in me for my afternoon tease.

"Parker boy, women like men who are active and classy. We show that in your profile."

I pose for her cell phone before the green Lamborghini that just arrived for detailing. The journalist in me spots a black strap protruding from the closed boot and alerts her.

"That's an eyesore."

"No, *lah*, Parker boy. I put it there. It makes it look natural."

Tinder buzzes when we reach home. I regret not seeking Su's help earlier. With her help, I will find my girls in no time.

> You have a match!
> Anastasia
> Age 28
> 9 km away
> *Be warned. I ride hounds, lash lions, tame hulks.*

Anastasia's profile description brags about her adventurous spirit while her attire and long nails reflect the psyche of a comics fan. My brain sifts through the DC Comics universe and picks out Catwoman as her matching superhero. She opens our chat like she has known me for fifty years.

Are you Christian?

Yes, I reply to the astute lady who guessed my religion correctly. How did you know?

I know everything, Mr. Christian. Aren't you here to rip me up?

My blood warms up and flows to the softest destinations. I love how she indicates I'm here to rip open her heart and enter.

By the time Su is out of the shower, Anastasia and I are discussing our first date.

I want to devour you right now.

Now?

Yes, don't worry. I have everything set up.

I foresee a room smelling like rose flowers, with candles, fruits, and red wine, for my first union. Su grabs my phone.

"Parker boy, let me handle this, OK. I don't want you to ruin this."

Five minutes later, Su is commanding me. "Faster! Go, change into your best clothes. She's waiting for you. I will drive you there and pick you up tomorrow morning."

I spring up from the couch and hug her tight. "You are awesome, Su."

"Parker boy, sure, no problem." She winks.

It's fun time, says Bhagwan from his seat in my heart.

An hour later, she drops me outside a gray-painted bungalow with blue-flowered plants creeping over its facade.

"Madam is on the second floor." The security guard, nearing his sixtieth birthday, accompanies me to the carved wooden door and points to the stairs.

I thud-thud on the mahogany stairs and arrive at an extra-large room that challenges me to decide if it's a gym or a drama set. At the center of the white room sulks a lone chair with two straps hanging on its arms. Behind it stands a pole with a handcuff hooked to it. On the wall far behind are masks of Guy Fawkes. I count six of them.

"Look who is here." Anastasia emerges from an obscure door in her Catwoman attire. A black whip is on her left arm, ready to be unleashed in the air.

"I'm a leftie. Is that a problem, Mr. Christian?"

"No. Not at all." I swig saliva, torn between admiring her chiseled figure or fleeing.

She takes a few steps forward. I can smell the lavender in her perfume. "Is this a role reversal for you, Mr. Christian?" She reaches for my collar.

I'm about to congratulate myself for packing formal attire when she yanks open my shirt. Three buttons eject and roll on the floor like little minions.

"Imma whip you like a dog. Oh, you'd love it, wouldn't you?"

Drops of liquid trickle down my inner thighs. I can't tell if it's sweat.

It doesn't matter, son. Run, advises Bhagwan.

I turn back and skedaddle, ignoring her calls from behind.

The security guard opens the gate with a blank face, as if he has seen many Parkers before.

I hit the street in the direction we came from. The green Lamborghini screeches to a halt beside me. Its window rolls down, and Su's voice reaches out.

"Get in, Parker boy."

I don't ask her how she knew I would be back so soon. Instead, I focus on getting some air in my lungs while a Davidoff Exquisitos lights up between the lips of my chauffeur.

Chapter 24

Ten days until June. I still haven't dipped my toe into the kizomba bar. As Svetlana said, the only way to become a pro is to dance in Kuala Lumpur's bars. And dancing is the quickest way to find my girls! *Why should I forgo the opportunity?*

Su drops me at the bar in Bukit Bintang.

"*Walao*, I don't want strangers to rub on my chest, very *geli lah*." She declines my invitation to join, then adds a diktat: "You don't enter my home smelling like cheap-cheap women's perfume, OK?"

I promise to return smelling like me.

The bouncer on steroids guarding the stairway to the loft refuses to believe I'm here to dance. I take a deep breath, smile, bat my eyelids, and offer to kizomba with him. It works like magic; he shuts his eyes and gives way.

I learn something new. This is how people like Isakki survive. Maybe all the scary stories of her powerful spells and charms are just manipulations of time and words? And skillful deployment of the eyes, jacked up with eyeliner darker than her eye contours? Well, the good thing is that I'm four thousand miles away from the dark witch and her buffaloes.

People drink around pub tables on one half of the loft; the other is vacant, ready to blossom into a dance floor. I wade through the crowd, scoping for welcoming eye contact. Five minutes later, I spot another Indian drinking a Diet Coke. Can't say if the look on his face is warm or cold, but I hear a greeting.

"Franklin." He stretches out his fist with a lopsided smile.

"Richard Parker." I reciprocate, and we bump fists. I sit on the empty barstool beside him.

He inquires where in South India I come from. The student in me wants to know how he was sure I'm an Indian from India and not a Malaysian Indian.

"That failed attempt to keep the curly hair well combed, lack of piercings in the ear, and many more."

I look at his balding crown. Wavy hair, zero piercings, and many more. "You are South Indian, too."

"Yes, from Kanyakumari," he says, rocketing me from the barstool. But I spot no change of emotions in him when I reply that I'm from Kanyakumari, too. Instead, he continues sipping the fake sugar drink.

I learn he's from the western side of the Kanyakumari district, at the border of Kerala and Tamil Nadu. People there speak a funny dialect, which we consider a corrupted Tamil while they mistake it as mellifluous. He works for some university in Miri, Sarawak. My eyes widen when he mentions Sarawak. When he stops talking, I restore my eyes to their former state and narrate my story.

"I'm from a small village toward the cape. You might not even have heard its name."

"Oh . . . Kuttithamaraikulam, that tiny enclave with lotus ponds." He shocks me for the second time.

I prepare for inquiries about Little Lotus Pond. Instead, he drags his Diet Coke can on the table, drawing imaginary Mona Lisas. I sit tight.

"Hello, young man. We have met before," a familiar voice wades in, breaking the tension.

I turn around to see Mariyam standing with one hand on her elegant waist. Her other hand flaunts a glass filled with red wine. This time she's in a free-flowing sky-blue dress with a matching beaded necklace that reflects the warm lights, giving off a peculiar tone. I rise and hug her.

She asks for hints on where exactly we met. "Thailand," I reply, then introduce her to Franklin, who shakes hands with the same lopsided smile as before.

The DJ spins a Portuguese kizomba song, and couples gather on the dance floor. The music drowns our voices. We excuse ourselves from Franklin and step out to the balcony overlooking the road.

"So, have you been practicing your dance moves, Parker?" Mariyam asks.

I reply in the negative. To my surprise, she offers to teach me if I sign up for her private classes.

"I thought you just began learning kizomba?" I remember her words from our first meeting.

"Oh, that was back then. But I have been dancing in this pub for two long weeks. I'm a pro now. Look at this . . ." She swipes her phone and shows me her Instagram. I forget to blink as images swipe by. She has a standard pose: red wine in one hand and some dude's shoulder in the other. In one photo, she is on the guy's lap, flaunting the wine. "Extremely tall guys." She puffs her cheeks.

I agree she's a pro.

"I wish I had two weeks more in this beautiful city. Unfortunately, the road calls," I say.

"Leaving soon? Oh, Parker. Where would you be going to?"

"Sarawak!"

"Sarawak? My God. Have you met Jenny yet?" She drops a name.

"Pardon me, Mariyam, not yet. Is she an instructor, too?"

"Not yet, soon to be. Hold on for a moment, please," she says, reminding me of dog trainers telling their puppies to stay. Of course, the puppy always stays.

She dives into the dancing crowd and disappears from my sight. Moments later, she reappears on the dark horizon beyond the dancing heads, leading another damsel by her arm. They look like identical twins from a distance, but as they come closer, the six differences are apparent, with the burgundy-dyed hair of the new entrant being the prominent one. Twin delights!

"Meet Jennifer, a.k.a. Jenny. Jenny, Mr. Richard Parker." She introduces us, and Jenny leaps forward to hug me, rubbing her wine-flavored cheeks against mine. I pick up a second scent—some imported jasmine perfume.

Mariyam tells her my intention of journeying to Sarawak.

"What a coincidence!" Jenny clasps her arms and makes small fake jumps, reminding me of Rachel.

"Are you going to Sarawak, too?" I ask, trying to guess the three factors driving her hourglass body to bounce nonstop.

"Going to?" She stops smiling and rolls her eyes, faking anger. "I'm from Miri, in Sarawak."

It's my turn to jump for joy. Three people mentioning Sarawak couldn't be a coincidence. It begins with Su, then Franklin, and then Mariyam. Here I am talking to a Sarawakian from Miri. This is not a fluke but a sign.

"You guys keep talking; I'm hitting the dance floor." Mariyam excuses herself.

"Have fun, babe." Jenny kisses her. I wish it will be my turn next, but no luck there.

Jenny asks me about my journey so far.

I describe my adventures. "Looks like Sarawak is where the wind takes me from here."

"When would that be?"

"June first, most probably."

"Great. I will be there, Parker. Going home tomorrow; my boyfriend is coming, and I want to introduce him to my family. It's going to be a special occasion." She drains my enthusiasm.

"Wow, I'm thrilled for you, Jenny. He is a lucky guy." I swaddle my disappointment.

"No, *lah*." She waves her index finger before her face. "I'm the lucky one. He is my godsent knight, the perfect match God made for me. Look at this." She swipes her phone to a picture of her with a white dude.

It looks like shoddy Photoshop work. I glance at her, speculating if it would be polite to ask. But she saves me the trouble by unraveling the mystery.

"I know what you're thinking."

That is not a surprise; everyone around me seems to have a knack for reading my mind.

"I photoshopped myself into the picture because this is my only picture of him. Do you know we have never met?" She begins her story with the quintessential question of our era.

I listen to her tale of how Tinder gifted her this amazing man from Grasse, near Cannes. A man who sold his Ferrari, vineyard, and brewery for the love of Southeast Asia. They found love. He wants to learn kizomba, too, and they plan to set up a studio and a café in Miri. She shows me the blueprint of the café and studio. It's all detailed, including pictures of the interior.

"Patently Bornean." She grins, raising the glass and letting off a wine-flavored burp. "I wish you could be our first student, Parker."

I'm to be her first student, her good-luck charm!

Parker, take a leaf out of her book before she gets drunk and pukes all over you, Bhagwan says, reminding me of my duty.

The diligent student in me obliges.

I awe her with details of my mission, and when she has finished saying "Wow" multiple times, I lay the hook: "It's our destiny to meet, Jenny. The seeker in me yearns to learn more about your inspiring saga."

She nods twice, downs the remaining wine, and balances the empty glass dangerously on the newel post.

"It's a long, long story, Parker." She turns around and peers down the almost vacant road, flaunting her low-cut back with X-shaped straps to me. "When I was at school in Miri, my bestie's sister got an *ang moh*, a handsome white boyfriend. Jealous and curious, we gawked at their photographs beneath the Eiffel Tower and grilling elk meat somewhere in America. I tell you, Parker, I'm prettier than my bestie or her sister. My classmates always said I shouldn't waste my talents for a low-life Asian." She taps her hands on the handrail and continues. "I want an *ang moh* boyfriend whom I can take to my *kampong*, one who will make every bitch look at me with a burning stomach. And it's happening now." She giggles and continues the narration.

Jenny and Mariyam were classmates in Perth, where they first met. She opted to study business as her parents wanted. Because it was the community tradition—to make big bucks and pay taxes on time. Stuck in the rut of assignments and exams, she found solace in three boys: Oliver, Ethan, and Mason. Fascination developed into crush, crush into obsession. But she lacked the mettle to approach them. It was a tough time—most guys were with boring girls who were into books, guitars, or dancing. Jenny was the prettiest in class. Her waist was as slim as her grades, and her bottom as enormous as her rice bowls. Yet nobody appreciated Jenny.

"I wrote secret letters to them, which I never posted. They all ended up in my closet, Parker." She sighs and continues. "I don't celebrate Christmas. It is offensive to Mariyam and her community, you know. But I wished Santa would somehow shrink them all and drop them into my Christmas socks. Of course, without the knowledge of Mariyam, *lah*." She sighs again.

I stand spellbound, facing her low-cut back, listening to the storytelling. It would have been nice to see her facial expressions, but no complaints—her words are audible enough.

"There were many Asian guys interested in me, *lah*. But, *meh*, all not my type. The Indian, so ugly and dark; the Malaysian one, so fugly. The Singaporean, all mama's boy, and the Thai guy, so cute, but I know he wears skirts in his room." She chuckles. "No way I could date them. But something happened!"

That something was Mariyam discovering the letters while sifting through Jenny's closet to borrow her lucky rainbow leggings. The word was that a girl who wore those leggings to a Friday date would have them peeled off by the dude. Jenny's letters ended up in the hands of Oliver, Ethan, and Mason.

The plot gets gritty. I'm sweating, adrenaline outrunning the blood in my arteries. It feels like the rustic rails have disappeared, and I'm left at the balcony's edge.

"Whom did you choose, Jenny?"

"All three, *lah*! I spend so much energy writing those letters. Cannot waste."

"Oh." The plot gets quadrangular.

"I dated all of them . . . damn, moda fucka." She chortles, turns around, and approaches me in slow motion. When she is closer, she raises her index finger and flicks it before my eyes. "But I never kissed them. In fact, I have never kissed a man on his lips in my entire life."

"Wow, you are a virgin. That's a rarity!" I congratulate her for resisting the temptation to have her flower visited, despite the dating spree.

"Duh, Parker." She rolls her eyes. "I only said I never kissed. Remember, I have a lucky legging!"

I rub my forehead, trying to decode the information overload. She steps closer and places her hands on my shoulder.

"I have told Louis, my fiancé. He can do anything he wants to me, but our first kiss will be in Paris, right under the Eiffel Tower. I want to live stream it on my Facebook. Let all the bitches burn!" She laughs. "Time for another drink, another dance."

We down two more glasses of wine. She curves her left wrist outward and points her wineglass at a small tattoo. I'm now looking at a mail icon.

"I have come a long way, Parker. The unisex hostels I backpacked to, the Kuching Rainforest Music Festival, Koh Pha-Ngan moonlight festival . . . all in search of my man." She smacks her lips, adding more gloss. "Do you know Mariyam took me to the beach and made me pose under the goddamn sun? Do you know how much I had to spend to remove the fucking tan, man?" She lets out a sigh. "I love the outdoors, the sun, the beach, and the forest—can't imagine the shit I wrote in my Tinder profile for the sake of love. The ordeal is finally over." She closes her eyes, flips her hands, and sighs a moment's relief. When she's done, she picks up the empty glass and says, "Show me some love."

I pour some wine from my glass.

"Raise your glass for me, Parker."

I raise my glass toward hers, acknowledging her long and tiresome journey.

"To all the boys I loved before but never kissed."

The music stops, and there's a chill in the bar. Not even a breath sound is heard. Then it resumes.

"I have seen a lot, Parker. Haters and bitches and their gossip. But I held my head high, and it's time to celebrate!"

She gulps the wine in one go and leads me to the floor. I lift her right arm and send my other arm to her back. And we dance; she is always two steps ahead of me.

"Wow, Richard Parker! You're an amazing dancer. You so light on your feet, like that tiger. I enjoyed it." She hugs me tight and rubs her smooth cheeks on my bearded one. *I'm making progress; the magic of Kuala Lumpur has just begun!*

"That was funny. Damn funny." Franklin shakes his head at me when I return to the table. I see jealousy written in green all over his grim face.

Don't fall prey to silly mind tricks of the world, Parker. Stay alert, Bhagwan calls out.

"She's an amazing dancer, Franklin. A wonderful human being, too. Someone who knows how to treat people the right way. Besides, you don't know her story." I am ready with an explanation for my statement because 80 percent of Indians don't get sarcasm.

"Amazing dancer? She said that?" He chuckles.

I tap my knuckles on the table to hide my irritation.

"OK, she's coming this way."

I'm about to turn back when he touches my wrist.

"Don't. Don't turn back. Just listen to me. You're either getting a dance festival ticket at a promotional rate or an offer to join a tour group where you can travel for free for recruiting five members. Since you're a he, him, I'm ruling out slimming belts, fairness creams, and silicone push-up bras. Likewise, I'm also ruling out tickets to sarong parties because we don't qualify."

I ignore his self-pitying rant and turn back and wave at Jenny, who is closer now. She waves back and treats me to another juicy hug.

"Drink?" I lift the empty glass.

"No, thanks. I just wanted to ask you something."

"Yes, please."

"Where are you traveling to after Sarawak?"

I sit up, sensing the coming of a sign. "Haven't decided yet, though I have to return to KL."

"You know what? I was thinking of this epic travel of yours, and this idea pops up. Why not Bali?"

Bali! Why wouldn't I? No spiritual odyssey would be complete without Bali. If the signs take me to Bali, I should find the legendary shaman whom Jayden and Stijin mentioned. I thank her for the excellent suggestion.

"Awesome. You're lucky, Parker. I have tickets for this ten-day dance festival there. It's $2,990, but you get a ten percent discount when you purchase from me. Think of this: you save $290. You could do a lot with that money."

True! I could do a lot with $2,700.

"Excellent, Miss Jenny! Mr. Parker here will appreciate this. He was indeed looking for a similar package." Franklin smirks.

"I know. He's an awesome guy. Cool dude, good listener. I like him," Jenny says, not getting the sarcasm there.

I learn something new. Seventy-nine percent of Malaysians don't get sarcasm.

"Rule number one on a dance floor: if you see that girl who smiles for no reason, gives you boobs-pressing hugs, compliments you, and encourages you to keep on dancing, then she is an event promoter or a multilevel marketing agent," Franklin says when Jenny has left, after giving me her phone number.

Those were profound words because I'm flooded with generous offers to attend festivals in Lisbon, Vienna, and New Delhi, all at a 10 percent discount, from other promoters who are also in awe of my dancing skills.

I don't turn into a pro magically. The magic of Kuala Lumpur doesn't rub off on me. It's a sad realization that gradually turns into a happy thought. Maybe I'm magic-proof. If Kuala Lumpur's magic doesn't work on me, then Isakki's won't work, either. When I visit home, I can stare straight into her eyes and challenge her. And yes, I can finally seduce the widow Shanta, too. I look at Franklin and smile.

"So, you are returning home!" he says, still fidgeting with the empty Diet Coke can.

I rub my forehead. *Isn't my destiny here in the East?* "No way. I'm here for a reason. This is where my destiny lies."

"Ah, OK. My best wishes, then. I'll see you in Miri." He stretches out his fist.

We chat longer. I mean, I ask questions, and he replies in monosyllables. Every time I abandon the conversation, he warms up with unusual friendliness, only to slip back within a few minutes. Amid this rollercoaster dialogue, I manage to sift some information. One, he works with the hunter-gatherers, documenting their ways of living; two, he's a classic introvert, using the dance floor to pull himself out of the cocoon; three, he's a writer, too, debuting his indie novel soon.

"It's going to be a hit, Parker, a hit," he assures.

Eleven dollars and forty-five cents—I remember the earnings from my super-hit book. With empathy, I ask him more about the hunter-gatherers because they might hold the key to moksha. Well, meeting the Hmong of Vietnam guarantees enlightenment. But the signs don't point that way. So, I must explore alternate possibilities.

"What's the relationship between you being a writer and the hunter-gatherers?" he asks.

Franklin only gets to know my author agenda, I decide. I am not disclosing the possibility of achieving fame as a tribal king.

"You see, writers traveling to Southeast Asia visit indigenous communities. No writing quest will be complete without some cross-cultural comparisons. This exercise is a decisive moment in every author's life. Equate it to a photographer meeting his first old man with a wrinkled face or the old lady with heavy earrings dangling from her earlobes."

The poor guy is still at a loss. I explain further. "Imagine I visit the Hmong people; I can write a few paragraphs about their lives, relating them to mine. It's like those progressive Tinderites posing with African, Cambodian, or Indian kids. That's the trend, Franklin. We must go with it." He needn't know that if I become a tribal chieftain, it wouldn't be a few passages but a complete blockbuster book with a deeper insider's perspective on the tribe.

I might sound like a writing coach to him. But as an experienced writer, I have the moral right to mentor him. I expect him to show some gratitude. Instead, he pulls out his business card and slides it across.

"If you ever make it to Miri, give me a ring." He rises. "I think I should go back now. One of us is too drunk."

Funny world—people get drunk on Diet Coke!

Chapter 25

Su texts me on Tinder, saying she's close by and can pick me up if I'm still sane and smelling good.

"Come close, Parker." She lunges at me soon after I get into her car. "Smell like rotten jasmine, white rose, some musk." She drifts from my neck to shoulders. "And summer cherry blossoms." She pushes me back to my seat and shrugs her shoulders. "You smell like cheap perfume. Parker, can have some class in choosing girls or not?"

I want to tell her Richard Parker doesn't pick his girls; the gods do. Instead, I promise to dance with a lady who smells like a vintage car next time.

Su's face lights up like the evening sun. "Parker boy, you know my taste. Making progress, *wo . . . good . . . fuyoh*, I like that."

I thank her and summarize my meeting with Franklin, Mariyam, Mariyam's friend Jenny, and the other generous ladies.

"You met a few girls, right?"

"Yeah, but I don't think any of them are virgins, you know."

She prods the cigar on her lips for a while and asks me with a straight face, "Tell me, Parker boy, is the vagina a wine bottle that loses its flavor once opened?"

I say nothing. That's how the evil lady killed my hanker for virgins.

We only hear the roars of traffic until she exhausts that cigar.

"I want to surprise you," she says, breaking the silence. "Open the dash, Parker."

I open it and find a white envelope below her Davidoff Exquisitos. Su leans over and grabs the box.

"It's your envelope," she says, dividing her attention between the road and the cigar box.

My attention is on the open envelope in my hand. I see printed air tickets. One is a return ticket to Sarawak, and the other is for Bali. The Bali flight leaves six hours after my return flight from Miri lands in Kuala Lumpur. There are two passengers: me and Su. We are flying to Bali! This means I can also meet the shaman. Now that I have been making little progress in finding my girls and enlightenment, he could help me.

"Yay! This is great news. What a surprise!" I feel like dancing.

"Yes, I suddenly change my plan. After we come back from Bali, then only my condominium will be ready."

I whistle as beaches, girls, and magic rituals flash before my eyes.

"Our agreement remains valid," she reminds me.

The images disappear, and I turn to look at her.

"We will meet, same place, same time as planned. If you not show up right, we will never meet again." She puts another cigar to her lips.

I look at the ticket to Sarawak. It is for June 1, as she'd mentioned before.

Neither of us speaks after that.

Worry not, my son. Our girls are waiting for us on the golden sands of Bali. Together, we shall rock toward enlightenment, says Bhagwan.

I hate how he emphasizes "we," sounding like an orgy. I must find some way to bid him farewell forever. But for now, I remain mum, as I am yet to be enlightened and still need his advice. Besides, what if he reads my thoughts and jinxes the plans?

Days fly past, and June 1 pops up on our calendars.

My flight to Miri is in the evening. That gives us a whole day together in KL. In the morning, Su wants to take me to a photography exhibition. "Richard Parker, you sure will love this one!" she says.

I don't want to go, but it's impossible to say no to her. Photography isn't a thing anymore. During the early days of my journalism career, we ran from desk to desk, pleading for photographers to join us while we interviewed gurus, organic farmers, and animal rights activists. Trust me, it wasn't an enjoyable experience.

"Nah, my camera doesn't love that kind of shit," said a guy who photographed real shit in the slums.

"I'm busy photo-documenting illegal sand mining."

"Sorry, bro—I have a date with birds and flowers for the magazine section."

"Oh, Parker sir, it's going to be dark soon. I don't do flash photography."

They all vanished soon after we purchased our first digital cameras. Two years ago, I met Palani, whose camera worked only under natural light. I caught him working with a photo lamination shop in T. Nagar, Chennai. "Do you know you can upload photos to a website in the US and have an excellent print mailed from Shanghai?" I asked him. That washed-out look on his face! It was a beautiful evening.

The meek reek of vengeance. The strong ones keep moving, up and higher, Bhagwan calls out.

I draw a cross over my chest and apologize to Palani. *May Lord Ayyappa find him a secure job.*

"Mr. Parker, you finished praying for a safe drive or not?" Su nudges me back to the present. We are on the way to KLCC, where the exhibition is.

"Parker, come on, let's play a guessing game. Tell me what pictures we'll see today. I give you one clue: this guy, right, he is a self-made man."

That's no big deal for me. I've been a journalist. Journalists are the first to read the pulse of the people. I roll out my guesses:

> A child on a buffalo, silhouetted by the morning sun
> An East Asian lady half immersed in some lotus pond
> Mug shot of an old man with missing teeth and frosted spectacles
> Rural African or Indian women carrying empty pots
> A nursing mother weaving handlooms
> A sailor kissing a nurse

"I could name more. But these are good starters." I grin.

"Hmm, you think like that, *arh*?" she asks. "Very nice. I guess it should be very amazing."

"Yes, unless we imagine ourselves in the shoes of a nurse violated by a stinking sailor, a mother whose love for her infant turns into some stranger's money-minting shot, or women on an arduous search for water."

She gives me a bemused look.

"You know? Once, some photographers visited Little Lotus Pond to click the wild beauty of our girls bathing in the mother pond. Their cameras shattered, and they ran for their lives. They didn't know we had a witch in jeans."

"Witch in jeans? Isakki?" Her eyebrows rise and fall.

"Yes, the talk of the village is that the ground they ran through is still barren, totally nuked!" I struggle to suppress my laughter. "I wasn't there. But every time someone narrates it, I feel as if I was there, right amid the action. Today, everybody in Little Lotus Pond knows there are one hundred and eight *varmam* points in the human body; twelve of these pressure points are deadly *padu varmam*, and the rest are milder *thodu varmam*. She played with those points like a child tearing apart her ugly toy." I snort.

"That would have been a sight to see, oh boy!" Su pauses for a few minutes and then looks at me. "Parker, I like how you say it in words. You show much admiration, *wo*. You adore her, is it?"

Adore her? No way. Not a nanometer, not a milliliter. Not an inch, not a morsel. "Have you met anyone who idolizes their nemesis?"

"No, *lah*, first time for me." She chuckles.

"How did you come to know about the exhibition?" I change the topic.

"Here is Kuala Lumpur. You know, we not just have bars and pubs only. We have many other beautiful art and culture scenes. You know what, most local people not even know the pubs and bars; they are open for tourists, not for local people."

"I see..."

"Parker," she calls. "Do you know you can become one feminist? You think about it before or not? The intellectual is asleep inside you, right?"

"Intellectual?" I shiver.

"I think it's time now, Parker. You need to wake up and discover who you are, OK?"

Men with unkempt hair and long beards, women in men's attire, sipping black tea and discussing neoliberal economics. *Is that the destiny I came in search of?* A long journey to become a Communist, to speak jargon that nobody understands? The bottom of my stomach churns, and I rub it.

"I see your underbody chakra is working." Su points her unlit cigar at my abdomen.

I'm in no mood to laugh. The idea of me returning to Little Lotus Pond in a long tunic, with a cloth bag and unkempt beard, is nauseating. The first thing to do on reaching Miri is to shave off the beard, I decide.

We arrive at KLCC. Remember my long list of guesses about the exhibition? Irfan's photographs tick none of the above. Irfan towers over me as a lanky, black-frame-spectacled photographer with a goatee who explores little creatures through his lens. "Hundred Little Dances" is the title of the exhibition. A sizeable crowd has gathered around him while he explains his philosophy, pointing to his picture before an anthill.

"I was there for two hours, waiting for the moment. I love it that way—the experience, the pain, the sweat is as important as the photograph," he says, adjusting his glasses.

"Uncle Irfan, is it true that we can refrigerate a butterfly and then put it under the sun to get a good picture?" a school kid asks with oodles of innocence painted all over her face.

"Yes, we can. But I don't think we would be happy looking at those photographs." He goes on to explain the ethics of photography and finishes to reverberating applause. Su claps; so do I.

Portraits of ants, frogs, butterflies, moths, dung beetles, and dragonflies, all captured in different moods, line up as we walk farther in. Su has stopped talking. She spends a long time before each photograph, scrutinizing them as though they were all vintage cars. My favorite photo is of a tadpole just below the water's surface. Taken from the waterline, it anthropomorphizes the larval frog. I can even feel the yearning in its heart—the desperate wait to take to the land.

The only photograph different from the others is that of a pair of eyes, a cliché. Every photojournalist wants to shoot at least one pair of eyes, like those of Sharbat Gula, the Afghan girl orphaned during the Soviet bombing. As far as I know, their masterpieces all end up as cheap stills stuck to the rear of autorickshaws. My hands itch to peel it off the black canvas.

"*Walao*, I wish I was his camera. Parker, we have been here for two hours already—you know that?" Su says as we exit the hall.

Su wants to congratulate Irfan, but I'm hungry. I want to tick one last item on my buccal list for Kuala Lumpur—*mee jawa*. The Java noodles have been on my list ever since Su suggested it. She insisted it would be an excellent prelude to

Indonesian cuisine before I set foot there. Su keeps talking about the exhibition; I salivate at the thought of food.

"There were ninety-eight macrophotographs. But only two human portraits, one at the beginning and the other one at the end. Very weird," Su turns back and says.

I don't reply. It's not up to me to worry about what goes on in a photographer's head.

We are before the restaurant, and there's only a glass door between us and good food. Su pulls the door and holds it open for me. "After you, Mr. Richard Parker, the great saint." She bows.

I put my hand on her forehead and bless her. "Live a thousand years if you can, my child."

We both laugh.

I take a step, and her grip slips, and the door slams into her from behind, yanking her toward me. My reflexes act fast—I turn around in a microsecond and hold her. The door swings ahead and hits the glass jamb while we struggle to stay balanced on the freshly mopped floor. It's as if time has stood still. I am yet to regain footing, but my eyes lock on the center of the quavering glass door, where an image takes shape. When it assumes form, I see that pair of eyes peering straight into mine.

"You are very lucky, you know. You can continue your journey in one piece." Su giggles, releasing herself from my hold and balancing herself. I don't reply.

"Parker, you OK or not?" I hear her repeating, shaking me by my shoulders.

"Those eyes, Su. Those eyes with the dot in between." I pull her arm. "Let's go back. I want to take another look."

I hurry back toward KLCC, with a perplexed Su trailing. I'm not hungry anymore.

"There was no round dot," Su disagrees from behind. I'm sure the *pottu*, the dot adorning the third eye of Indian women, was there. If I shut my eyes, I will see them again. They were peering at me and mirroring the pace of my strides as if they were leading me.

Su says I'm delusional out of hunger and deprivation of the female body. She's right; the laser dot is not there in the portrait. I scrutinize the photograph, ignoring Su's taunt not to behave like a pervert.

I shake my head. "These eyes, Su. I have seen them."

"*Mangkuk*, you empty cup," I hear her tease.

"Your friend is right."

We both turn toward the voice. It's Irfan. "There is little chance you might know her. She's a secret." He stretches out his hand. We take turns shaking hands with him, not a firm grip but more of the gentle touch I have gotten used to in Malaysia.

Su summarizes our disagreement over the *pottu*. I don't know why she makes it sound like an ordeal.

"I have other pictures of her with the dot," he says. "Unfortunately, I can't put them on display because of cultural and political restrictions."

I try to rub my forehead, but Su grabs my arm.

"That was my first time shooting boudoirs. My friends who do intimate photography wouldn't even talk of models with unwaxed skin. Yet, there I was in a little village somewhere in South India, filling my memory card with sheer feminine energy, complete with hairs and scars and marks. Some ask me if I got aroused. Looking back, I think I felt like a toddler before his mother."

I look at how he rubs his goatee as he speaks. We know all geniuses are eccentric. But all eccentrics are not geniuses.

"Where in South India was it?" Su asks, passing a glance at me.

My feet drag two involuntary steps backward, pulling Su. She judders and releases her hold on my arm.

It's as if my heart knows what's coming.

Don't tell me it was Little Lotus Pond, Irfan. I don't want to hear it's that witch in jeans. Don't tell me it is she to whom you lost your sanity. Tell me it's not she who makes you the odd man in the crowd, speaking a language that nobody understands.

Irfan doesn't answer the question. Instead, he fixes a penetrating glance into my eyes, caresses his goatee, and says, "Eyes that kill, hands that know every pressure point on the body. Despised queen of magic and a benevolent witch who touches to cure." He smiles. "I think I was wrong earlier. You know her, don't you?"

I don't utter a word. My legs have begun their retreat.

Chapter 26

I know—I shouldn't have walked off. It was rude to leave Su behind. Here I am, next to the car, concocting excuses, from an out-of-body experience to an urgent call from nature, rehearsing them to perfection. Su arrives, acting as if nothing happened. But the way she talks about Irfan, rubbing the cigar stub over her glossy lips, shows she is smitten.

Su is an expert in eliciting responses. She can induce one to narrate their entire history with a teasing remark. Her smart brain would then match the zigzag puzzles for the bigger picture. It's easy for her, just like assembling a vintage car from scrap.

It was a naturalist photography expedition. The team members were all from the north of India, except the Malaysian Irfan and Nguyen from Vietnam, she says.

At this point, I intervene. I had met Nguyen at a journalism workshop in New Delhi. He sounded like the mechanical shutter of medium-format film cameras when he spoke. I predicted back then that he was destined to pick up photography someday.

"Shut up, Parker. Every third person you meet in Vietnam is Nguyen. It's a popular surname!" Su continues talking.

Every time they stopped at a national park, wetland, or plantation, the team spread out, looking for their subjects of interest. Birders scanned the treetops and bushes while macrophotography lovers stuck their eyes close to the ground. But when they arrived at Little Lotus Pond, their interests changed from birds and insects to our girls bathing unaware in the pond. Irfan, Nguyen, and a couple of others protested and stayed away. But the voyeurs continued clicking until Isakki spotted them while returning from her field with the buffaloes. While she stood staring at them, as she always did before acting, somebody wished aloud that he'd like to see her bathing naked. The rest is history—folk history or oral history, whatever you call it.

Those photographers who stayed away escaped Isakki's wrath. She later stopped their van on the highway, singled Irfan out, and rewarded him with an exclusive boudoir session.

In the part of Tamil Nadu that lies on the leeward side of the Western Ghats, you will find little commemorative temples at the village entrance. Most are just white platforms with saffron stripes on which they erect the idols. These are for heroes who died defending the village from evils or invaders from other castes. Some of them are venerated along with their dogs and horses. Luckily, Little Lotus Pond is in the Kanyakumari district—the only district of Tamil Nadu on the windward side of the Western Ghats, where no such practice exists. Or else Isakki would've created history by being the first heroine to be worshipped while still alive. "You should be proud of her, Parker." Su ends the story with some advice.

I don't reply. My stomach is filled with three-quarters acid and one-quarter of the Irfan–Isakki story. But the buccal list must progress.

We move on to find *mee jawa*. The yellow Java noodles bathed in potato, beef soup, and tomato sauce ticks off an item on the list. Su keeps her monologue on Isakki going. She thinks she knows more about the Isakki thing than I do. To top it off, she has taken Irfan and Isakki's numbers. I know she can reach Isakki only when the witch in jeans ventures into civilization where cell phone coverage exists. But I don't tell her that. One day, she will learn this. That day, she'll realize Richard Parker knows more about Isakki than she does.

"It's her landline number."

I swallow the soup.

The soup burns my buccal cavity and throat, inscribing its name with fire. In my overenthusiasm, I had ordered it extra spicy, ignoring Su's reminder that *mee jawa* is best in its original spicy-sweet form.

I learn something new—respect local knowledge, especially on spicy food.

"I suggest an ice cendol, Mr. Parker. It soothes the burned throat and the to-be-burned butt."

Su is correct again. Ice cendol tastes good on a burned tongue. As for the other part, I hope it never happens.

All along our drive back, she can't stop talking about Little Lotus Pond and Isakki. At one point, I ask Su if she is bisexual.

"Just asking for a friend." She winks.

"Oh, you have a friend who might be interested in her?"

"Parker," she calls out in a high-pitched tone. "Can I take back my words?"

I grin, tasting victory. "Yes, please. Thanks for reverting your opinion on Isakki."

"Not that! I recall my observation that you could be an intellectual in Parker's skin."

I sigh in relief. "Please do. My Little Lotus Pond and I shall be grateful to you."

"I like the way you say 'my Little Lotus Pond.'" She laughs as though it is the joke of the century, annoying me further.

The world will test your patience. You must stay calm and alert. Bhagwan appears on the scene.

I take a deep breath.

"Inhale. Exhale. Do it a hundred times, my boy," Su teases.

Don't listen to her.

I remain focused on my breath.

She maintains tempo until we reach home. After a warm bath, I check my bags.

"Have you informed your dates here about your departure?" the mind reader teases.

"No, but I have informed my Sarawakian girls. They know I'm arriving soon."

We arrive at the parking lot of KLIA-2. I have dreaded this day for the tears and heaviness it will bring forth. But it's arrived, just like any other day.

"There you are, Saint Richard Parker—the first monk to travel with a bag on wheels," Su says, opening the boot.

I thank her for the compliment. The prophecy is coming true. Soon, more people will realize I'm a trendsetter.

We walk to the check-in counter, and I drop my duffel bag.

"Sir, just to confirm, you can only remain in Malaysia for another ten days," the lady in red explains after going through my passport while I wonder why there were no special offers this time.

"Yes, I'll be back in Kuala Lumpur in nine days and fly straight to Bali with my friend." I point to Su standing beside me.

"Ah . . . ," she says, shuttling her gaze between us while her mouth sucks air.

Su stands with folded hands, surveilling the red-uniformed lady as she sticks on the check-in tag.

We still have two hours to spare. We must now choose the rendezvous point—our gateway to the golden sands of Bali. Su leads me to level two of the Arrival Hall. I can tell she has already decided on the location.

"Your flight will land at pier J or K around 12:30, lunchtime. It will take thirty to forty minutes to clear immigration and collect bag. An arrival gate would be more convenient for you."

"What if my flight is late? What if it is canceled?" I'm fishing for her phone number.

"There are apps to track flights, my dear Parker. And no, I'm not giving you my number." My hopes deflate like the balloons at the Friday market. They fly high in the morning, go low by midday, and by evening, they are on the grass, shrunk and wrinkled to a quarter of their original size.

"Here." She points to a signboard that reads OLD TOWN IPOH COFFEE. "I'll be here at one o'clock, waiting for Saint Parker."

My eyes prepare to cleanse themselves. Going by our Bollywood tradition, this is the occasion for a sad background song. But she's cool as usual.

"You need this. It's freezing at the airport and on the flight." She pulls out a rolled shawl from her handbag. "I couldn't find a good winter coat. This should help for now."

I look at the tag on the silky ribbon: *Adventures are routine experiences encountered outside our comfort zones.*

It sounds profound, but I am in no mood to ponder over it. I rain-check my thoughts.

We hug. We part.

"See you soon," she says, then turns back and walks away.

I watch her disappear beyond the glass door, hoping she turns back to wave, but she doesn't. That's Su. Turning back would be uncharacteristic of her. I also know that she will have unmatched me on Tinder by now. I'm right. My Tinder match list is back to zero.

I clear immigration and enter the secure area. This means that there are physical and legal barriers between my ground and the world where Su drives her vintage Proton Saga. Damn! I wish I could abandon this trip and go back to Su's place to sleep happily in the company of cartons.

Adventures are routine experiences encountered outside our comfort zones, Bhagwan reminds me.

The LCD screen confirms my departure gate. To go back is to quit my quest. Had I remained in Little Lotus Pond, I wouldn't have met Rachel, Nita, and Su. Yes, they were all encounters of different kinds, but valuable ones. Bhagwan is right; so is Su. I should tread into the unknowns.

Su had chosen the right gift. It's cold inside the airport, so cold that my eyes remain wet. I take the travelator, sidestepping the elbows of slow walkers and window-shoppers, smiling at children playing merry-go-round around their parents.

I resist my craving for tea and buy a coffee and settle on a steel chair with my laptop. Because airports are productive places to write, and writers who drink coffee write better.

Opposite me is a tall man clad in blue jeans and a blue T-shirt. He has long arms and a cold stare. He cares for no one. He has no credit cards, no wallet. He has nobody to care for. He visits the same spot many times a day. He has been selected for his observation skills. His entire career is about observing details. He carries a long tool in his left arm. He bends down, cocks his head, and sends the device underneath the chair, sweeping out pieces of trash. He's Reacher, Zack Reacher. His job is to look out for small things people drop and sweep them away. It's just another busy evening in his long career. His eyes sweep the floor before his mop does. Reacher, the perfectionist.

A notebook-bearing man follows Reacher. *Lee Child*, his name badge reads. His job is to note down everything Reacher does. But Reacher is the only one doing real work. Reacher, alone and efficient.

I bring the coffee cup to my lips. The first sip excites my nerves, but the second sip hits my gut and sets off a tiny cramp. There's no third sip. I splatter the coffee in the plastic-wrapped bin and dart to the *tandas*, only to find an A4 sheet of paper stuck on the toilet door. "Toilet under renovation. Next toilet three minutes' walk away." The sign even has a tagline: "An amazing experience is coming." I rush to the next toilet to prevent that amazing experience from coming. The walk proves to be my toughest; they have blocked access to the next three toilets as well. Fortunately, the fourth one is open, and I stay civilized without fertilizing the marble floor. But I spend the next forty minutes walking in and out of the toilet cubicle. By the time the spices finish burning my alimentary canal, I have no energy left. Su was right. It wasn't a good idea to prove my Indianness by asking for extra spicy *mee jawa*.

Walking on the floor is like I'm on the travelator, with objects and people speeding by. Twenty minutes until my flight, and I am struggling to stay on my feet!

Three questions come to mind: One, how come the oracle never predicted this amazing experience? Two, why haven't I heard from Bhagwan while running from toilet to toilet? Three, why are there only two points when there are supposed to be three?

I throw my daypack into the carousel for the last check, ignoring the security personnel's grumbles. "You are lucky it's the Red Airlines. Those cheapskates open gates only ten minutes before departure."

The flight is only half-occupied. I ignore the stares and teeter toward 17F, my window seat, apologizing to the shoulders I bump. On the aisle sits an elderly lady, around seventy years old.

"Excuse me," I say, pointing to my seat.

"You . . . your . . . your seat, *ah*?" She locks her trembling knees and tugs down the hem of her skirt.

Having spotted the signs of a panic attack, I am about to summon the stewardess. But her emotions downshift to disgust as she puckers her face and retrieves her handbag from underneath the seat.

I tuck myself into the seat gap behind me to make way for her. She pinches her scrunched-up nose like someone who sniffed excreta and crosses me, taking extra care not to rub against me.

I dump my daypack in the overhead compartment and sink into my seat.

Parker, brace for the storm.

Bhagwan's voice rings from some canyon while my co-passenger struts to the air hostess and demands a seat change. I expect the flight attendant to approach me with an apology on behalf of her guest. Instead, she calmly proceeds with her tasks. I realize this is nothing new to her.

The floorboard shifts beneath my feet like quicksand. I fasten my seat belt, lean against the fuselage, and slip into the abyss.

Two hours fly by; I can't tell if I was sleeping or passed out. I'm not feeling great, but it doesn't hurt, either, as if deadness has set in. Perhaps the pain might have been sharper if Bhagwan had not cautioned me in time.

But as the oracle said, I must keep going.

Chapter 27

Although a part of Malaysia, Sarawak has its own immigration policy. Sarawak controls everything moving in and out of its borders, except the fossil fuels the federal government extracts from their territory. Even Peninsular Malaysians should secure immigration clearance. Su gave me an idea of the immigration formalities involved.

I shut my eyes and take a deep breath, expressing gratitude for landing in this generous land. The immigration queue is not as long as those we saw in Kuala Lumpur. What is striking to me is that the female immigration officer has features resembling those of Northeast Indians. Unlike the rest of India, which is in South Asia, our eight northeastern states lie in Southeast Asia. People there are mostly Christians, and we have a love-hate relationship with them. When they come out of the Northeast, Brown Indians make racist jokes about them, about the way they look different. When we go to the Northeast, they make racist jokes about us, about how we look dark and ugly. The parallelism stops there because they can sue us for calling them names, but we can't do the same.

The immigration officer asks me if this is my first visit to Sarawak. She smiles when I reply yes, then stamps my passport, adjusting her golden bracelet. The bracelet charm catches my eye—it has a fern motif with a cross in the center.

Son, do you see that?

Bhagwan points out the coexistence of Christianity and indigeneity in East Malaysia. Looks like Bornean Christianity has learned its lessons from the violent Latin American experience.

The hostel Su picked for me is in the city's heart, twenty minutes' drive from the airport. "It's close to Zing Café, the most happening place in Miri," she told me. Apparently, it's customary for every traveler to take a piss in their loo that smells like stale beer. She also added that they welcome foreigners with open arms and frothing draught beers.

"You are Richard Parker?" the driver inquires the third time. I haven't even stepped into his taxi yet.

Surprise, buddy!

"Sorry, *ah*. Don't mistake me, boss. So far, Meeri travelers come with backpack. First time I see traveler with wheel bag," he says, slamming the boot door.

I like the way he pronounces Miri. I also like him for recognizing my uniqueness. Good passengers chat with the driver. I'm tired, dehydrated, and sleepy but decide to make his day better. From his corner in my heart, I hear Bhagwan applauding.

"So, how's business today? Got many customers?" I begin.

"Yes, business so far today, *ah*, so good. You my nineteenth customer. Ten ladies, nine males. Got rain two times today. Yes, I ate lunch and dinner o'ready. You my last customer today," he says, taking the U-turn toward the city.

"That's damn impressive." I appreciate his foresight into the questions I had lined up in my mind.

"My standard answer, boss. Everybody asks same question. By evening, o'ready tired of answering. So, I tell everything in advance." He laughs.

For a moment, I think it's better to push my seat back and nap, as my body wants to. But Bhagwan reminds me to keep engaging. We are at the first roundabout of the trip, one with a seahorse statue.

"What tourist attractions would you recommend to a traveler like me?"

"Banana leaf," he says after an *umm*. "Your stay in Meeri center, *oh*. No problem. You step out from hostel, turn right, walk ten minutes, got banana leaf restaurant. Got good *thosai* there. Just now you see the airport? Got one temple there. Meeri not many Indians. Maybe you meet Indians at banana leaf, make friends."

"Anything adventurous? I mean, for an adventurous person like me?"

He takes his eyes off the road to glance at me and then points to the traffic light. "You see tha' traffic light, *ah*? Most adventurous place in Meeri. Three big people already shot down in daytime."

I taste hydrochloric acid in my mouth. "Any writers on the murdered list?"

He taps the steering wheel for a moment. "So far, no, *lah*. But you never know."

I realize I'm not that adventurous. "How about Zing Café, bro? I mean, just for some exotic food."

"Zing Café, oh? I don't know. I won't recommend, *lah*. That one, only locals and foreigner go for drink beer."

I rub my forehead. That's too much information to process. I decide to rest my brain for a while.

It's close to midnight, but the hostel's vicinity is alive when we arrive. A food court, pubs, and burger stalls all spill out their versions of music from the other side of the street. But the guitar notes floating down the hostel stairs are soothingly distinct.

I pay him and refuse to take the change. "If you want taxi, call me, boss. I give you good price." He hands me a brown slip with his address stamped. "*Terima kasih.*" I thank him and drag my luggage up the stairs.

I arrive at a tiny lobby, spot the "press me" switch, and comply with the instruction.

A midsize lady in a sleeveless top and shorts appears. She introduces herself as Agnes. "Agnes all-in-one." She laughs, revealing her lone dimple on the right cheek. "Welcome to the community. Once in, you are never out," she adds after securing a photocopy of my passport.

Agnes opens the glass door flaunting orangutan and rafflesia posters. The dorm is twice as big as the lobby, and I spot two men and two women on the floor. The men have tattoos, as expected. One is on the guitar while the other is scribbling something on his notepad. The two ladies sit opposite them, facing the entrance. The lady with tattoos on her belly and forearms is busy scouring her fleshy biceps for new spots to tattoo while the other fidgets with her long white T-shirt that neither covers her shorts nor eliminates the need for them. Her angular chin points downward to her well-toned body. She takes her eyes off the guitar guy to glance at me and returns to him again.

There's a walking piece of God's wonder over there, Bhagwan says. I don't respond because I noticed her before he did.

My bunk has the number eighteen stuck above it. It's three rows from the door that opens to the shower and smoking area.

"There's a balcony with a tin roof above." Agnes warns that venturing there during the hot daytime is injurious to health. Luckily, the air conditioner is set at 25°C, making the hostel habitable for me.

I had hoped to say hi to the four other guests after my shower, but they had gone out.

Son, never lie before going to bed, Bhagwan reminds me.

Allow me to correct myself. I wanted to say hi to the lady with the sexy chin.

Like a battered log, I sleep until eight in the morning. After a quick shower, I appear at the breakfast table. Agnes switches on the toaster and tells me that the other occupants have gone to the forest department for some permit. She points to a long wooden pipe stuck diagonally on the wall. It has a rustic knife tied to its top with bamboo-bark twine. I guess she's hinting at some connection between the tube and the quartet. My brilliance is being tested, and I must rise to the occasion.

"Wow, cool. They are into fishing! I love fishing, too," I say, remembering the good old days of fishing with plastic threads pulled out from mosquito nets.

"Oh, no. It's a blowpipe." She hollows her hand and blows air into it.

The toaster pops the bread slice.

"Wow, glassblowing! I love artisans," I say, spreading red jam over my bread.

"Well, yes. Kind of." She smiles, pouring some tea into her cup. "Our foragers use the blowpipe to shoot poisonous darts."

I step close to the blowpipe, with the plate in my hand, bread in my mouth, and awe in my eyes.

"The other guests you were inquiring about before? They do research in the Highlands with the hunter-gatherers. This blowpipe was crafted by an artisan from the community." Her voice rings loud.

I spot the sign.

Chapter 28

Nine more dawns to go in Miri.

The signs beckon me to the Highlands. I must reaffirm it because this could be the pivotal point in my quest.

I text Jenny, whom I had met at the kizomba pub in Kuala Lumpur. Hi Jenny, I landed last night. Here for another nine days. Hope to drop by your studio sometime. The double tick does not appear. She must be out of the coverage area, swimming in some jungle brook with her white boyfriend.

Since Jenny is unreachable, the hostess, Agnes, becomes the starting point for my Miri itinerary. I don't want to seek Franklin's help. Some people are like magnets: they leave us hankering for another meeting. And then there are Franklins.

Only three of us are in the hostel—me, Agnes, and a cat in its cage. The cat sends its meows from the tin-roofed terrace. Agnes is bent before the sink, washing dishes.

"Agnes, I'm drawing up a list of things to do in Miri. Wondering if you could give me some ideas?" I ask, broaching the topic.

"That's my job, helping people. It all depends on what you want to do," she says, working up a lather on the pan.

"I'm not a regular traveler. I want something offbeat," I say without sounding boisterous.

"You're in the right place, Richard."

She plunks the pan into the drainer and pulls out a paper towel to wipe her hands. "Why not sit down and talk?" Agnes points to the dining table. I oblige.

"You can begin with the crocodile park," she suggests.

My energy level spikes. Crocodiles!

"And savor a delicious crocodile satay." She sends it plummeting.

I control the nausea attempting to spoil my day, just as diarrhea ruined the last evening. I had already declined to partake in Rachel's crocodile tail soup party in Singapore.

Agnes continues. "Fly down to Mulu caves, trek to the pinnacles, and arrive in Limbang on day five. You can sleep in a camp, a longhouse, and an open jungle."

I ask for adventures, and Agnes gives me suicide recipes!

"The Mulu trip and headhunters trail sound so exciting. But I only have nine days," I say, tucking in my tummy.

"Well, you can take a two-and-a-half-hour drive down to Niah caves, stay at the longhouse, and see prehistoric art paintings." She waits for my reaction, but I stay mum. That brings out her best. "Better, Richard, fly to the Highlands, meet hunter-gatherers, shoot blowpipes. The Highlands is also famous for good food, pretty girls, and unspoiled natural beauty. Besides, they love foreigners."

This is the sign, my kind of offbeat adventure. I grab it without betraying my emotions.

"Sounds good. But is it doable, Agnes?" I ask, stroking my beard.

"Yes, if you plan well. I shall pass you contacts of a homestay in the Highlands. They regularly host foreigners and also take visitors to the hunter-gatherers. It's just a three-hour trek from the village center."

Everything sounds perfect except the three-hour walk.

She scribbles the contacts on a paper slip and hands it over with a tourist brochure. I thank her thrice—once verbally and twice in my heart.

I connect my laptop to the Wi-Fi and book return tickets to the Highlands. The plan is to spend three days more in Miri and then fly to the Highlands for another three days. I leave the last four days for the gods to fill in.

"Ah! I forgot to say, if you're lucky enough to get a visa, Brunei Darussalam is worth a day's visit. You have come this far anyway." Agnes reappears on the scene, prodded by my destiny.

I thank her and take directions to the travel agent.

The travel agency is inside an old shopping mall with no elevator. I take the stairs that remind me of some villain's mansion in Bollywood movies. A plywood board partitions the shop into two; one half is occupied by a men's salon and the other by the travel agency. If not for Agnes's recommendation, I would have run away without stepping in.

The gentleman introduces himself as "boy," though he looks like he is in his fifties. I hand over my passport and tell him my requirements. He takes my passport and flips it open. His face now lights up like a comet.

"Richard Parker!" He springs up from his seat. "Oh, what a pleasure to meet you. Never met a Richard Parker in my entire life, I mean a human Richard Parker." He stretches out his arm.

If not for his glowing face, I would have mistaken his words for sarcasm.

"I'm boy," he repeats.

"I was a boy, too, once."

"You so funny. I mean, my name is Boy, *lah*."

I apologize.

Boy upshifts his curiosity and inquires about my journey. I give him a fair idea of Little Lotus Pond and a vague idea of my mission. We speak for half an hour—the longest I've talked to any travel agent. I learn three things: one, he's a man in his early fifties but also a boy because his name is Boy; two, he is an international traveler who drives twenty kilometers every weekend to visit Brunei Darussalam; three, his dream is to visit the Taj Mahal, whereas mine is not to get anywhere close to the traffic snarls and the slums surrounding it.

I sign where he asks me to and pay him 150 ringgits. He promises to try his best to get a visa for me, but he says I must be prepared for disappointment. That's because Brunei Darussalam is that rare country with no tourist visa. Approval of a social visa application depends on the immigration officer's ability to spot the goodness in the applicant. Anyway, my nine-day tentative itinerary is ready without the help of Franklin.

In the afternoon, I walk to the mall like any modern-day traveler. What they call a mall in Miri is one-tenth the size of those in Kuala Lumpur. I can't compare it with malls in Kanyakumari, as we have none. They have a Bata store here. Well, there's a sizeable market for disposable shoes everywhere. The cinema is on the top floor. Before you judge me, let me say this: I'm not the only traveler watching the dust fly in *Mad Max: Fury Road*. In front of me are five noisy Chinese tourists.

When the streetlights turn on, I walk to Zing Café. The expensive cars lined up outside testify to its popularity with the locals, while the white tourists socializing under its awning attest to its popularity abroad. I spot some Indian men, too. The gigantic clock on the fake brick wall shows eight o'clock, and I see no empty tables. Even if there are, I don't think the waitress will be happy to see me usurp an entire table. I turn back.

"Richard Parker." The voice stops me. I turn around and catch the four researchers from the hostel.

"Would you like to join us?" The one with more tattoos moves closer to his buddy to make space for me on the wooden bench.

I thank him and take that space. A wooden log split into two is our bench. The live-edge table that separates us from the two ladies is also unpolished. The log furniture, a lit candle inside a jar, black bottles of beer, and a warm light hanging above create a varied ambiance.

"Agnes mentioned you, and I was telling Hillary you have a handsome name," the lady with the tattoo says, referring to the pointed-chin damsel next to her. "By the way, I'm Dora; that's Andy for Andrew and Mike for Michael."

"Dora for Dorothy," Andy adds.

Dora paints an angry emoji on her face.

"She hates her name," he says, guarding his mouth with his hand, pretending to share a secret. I like the way I'm instantly welcomed. The three continue talking, laughing, and gulping mouthfuls of beer. Hillary seldom speaks, and it doesn't seem to bother them at all.

"We're on our way to the hunter-gatherers." Mike gives me an idea of their mission—to set up a community-based ecotourism venture. "Parker, they are amazing humans. They speak very few words. It's funny in the beginning because, for any question we ask, the answer is 'I don't know.' Even if the question is 'What's your name?'" Andy laughs. "But you make friends, and oh boy, they fatten you with wild pig fermented inside bamboo tubes."

I sneak in my agenda and ask them if I could join. But their research permit doesn't allow that.

I narrate my mission, including the writing part, ensuring that my eyes meet Hillary's as I speak. She is attentive but does not utter a word. The others can't stop bombarding me with their inquisitiveness. Two beers down, my bladder cries, and I respond. Yes, I have been to the toilet of Zing Café, and there, I peed like every traveler is supposed to.

While walking back, I stop to scan the bulletin board—photographs of all visitors except Brown and Black. *This place is surely elite!* I laugh and laugh. The server passing by with a bucket full of Carlsberg doesn't even notice me. I'm just another drunk fellow to him.

The quartet is ready to leave. They have another meeting to attend with a supplier. I was hoping to walk back with them—and in the process, talk to Hillary. But it rains—both on my plans and on the rooftop. After we split the bill and part ways, I walk to the clubhouse next door. A club isn't on my itinerary, but between getting drenched in the rain and sitting inside a club, I choose the latter. It's ten o'clock, and there's only one table occupied by some stags. The stage is empty except for a lady in jeans as short as a bikini bottom, scratching her iPad.

I choose a small bar table in the middle, order my third beer of the day, and pretend to sip it.

"Mic testing . . . *satu, dua* . . ." a voice breaks, setting the stage for the night. Revelers hobble into the darkness punctuated by laser lights. Two classy women in suits appear at the entrance, with hands shading their eyes from the laser light, and sink into the crowd. Moments later, they pop up at the table next to mine.

I smile, spotting the sign.

The world belongs to the bravest, the three beers in me encourage. I know the drill. I walk to their side and stand still, pretending to watch the band.

The lady who was on the iPad before is now at the microphone. "But I set fire . . . check, check." She turns around to the DJ and mumbles something.

I turn to look at the young ladies. "Looks like we're going to have some wonderful songs."

I'm sure I was audible. But both pretend not to hear. I try again. "Have you heard them before? Sorry, I'm new here."

Nothing.

Gentleman, take the hint, advises Bhagwan.

I retreat to my spot. Outside, it's still raining. On the stage, the singer sets fire to the rain. She's no Adele, but she's not bad, either.

I look around. One thing is clear—the place isn't for making new acquaintances. People who walk in together stay together, smoke together, and drink together. The bigger table next to me is now occupied by three men, three ladies, and lots of smoke. They look like working professionals on a get-together. The tall lady in the group occasionally raises her ringed finger to the guy opposite her. *That's the red signal, pal.* The only one noticing me is the shortest dude in the group—the one in a white shirt with green flowers. I smile back. He is a misfit in the group, a gifted human, just like me.

He waves at me, and I wave back, taking two steps closer to him. *I just made a new friend.* Remember, two other ladies haven't raised their red signals. Maybe they are single!

The dude utters something that gets drowned in the music. I tap my ear to signal *can't hear*. He draws a tiny notepad from his shirt pocket, pulls out an equally tiny pen, and scribbles something. He then tears off the page, carefully rolls it into a little scroll, and gives it to me.

I open it.

Can I suck your ****?

My fingers free their grip, letting the paper fly into the smoke. I turn around and walk back to my table. No, we aren't the same kind of misfits.

The music continues, except for a ten-minute break every forty minutes. The rain outside tilts my indecisive mind toward staying behind. Besides, it's too early to give up!

Bodies bounce and bounce around me, elbowing each other. I watch them, hoping to pick up a few moves while the two young ladies maintain their state of eternal stiffness. The Lord must have fortified them against temptations. The tall guy from the other group moonwalks backward and places himself next to the two ladies. He inserts his hands into his jeans pockets, looks at the stage, shakes his head, turns sideward to them, and says something like his predecessor—yours truly—had done before. They pretend not to notice, exactly as they did to me.

A warm feeling sidles into my heart. I take a deep breath. It feels good. I take another deep breath, then cough.

Learn the difference between cigar smoke and happiness, says Bhagwan. The master is always right.

It's past midnight, and the rain has subsided. My eyelids are romancing gravity, and the alarm in my head reminds me it's time to get out. I walk sideways like a crab on two legs, squeezing myself between the back of the lady and a drunk soul leaning like the Tower of Pisa. Had he tipped over, it would have been an enactment of the classic hound position of the Kama Sutra. I emerge on the other side. I still must wade through a maze of sweaty bodies at the entrance before I can get out.

Suddenly, the crowd falls silent. My kindergarten teacher used to call it pin-drop silence. Never did I expect such a majestic send-off for being a civilized pub-goer. If not in my entry, then at least in my exit. Happiness and gratitude overwhelm me. I bow my head in acknowledgment, only to realize that they have their bodies and eyes turned toward two white men at the entrance. My mind digs its fossil sediments to recognize one—Smith, the begpacker. He has no guitar in his hand. The world is indeed small!

The crowd splits like the Red Sea, making way for them. Smith walks past me, looks into my eyes like a king gracing his subjects, but doesn't recognize me. My eyes follow the duo, but my legs snub my request to move. When my head can't turn anymore, I twist myself to keep my eyes on them. It's as if two gods appeared amid hungry believers to feed them chicken wings and beer.

And then, magic happens.

The two classy ladies sitting tight rise in slow motion with their beer bottles. Smith nods, and two become four. I can't hear what they say, but they are clearly introducing themselves. I shake my head twice. The group swells in the next ten seconds, with three more ladies ditching their men. I want to shake my head again but decide against it because so many things can happen in that split second.

I turn around and begin walking. Behind me, the music resumes.

I put my hands on my head while emerging from the door to avoid the rainwater dropping from the eaves.

"Richard Parker." I hear my name. I pinch myself to ensure it isn't my imagination.

"Parker, it's me!"

I turn around. It's Franklin, behind me, at the pub's entrance. *How the heck did he get in there? Did he walk past me just now?*

"Hey, Franklin, what a pleasure to see you!" I lie. He is right below the roof eaves, and I pull him a little to prevent him from turning into a rainwater-harvesting structure.

"You just arrived?"

He looks at his watch and says, "Yes, around ten-thirty last evening."

What a perfect time for sarcasm! I stop my facial muscles from displaying cringing emotions.

"Hey, listen, want to grab a burger?" he offers.

A beef burger with a double serving of cheese and sarcasm. That's the worst to have when your body is struggling to stay awake.

I look at the burger stall on the footpath between the road and the pub. The lights are off, and the vendor is cleaning the pan top. My savior!

"Not here. There's one across the road." He points toward the waterfront area.

We cross the road and walk to the waterfront through the dimly lit corridors. The only signs of life are at the massage joints, where middle-aged women in thick makeup and miniskirts work hard to pass themselves off as young girls. I avoid eye contact, as I learned from the Kuala Lumpur chapter.

"That's my favorite pub. I come here often for inspiration," Franklin says.

We are on the road before the waterfront. I don't ask him what kind of inspiration he finds there. But he continues his one-sided conversation.

"A pub is a place to find stories. Men getting shooed off, pimps fishing for clients, revelers on watered-down liquor getting high on the nicotinized indoor air, and much more. You talk, you lose the story. Take a corner and observe like a keen student," he says, sounding more like Bhagwan.

"Oh, I see," I mumble.

"Occasionally, men also get hit on by gays in floral shirts."

I divert my gaze toward a random shop that looks like a pub.

"But Miri is safe. Rapes are rare."

I say nothing, though he would have seen the cringe on my face had he bothered to look. "Tell me about the food here." I divert his attention from himself.

"Oh! Street burgers, *laksa, kolo mee.* Sarawak *kolo mee* is unique because it's a Chinese dish born here," he says, making a bowl shape with his hands.

"I love ethnic food. I want to try them all."

"*Ayam pansuh*—chicken cooked with rice in a bamboo tube. *Pakis*—fern stir-fried with *belacan*, a sour shrimp paste. Rice cooked in pitcher plant. *Babi hutan*—wild pig barbecued. That's the ethnic food you are looking for," he continues with his thumbs up in the air. "You won't find them at a restaurant but in the longhouses or the *kampong*, where the soul of Borneo is still alive."

I nod, adding them to my buccal list.

The burger cart stands in the corridor between two seafood restaurants. It's very much alive, even in the middle of the night. The waterfront isn't a pleasant sight, though, as the skeleton of a skyscraper towers over. Franklin says it's a new hotel sprouting on reclaimed land. I question how one could dump mud on the sea, alter its natural state, and call it reclamation.

We order two beef burgers, both without mayonnaise.

"*Tunggu sekejap*," the burger maker says, pointing to two young couples. We are in a queue.

"You see, Parker. Borneo was linked to continental Southeast Asia until fourteen thousand years ago. The rising sea level flooded most of the Sunda Shelf, isolating Borneo into the world's third-largest island. Politicians are only reclaiming what is theirs." He thrusts the tip of his tongue into his cheeks and continues to present the various theories on animal evolution, human migration, Chinese migration to Borneo, loss of rainforests, and the birth of palm-oil culture.

Fortunately, the burgers are ready. I take a bite.

"I like to take small bites and swallow them slowly to let the pan-heated butter flavor fill my mouth." He unwraps his burger from the butcher paper. "Did you contact Jenny, the kizomba promoter we met in Kuala Lumpur?"

"Yes, I did. But the message is in the server, awaiting delivery," I say while my left hand frees itself from the burger to fetch my cell phone from my pants.

"It won't be delivered." He chortles.

"Why would you say that? She's a nice lady," I say, remembering her kind offers, including the discount on the Bali trip.

"Of course she is. This has nothing to do with being good or bad. It's just about a misfortune that came her way." He pulls out his phone with one hand, unlocks it with his thumb, and swipes it.

"Oh ... Oh. I'm sorry," I say in advance, trying to guess what that misfortune could be.

He hands the phone over to me, and I look at the screenshot of some online newspaper.

Artist loses RM100,000 to parcel scam

Miri: An entertainment artist lost RM100,000 in a parcel scam after she believed it was a gift from her boyfriend whom she met on a popular dating site. Miri OCPD Robert Liew said that the victim, twenty-eight, fell in love with a man who introduced himself as Louis Venton from France. She and Louis had planned to get married soon and settle in Miri, where they would set up a studio and a café. He had shipped her a parcel with expensive French antiques for furnishing their café. Two days later, the victim received a call from a lady who identified herself as a customs officer, informing her she had a large parcel with declared items worth one million ringgit. The victim was then asked to pay a 10 percent customs fee, which amounted to RM100,000. The victim, who was living in Kuala Lumpur, used her savings to make the bank transfer and flew down to Miri. However, after the payment, Louis disappeared, along with his social media profiles. The victim then realized that she had been conned by someone who used the name of a popular handbag brand, and she lodged a police report. Miri police have registered an FIR, and the case is being investigated under Section 420 of the Penal Code for cheating. The Miri OCPD added that it is unknown why such parcel scams are common in Sarawak and asked the public to be vigilant.

I return his phone, wondering what its relevance was.

"Here." He swipes it once again and returns it to me.

It's a photograph of the lady at the police station, published along with the news. The face is blurred for anonymity.

"Zoom in on her hand," says Franklin.

I oblige, and the image gets pixelated. But I can make out that mail icon tattooed on her wrist. Jenny!

I take a deep breath. "Really sorry for her. Such a kindhearted lady." I sigh as heaviness creeps into my heart. She did mention Louis, I remember. I also recollect the joy in her eyes, the pride of finding someone worth flaunting. I send her an imaginary hug wherever she is.

My last chance of becoming a kizomba dancer has disappeared with the parcel. A dance floor now appears like a distant dream. But the journey must continue. I wipe the butter off my fingers.

Franklin is right. Burgers come as a package. You stand next to a street burger stall and watch him press the patty to the buttered pan surface. Then you take small juicy bites, the flavors hit the roof of your buccal cavity, and the visual memory now co-acts with your taste buds—memories of the pan, the street, the burger man. That's an experience worth the butter.

I tell Franklin about my three hostel mates who work with the hunter-gatherers. I stress the last part to take a pinch off his frigging ego.

"Strange," he says, exploring his cheeks with his tongue. "Hillary said she was staying there, too."

"Oh yes, that must be her. There was a fourth lady. Not sure if it was Hillary. I didn't speak to her," I say, looking straight into his eyes. Batting eyelids are telltales of lies. But I know how to mask them.

"Strange! She talked about having a beer with Richard Parker."

Weird lady! She doesn't dole out a word while I'm there. I decide to be silent. He doesn't pursue the string further. Instead, he drops the bomb.

"The house opposite mine is like a homestay. I know the landlord, a retired headmaster from Ulu Baram, who uses the master bedroom. I can get you a room there. It would give you a genuine taste of Miri life. Also, why pay for the dorm when you have affordable options?"

I accept his offer and look up to the sky, wondering what else the gods have in store for me.

Beyond the reach of the sodium vapor rays and cool white lights, the full moon shines in her fullest pomp.

Chapter 29

I couldn't refuse Franklin's offer for three reasons: one, Bhagwan says the ideal pupil accepts anything offered with love; two, Franklin said I could use his car when he is back from work; three, Hillary woke me up before leaving for the Highlands, saying she would meet me there.

Behind every successful man is a woman or women who speak(s) motivating words, just like Hillary did. No, it wasn't an early-morning wet dream. I know because I hit my head against the bunk bed, springing up in response to her wake-up call.

Who am I to refuse the sign that comes my way?

Franklin's rented house is in Senadin, a new residential area around ten kilometers away from the city center. It's a one-story semidetached house in Malaysian parlance. But that's not where I stay. The house of my host, Mr. Roland, is opposite Franklin's, the last one in a chain of houses. It is also the opposite in design. They call it intermediate terrace housing.

Franklin's house has a traditional tile roof with a top ridge where opposing roof planes meet. Mr. Roland's house has no ridge. The roof floats in almost flat patches—one patch above the other.

I'm happy that Franklin chose a trendy house for a modern person like me. Mr. Roland has added two additional rooms to the distal wall and expanded the kitchen. His family uses the master bedroom whenever they come to Miri from Ulu Baram, the inner Baram. He rents out the rest of the rooms.

You might wonder why Franklin didn't invite me to stay with him. I did, too, until I saw the interior of his house, painted dark brown. He calls it "earthen color," omitting the "depressingly dark." But he has a cool car in which he picked me up earlier. The Kembara, a rebadged version of the Daihatsu Terios, is another testimony to Malaysians' expertise in rebranding Japanese cars. The Terios was the world's first compact SUV, thanks to the Japanese love for miniaturizing everything except their payrolls. Franklin calls it the poor man's SUV.

Franklin drops me at the house early in the morning. Mr. Roland isn't there, but I am let in by the caretaker, who makes a brief cameo. I recommend Johnny Depp, minus the rags and eyepatch, to enact this role in the blockbuster movie version of this novel. Mr. Johnny Depp Br—*Br* here stands for *Borneo*—hands over a pack of cigars to Franklin, which he shoves into his dashboard that's already crowded like the autorickshaws back home. My joy at discovering one of Franklin's many weaknesses is short-lived when he pulls open the dash and retrieves the pack to show me its cover. I rubberneck like an ostrich through the crew-side window and find my name, age, and flight number written below the disgusting pictures of a cancerous tumor.

"Mr. Roland wanted those for his records, and I didn't have a notepad. This dashboard harbors many secrets that my married colleagues hide from their lovely wives, and these cigars are one of them." He shoves the cigar pack back.

"Hey, be here around six-thirty. I shall take you to Rumah Asap," he says, bringing the engine back to life with a roar.

"Rumah Asap?"

"The smokehouse. One of Miri's best-kept secrets. They serve grilled pork and chilled beer. Miss it, and you'll regret it for life." He raises the window glass. The Kembara roars forward, emitting obnoxious black fumes.

I'm ready for my new base, aided with gigabytes of unsolicited information Franklin uploaded into my head while driving me to Senadin. I don't want to use the kitchen because it would deprive me of the opportunity to socialize with the locals. Besides, eating out in Malaysia is cheaper than cooking if you avoid the fine-dining places. With around 3,000 USD left in my account, fine dining is beyond reach now.

Franklin has given me an idea of the eateries in the shopping lots within a four-minute walk. According to him, food here is like medicine if one knows the right food for the ailment. "If you feel constipated, go to the Pakistani restaurant. Have diarrhea? Choose the Indian one serving Indonesian food because the cooks are

Indonesian. If you have hypertension, go for dim sum at the Chinese *kopi tiam*. If you feel normal, wait for the hawkers to appear with durians, rambutans, and *mata kucing* in the evenings," he advised.

After transferring his pearls of local knowledge to my buccal list, I spend seven ringgits to buy *roti canai* from the Pakistani restaurant and chicken curry from the Indian restaurant, enough for both breakfast and lunch.

Bravo! That's my intelligent disciple, Bhagwan says, appreciating my balancing of yin and yang.

Looking at the food inside the plastic bag, I laud myself for saving a walk under the midday sun later on. Mr. Roland arrives at ten, sparing me from stalking the Chinese elder tending to the saplings on the avenue. He is lucky to have a government that remunerates him for looking after the avenue trees. Got to give it to the Chinese for finding business opportunities in trivial stuff!

Mr. Roland exudes his charming smile, which lifts his glasses by a centimeter and amplifies the wrinkles gifted by his sixty-plus years on earth. Behind him stands a little girl, around five or six years old, in a white tee and blue jeans, clutching a yellow stuffed animal—a big fat bumblebee. Stand them miles apart in a crowd, and you'll still be able to tell that she is his granddaughter.

He speaks, I speak, and she prattles.

"If you don't mind, can I walk into your room, please?" he requests after the small talk. I'm surprised he sought my permission. He pushes the plywood door and walks to the corner away from the single cot. After examining the ceiling, he gives a gratified smile.

"Looks like it's working, Mr. Parker. Every time I come to Miri, some corner of the roof is leaking." He removes his glasses and wipes them on the corner of his T-shirt.

Lucky for me, he says that before I congratulate him on choosing such an aesthetic design. The roof is not a rain-friendly one, he explains. He also illuminates me on Malaysia's homegrown philosophy behind the roof's structure.

"They said it's based on the philosophy of *ke sana, ke sini*, meaning 'toward there, toward here.'"

I learn something new. If Confucianism is China's gift to the world, Stoicism that of the Greeks, then *ke sana, ke sini* is the Malaysian entry into the encyclopedia of the world's philosophies.

"But I learned the roof is not the place to apply the philosophy, Mr. Parker. There are good reasons for having roof ridges in the wet tropics." The retired headmaster lets out a deep sigh. "They provide the right slope for roof water to run down. Can you believe it, Mr. Parker? This *rumah* leaked the very first month after its housewarming. I had expected this—but not so early. These roofs just don't have the right slope." He points to the ceiling.

"I'm sorry," I say, not out of sympathy but regret for my euphoria over a faulty roof design. We walk back to the hall.

"Please sit." He points to the bare-bones rattan couch opposite him. I thank him and place myself on the rattan. Su would love such a couch for the ventilation it provides to the bottom. The tiny tot darts like a jet to the kitchen. "She likes this kitchen so much," he says and laughs. Like you, I, too, await the story to unfurl.

"I was twenty-three when I reported to my job in 1972. It was soon after the government realized that learning in English was the biggest evil facing Malaysia." He laughs. It's his perfect row of teeth that adds to the charm of his smile, I notice. Not long after joining, Mr. Roland was promoted, along with a transfer to Miri, which was still a crude-oil town. With all its sinful pleasures, Miri was the Valhalla of people in the interior. A young teacher back then, he opted out of the promotion and the allure of Miri and continued to educate the young minds of his community in Ulu Baram. When he retired at fifty-six, Miri had become a city. Oil palm plantations had eaten away most of Sarawak's forests by then, displacing the natives to the city. Mushrooming nightclubs in the well-lit corners of the city upped the adrenaline and alcohol in the youngsters while reflexology centers in the shady lanes helped young men let off their steam. These clubs and the reflexology centers together formed the yin and the yang, restoring balance in the city. Miri was also an education and a transit hub by then, attracting his children. His only savings were his children's education, a pickup truck, and his Employee Provident Fund. Despite withdrawing his Provident Fund, he could not afford a house with a traditional roof and had to settle for a cheaper one with unconventional roofs. He waited for another five years for the construction to be over. "If I sell it today, it won't even fetch me half the price. All my life's savings!" He removes his glasses and wipes the corner of his eyes with his finger. The young girl, who has returned to his side by now, leans over and hugs him. He hugs her back.

I can't sit there anymore. I walk to the entrance and stare at the road. The sun is scorching the street, replacing remnants of last night's rain with mirage waters. The Chinese elder is nowhere to be seen, and cars with jacked-up silencers boom by, piercing the silence of the blazing street. Franklin's house remains locked.

I feel a tiny hand on mine.

"Uncle, does your house have a proper roof?" the little angel asks. Had I married twelve years ago as my parents wanted, I would have had a precious child like her, to whom I would be reading bedtime stories.

"Yes, my friend," I say, squatting to meet her eyes. She doesn't know that most Indians are obsessed with concrete slab-roof houses that are warm in summer, cold in winter, and leaky in the monsoon. I don't tell her that had the oracle not found me, I, too, would have demolished my tiled-roof house to build a slab-roof house.

She sits on the doorstep and points her bumblebee toward me. "Do you want to hear my bee story, Uncle?"

"Why not? Let's go." I sit next to her.

"G'andpa says honeybees are spirits, Uncle. They dance; they sing; they take care of their babies. They have secret lives that we don't know. You know Leesa, my friend? Her uncle went to God. G'andpa's friend who came home says it is because he disturbed the homes of the bees and . . . and the spirits got angry," she says, nodding her head more than any Indian kid would.

I laugh and pat her back. "That's so cute, my friend." I know her grandpa is listening to our conversation from his rattan couch. The responsibility of teaching this young mind what's true and what's not is now on my shoulders, I realize. "Honeybees don't have spirits, my friend. They are mere insects driven by instinct."

She shakes her head in disagreement, twists her body to face inside, and calls out, "G'andpa . . . Uncle says honeybees have no spirits. Your friend was to-ta-llee wrong."

I, too, turn back to see what Mr. Roland has to say.

"Uncle is from a different culture, Angela," he says.

She darts toward her grandpa. I follow her and return to my spot on the couch to face Mr. Roland.

"In some cultures here, Mr. Parker, honeybees have spiritual significance. They are ancestral spirits, and the trees where they set up their hives also assume spiritual value. We have one tall tree here. Our people call it *tanying*. But once the honeybees set up hives, we call it *tapang*, meaning it is a spirit now."

I bite my lip to muffle my laughter and avoid offending him. Luckily, his phone rings before my laughter bursts out.

Mr. Roland bids me goodbye, as he has to leave to attend to something urgent. I don't concur with his folktale, but I enjoyed talking to him.

"Bumblebee says bye, Uncle." The little angel waves her bumblebee. I wave back and send a few kisses flying.

I rest on the rattan couch for a while, caressing my beard. Then I remember the salon at the shopping lot and my plans to get a shave. But I have already decided it's too hot to walk. So, I wait till the pendulum strikes one, have lunch, set my cell phone alarm to four-thirty, and slip into a nap.

The singer, the begpacker, and the two smart ladies appear again in my dreams and drive away in a cycle rickshaw, ringing the bells. It takes me five minutes to realize it is my alarm sounding. I sit on the edge of the bed to let the grumpiness evaporate and reality sink in.

Human friendliness is not a virtue of the Bornean sun. It's milder than noon but still hot; I wonder if I should remain indoors until five. But as they say in Little Lotus Pond, it is a bad omen to retreat once you set out. These omens and beliefs frame our lives back home; the only human who flouts them is Isakki. Her buffaloes are more disciplined than her—nobody has ever seen them walking into an unguarded field, even when left unchained. You can see them waiting at the namesake bamboo gates of the harvested paddy fields. They jump in only when the farmer hoots, their happy bleats reverberating against the white hills beyond Isakki's backyard.

So, your beliefs are worthy while somebody else's aren't? Bhagwan asks.

Bhagwan, wouldn't ye, the learned soul, know that humans are the only sentient beings? How can ye equate human beliefs to the spirit in bees?

There is no answer. Sometimes, he's more of a hit-and-run type.

The salon is closed. So, I drop by the Javanese eatery to have *teh tarik india*, the Indian tea you won't find in India. The restaurant is empty except for its workers. The tea puller is an Indian, uprooted from central Tamil Nadu. Over his round-neck T-shirt hangs a faded fake gold chain with two pendants, one a cross and another with the image of Lord Murugan on his peacock. There should be a third pendant because I see an empty link hanging. I ask him about the missing locket.

"*Shh.*" He puts a finger on his lips. "It's in my trunk. Will wear it when I return to India. Boss says it's an offense in Malaysia to consider all religions equal."

I don't reply as a humming sound interrupts the conversation. The buzzer is a honeybee on the table, right next to my empty tea glass.

"They are here for the sugar. Nobody disturbs them," he says, as though I might swat it.

The bees with spirits! I laugh as it takes off.

The tea puller and I talk for around five minutes, and then he excuses himself to attend to the customers filling the chairs. "Franklin sir's university colleagues," he says before taking leave. I look at my watch: 5:35 p.m. I pay my bill and step out. Another bee hums by my ear. I laugh, startling a random guy.

The sun has recovered its milder manners. I take a detour back home—through the tarmac that coils around a circular patch with nothing but tall grasses. You could call it a roundabout, but to me, it looks like a placeholder for another seahorse statue. I trace my steps through the periphery of the roundabout, which is busy with vehicles flowing in from the university and exiting at the three o'clock side. Ten meters away from the roundabout, I hear another bee buzzing by. I pretend to take aim at it, holding my hand like a Ping-Pong racket. Five steps later, another buzz, this time close to my ear. I stop and squint at the buzzer, wondering if I should hit it for real this time. But this bee isn't alone; a few more are behind him, executing their war dance. Behind me, amid the vehicle grunts, grows another roar—the sound of a swarm, the war cry of the bees.

A sting lands on my left arm, and it shakes itself like an autonomous unit. The pain sets in sharp, like a rotten tooth awaiting its white-cloaked Darth Vader.

Run, Parker, run, I hear Bhagwan yell.

I thrust my legs hard on the asphalt and run with all my might, looking around for bushes or shanties or discarded boxes to seek asylum. A pickup honks and swerves to avoid me. I jump in the air, taking a few more stings. A Mercedes squeals before me, its bonnet two feet short of pulping me. I jump to the roadside, and the vehicle farts away, followed by an Audi. I raise my hands to shield my face, but more stings land on them, puncturing my defense. Two more buzzers hit my neck. My mouth cracks open, and unidentifiable sounds formed at the bottom of my gut burst out. Another car rattles by and screeches to a halt a few meters away.

"Jump in!" a voice reaches out to me.

I dart forward, connect my hand with the rusty door that looks like it will fall off at any time, jump in, and slam the door. *"Aiyoh."* The driver stretches and then crouches like a question mark, clutching his waist. He is stung, too. I strap on the worn-out seat belt, curl forward, and hug myself like a snail. The dashboard hangs off by an inch. The poor guy should have bolted it up himself.

"Boss, I bring you hospital, can *ah*?"

"Can . . . can," I blurt, hugging myself even tighter.

"You want *rumah sakit* or *klinik*?" he asks.

Our strength lies in our ability to think clearly in tough times. My brain rises to the occasion and does a quick translation using the meager words it has picked up—*rumah* means "house," and *sakit* is a word I'm yet to pick up. He is my savior, my angel, my Vladimir Putin for the moment. But going to his house, or any stranger's house, isn't wise. I choose the clinic.

The clinic is six hundred *aiyohs* away, calculated at one *aiyoh* per second, without counting for the lone *aiyoh* from my savior. It is a regular shop converted into a three-room clinic with large glass panes advertising health food supplements and vaccines. The nurses direct me to the procedure room next to the doctor's room.

The doctor comes trotting from the inner door that connects the procedure room with hers.

"Do you have over ten stings?" she asks, pulling the stethoscope from underneath the scarf that merges her head and neck.

I apologize for not counting. Even on a glorious day, I would fold my fingers underneath the desk to count from one to ten.

She puts the scope on my back and chest, asking me to breathe deeply. "Your breathing is normal. Show me the stings."

I show the spots one by one. She counts nine of them.

"Lucky you, *ah*. More than ten means a greater chance of developing anaphylactic reaction." She scribbles me a tetanus shot and mefenamic to kill the pain and directs the nurse to remove the stingers. "Nothing to worry about. Just relax and take deep breaths. We will keep you under observation for two hours, and if nothing serious happens, we send you home. If something reaction happens, *ah*, we send you to *rumah sakit*," she tells me. I want to ask her whose house it is, but the nurse has pressed her finger on the sting spot on my neck by then. There goes my six hundredth and first *aiyoh*.

"*Sakit ka?*"

My in-pain brain spots the word. "*Sakit?*"

"I mean, are you paining?"

My brain is confounded with the word it has just learned. *Rumah sakit*—house of pain.

The nurse finds one stinger there and then moves to other spots. "You lucky, sir, got only two stingers inside. You pull them out, *ka*?"

I shake my head. The only thing I would have pulled out is my hair.

Another nurse tiptoes in to collect my personal details. "For your information, sir, our data policy conforms to the Malaysian government's regulations. Do you want me to read the regulations, sir?" she offers.

"No, but thanks." I thank her for the perfect timing.

The first nurse gives a shot on my biceps. "Very smooth, *lah*. Nice arm. If got muscles, very difficult to inject," she adds.

A goddamn day of coordinated attacks, I swear. She then forces me to lie down, pulls the curtain over my raised bed, and leaves.

Moments later, the face of another nurse appears through the slit in the curtain. "Your friend wants to talk to you." She also hands over a pill to kill the pain and a glass of water that I send straight to my gut. Moments after she disappears, my savior appears, clearing the curtains to fit his healthy build. I sit up and clutch his hands. "Thank you so much, my friend. It was a timely help." Tears glisten in my eyes.

"No problem, *lah*," he says, touching the cotton swab stuck to the back of my neck. That's where one of the two stingers was. I look at him. A knight in an old car, a total stranger in an even stranger land. He could have driven past me as others did. Instead, he stopped for me. As the doctor said, another sting, and I would have got an ana-phy-lactic reaction and been admitted to the house of pain. I don't know what that house would have done to me. But it sounds terrible, like the smokehouse where they grill pork. This is the Good Samaritan Christ spoke of 2,015 years ago—the passerby who would stop his old car to rescue you, even when a new pickup, Mercedes, and Audi drive by without giving a damn. The world revolves only because of such kind souls. I pull out my handkerchief and wipe away my tears.

"Very pain, *ah*?"

"Little bit," I say, guilty that I didn't even ask for his name.

"Sorry, *ah*, bro." His empathetic arm is over my sore one. "Look...look." He lifts his T-shirt to show a red patch on his belly, from where his only *aiyoh* came. "Very pain there, oh," he says, contracting all his facial muscles. "I had appointment with one friend. He promised to buy my car. Now, canno meet him, *lo*."

I put my hand on his arm. "Sorry, brother. I'm grateful that you stopped to help me. Without you, I don't know what would have become of me."

He pulls his arm away and turns to face the only other bed in the room, where the nurse is working hard to pull down the trousers of a toddler clinging to his mother.

He stands still, scratching his chin. I can see some deep thought in progress. Then he turns toward me and says, "I bring you here, bro...got expense...fuel ...lost business. You pay me, *lah*."

I look at the Good Samaritan, who lost business because of me.

"Not much, *lah*. Just one hundred ringgit and fifty."

"One hundred and fifty ringgits?" I dab my eyes with the handkerchief to absorb the tears that have appeared again, this time for a different reason.

"Not much, bro. You see, *ah*. If I no come, you get more bite. Bite, bite, more bite...later go *rumah sakit*, pay more."

He talks perfect sense. *But 150 ringgits*—that's a precious amount to forego now. I wish Bhagwan would help me out. These are the times when a guru bails on his disciple.

The ideal guru he is. He responds to my call.

Richard Parker, this is a genteel soul, your guardian angel who saved you in the nick of time. Now it's your turn to repay his kindness.

"*Sakit*...*sakit*," the kid on the other bed in the room cries, clutching his bum from where the nurse's syringe is retreating after the assault. My mind reminds me of *rumah sakit*, the house of pain, and why I should be grateful for escaping that dungeon.

The gods speaking through the child's bum!

I pull out my wallet and pay him three fifty-ringgit bills. He thanks me, and I thank him. He doesn't ask for my name, and I don't ask for his.

I watch him draw back the curtains and wave his hand one last time—the Good Samaritan who saved me from the bees, for a fee.

Chapter 30

The nurse pokes her finger into my tummy to check if I'm dead or alive. "Your friend is here," she says, exuding satisfaction.

The Good Samaritan is back to drive me home! I shuttle my glance between her and the mini-volcanoes on my arm. The painkiller did a good job, like the road contractors back home.

"Where is he?"

She points to the doctor's room. I step down from the raised bed and hobble over.

The nurse opens the door for me, and I gaze at the doctor's laughing face. Across from her sits Franklin.

"Here he is. Safe and sound." The doctor invites me to take a seat.

"Professor Wong saw you getting stung and speeding away in some car. I had to call a few clinics to check if you were admitted," he says.

"Thanks for checking. I should have called you," I apologize.

I ask Franklin if our dinner plan is still on. The doctor also wants to join us.

Franklin is reluctant. "Change of plans, Doctor. Not a good idea to bring him there now. Besides, it's forbidden in your faith. We could meet some other time for some nice Islamic halal-certified food."

I realize they must have known each other for some time. She discharges me, asking me to report back only if I develop any allergies.

In the lobby, I pay using my debit card and thank the nurses.

> *Timely help from those who ne'er received our help,*
> *Cannot be repaid even if we gift them the heavens*

That's Bhagwan reminding me of my debts. But this one is familiar. I rub my forehead to work up my memory. Yes, that's the Tamil saint Thiruvalluvar speaking about gratitude. I learned it sitting on cracked wooden benches back home. One of those benches even had my first crush's name scribbled over it. The last time I saw her, she had a twenty-year-old daughter and wrinkles like that bench. I thank Lord Ayyappa for guiding me toward a well-read spiritual mentor. The only soul left to thank is the mysterious Professor Wong.

"Who is Professor Wong? How does he know me?" I ask Franklin, who is busy training his puny muscles on the steering wheel.

"Professor Wong is a retired professor. Without him, our street would be barren. He planted the trees and bushes, and he waters them every day. Months ago, when he was down with pneumonia, the entire street was there for him."

I rub my forehead. The Chinese elder whom I saw in the morning is not a gardener!

Jump ye not into conclusions, Bhagwan says, handing me my takeaway for the day.

We skip the smokehouse. Instead, Franklin drives me to a Chinese *kopitiam*. I request him to drive through McDonald's when it appears on his side of the windshield. He refuses and turns left at the following diversion, saying food chains run by global conglomerates are not in his book. I wonder what that book is as flashes of red skim before my eyes—red flags, red caps, hunger strikes, *gherao*, and pickets. The Kembara pulls up outside the restaurant.

I turn toward him and ask, "Are you a Communist?"

He pumps hard on the brake, pushing my sore body onto the dashboard. I clutch my neck, which just suffered whiplash.

He yanks the hand brake toward the roof and puts a finger on his scrunched mouth. "Shh. Communism is banned in Malaysia, and so is atheism. Don't get me killed with your fantasies."

Good for Malaysia. I jump down from his fake SUV.

He orders grilled pork for himself and rice porridge for me. "It will help you recuperate," he says.

My hands are still on my neck, above the X-shaped bandage, while my brain oscillates between prioritizing the stings, the whiplash, or the porridge before me to mourn.

He takes to the pork, the sound of chewing hitting my eardrums without my permission. I swallow the porridge. After the dinner—his, elaborate; mine, measly—we drive straight to Professor Wong's house to express my gratitude. But he isn't there. "We can come back after your Highlands trip," Franklin says, his breath still smelling of pork.

After reaching home, I dial the number Agnes had given me. Introducing myself as a traveler, I request accommodations. "Yes, Mr. Parker, we can reserve the best room for you," the fine lady who introduces herself as Magdalene says, offering some positivity to end the fucked-up day.

It's just for two nights, so I pack just two pairs of short pants, jeans, T-shirts, inner protection, and toiletries. A strange thought occurs: Will there be enough food in the Highlands? I decide to pick up some food on the way to the airport in the morning.

The car icon on the app twitches and turns at the end of the street. I clutch my daypack, shut the door, and squeal the gate closed as a white Perodua Myvi—a rebadged version of the Daihatsu Sirion—pulls over.

I dump my daypack in the rear seat and park myself in the crew seat.

The driver pretends not to notice my swollen face and arms and makes a successful U-turn on the second attempt. I tell him to stop somewhere on the way for snacks.

"Sure, there are two 7-Elevens on the way." He grins.

I note the avenue trees flashing by. The last tree stands two streets down—the final point to which Professor Wong's aging legs can lug the bucket. I sit back, close my eyes, and take a deep breath. I'm not the chatty, jovial, and friendly passenger I once was.

It's too early for the traffic to peak, which shrinks our travel time from forty to twenty minutes. We stop for five minutes at the 7-Eleven near Pelita. I pick up six cup noodles and three packs of crispy potato fries.

I pay the driver two ringgits extra. Here I am, following destiny's call to the Highlands. I pass through the automatic door, then the humongous check-in baggage scanner in the foyer, and wiggle to the counter that says MASwings. Two ladies are before me: one elderly, flaunting her wrinkles and ear hangings, the other one younger, perhaps her daughter, clutching a rattan basket. The ground staff asks them to weigh themselves.

I learn something new: in Sarawak, they value every gram of flesh you carry.

The daughter leads her hunched mother away, and I present myself behind my ticket. The ground staff looks at it and then at me, then at her long, old-fashioned notebook and says, "Sorry, sir, all seats full."

"But I have a confirmed ticket." I shake my head and register my protest.

She puts a smile on her lips, apologizes, and explains in a sweet tone that sounds like speakers inside the church bell.

My learning continues: people of the Highlands board first, even if they don't have confirmed tickets.

"Your ticket is still valid for tomorrow, sir," she says, neutralizing the acid in my stomach.

> *Ask not why bad things*
> *Happen to good people,*
> *Ask what good people do*
> *When bad things happen to them*

I hear Bhagwan reciting one of my favorite slogans from the Bhagavad Gita.

Good people stay calm, like Parker, Saint Richard Parker. An eerie calm befalls me as I lean against the window glass on my way back. The micrograms of bee venom stung into your skin contain twenty-six amino acids—enough to have therapeutic properties. A journalist reads every topic under the sky, and this knowledge helps to sedate the venom.

Shut up, Parker—it's the painkillers doing the work, Bhagwan chastises.

I hobnob with sleep for the rest of the day and night. At five, I wake up and meditate, beseeching Christ and Ayyappa to lead me to the Highlands. I remind Ayyappa of his failure to get me to his abode and seek a seat on MASwings' nineteen-seater Twin Otter that flies just above Sarawak's last rainforests. I take a deep breath and end my meditation with the Lord's Prayer on my knees.

You should also pray to Lord Krishna, my previous avatar, reminds Bhagwan.

I will, when you stop telling people you are Krishna, I reply.

Every scene from the day before reenacts faithfully. This time it's a different driver, but he has a similar white Myvi. I tell him to stop at 7-Eleven for snacks and then cancel it, remembering the snacks in my daypack. The trees flash by, reminding me of Professor Wong once more. Roads clear, time contracts, and I tip him two ringgits. I look for a ringgit more to break the jinx but can find only two. The force majeure of déjà vu!

I don't wiggle like yesterday. I hold myself steadier. The volcanoes on my skin have receded to tiny pits. If they retreat further, they'll look like the hundreds of ant-lion burrows beneath the roof overhangs. As kids, we used to drop little spiders and ants into their burrows and watch the ant lions bury them alive to snack on later. Cousin Mercy was the one who taught me its local name—*kuzhi yaanai*, meaning "pit elephant." She convinced me these minuscule creatures could grow into jumbos and we could have an elephant farm. For some time, our barn had dozens of mud pots with sand and ant lions. She was such an inspiration!

It's a better day, I tell myself, slamming déjà vu back into its cave. I present my ticket at the counter. It's the same ground staff. She recognizes me, gifts me a smile, and chimes, "You are on, sir. Please weigh yourself with your backpack."

I honor the weighing machine. Seventy-three, it reads. Remember, I have my daypack on. The ground staff notes it in the same long notebook, stamps my ticket, and hands it over, wishing me a pleasant journey.

I thank her for helping me defeat déjà vu. I hold my head high above my neck like the flamingos that visit Little Lotus Pond in December.

Two ladies in identical T-shirts and short skirts swish by me to the escalator ahead. I pause for two to three seconds, looking up to forgive them for overtaking me. Then I realize it's a blessing in disguise—some escalators come with a view!

The view disappears beyond the horizon. Three seconds later, I land on the first floor and follow the short skirts to the security queue. My turn comes. I drop my daypack into the carousel; place my belt, watch, and wallet on the scanner; step in through the metal detector; place the ticket on the steel desk with my driver's license; and raise my arm sideways for the sweep. *Bring it on!* my heart tells the officer.

He looks at the ticket and asks me, "IC *di mana?*"

"Sorry?"

"Passport . . . your passport?"

"Passport? I'm just flying to the Highlands. It's within Sarawak. That's my driver's license for identity," I explain.

He scans me from head to toe. "Sorry, sir. License cannot. For foreigner, need passport."

I look at the two-legged portcullis standing between me and the next episode of my epic journey.

"Your bag, where?"

I point to the orphaned bag at the end of the roller conveyor. He picks it up and takes my arm. I collect my belt, wallet, and watch. He leads me back to an area behind the barricade, sidestepping the detector. I avoid looking at those in the queue.

"Terrorist, *ka*?" Someone in the queue has her eureka moment. A spring of acid opens inside my gut, and I regret not shaving my beard. I explain to the officer that my passport is with the agent.

"Receipt *di mana*?" he asks, and I have no answer. I didn't ask Boy for a receipt.

"Sorry, sir, I cannot let you through." He shrugs and turns back.

I drag my daypack to the oversize stainless-steel chairs. I drop myself into one first and then fall to my knees. Prayers in vain, two gods with their backs to me. Blue mountains, flowery meadows, and tall trees fly past me until an empty desert presents itself. I crunch my eyelids.

"Mr. Richard Parker?"

I clutch my knees. I want a diversion of thought and not a stab from my destiny.

"Mr. Richard Parker?" I feel an arm on the back of my shoulder. I lift my head and look up into the face of Boy, the travel agent, standing with his leather sleeve tucked under his armpit. His figure looms over me like a benevolent giant. He asks me what I'm doing, and I tell him my bad luck. I tell him I should have at least asked for a receipt.

The best of lights appears in the deepest of darkness. He smiles and relaxes his armpit. His bag drops in slow motion, which he nets with a backhand catch. He zips it open, pulls out a journal, and conjures a slip of paper.

"This is my office. The one you saw there is just a room." He smiles, patting his sleeve. He takes my right hand and places the receipt in it.

"Come—I can explain to the officer." He leads me by my arm, and I cling to the paper for dear life.

The officer steps out to shake hands with Boy. He listens to his explanation with his hands in his pockets and nods, looking at me. I present the receipt with my driver's license.

"You can proceed, sir." He points to the scanner after scrutinizing both.

I thank Boy again and again. He promises to have the visa ready for me soon, turns back, and walks away. I watch him descend to the foyer, and then I line up for the security check. This time, I walk through.

After forty minutes of waiting before the stall that sells overpriced handicrafts, I hear the muffled boarding call. I walk into the next episode, pondering why airports deliberately choose poor audio systems.

Chapter 31

The nineteen-seater Twin Otters offer three significant advantages: one, they can take off and land on the short runways common in mountainous terrains; two, they are economical to operate in low-traffic routes; three, they help people overcome claustrophobia. You have only two options—to cure yourself or jump into the woods below. And only one of those options guarantees survival.

I squeeze myself into the narrow window seat and tuck my daypack between my legs. The seat beside me remains empty. The pilot's voice cracks through, and I pick up words here and there: "seat belt," "miles," "landing."

"Mommee, can I see or-ang-utan?" I hear a child's voice. I spot him in the adjacent row, prodding his mom's chin. Seats apart but united by our love for nature. My mind tells me that one day, he will grow into a celebrity like Richard Parker.

The flight roars over the runway and winces into the air. My ears question whether they really pressurized the cabin. We hit altitude within a few minutes, and I free my tummy from the seat belt. I glance through the tiny window; the lush green oil-palm forests are still visible, and I can tell apart the individual trees. *If this is the height we fly at, how will we cross the mountains?* A logical question comes to mind.

"A big one coming there; turn left," I hear a pilot babble from the cockpit, and the aircraft veers to the left to avoid the cloud. It shudders, reminding me of the 1½ route bus from Nagercoil to Little Lotus Pond.

Bang!

My daypack pops. I erupt from my seat, clutching my ears.

Bang!

Another pop goes off, again from my bag. Clutching my ears, I look around; the kid, his mom, and the elders on the seats in front of me all laugh. I hear the pilots laugh, too.

"Uncle, here." The child extends his arm. I look at the safety pin in his hand and then at my bag, trying to establish a wireless connection between them.

"You got potato chips, *ka*?" his mom asks.

I nod.

"You make hole, release pressure," she says.

I pick the pin from her son's hand, return to my seat, pull my bag over, and puncture the remaining packets. The flight now smells like potato chips.

"Yummy," somebody says, and there's laughter all around.

I learn something new: always puncture nitrogen-filled chip packets before boarding a low-altitude flight.

Fifty minutes after takeoff, our bird lands on a tiny tarmac strip that shines like a magnet. The tarmac and the sign saying THE HIGHLANDS AIRPORT above the blue-roofed cottage save you from mistaking it for a farm barricaded by hills. The genius who discovered this flat piece of land in the undulating terrain deserves the Indiana Jones of the East award.

"Uncle, thanks for the pop," the little boy says with his tongue in his cheek as we walk toward the cottage.

"You're welcome," I reply.

"Johnny, don't show disrespect to Uncle," says his mom.

I rub my forehead, confused about which among the above qualified for a jibe.

I walk to the foyer, passing the guard in green with the name tag *Rela* stuck to his left chest. Finding Magdalene is easy. She has a square face and a square paging board with my name scribbled on it. I give her the shock of her life as I introduce myself as Richard Parker. Her eyes widen, her mouth opens, and her shoulders rise and fall. Her free hand reaches to push back the silvery strands from her receding hairline to the knot at the back.

"You . . . You Richard Parker?"

"Yes." I smile.

"Sorry . . . sorry . . . I thought you were British," she says like someone who just bit into last year's Deepawali sweets. She then corrects herself: "Sorry, most of our guests are from Britain."

Meet Richard Parker, the unique! I smile in glee.

I follow Magdalene to her smoky gray Hilux. She pulls open the door and throws the placard onto the rear seat. It falls face down, hiding the name of the future saint. I get to the crew side, drop my daypack to my feet, and lean back. The smell of mushrooms envelops me.

"Sorry, it's musty. Always rains here. Difficult to keep the car clean." Magdalene turns on the ignition and reminds me to wear the seat belt.

I am about to ask her if it is mandatory even in this corner of Sarawak, but I drop the idea as the pickup jumps over a pothole, reminding me of the fragility of my joints. The vehicle dances along, rocking us through the bumpy tarmac lined with bushes of purple-colored flowers. We pass through a hamlet, where she brakes next to a pickup hauling wooden planks to talk to its driver.

"This is the central village," says Magdalene. "That's my second cousin; he's building a new house."

We rock forward again. I count sixteen pitcher plants climbing up the barbed-wire fences. I open my bag and retrieve my journal, where I note the number of pitcher plants. The pickup now smells like potato chips laced in mushroom sauce.

"Hmm . . . potato chips. Yummy," Magdalene says, scrunching her nose and lowering her side of the window.

I take the hint and zip my bag.

If Hillary is part of my destiny, then I will see many more pitcher plants. We will explore them together, and she will name the new ones after me.

"Do you know Hillary?" I ask Magdalene.

"Of course, every homestay owner in the Highlands knows Hillary and the team." She pauses, sighs, and continues, "But so sad."

"What happened?"

"They were sent back this time. Someone complained they were inciting the hunter-gatherers against the logging companies."

The pitcher plants in my mind turn brown and wither.

"I spoke to Hillary. She is meeting someone high up there to appeal. You might meet her when you return to Miri." Magdalene resuscitates the pitcher plants in my heart. They grow to human size and dance on green meadows, just like in Bollywood movies.

Twenty minutes after we started, the pickup makes a sharp right turn into the courtyard of a wooden bungalow on stilts. "If you drive straight, you will reach the riverside village, my mother's place, after which I named my homestay," says Magdalene as the car pulls into her garage.

I open the door, and a breeze of wind carrying sounds of the gentle river caresses my face. "It lives up to the name," I say. The proud owner of Riverside Homestay grins in acknowledgment.

We take the stairs to the wooden house elevated from the ground by eight-foot-long stilts. She pushes the unlocked door, and it opens into a large hall, one half occupied by three large dining tables and another by multiple laundry lines running crisscross. Magdalene explains that the large tables are for the occasional feasts. I follow her to the first floor. There is a framed copy of Warner Sallman's white Jesus Christ on the plank wall. She opens another unlocked door, and two ginger cats with tiny heads and oversize ears greet us. We continue through a narrow plank corridor and stop before the last room. Next to the door hangs a festive black skirt with white fern motifs on its hemline.

"You can use this, Richard." She opens the door.

I step into the room, which has little space left for anything other than the double bed.

"The toilet and bath are at the other end of the corridor, to the left of the door we walked in." She points in the direction we came.

I toss my bag onto the bed and unzip it, filling the room with potato-chip odor.

"Ah, Richard," I hear Magdalene again. "Forgot to say. No food in the room because food attracts rats, and rats attract snakes."

That sounds logical. "Yes, yes. Copy that." My flaccid chip packets and I return to the dining table.

Magdalene pours some roselle wine into a glass for me. "Homebrewed by my first cousin, a delicacy of the Highlands," she says. The rosy fluid blesses my taste buds and enters my buccal list. When our glasses are empty, she clears the dining table, spreads a hand-drawn map, and hunches over it. "The salt spring in the east, the wildlife sanctuary in the northeast, the central village in the center . . ." I follow her index finger as it runs through the three major attractions in the Highlands.

"A walk to the salt spring and back will take half a day, the sanctuary a full day. But your flight is tomorrow afternoon." She scratches her chin.

I pick the salt spring for the afternoon and a visit to the hunter-gatherers tomorrow morning. "Hunter-gatherers? Doable in half a day?" I probe.

Magdalene straightens up and looks at me. "Tomorrow. Got one day. How, *ah*? I don't know." She scratches the wrinkles on her forehead for a moment and then says, "I can ask my cousin Esther. She will be here for lunch. She's your guide."

Her cousin! The party street in my heart lights up in neon.

The cousin arrives at twelve, but the party doesn't. Esther is at least a half century old.

Magdalene serves us *nasi goreng highland*, highland fried rice. I pick up shreds of pandan leaves and a mysterious gingery flavor and glide it into my buccal list. Esther tells me the Highlands is a land of chosen people where, one, a dozen wild ginger species and tasty pineapples grow; two, eligible spinsters marry relatives of the Duke of Edinburgh; three, prayer battles happen often—the last one was between Manchester United and Swansea City supporters. Swansea City had nobody to pray for it, and you know the result.

Chapter 32

A long time ago, long before the forest-devouring machines arrived in Borneo, highland salt was an important trading commodity. Today, it's a souvenir. We walk for two hours to meet the last salt maker conjuring salt from the spring water.

"Our ancestors spoke to deer. The deer spoke to the spirits," says Esther as I stand baffled, trying to connect the deer and the salt pan.

"The deer led our ancestors to the salt springs in the mountains," she explains. I have heard such stories back in India, too. Foragers speak the language of birds and animals. For us, they are animals, but for them, they are sentient beings. Our world subjugates these animals into edible and nonedible, wild and domestic, while indigenous people embrace them as kin. I sense a halo growing around my face. Esther must have spotted that. I can tell from the way she glances at me.

I remember the indigenous people adorning the used copies of *National Geographic* magazines I salvaged from Chennai's bazaars during my college days. Some came with library seals. I chuckle, remembering the British Library seal on one of them. But a dark figure looms over my mind—someone who treks into the Western Ghats forests to learn sorcery from the tribal sorcerers. The witch who strips to summon dark spirits in the jungle, where even the midday sun fears to penetrate.

"Richard Parker." Esther's voice rings from the jungle. I shiver and open my eyes to look at her shaking me by the shoulder. Behind her stands the salt maker, with fear in his eyes. "Oh, God! You scared me, Richard." She steps back.

"I'm all right . . . perfectly all right. Was brainstorming something."

"God!" She crosses her hands over her chest, looks up to the sky peeping through the canopy, sighs, and then looks at me. "Do you always space out like this?"

This is the problem with the common folk. They can't tell an enlightened soul from the ordinary. But I must assure her fragile heart that I'm OK.

She asks me to smile, and I smile. Then she asks me to raise both arms, and I comply. "Where does the sun rise?" she cocks her head and asks.

I explode into laughter, recognizing her humor.

She flicks her hair and blows air into her cheeks. "Let's go back."

I realize she's tired. We turn back. As we negotiate the slippery trail, I ask her if she can take me to the hunter-gatherers. She says it's impossible to do that in half a day. I tell her I'm a writer and my book would be incomplete without meeting them. She shakes her head and refuses again.

She treads before me in silence, occasionally turning back to check if I'm still there. An hour later, she stops where the trail widens and the sand below our feet is visible. I learn we are close to her hamlet. I ask her about her family and husband—and why she did not marry a Briton like everybody else.

"I loved Marco and these mountains since I was a child," she says, then drifts to her son and daughter, studying in Kuala Lumpur. "They are lovely kids. My mom used to love them a lot." She looks up to the sky. We are on the tarmac now.

"I'm sorry," I sympathize. "I lost my mother, too, and not a day goes by without remembering her."

She stops and glances over her shoulders. "Tell me about her."

I tell her about my parents. My mom's love for all creatures, her knack for finding abandoned puppies and kittens. Her fish curry that makes me salivate at the memory. Dad's love for shoeflowers, how he planted varieties of them beyond our courtyard. I want to tell her about their love for farming, too, but a ball of emotions chokes me in my throat.

"I'm sorry," I hear Esther say. "The vacuum they leave remains forever."

I nod and look at her. She has stopped walking, and I see her staring at the purple flowers to the side of the road, lit by the evening sun. Two hummingbirds rise and chirp away to the right. Esther turns back to look at me with her hands on her hip. "I think I can take you to the hunter-gatherers."

My face lights up more than the evening sun. I turn my ears toward her like a donkey.

"If Cousin Magdalene can drop us at the central village at seven in the morning, we can make it."

I agree to talk to Magdalene over supper.

Supper is served after prayers in the Highlands. So is breakfast, lunch, and pretty much anything that passes beyond the tongue, including drinks. Magdalene serves rice and meat from her casserole. I ask her what meat it is. "Specially slaughtered lamb," Esther jumps in.

I thank Lord Ayyappa and Christ and take a bite. For the next five minutes, the piece of meat stays in my cheek while carts of rice mixed with Highlands pickles pass through. Esther and Magdalene are more adept. They take to it like fish to water.

"Hard to chew, isn't it?" Esther says, still chewing.

"Yes, a bit," I say, though *can't chew* would have been appropriate.

"It's wild pig. Bearded pig, to be precise." She giggles. "Marco hunted one yesterday, just in time for you. It's a mature one, but it's the only one we could get."

Mature or tender doesn't matter because something is better than nothing. I have never tasted wild pig or wild boar before. But I've heard that wild boars were once abundant in the hills of Little Lotus Pond before the poor shaved the forests off for firewood. I vow to finish the pieces in the ceramic bowl before me. Supper thus gets extended by forty minutes.

"The last three times, he returned empty-handed from the hunt. This time, he says, the pig was just waiting for him. It's a sign, Richard. God welcomes you to this blessed land."

I can sense my journey is close to its purpose. The signs are here, and even Esther, who didn't know that Richard Parker existed three days ago, can see it.

I thank Magdalene for cooking it and Esther and her husband for hunting it. I also thank the poor creature for sacrificing its life for me. It would have died happily knowing that it has realized its life's purpose—to accrete with a saint.

We Indians grow up listening to stories of curses lifted through death. Let me tell you one such story. Huhu, a celestial king, and his consorts were bathing in the waters where Saint Devala was offering sun salutations. Pushed to musth by his consorts and fate, Huhu pulled the leg of Sage Devala. An infuriated Devala transformed him into a crocodile. Crocodile Huhu waited for ages for Lord

Vishnu to slay him and liberate him from the affliction. Without the curse and the slaughter, Huhu would have never met Lord Vishnu.

"Richard . . . Richard Parker." I hear a shaky voice, and I open my eyes to look at Magdalene, her eyes wide open and her glabella showing a thousand contractions.

Esther is cool. "Don't worry, cousin. Richard often gets lost in his thoughts," she says, waving her fork like it was some victory medal.

Mortals!

Magdalene sighs. I smile and vacate my seat with an aching jaw and a sore bum. When I'm back in my room, I jot down the events of the day, then slip under the duvet.

We eat cornflakes and milk for breakfast at six.

"We, the Highlanders, are a fine blend of modernity and tradition today." Magdalene explains the story behind the breakfast. It passes through my mouth but fails to enter my buccal list. It isn't easy for every shred, flake, and crumb to make it onto the list.

Thirty minutes later, we arrive in an open area that might have been a paddy field once. Magdalene yanks the hand brake, and the car sinks by an inch. She notes down the odometer reading. I'm a tourist, and everything has a cost, so no surprises there.

I step down from the pickup, followed by Esther. Esther looks at Magdalene, and Magdalene nods back without uttering a word. I stand mute, unskilled in deciphering the wordless communication between the two. Magdalene's pickup draws a jarred semicircle on the soggy ground and disappears.

"Let's go." Esther swings her daypack over her shoulders and points to a footpath that snakes through a log bridge across a runnel. The mud splattering from her sneakers threatens to transform me into a terra-cotta statue. I preempt it by maintaining a healthy five feet of distance from her. Two buffaloes on the other side of the runnel bleat to announce our arrival. They sound like Isakki's buffaloes, as if they were cousins.

Our footpath runs along the runnel and disappears before an opening carved into the jungle. Esther announces the official amalgamation of the runnel and the footpath. My shoes soak up the cold stream water, and pins and needles make merry inside my wet feet. The world around us appears like a giant refrigerator, with rattans and palms and lianas and trees with weird buttresses.

"The entire land belongs to my community," says Esther, extending her arm to swipe an imaginary one-eighty-degree pie.

I look around and ask, "You mean the jungle?"

"Yes, the hunter-gatherers are squatters here. We're generous to them. Poor souls," she says as we balance ourselves on the wet, butter-smooth rocks. "We were the first settlers here. The fields we crossed before entering the jungle were all under our paddy cultivation for centuries." She stops near what looks like an overgrown ginger plant, with bright-red coneflowers popping up from the ground. She stoops down, nips a piece of the flower, and sniffs it with a hum. "It smells like my people . . . smells like the Highlanders."

I pinch a piece and take it to my nostrils. A delicate blend of cardamom and ginger rises and sings to my senses. That attests to one-half of what Esther says. The other half I never will know, as the last spinster in the Highlands had just got married.

We walk for another ten minutes and step aside to make way for two young ladies. Both are in white T-shirts and blue jeans, wet from the icy waters, rolled up to the knees. I provisionally identify the one in the front with a snow-white complexion and golden-brown hair as a German and the black-haired one as a Canadian. Esther shakes hands with them and talks in her language. They must have been living here for quite some time. The two ladies walk past, and Esther says, "Congratulations, Richard Parker, you just met two fine ladies from the hunter-gatherers."

I stop walking. "Seriously?"

"Surprised, *ah*? Their girls are beautiful, and men so handsome. Just wait and see."

A ball of zeal puffs up in the cavity below my diaphragm like the pufferfish on Kanyakumari beach. Streaks of light sneak in through the canopy and glisten the miniature waterfall before us. Cicadas rise to the occasion with their orchestra.

A barely visible path to the right of the spillway gleans us away from the runnel. Esther stops again to shake a rattan. It rattles. She points her longest finger at the black ants running up and down with their antennae raised to the heavens. "The sentinel ants, warning us to stay away from their plant." She reminds me of the lessons on mutualism.

I wipe the moisture off my watch's face on my damp T-shirt. It reads 8:00 a.m. Five minutes later, we are in a well-lit patch of forest, as though someone had cleared just a few trees to let the desperate light in.

"There . . . can you see their huts?" Esther stops and points ahead. I squint but see nothing.

"Where? I'm sorry, but I see nothing."

"Look behind the large tree with the smooth, whitish bark."

I strain my eyes further. They wander beyond the tree and land on a few triangular bundles of sticks and camouflaged tarpaulin on stilts, around a hundred meters away. I count five of them looking like overgrown emus, not more than four feet wide and six feet long.

"What's that?" I quip.

"Wait." She raises her hand, signaling me to stop, and tiptoes to the first one. We are twenty meters short of them, and I notice the flimsy ladders hanging from their short sides. I look at Esther and the Lilliputian ladders. My world now seems to be scripted by Jonathan Swift.

Esther approaches the ladder, placing her feet softly as if we were in some meditation session. I stand still, waiting for her next signal or scream—whatever comes first.

She slides her hand between the matted bamboo above the ladder and pulls it. It raises, magically transforming into a flap door.

Don't ask me how it happened, but I'm now just ten feet away from the door. I count five black fur balls turning clockwise and anticlockwise like they are fixed to some mechanical gears. Then I hear giggles. A fur ball gently rises and turns, and I see a face, a human face. I take three full seconds to tell apart the five humans crammed there. Esther speaks to the head facing her, and it lifts farther, revealing a man of fifty rising on his elbows in the classic *bhujangasana* or cobra pose. Two feet emerge between his elbows and touch the ladder. My jaw drops, and the jungle air moistens my tongue as he descends nimbly on the ladder.

I shut my mouth to stop mushrooms from growing. Esther is animated, her arms flinging in all directions—head moving up, down, and sideways. The gentleman says nothing; he just shakes his head in response. Then Esther walks toward me.

"He is the leader of the group. He first wants to take a good look at you."

"Really? Did he say that?"

"Of course he did."

"I saw only you speak," I say, looking at the skipper rubbing his six-pack abdomen.

I learn something new: when you speak to the hunter-gatherers, listen to the miserly words, observe the movement of the head and arms, and then guess the rest. Basically, you need to play a fill-in-the-blank game inside the jungle. Now I know why the gods brought the Dutch English–speaking Jayden and Stijin to Kuala Lumpur and made us cross paths. It was their way of priming my comprehension skills for this moment!

The gods have set an opportunity for enlightenment through spirituality! *I'm about to become the hunter-gatherer chieftain!*

I step forward and stretch out my right arm. He touches it and withdraws. I'm unable to hold back my laughter. It's now up to me to discover why the gods brought me here.

I hear a kid laugh and turn to see a chap in oneness with nature, grabbing a miniature blowpipe in one arm and his future conjugal pipe in the other. My eyes wander further, and I spot three women who look like aunts or mothers of the ladies we met on the way and at least a dozen carbon copies of men behind them. The only explanation for their sudden appearance is their ability to materialize from air.

I'm a journalist, a people person. I know the key to people's hearts is via the youngest of the souls. It's an age-old technique that many wouldn't know. I squat before the kid and take the hand holding the miniature blowpipe. You are to learn the second secret in my arsenal—children understand any language.

"How are you, little master?" I ask in Tamil, my mother tongue.

He nods his head and takes two steps backward in respect. I understand that.

"Your land is beautiful," I say, involuntarily wiping the beads of moisture off my beard. He nods again and retreats farther until the arms of the lady in the center pocket him.

I stand up. Me, Esther, the hunter-gatherers, and magic! The cicadas lower their decibels as if their choirmaster's arms have dropped in fatigue. I close my eyes and take a deep breath to ground myself in the moment I have been yearning for, the moment that has been foretold.

I open my eyes, and the woman and the kid disappear. The men now hold black seven-foot-long blowpipes with spear blades attached to their tips. This meeting has been long foretold, but this rousing welcome was not. I raise my chest, stand like a king, and wave at them. They don't wave back because we don't share the same sign language. They, of course, nod their heads, acknowledging my presence. I nod in reciprocation. I can now see through their warm, sparkling eyes. Just a couple of hours more before I speak their tongue!

I give Esther the look to tell her she's just a medium for this meeting. She stays still, her eyes betraying the pleasant shock that has just jolted her. *Earthlings!*

The man at the center pulls out a dart from his quiver, loads it into his blowpipe, and points it at the tree behind me. His stomach muscles contract, cheeks puff, and the dart whooshes ten feet above my head. I cheer.

Esther continues to be in her standing corpse pose. Stupefied by the unraveling show, I'd say. There's a saying back home: the jasmine in our courtyard smells like nothing. Esther, though a guide, wouldn't have bothered to watch a dart, precision-carved from the rattan of Borneo and shot by the finest shooter, swish by.

Esther resumes talking, shaking her head and flinging her arms. The shooter pulls out an old Nokia cell phone from his quiver and begins speaking in monosyllables, like a talented ventriloquist. It takes a sharp eye like mine to notice that.

Esther continues talking, but her legs have retreated toward me. When she's close enough to whisper, she says, "Parker, we're in trouble."

"Trouble?" I ask her to check if I heard right.

"Yes, text messages have been going around saying the policemen are here to kidnap their kids."

"Really?" I remember the innocent face of the kid moments ago. Richard Parker, the journalist, recognizes destiny's frantic call and springs into action. "Ask them where they are. Tell them I'm a journalist, and I will make a newspaper report."

She swivels her head slowly to look at me. Drops of sweat appear on her pale forehead and mix with the rainforest moisture to give up a strange odor. "They . . . they believe you are one of them," she says and turns to face them without stopping the hush-hush. "They say they know you . . . like . . . they have prior information about your arrival and your intentions."

A spring of sweat pours from my armpits, and a shiver runs through my spine. I now smell like Esther.

"That shot above your head was a warning. Not a sign of welcome," she says, taking care to maintain eye contact with the sharpshooter.

"What . . . what . . . do we do now?" Words froth in my mouth.

"We need to go," she whispers.

A stream of wetness flows down my inner thigh. Hot blood overtakes it from beneath and hits my foot. I rotate on my heels, aim in the direction we came, and take off. I run like crazy Lucas of Little Lotus Pond. My tongue is out, my eyes blur, and every tiny sac in my lungs craves air. But my legs keep going like autonomous bots. I hit the miniature waterfall and jump across its pool.

Thudddd.

My feet land on the other bank and sink in, but my torso is late. Instinct twists me on my waist.

I drop like a flat stone.

Chapter 33

"I have fought the good fight. I have finished the race. I have kept the faith. Now there is in store for me the crown of righteousness, which the Lord, the righteous Judge, will award to me on that day—and not only to me but also to all who have longed for his appearing."

Father Cornelius reads Timothy before my swollen corpse, stiff inside the coffin. My eye sockets have been carved out by the tiny fish of the Highlands, and unknown chemicals have robbed me of any remaining handsomeness.

A hundred people have squeezed themselves under the tin roof of the church. Widow Shanta, the dark witch's friend and the preacher's paramour, is nowhere in sight. Thankamoni and Susheela stand in the front row with their daughter between them.

"His elimination is God's blessing. We need not pay the lessee fee anymore," says Thankamoni.

"*Appa, the banana farm is ours now?*" asks his progeny, gaping at his greasy face.

I zoom out for a bird's-eye view of Little Lotus Pond. Under the banyan tree, people with folded wet umbrellas wait for bus number 1½. In the bathing ghats, women with lungis knotted across their round breasts beat frothing laundry. I direct my gaze toward the farmlands. Isakki is slurping rice congee from a jack-tree-leaf spoon. In the field before her, freshly transplanted paddy saplings flaunt pearls of raindrops.

I shudder. I'm sinking. Had I learned to swim, I would. Even if I were afloat, the raining darts of the hunter-gatherers would have penetrated every cell of me. *Is this watery grave my destiny? Where are the promised girls? Where's the enlightenment I came looking for? Am I just another corpse displayed to satiate the peasants of Little Lotus Pond?*

You know what? I don't want to sign off as a corpse at all. I deserve a *maha samadhi*—death in a seated position, like any saffron-clad Indian sage!

I roll over and rise on my elbow. I learn some things: one, muddy water tastes like fermented rice; two, my right knee is hurt from hitting the only boulder in the pool; three, the pool is just two and a half feet deep.

I sit with half my torso above water and my legs stretched over the debris. Some nameless bug crawls under my stiff right leg. A shoal of little green fish gathers above my waist with scant regard for the living human.

"Richard . . . Richard . . ."

I lift my head and see Esther standing there. Tears merge with the water dripping from my forehead.

"Esther. Esther . . ." I choke. "I'm injured. I can't walk. You save yourself. Run! Don't worry about me."

She puts her hands on her hips. "Run? From whom?"

"The hunter-gatherers—they will be here soon. Run, Esther, run. Save yourself. You have a family."

Esther face-palms. "Nobody can outrun them, Richard. We would have been dead long ago if they wanted to kill us."

"Really?" I rub the debris off my forehead. "But you said they were going to kill us."

She face-palms again. "Oh, Richard, I only said they wanted us to go back. It was just a warning."

I ran like a nutter and broke my leg for nothing?

"Come on—get up!" Esther places her feet wide apart carefully, balances herself on them, and extends her hand. I take it, and she pulls me to the bank. My knee reminds me of the entrance to hell I just missed.

I roll the hem of my jeans up and examine the pink patch on my knee. Like bird shit on a fresh shirt, it ruins the beauty of my washed knee. I have never realized how fair my legs are before. Pinheads of blood appear on it and enlarge.

Esther pulls open her daypack and retrieves a small box with a Red Crescent sign.

"Do you always carry it?"

"No, only if I anticipate a need." She hands over an adhesive bandage. "This will suffice until we get back. It's just a bruise."

An adhesive bandage for a battle wound?

"Shouldn't we rub some alcohol on it first? What if the pool is infected with anthrax?" I ask.

She stares at me for a moment. "Well, in that case, I must leave you behind. We can't afford to spread it in the Highlands."

I stop talking and take the bandage strip. She swings the daypack back, pulls the straps to her shoulders, and leads me through the runnel. I limp behind her. My mind jiggles brave tales to narrate—first to Su and then to my future one million followers. But I need a frame for the narrative.

"I didn't expect them to be so ferocious," I say, stitching the frame. "Thought they would be warm and friendly."

She stops and pivots on her heels to look at me. "I have come here at least twice a month since I turned eighteen. Never had a bad experience with them."

"But I have never been here. Not even to Malaysia before."

"See, Parker, they have dumbphones that can receive only text messages. That, too, only in certain high points in the jungle. The rumor is that the kidnappers are . . ." She scratches her nose and shakes her head. "Never mind, *lah*. Forget it. We're safe now."

"It's OK, Esther. I can stand it. You can be honest with me."

She eyeballs me from head to knee, pulls her tightly closed lips to one side, releases them, and then says, "The SMS says the kidnappers are dark, short, and ugly, with messy hair."

The framework I etched shatters into pieces.

"It's curly . . . curly hair," I correct her. "Besides, I'm not that dark."

Esther pretends not to hear. She turns back and drags her feet through the waters again, muddying it. A brown frog with weird horns leaps from one bank to the other. "Kalimantan horned frog," says Esther without even looking at it. Two minutes later, I hear a helicopter flying low. "Rhinoceros hornbills whooshing by." She looks straight and speaks. She can tell everything from afar except for the mood of the hunter-gatherers!

Remember, part of your mission is to unravel the mysteries, reminds Bhagwan.

I press my hair to my cranium to drain the water and then shake it off. It's time to get to work.

"I heard your father was a famous man." I set my hook. In journalism, we call it open-ended interviews. We steer the conversation using strategic leads. It always works for me.

"Whoa... you heard that, too?" Esther bites into my first bait. She narrates her father's valor—how he and other natives in the Ant Army helped the white man defeat the Japanese in 1945.

"Wow, I'm sure the British felt indebted."

"Ummm... well, kind of."

She continues after a pause and explains how, as a token of appreciation, the British prime minister, Harold MacMillan, granted an audience to delegates of Sarawak and Sabah in 1962. The representatives were seeking guidance on the postindependence path to pursue. MacMillan convinced them to join the Federation of Malaysia, giving up their oil and gas resources for the development of Peninsular Malaysia.

My premonition wakes up. It's happening; the reckoning is happening now! After five decades, the natives have realized that the white man has conned them. Nature has brought me to witness this decisive moment, not to become a chieftain. I have finally met Asians who despise the whites!

Proud of you, my son. You are close to becoming Richard Parker, the enlightened, says Bhagwan, subtly reminding me that the journey is far from over.

"*Oi*, Richard. Spaced out again?"

I open my eyes and see the earthling standing with her hands on her hips like a kettle. Poor soul! She knows not the plans of gods, sees not the future saint standing before her, and feels not the beckoning of enlightenment. I pardon her with a smile.

Esther shrugs her shoulders, shakes her head, turns back, and resumes walking.

"So, you guys hate the whites for conning you. Don't you?"

"Conning us?" She stops, turns back, and mouths a capital *O*. "The whites don't cheat, Richard. They are our superhumans. Haven't you heard even God may err?"

"Superhumans?" I scratch my forehead.

"Oh my, Richard. You're like a child. Let me explain." She shakes her head. "Deep inside the jungles of Bangalla is a hero who saves Black lives. Who is he?"

"Who?"

"Phantom, a white man." Esther shuts her eyes for a second to mark that profound moment and continues. "When aliens invade the world, a hero rises from the slums of Mumbai. Guess who?"

"Hrithik Roshan, an Indian," I say without the customary hurrah.

"No, it's the Hulk, a white man, hiding in the slums."

"Superman, He-Man, other men—they have one thing in common. What's that, Richard?"

I spot the changing hue in her tone. Naughty lady! "I got this . . . It's that . . . that male thingy, right?"

"Huh?" She drops her jaws. "No, *lah*, Richard. They are all white!"

My confusion continues.

"Why Africa? Imagine someone kidnapping an Indian kid to Bangladesh; you would need a white mercenary speaking chaste Bengali to extract him."

My head freezes while my vision does a three-sixty-degree rotation. I take a minute to regain normalcy.

As if she had been waiting for me to gather myself, Esther resumes, pointing at the runnel where we stand. "Forget everything. The land where we stand, you know to whom it belongs?"

I drag my leg through the water and stir some dirt. "Well, isn't this so obvious? Of course, it belongs to the natives—you Sarawakians."

"Huh?" She puts her hands on her hips and shakes her head. "No, Richard, no. That's what every foreigner mistakes. This land belongs to our beloved white rajah, James Brooke, and his descendants. We are all humble vassals awaiting the return of their golden reign." She gives me a crash course on the glorious reign of the Brookes—how for more than a century, they averted the kakistocracy of one Sarawakian ruling another by eliminating many indigenous insurgents. "Can you believe we stand on the very white man's land and call him a con man?" She ends with a kaboom.

My vision blurs as my lessons on decolonization swirl around me. I take a complete two minutes to regain composure this time. Thankfully, Esther ends the question hour, rescuing me from premature death. We emerge out of the forest smelling like decayed wood. *Mushrooms grow on decayed matter*—I remember my biology lessons. An itch in the crevices of my wet groin signals the sprouting of a fungal spore.

A saint has control over his anger and itches, says Bhagwan.

I pull back my arm from its secret mission to scratch the itch.

We continue walking, smelling like dung, pure cow dung.

"Parker, I hope you get time to shower before the flight," says Esther.

I fume at her for singling me out on this dung-scented walk and search for the right words to tell her she should also bathe. But loud sniffs startle the train of sentences lining up inside my head. I turn back to look at the forehead of a buffalo chewing the bottom of my wet T-shirt. Behind him is another one waiting for his turn. I jackrabbit and appear five meters ahead of Esther. She raises her hands toward heaven to mean *What the heck?* and then spots the buffaloes. She drops her shoulders and gives the front one a gentle rub behind his ear. "Oh, my boy, missing momma, *ka?*" she asks with unbound affection, bringing tears to my eyes. Then she looks at me, jolts her eyebrows twice, and says, "They belong to my cousin. We are fattening them for Christmas."

My eyes are not wet anymore.

We cut through the field where Magdalene dropped us and walk toward the central village. At the left end of the horizon, a mountain rises with every step we take. I want to write about how menacing it looks as it rises. But Bhagwan alerts me that a white man called Wordsworth stole those words from me long ago.

Esther stops for a few seconds to look at the mountain in silence and takes a deep breath. "It was May 2013 when our country went into a general election." She fills me in on the power of prayers. "The world stood still, and the night was chill. We were all praying for the results."

She still looks at the mountain, ignoring the buffaloes and me behind. "Most folks believed change was in the air. Old-timers like Magdalene and me alone believed our ruling party would return. We prayed; they prayed; everybody prayed."

Her breathing speeds up, causing her sagging breasts to rise and fall in a quick rhythm. My fingers curl inward, like I'm at the edge of some cinema seat.

"The radio announced that the opposition was winning. Our opposing prayer group stopped praying and began disbursing sweets." She turns to glance at me in a determined way. "See, *ah*, Richard, never let your guard down. The battle is raw until the last second."

I rub my forehead to step up my comprehension skills to the level of the Highlands people.

"There was lightning in the sky, Richard. Like God was signaling to us. The radio then announced that recounting was on for many seats. And then . . . and then a blackout happened. A massive nationwide blackout." She stretches her arm sideward and scrunches her eyes with her face up to the sky. "Our Lord cut off the power. And when the power resumed after thirty minutes, our party was cruising back to victory." She slows down her breathing and smiles.

I shake my wrists and blink a few times. I can feel my breath again. "Wow, Esther, that's a miracle."

Esther takes measured steps toward me, as if she is testing the maximum depth her feet can sink into the wet earth. She stops before me, clutching the straps of her daypack, and looks into my eyes. "The miracle was just beginning, Richard. For every seat we won, a corresponding soul from the opposition prayer group converted. In the end, when our party won, not a single soul remained on the other side. We were all together, relishing the same sweets they had distributed before. But this time, for the right reason. Our Lord is powerful, Richard."

I nod my head. Behind me, I hear the bleating of the buffaloes.

We reach the central village. Esther leads me down a concrete path between two rows of wooden houses until we reach a longhouse. The discolored wooden planks and the rusty tin roof proclaim its age before Esther does. We remove our sneakers and smelly socks and thud-thud the wooden stairs to arrive on the long veranda, interspersed with furnaces, above which are large racks of firewood. The first furnace has a kettle whistling over a live fire, its smoke rising through the firewood and disappearing into the chimney above. "An ingenious way to dry firewood," Esther explains. I note it down in my head for transferring to the book.

She introduces me to a grandma who could pass as a thousand-year-old if a person's age were determined by her wrinkles. Her earlobes stretch downward with the weight of the adornments. They look like they could pull a train, as you see in Guinness World Records book stunts. We shake hands and speak in mutually intelligible languages. She lets out a giggle.

Esther leads me farther through the veranda. We cross five deserted kilns and stop before the sixth one.

"Welcome to my parents' home." Esther points to the shut door. To its right hangs a diagram of her family tree, surrounded by at least two dozen hats of multiple colors. "My dad was into collecting hats. My sister's white psychologist friend says it's a remnant of our headhunting memories." We turn toward four large photo frames hanging to our left.

"My late parents." She points to the first, with two elderly souls in their traditional clothing. Her father wears headgear with a feather tucked into it. Her mother has her arms crossed across her stomach, a symbolic statement of the darlings she brought into the world.

"My eldest sister, married to the Earl of Wessex's extended family." Esther points to the second frame.

I don't ask how extended the node is in the royal family.

"My second sister, married to O'Connor," she says. "Descendants of King Conchobhar of Connaught."

I notice the pride in her eyes.

"That's Marco and me." She points to the last and only color photograph in the series. I'm curious why she skipped the third one of a guy with a big mustache and curly hair, standing next to a lady.

"That's . . . that's well . . ." Esther fumbles and rubs her hands.

My curiosity roves further, threatening to rocket off through the roof at any time.

"I can see that she's your sister." I cast my hook. "But the man?"

"Yes . . . ehmm." She scratches her chin as though she's about to introduce the kingpin of Bangkok's underworld.

I look again. I don't know him, and I know not his story, but something about him is familiar.

Esther rubs her hands again, and I stop her before sparks fly and burn down the longhouse.

"He's also a *keling*. Isn't he?"

"Yes, yes . . . well, no." She clenches her fist, bites her lower lip, and shakes her head. "Well, yes, he's a Malaysian Indian. But mind you, he is a top-ranking officer in the Home Ministry." She looks down at her feet, prods her jaw with her clenched fists, and continues. "He broke Dad's heart, Richard."

It's the first time I see Esther standing with drooping shoulders, painting a picture of humiliation.

"Dad hoped she would keep the family legacy alive. My sisters wanted to introduce her to eligible bachelors from great families. But she . . ." Esther bites her lips and draws in a breath. "She threw away all that and married him, Richard. This is the only time, in our entire history, a prayer went unanswered."

"Prayer?" I rub my forehead.

"Look, Richard, we are not racist or anything. My sister is a smart, beautiful woman. She had just discontinued her undergraduate course in Kuala Lumpur and begun working at a supermarket." Esther pauses for a second, sighs, and continues. "Her life changed the day he dropped by for grocery shopping. My sister wouldn't have fallen for him. They say he consulted some Indian sorcerer in Seremban and seduced her with some love potion. We prayed for her, but maybe we didn't pray enough—because it didn't work. He tricked her into marriage, Parker."

Questions flash through the screen of my mind: One, why wouldn't a top-ranking bureaucrat be a good match for the family? Two, why would a smart lady drop out of her undergraduate course? Three, where can I find that sorcerer?

The sound of Magdalene's pickup rattling on its chassis is now audible. Fresh raindrops hit against the tinned roof, upping the melodrama. We pick up our muddy shoes and run barefoot to the pickup. The rain cleanses the stench of our morning's adventure. I know we can make it to the Riverside before the stink returns with a vengeance.

Esther parts ways soon after we reach the Riverside. I pay her 150 ringgits as a guide fee, as suggested by Magdalene.

"I wish you all success in whatever you're looking for, Richard," she says before stepping out into the rain under the extra-large umbrella.

I thank her for her kind help and for being a part of my journey. There's no time to shower. So, I grab my belongings and dash to the pickup, disregarding the throbbing knee.

People cross our lives for a reason, and every soul offers something to ponder. My takeaway question is: *Could I have visited the Hmong people, as every famous writer has done?* I close my eyes and bounce with the pickup, wondering why the sign didn't take me to Vietnam. Then I remember the lessons I learned and curse my ungrateful self.

You can go through self-realization without cussing, says Bhagwan.

"You're effing right," I reply.

"Is everything OK?" asks Magdalene.

The clouds burst to test Magdalene's driving skills on the way to the airfield. She holds the steering wheel with grit, even when the tires skid, miraculously stopping short of a gorge. I sit tight with my hands on the grab handle and my heart in my mouth.

The rain retreats, clearing us for takeoff. There's nothing in my bag to pop this time. So, I let my eyes sweep the forest canopies beneath us. But my thoughts keep returning to the hunter-gatherer kids, the *keling* in the framed photograph, and my wet clothes decomposing inside plastic bags.

Chapter 34

Miri is dry, and I thank the gods for that.

I wash my clothes and hang them in the late-afternoon sun. My sneakers also get a bucket bath, but the malodor remains. I stick an adhesive over my war wound and let my fingers romance my laptop keyboard. A new chapter titled "Adventures of the Keling" takes shape.

Franklin appears at half past seven to liberate my arched back, numb fingers, and sore bottom. We walk to the shopping lot.

"Was it worth the trip?" he asks, hands locked behind like Kim Jong Un.

"Worth every penny," I reply without detailing. He will know one day for sure.

"I was asking Magdalene about the researchers working with the hunter-gatherers. She knows Hillary and company; so does Esther. But they haven't heard about you. I thought you worked with the hunter-gatherers?" I lodge the spear in the right place.

He returns a few steps of silence, then says, "That's why we have research assistants."

"I see . . ." It's my turn to lock my arms behind me. "So, you're not the researcher?" I pretend to admire the streetlight-lit satin-tail grasses on the vacant housing lots.

He stops walking, looks up at the stars, and laughs. "Parker, oh, Parker." He lowers his gaze toward me, squints, and laughs again. "Imagine you live in some tiny East Asian village. Two anthropologists knock at your door—one a tall white guy and the other a tiny Brown Indian. You have only one choice to make. Whom would you welcome into your home?"

I stop walking.

"It is a white man's world, Parker. For the Browns and Blacks, survival in East Asia is an everyday struggle. A white guy merely has to grace the chair by occupying it." He looks up to the sky again, laughs, and draws a deep breath.

I spot signs of an imminent lecture.

"When a white man goes to the pub, he is a socializer; a Brown man in a bar is a drunkard. A white arrogant man is an alpha male; headstrong Indians are pricks. A white man sleeping around is a lover; an Indian on multiple dates is a womanizer. White men make love, we Brown Indians fuck." Franklin shakes his head and draws another breath. "White fever and Yellow fever are pervasive, contagious, and incurable. Like the opposite poles of magnets, they are inseparable."

We don't talk until we reach the Javanese restaurant that smells like a mixture of curry and seaweed. I recollect Franklin's take on white privilege and juxtapose it against Esther's white-hero worship. It's as if the gods had dispatched them to balance the yin and the yang, the hot and the cold.

I also learn something new—the secret behind Franklin's singlehood in Borneo.

Franklin orders a seafood *mee bakso* while I run my fingers through the noodles, *laksa*, and rice on the menu. Nothing appeals.

The smell of rice batter frying over the hot pan lures me. I order a *thosai*.

The first bite sends the golden fried rice flour–coconut chutney flavor rocking upward to my nasal cavity. Mom's *thosai* were thicker and never crispy. Crispy *thosai* are unhealthy secrets of restaurants. I remember the first time I ate one on a picnic at the Vaigai Dam near Madurai. We were taking a day off amid Dad's business tour in the town. My first *thosai* came rolled at one end into a cone, and I sat confused about where to extract my first pinch. Mom flattened the cone into a triangle and helped me pass the first hurdle of being a modern Tamilian.

I spot round balls floating in Franklin's soup. He pokes his fork into one and downs it.

"What's that?"

"Fish ball."

I learn something new. Malaysian fish have balls.

"What are your plans for tomorrow?" he asks, ignorant of the discovery I just made.

"Going with the flow for now. If nothing turns up, I might go to the mall like any local."

He sends the noodles to his mouth and grinds them. "Hillary is visiting the Niah caves. She asked if you wanted to join her."

"Hillary? Niah? Me?" I taste honey on my *thosai*. "Of course, let's go."

"I can't join. You can take my Kembara. I have made alternate arrangements for my transportation."

How did he know I would go for sure? Whatever it is, I'm going. Caves, mountains, or cliffs. Richard Parker is ready for anything.

I sense adrenaline squirting underneath my tummy.

Don't be stupid. Adrenaline is not produced there, says Bhagwan.

I ignore him.

Chapter 35

"No man steps in the same river twice. He's not the same man, and it's not the same river." I quote Merrill when Hillary points to two men fishing in the creek.

"That's so profound," she replies, fidgeting with the cheap compass stuck next to the air-conditioning vent.

The air gushing in through her window picks up her mysterious scent and taunts me. It's six in the morning, and from the lone CD in Franklin's collection, John Denver sings his perfect number for the country road.

I remember the lecturer in my Philosophy of Journalism course. "It develops critical thinking," he said. He was right because, after classes, we debated why we had to memorize the nature of truth and its meanings. In the end, the editor and his patrons decide what truth is and what's not. I didn't know what good Merrill's passages would bring until moments ago. See, everything has a purpose in life.

I lower the window on my side, too.

"Yes, Richard. Let's savor the fresh air before the sun rises," she says, running her hands along the seat belt. Since we started, those slender hands have never remained idle. When they are not playing with her green tank top, they are either drawing strange figures on the misty windshield or combing her brown hair. Twice they caressed the hand brake, twisting nerve knots in my gut. I bet those hands never fall asleep.

Occasionally, I look in the rearview mirror to see if the Honda CR-V carrying Dora, Andy, and Mike has caught up with my driving. But even after forty-five minutes into the drive, there's no sign of them.

"Do you think we should pull over and wait for them?" I ask Hillary, who is busy tying her ponytail for the umpteenth time. You see, the best way to get into a girl's heart is to show how much you care for her friends.

"Pull over?" She rolls her eyes like a doll. "They drove past us. Andy drives fast."

I floor the throttle, and the Kembara protests with a disproportionate roar. I give up and come to terms with reality's piston. By the time we arrive, Mike has completed thirty minutes of bird-watching along Sungai Niah.

"We saw two muggers there." Andy points to a man fishing next to a red sign that says BEWARE OF CROCODILES.

"This is Borneo. There's a fifty percent chance of finding crocs in rain puddles," Hillary says with a laugh, pulling on a green poncho.

We pay a ringgit per head for a thirty-second boat ride across the river.

"A simple suspension bridge would solve the problem," I note, showing my ingenuity.

"Yes, but it would deprive the native boatmen of whatever little income they get," replies Hillary, her hands tucked into her poncho's pockets. Her hands have shed their hyperactivity and now behave.

"The genius mind behind the slippery footpath would have gone bankrupt from multiple litigations had it been the US," says Dora. Her hands are also inside the waist pockets of her poncho. I look at Andy and Mike; their hands are tucked in, too. Weird people with synchronized hands!

The slippery concrete path transforms into a mossy wooden trail elevated on stilts over the swamp. Andy and company stop for bird-watching. I pretend to be excited, too.

"Oh my God. Look at him . . . how handsome! That's a black-bellied malkoha." Hillary points to our right. I scan the tree with plenty of ferns stuck over it but spot no bird.

"Yes, yes . . . look at him. Such a marvel," I echo.

Liars go to hell, I hear that familiar coarse voice inside me say.

I hit the ignore button.

Forty minutes later, we arrive at a handicraft market set up by the longhouse people. The group buys bead necklaces, bracelets, and baskets. "I don't need them. Just supporting the locals," Hillary whispers in my ear, her breath enhancing the smell of the butter cookies we just shared.

I take the hint and pick a long beaded tassel. If you are in Miri, look out for Franklin's Kembara. You might see the tassel of yellow, red, and blue beads hanging from his rearview mirror. Not sure if it's legal in Malaysia, but who cares?

I lean against the wooden railing. Hillary turns, and I notice the shock in her eyes. Before I can wonder what's wrong, she lunges forward and yanks me away. "That centipede is damn poisonous, Parker," she says, pointing to the railing from which I was violently separated. I look at the red millipede and suppress my giggle from exploding into laughter. Even kids would know millipedes are harmless. But you must appreciate it when someone shows concern for you.

"Hmm. It's a millipede," I say in a calm, polite tone.

"Not that one." She cocks her head and points underneath the railing, from where a tuft of hair protrudes. "Long-legged centipede. You don't want to touch one." She tucks her hands into her waist pockets.

"Oh boy, it's equivalent to a thousand bee stings," says Dora.

Oh, the bee stings! It's weird how the forces of the universe remind us of our misadventures. My hands stay in my shorts' pockets from then on.

We climb the stairs and arrive at the gigantic Great Cave. My knee tries in vain to remind me of the bruise. No injury is bothersome when a lady is around to ease it.

Hillary points at the fenced-off area where Tom Harrisson excavated the thirty-eight-thousand-year-old Deep Skull. She details the skull's archaeological significance and the many other adventures of the Indiana Jones of the East. Our conversation drifts to the numerous bamboo poles hanging from the ceiling. "Local tribesmen once scaled them to harvest priceless bird's nests. And then, the hardworking Chinese entrepreneurs arrived with their artificial swift farms." She winks.

You appreciate the true worth of a poncho in a cave, where it rains guano and you don't know what lurks in the stalactite drips. Water drops bounce off Hillary's poncho hood with a thud. When they hit mine, they just creep in through my hair mat with a soft sound, as if someone threw a pebble on buffalo dung.

We lug ourselves up the wooden stairs and into the darkness of the cave. The place smells like ammonia leaking from a million battery cells. I'm treading the same guano as Tom Harrisson—unbelievable! Headlamps appear on top of the quartet's heads. "Please go ahead so that you can walk in my light." Hillary's poetic words echo on the cave walls and sing to my eardrums. The ammonia-induced nausea recedes to some corner of my gut, and newfound energy seeps down to my knees.

Do you see the signs of the prophecy? Because I do.

Hillary directs her headlamp to the cave's roof, where bats hang from tiny bat tunnels and apse flutes. "The warm carbon dioxide exhaled by the bats hits against the cool cave roof and condenses into carbonic acid that erodes the limestone. That's how these structures form." Hillary's statement makes me rub my forehead.

The wet wooden trail snakes us up and down through the cave floor, testing my mettle. We arrive at the painted cave after an hour or so. I climb over a small mound to look at the fading prehistoric paintings beyond the iron gate. Much of the red hematite paintings has been engulfed by green algae. Yet the feeling of standing in the space once occupied by prehistoric artists is so intense.

"The rumor is that the government doesn't want to develop this, as it would compete with the privatized Mulu caves," Hillary explains, removing her poncho in Hollywood style.

My eyes slide down her pointed chin to the pearls of sweat lacing her turmeric neck. I struggle to hold my gaze there and give up. It slides down to the valley of happiness, where the goddess of femininity has pitched in two perky tents. Her sweat-soaked tank top has now ebbed into the contours of her petite body, leaving those sharp breasts trained on me.

"Look what I have found." Andy's voice jolts me out of my ecstatic state.

I pull my neck up, and my eyes are now tangled in Hillary's. A thousand volts of energy strike me. When I'm back to half my senses, her warm breath is tunneling into my neck. Her arms circle my back, below my shoulder blades, drawing me in. I taste the sweat of her forehead on my lips, her nails digging into my skin. A swiftlet misses crashing into my ears by a whisker. She shudders and pulls back, bites her lip, and then lets out a deep sigh. "Tonight, I'm going to squeeze you in my arms, Parker," she says in a husky tone.

Andy's voice raises again from the mouth of the cave to interrupt us. He calls us to the second excavation spot where Tom's wife, Barbara Harrisson, dug up the burial ships.

"Say hello to the grand old spirits for me, Andy. We're walking back. See you at the park HQ," Hillary yells back.

Swiftlets buzz by, bats screech, and funny bugs shine in the light of her headlamp. She doesn't stop to explain their ecological significance anymore. Her poncho is back in her daypack, and her hands are now circling, rubbing, and pressing my hand like it was her Aladdin's lamp. The quantum of energy in her hands is so much that it could melt a nuclear reactor.

Fever sets in, and my temperature rises. If there were thermal scanners in this cave, you would see two hot red bodies ready to explode at any time.

"We should wash first, Parker. I don't want you to remember our first kiss for the guano." The tender female in her wakes up and loosens her grip on my hand.

We glide up and down the stairs. I smell no ammonia, no bird shit, and no archaic dampness.

A slight drizzle finds its way through the canopy. The handicraft vendors have returned home. It now makes sense why Andy and company purchased the craftwork on the way in. We walk for another thirty minutes and arrive at the park HQ after that thirty-second boat ride. We would have made a run for it had it not been drizzling and slippery.

Fortunately, the foresighted me came prepared for this trip with an extra set of clothes and a towel. Our arms stay hooked even while I open the boot to retrieve the clothes. A group of teenage boys circles us once, cheering and waving in a language that doesn't sound like Malay, and rides off. We walk to the showers.

"Too bad the showers aren't unisex," she whispers in my ear.

Her warm breath teases the delicate junction behind my ear, spiking my temperature further.

"You get two minutes, just two minutes." She relaxes her hold and lets me go reluctantly.

The water is cold, damn cold, but it doesn't quell my fever. I quickly wash, half dry my hair, and dash out into Hillary's arms. The L-shaped junction where the corridors of the washrooms meet recesses into a secluded space. Not that there are so many people around, but we know not who stands behind those window curtains of the park office. A wise lady knows the meaning of that space; so does a feverish man. I tighten my hug on her waist, lift her, and swivel her against the wooden plank wall. Her pink lips part ways, inviting mine in. I savor the rose petals soaked in morning dew.

"Ahem. We see nothing . . ." Andy's voice stops me from eating her lips for lunch as the trio giggles and passes by us.

Her grip loosens, and her hands slide down to my waist. She nuzzles me and shouts at their back, "Good for you, Andy. You get to live."

She is back at me with a hundred newtons of force. I kiss her neck, which has turned pink, and take a whiff of her pheromones tempered with soap perfume. "Oh boy . . . I wish it was the States; I would have had you right here." Her eyeballs sink into her eyelids. "Take me home, Parker," her warm breath speaks.

"How about your friends?" I whisper at the holy junction of her neck and ears.

"They are adults. We needn't worry."

I scoop her up, and she locks her arms around my neck. I carry her like a florist with an oversize bouquet and step out of the building. The boys are back with their bikes, hooting and cheering at us.

She looks up into my eyes, shakes her head like a doll, and says, "Hey, Parker, do you know Malaysia is a conservative country? People don't want to see us like this."

"What people? I see only you and me." We both laugh.

I bring her down to the earth and open the door for her.

"Good, that's how you treat your girl," she says, pressing my arm before getting in.

The boys are back to their best, circling us. I am sure they are part-time cheerleaders for some local soccer team. The guy in the front with a red cap lifts his hand to his mouth and flies us a kiss, displaying his leadership skills. "You so lucky! *Ah moi cantik*!" he shouts. They make one more circle and disappear into the road ahead.

Kids! I smile and walk to the driver's side.

On a typical day, it would be my lunchtime. But today, I have zero appetite for anything other than Hillary. Inside the car, both of us raise our fingers at the same time to rub our lips and then realize what we did and laugh.

"I know it's tough, but I want you to focus on the road. I will be a good girl and shall not distract you," she says as we turn left, entering the less bumpy highway.

But before I finish nodding in acknowledgment, she leans over and plants a wet kiss on my left cheek. The car wobbles, and we hear a loud honk from a truck behind us.

"Sorry, couldn't resist." She giggles as her hands tuck themselves between her thighs. My temperature rises further. You can now fry an omelet on my forehead. A headache creeps in from the back of my head. Hillary opens her water bottle and brings it close to my mouth. I take it and drink two mouthfuls, surprised at how fast she has begun reading my state. Her hands are back to hyperactivity. I imagine the havoc they will wreak on me this evening and smile.

The headache grows stronger. Hillary senses that, too, and offers a distraction. She talks about her life back in the States, where she grew up, how she made friends with the natives of Borneo, and the boyfriends she met and left.

"They were all jerks, Parker." She pulls her lips to one side and shakes her head. Her hands are drawing an imaginary line parallel to the glove box.

Beneath that bubbly, cheerful face lies a wounded soul, I realize, and I vow to soothe all those wounds.

"I cannot stand lies, Parker. I don't know why. But even a small lie hurts me." She rubs the corner of her eye.

I'm unable to say if she is dabbing a tear or if it's just a twitch.

She recollects all the lies that have hurt her: her professor's false promise of an internship with the Inuit people; her last ex, a Spanish macho, telling her he was at work while pumping iron at the gym.

"Where would you like to go for dinner?" I interrupt to wean her out of the gloomy topic.

"First, take me to your place, Parker. We can come back to the city for a late dinner. I want to celebrate with wine," she says and pulls up her legs, one after the other, toward her hips to form the lotus position.

My eyebrows hit my hair as I watch her do it effortlessly.

"The perks of doing yoga," she says, chuckling. "Sorry, I should have asked first. Do you drink? I mean, as in alcohol?"

"Of course, in moderate quantities. Tonight, I will drink for us."

"Yay," she says. We point our thumbs up, bump fists, and say cheers.

"Do you smoke, Parker? I don't, but I'd understand if you did." Her hands are back at the glove box, drawing imaginary stars on it.

"Smoke? No, never in my life have I smoked; never will I smoke." I know it sounds like I'm trying to impress her, but believe me, I'm speaking the truth.

"No wonder our kiss tasted so clean. Clean like morning dew." She giggles and pulls open the glove box.

A cigarette pack springs out and lands on her lap. It doesn't even take microseconds for me to realize what's happening. She flips it over and reads what's written there.

Richard Parker
Pp no. Z3186371 (IND)

She stuffs the cigarette pack back into the glove box and slams it shut. A truck carrying oil-palm sludge passes by, smearing thick slurry all over the windshield. I pull over to the left.

"Hillary, that's not—"

"*Shh.*" She raises her finger, staring out at the road. "Drive. Please drive straight to my dorm."

"Hillary, let me exp—"

She twists and leans back through the space between our seats and fetches her daypack. "All right. You can drop me here. I know how to get back."

"No. No, please . . . I shall take you to the hostel," I insist.

I lean back, bite my lips, and squeeze my eyes. The fever is gone; so is the headache. My hands and feet tremble from the lack of sugar in my blood. The damage has been done, and it's beyond repair!

I open my eyes and look at her—she sits still, staring at the road, her fists clenching the daypack. I pull up the lever to spray water over the windshield. The wiper does an OK job. Hillary leans on her window glass with her arm covering her eyes—a position she maintains until we reach her dorm.

"Thank you for the ride, Mr. Richard Parker," she says, then hops out.

Through the dirty windshield, I watch her disappear up the narrow stairs.

I wait for ten minutes, hoping Hillary will come running down the stairs.

My phone rings. I pick it up from the central console, praying it's her. But it's Boy, informing me that my Brunei visa has been approved.

Chapter 36

It's three in the afternoon. I drive straight to Boy's travel agency and pick up the passport. Boy also offers me a hundred dollars for 310 Malaysian ringgits.

"Brunei so rich. You enjoy, Richard," he says.

"Enjoy" sounds so distant to me now. But Boy's words bring up memories of workers returning from Brunei. Stories of oil, cars, and big houses, together with the sultan's status as the wealthiest ruler in the world, fascinated me when I was a kid. Now, I would trade a ton of gold for another drive with Hillary, whose pheromones still linger in the car.

The car! I curse myself for accepting Franklin's offer. For 150 ringgits, I could have easily rented a vehicle. I bang my forehead on the steering wheel. *I must get rid of this first.* The rpm needle hovers close to the red zone. A 600 cc pink Kancil with Hello Kitty stickers stuck all over zips by, mocking my misery.

Franklin's house shows no signs of life. It's still another thirty minutes to go before he returns from work. The gate is latched from the inside but not locked. I set the latch free and bring the car in. *Never am I going to step into it again,* I vow.

"Richard Parker." I hear my name and turn back. Professor Wong steps out of his car.

"Hello, Professor Wong." I walk toward him, forcing a smile on my face, and shake hands. I notice his car is a red Proton Saga that has turned brown. Su would be able to breathe new life into it.

"How did your date go?" he asks, caressing his gray goatee.

"Date?"

"Franklin told me he set you up on a date with Hillary this morning. I tell you, Richard, you're so lucky. That girl is beauty with brains."

Tears flood my vision. My airway chokes. It's like my brain has slipped into my throat.

Professor Wong doesn't notice my plight, as his eyes have drifted to the avenue trees he has nurtured.

"You should come home before you fly off," he says with his eyes still fixed on his tree babies. "I tried to match her with a boy from my church and another from West Malaysia. But she refused. What tricks do you have up your sleeve, Richard?"

I dab my tears before he turns back. My brain slips further down and begins pulsating like a balloon above my chest.

Professor Wong bids me goodbye and drives off.

I sit on the doorstep like a statue.

Chapter 37

Moments after I vowed not to step into that car again, I'm driving it to the smokehouse. This time, it's a gentle ride, well within the machine's capacity.

The smokehouse is almost empty, which isn't a surprise, as the place only comes alive after seven in the evening. Seven o'clock is still eons away, but I need a drink to stop my heart from exploding. Shops 13 and 10 are the only ones open. I skip number 13, as I have had my fill of bad luck today, and pick number 10. When the shopkeeper appears, I order a bucket of whatever beer she has and grilled pork belly.

Funny stares from passersby force me to rotate my seat and face the stall. They know not the pain of a soon-to-be-enlightened soul being beaten into shape.

I dip the crispy pork in the orangey sambal and crunch it with my eyes shut. Two beers in, and Bhagwan appears.

Parker, you are hurt!

He knows how to put tears back in my eyes.

Is that a joke? You saw me lose her over a cigarette pack I never touched, I mumble.

Remember, Parker, you are a seeker. Girls come like a breeze and leave like a tornado. But we emerge stronger and wiser.

I don't reply. But the mind master rips into me through beers and pork. He flashes images of Chandini, Rachel, Nita, and Hillary before my foggy eyes to remind me of the temporary nature of pain. I sit unconvinced, ready to order more beer, when he dangles the wild card—Su!

Count your blessings, son. Had you not been to the East, you wouldn't have met her! Remember, your mission is to love, expecting nothing in return.

The floodgates of my dam open, and tears gush. The shopkeeper comes running.

"*Sambal pedas, ka?*"

"No, no . . . the sauce is not that hot; it's me. I bit my tongue." I assure her all is well.

She runs back and returns with some ice cubes. "This one good for your mouth, *bah*," she says.

I thank her and wipe my tears.

Bhagwan is right; there have been so many blessings on this trip. An idealist who saw me as a part of her mission, a stranger who trusted me to find her boyfriend, a celebrity who picnicked with me, a hard worker who took me home, and a mystery guy who set me up on a date with his friend . . . It's all a matter of perspective.

The fog clears from my eyes, and the erratic rhythm of my heart calms. It's ten past seven, and while darkness has set in over the skies, my heart sees a new light. Perhaps this is what enlightenment looks like! I wipe away the last tear and pay the shopkeeper twenty ringgits extra.

As I walk out, I hear her calling from behind, "Not that way, *bah*. Road this side."

I turn 180 degrees and stumble to the Kembara.

The ride is smooth, as smooth as freshly churned butter. I'm closer to my destiny than before—that's what matters. I turn around toward the city and drive to the beach.

Miri's seas are popular for bioluminescent waves. But I spot no luminescence. The dark gets darker; the breeze brings a drizzle, and the drizzle brings a gust. I retreat to the beachside shelter and watch the oil platform flaming on the horizon. The night progresses, and I give up.

Before I leave, I turn back to glance one last time, and there it is, the faint, blueish glimmers of light on the roaring waves—the sign of God!

I drive back to Senadin, taking the same route. I'm surprised that Franklin hasn't called me yet. A hundred meters after E-mart and its smokehouse, I spot an old Pajero pushed by four people. I drive past but remember Bhagwan's sayings: my mission is to love and spread love. Indeed, doesn't matter if the path is sexuality or spirituality; love and compassion are prerequisites for enlightenment. Two U-turns later, I pull up a few meters ahead of them.

Saint Richard Parker at work!

A middle-aged woman is at the steering wheel. Another lady is pushing the car while also instructing the two young men flanking her. Her broad shoulders and thick thigh muscles tell me she alone could tug a truck out of a river. She spots me and slams her fist on the car, commanding it to a halt. The three go into a huddle, reminding me of a fight scene in some Jet Li movie.

It doesn't surprise me; I have learned enough from my experience with the hunter-gatherers. I smile at the driver, who gives me a guarded look, and walk to the rear, raising my hands to allay their fears. They look at each other and murmur something. The driver also joins them.

The strong lady nods. "Sir, our car . . . broke down. Our flight at eleven fifty. We go Kuala Lumpur." She looks at her watch and then at me—the kind of look you get from a refugee rescued from the ocean.

I realize my purpose in being there. This is my moment, and I'm not letting it slip by. My neurons rise to the occasion and remind me of the sticker on the Kembara's windshield with the emergency numbers. Somewhere in a corner of my mind, a red light flashes, reminding me of my depleting bank balance. I ignore it because I am closer to my destiny.

"Don't worry. Shall I get you a taxi?" I ask.

They pass around glances but don't reply.

"I can arrange for the car to be towed to the garage. You can pick it up when you return from KL," I suggest.

They huddle into another discussion. Poor things, my kindness must have shocked them. But then, that's my purpose—to show compassion when it's least expected.

After a lengthy deliberation, they agree, letting me inch closer to enlightenment.

"Thank you, sir. Hope no trouble for you." The lady wrings her hands.

"No, no. Not at all. It's my honor." I bow.

> We have found you a ride.
>
> Six minutes away.

After the taxi icon on the map moves, I dial the towing service. "I shall be there in twenty minutes," responds a sleepy voice after a long ring.

They retrieve their bags from the boot of the Pajero. The many patches on the bags tell me the story of economic deprivation. They note down the address of the towing agency and thank me repeatedly before boarding the taxi. I pay the driver in cash and instruct him to drive fast. A strange feeling tugs at my heart as I watch the taxi take the U-turn toward the airport and speed away. *Is this what inner peace feels like?*

The humming of a trailer grows into a fine tune that reminds me of a Jew's harp and fades off once it passes by. On another day, it would have sounded like the flour mill opposite the widow Shanta's house. This is what the enlightened state feels like. With eyes shut, I take my windpipe through cycles of deep breathing until the tow truck pulls over. I can't stop smiling, like my lip muscles can smile involuntarily. I pay the tow-truck drivers 250 ringgits.

After they leave, I spend a few moments at the sacred spot where the Pajero stood. I note down the GPS location on my smartphone map. One day, my followers will flock to this holy space to commemorate this moment. Until then, it's just another roadside spot for dogs to pee and travelers to upchuck their travel sickness.

I drive straight home, deciding against disturbing Franklin. I sleep for only six hours, but it's the most refreshing sleep I've ever had. When my watch reads half past six the next morning, I'm parking the Kembara in his garage. Franklin appears in his pajamas. I hand him the key and point at the beaded tassel hanging from the rearview mirror.

"A humble token of my gratitude."

He nods in acknowledgment. I linger, expecting him to inquire about yesterday's date—and the aura around my head. Instead, he asks if I'm taking the eight o'clock bus to Brunei.

"Yes, my return flight is tomorrow. And today is the only possibility."

He nods again. "Good luck, Parker. If we don't meet tonight, let's catch up tomorrow before you fly. And please don't book a taxi. I shall drive you to the airport."

Chapter 38

In the morning, I take an app taxi to the central bus station, praying all along that I get a seat. I can only imagine how packed those buses are, with everyone flocking to the gold-laden country. At the glass counter, I ask the gentleman if he has a seat for me on the Brunei bus. He gives me a sorry look—you know, the look you get when the guy before you in the queue purchases the last cinema ticket.

My Lord, the bachelor god Ayyappa of Sabarimala, and the bachelor god of the Middle East, Lord Jesus, please get your newest saint a seat, I pray in my heart.

My prayers don't go in vain. The guy pushes across a ruled sheet of paper clipped to a writing board. I scribble my name, passport number, age, and nationality on the seventh line. For now, I'm an Indian. Soon, I will be a global citizen, not chained by the political boundaries etched on our common earth.

"Hey, mister, what you looking? You like that paper, *ka*?" The poor mortal derails my thoughts.

I slide the writing board to him, collect my ticket, and strut to the chlorophyll-colored bus.

The bus dances on the bumpy road to the Miri–Brunei border. The guy on my opposite seat, with blackened teeth and a colorful Javanese turban, points to the tree line on the horizon and says, "Brunei . . . very green."

I learn two things: one, the land is indeed greener on the other side of the border; two, there are just seven of us, leaving enough space for a soccer team.

We cross the tollgate, and it pours. I learn one more fact: when it rains outside, it also rains inside the bus. Just like on bus number 1½ plying from Nagercoil to Little Lotus Pond.

The bus pulls over at the border checkpoint. We alight and line up to get our passports tattooed. Country number four, I update my count.

We enter Brunei, and the bus stops dancing. Green swamp forests run freely across the land, occasionally interspersed with fire-burned patches. I see no oil palms.

The road is straight and neatly laid, but our bus hums lethargically, letting even the tiniest four-wheeler cruise by us. We snail-roll into cloudbursts, only to be scorched by the sun again. The dry–wet joy ride continues.

Four hours later, the door swivels open, and we alight at the waterfront of Brunei Darussalam. I walk to the driver, who is wiping the shine off his bald head, and inquire about the return times. The bus returns at half past one to make it to the border crossing before 6:00 p.m., when it closes. I have just one and a half hours! But then, why would the gods bring me here? Surely, there must be girls, fame, or gold awaiting *the enlightened*.

I traverse the parking lot, cutting through a line of Chinese tourists in thick makeup and round hats. A hundred meters ahead, on the green waters, rows of houses stand on concrete stilts—the famous five-hundred-year-old water village of Brunei Darussalam.

A boat draws a crescent shape over the waters and muffles its engine before me.

"Boss, want go ride? Ten dollars, I take you one round," the boatman offers, drawing a fictional loop in the air.

I look up. The sky is gloomy, and it might rain at any time. There could be something awaiting me in the settlement, though.

"Would you also take me inside the settlement?" I ask him.

He lifts his blue cap, puts it back, and says, "Can, can. Two hours, boss. Thirty-five dollars."

"Two hours? One hour cannot?"

"One hour can take you around the village." He draws the loop again.

I back off because the oracle's prediction did not involve any mermaids. If something awaits me, it ought to be where there are beaches and people, not fish, crocodiles, and microplastics.

I turn around. The Chinese tourists whom I mentioned before now surround a guy with a messenger bag across his chest. He must be the tour guide—one who takes a few classes and pretends to know everything. He flings his hands all around like he is explaining chaos theory or something. The tourists are all agitated, though, especially the violet-dress lady squatting on the pavement. She screams in high pitch, pointing at the streetlamp behind him. Don't know why, but she reminds me of Rachel in Chinatown. Then it strikes me why Richard Parker the great is here when this moment unwraps. I approach her, squirming in through the perimeter of straw-hat heads.

I squat down to meet her eyes and whisper, in Morgan Freeman style, "I am Richard Parker, and I'm here to help you. Please stay calm and let me know what hurts you. I promise to do everything to make you smile."

She swallows saliva and tears, bites her lips, and mumbles something. The saint in me sees her anguish and anger. The snorts and mumbles stop, and she talks. I can see that she's returning to normalcy, but I can't comprehend a word because it's all in Mandarin. I gyrate my head back to the guide and ask for a translation.

"Boss, you no understand Mandarin, *ka*?" He face-palms and taps on the streetlamp pole. "She wants refund because this one not gold."

I get the story, though I wish he had avoided that facepalm.

It comes to me to reason with her and help her understand that golden streetlamps exist only in fairy tales. I turn around to meet her eyes, but she is now back on her feet, and I am glancing between her legs. I shut my eyes tight to avoid that pervert tag replacing my sainthood, and stand up.

My mere presence has solved the situation. The lady walks away to the monument with a giant number sixty written in gold; others follow suit.

The sun emerges out of its midday siesta. I walk to the streetlamp, looking around. After ensuring nobody is watching me, I fish a Malaysian ten-sen coin from my pants, lean on the lamppost, and draw it over the pole. A shred of black paint peels off, exposing the naked aluminum surface.

I feel her pain.

I cross the road and enter a shopping corridor. The fried chicken stall, the money exchanger, and the tailor's shop—they all lose the privilege of receiving me. A shop that claims to sell everything at the lowest price catches my eye. I push on the door where it says PUSH in bold. The sleigh bells on the door chime, announcing my arrival. The cashier lady looks up, her eyes twinkling like little stars. Stunned, stupefied, or spellbound—call it whatever you want—the awestruck lady looks at the saleswoman, kindling a glimmer in her eyes. I grace her with my smile and scour the Chinese plastics, with the smitten saleswoman following me. After wringing her hands for a while, she opens her cherry-red painted lips.

"Welcome back, sir. Long time no see." She flashes her dental braces.

A smile would make those braces sparkle. Must have been a tiring day!

The enlightened in me awakes and notes down the details as the sign unfolds. The way she rolls her tongue to flavor the *r* sound and the lovely braces tell me she is a daughter of the Philippines, another country of the East. Something about the way she looks at me tells me we've known each other for ages. Maybe she was plucking cherry blossoms for the consorts of the great Japanese emperor Minamoto no Yoritomo when Richard Parker san, the first samurai, passed by.

"Have we met before?" I cast my hook.

"Of course, sir, how can I forget you? I always think about you, sir." She takes the bait.

I take a deep breath. It's true; the first of my girls is here.

"My friend always thinks about you, too, sir."

There's a friend, too. The Lord has thrown a double rainbow after the Malaysian storms!

"You always come here before. Now, you don't come anymore, sir. Not good, sir," she presents a grave face. If the forty-three human facial muscles go constipated for three days, this is how they would look.

The glow on my face dims. Something doesn't sound right.

"Me? Come here before?" I rub my forehead. "I'm sorry, I think you've got the wrong person. Never been to Brunei before," I say, hoping she will light up and connect to our previous lives.

"I know, sir. Same excuse for all *bumbay*," she says and exchanges a look with the cashier, who is animating on the phone. "The girl is pregnant, and everything changes, including passport. But, *ah*, face no change, sir," she says, her tone climbing up the gradient.

Drops of sweat appear at every junction of my body. I realize that staying alive is more important than the prophecy.

"Sorry, I think I should leave." I turn toward the door. Sweat springs squirt as my eyes fix on the bald guy blocking the door. He is no taller than me, but with hands folded across his muscular chest, he looks as friendly as the Hulk holidaying in Mumbai. He glances at the cashier and utters some words. All I pick up are some instances of *ista* and *nglang*. The cashier points her finger at me, and the guy lunges straight at my collar.

His knuckles squeeze my windpipe, and I struggle to free myself, kicking my feet, which are now swinging one foot above the floor. My eyeballs roll into their sockets and begin seeing kaleidoscopic patches. I give up my fight, realizing that my countdown on earth has begun.

But a siren rings loud, and his grip loosens. I hear somebody shouting, *"Polis, polis!"*

The macho dude drops me to my feet and shuts my mouth. I gather quick gasps of grease-smelling air. A few white motorbikes pass by, followed by two cop cars. The cashier takes a glance outside and signals him *all clear*.

"*Tang ina mo*! You make my sister pregnant and run away?" he screams.

His hand has slipped down to my belt, pressing against my navel. I must act before it slides down any farther.

"I kill you, bastard Kumar!"

"I'm sorry for your sister, but I'm not Kumar. I am Richard Parker. Richard Parker from Little Lotus Pond." I tell him my story, gasping for breath in between.

"You think me fool? Some *tulala* say you go abroad, get many girls, and you go just like that, *ba*?"

He twists his wrists, knotting a pound of my belly fat.

"Ah . . . no, let me explain," I say, panting. "Not girls. Enlightenment. We writers come to East to eat, pray, sleep, and—"

He turns his wrist farther, darkening my vision again and pushing me against a rack. I hear random plastic stuff tumbling down. "You dare, *bumbay*. Come here in Brunei and Philippines, sleep with many, many girls and . . . and run away?"

"No . . . not that sleep." I clutch his hand and arch my stomach in. It hurts worse.

"Me give you nice treatment, *ba*. You never sleep with girl again." He relaxes his arm.

I can tell what's coming next. You know how his grip slipped down to my navel. I can tell you, my balls can't take an iota of that brutal power. I dispatch quick prayers to Lord Ayyappa and Lord Jesus, the only begotten son of God.

The doorbell jingles, and a female figure twice his size walks in. No, it is not any of my gods or angels.

"You see that, *ba*. My sister. The girl you made pregnant and leave."

I look at the new lady with blonde, dyed hair inching toward me like some time-freeze moment.

"Sister, I found him. I tell you, I find him and kill him. I keep my promise, *ba*," he tells her.

She is now five feet away from me, flanked by the other two ladies. I blame *Charlie's Angels* for this moment and hold McG responsible for my murder. I am also forbidding the media from publishing details of the specific organ that'd be crushed soon.

She speaks not a word, keeps walking, and places herself next to her sibling. Her hands go to her hips as her brother watches like Shylock of Venice, desperate to extract his pound of flesh.

She stares at me for a few moments and speaks. "Face same, hair same, beard same, skin also same-same, *ba*. But . . ." Her face extends forward like an accessory, takes two loud sniffs, and utters those precious three words: "But not this one, *ba*."

I give out a deep sigh. "Thank you, sister. Gracias for coming in at the right time and saving me." I put my hands together and thank her in the traditional Indian style.

"That one, the Kumar smells like curry, *ba*. This one . . ." She brings her face closer to my armpit and takes the best of her sniffs. "This one's *kilikili* smells like *amoy kanal* . . . like he fell in sewage, *ba*."

My arms drop, and I give her an icy stare. She knows not how many times I lathered the soap after the Highlands episode!

"Really?" He scans me from head to toe and turns to his sister. "Sister, you remember we children? When we naughty, Mama scare us, saying she call the *bumbay*. You forget that one, and date with *bumbay*?" He pauses, passes glances at all three of us, and takes a deep breath.

I read the signs, the body language, the emotions. I know he is readying to present some great wisdom. The seeker in me awakens even in the dearth of the moment, ready to seize the learning opportunity.

He takes another deep breath and speaks in a poised tone. "Listen to your *kuya*, sister. Got three type *kilikili*." He raises his finger. "One, that *kano* armpit smell like butter, burger, dollar; two, that Chinese *intsik* one smell like noodles, *siopao*, yuan; three, that *bumbay* one bad smell like roti, curry, rupee. Next time, find a *kano* who smells like butter, burger, or dollar. Curry not good. Rupee also not good, *ba*."

"Hey . . . you . . . stop!" The words jump out of my voice box.

I can forgive his onslaught on my armpit. But jacking my three-point philosophy? That, I will never tolerate. My temperature rises; my vision runs amok, looking for a weapon, and stops on a lightsaber.

My hand itches to wield the mighty weapon to teach him a lesson but cools off because violence is against spirituality. Besides, nobody has ever been hurt by a plastic lightsaber.

I'm still tempted to say many a thing in defense of curry, but I resist it out of respect for his little sister. She is still my savior, the goalkeeper who saved my balls.

"I'm sorry again for what you have been through. Now that the confusion is over, I must go, *ba*." I add the *ba* for that cultural touch. I don't ask who the *bumbay* are.

"You, *ah* . . . you wait!" He stretches his arm forward, stops me, and looks at her sister. "But still, sister, my hands itching, *ba*. I give two punch. Just two punch. OK, *ba*?" he asks, pointing to the pressure point below my beltline.

I fix both my eyes on the lady. She looks sane, unlike her brother. But my hope shatters when she opens her mouth.

"OK, *ba*. Don't kill him. Later you go jail, canno catch Kumar."

He smiles and nods satisfactorily before turning toward me.

Run, Parker, run, I hear Bhagwan say.

I push his Hulkish arm, swerve left to the alley between two racks, jump over the cheap plastic flowers strewn over the floor, and dart to the glass door.

The sleigh bells ding, and my legs pound the corridor.

I'm proud of my legs. They have seen many runs and taken enough bruises. They know the drill, the time-tested drill.

Chapter 39

You never know how far you can run with a bruised knee until you have done it. Thanks to my supernatural protection, the brother-and-sister duo doesn't pursue me, and I board the bus to Miri with an empty stomach and sweaty body.

To commemorate my escape from the mother of my kid whom I didn't father, I devour a bowl of Sarawak *kolo mee* after reaching Miri, and burp it off. When the clock hits half past seven, I am alive in my room. Mr. Roland's room remains locked.

As the warm shower washes off my fatigue, deep philosophical thoughts overrun my mind: now that I have eaten *kolo mee*, will I smell better? My co-passenger who shifted seats upon seeing me, will she sit beside me next time? Will women mistake me for a runaway boyfriend again?

Son, think of the single mother raising the illegitimate child of another Indian. Does it still hurt?

Bhagwan pops up with my lesson for the Brunei episode. He is right; our experiences, our pain—they are all contextual!

I pray to my gods that my next learning lessons arrive without the bruises and pain.

The shoes and the jeans I wore to the Highlands have become fertile ground for mold. I dump them in the garbage in the interest of my living cells. Having packed the rest of my belongings, I sit in silence to thank this beautiful land for the amazing moments I've had. Along with the bees in their hive and the hunter-gatherers in their unbelievable houses, Esther in her sweetheart's arms, Franklin under the roof opposite mine, Agnes in the dormitory, Boy, Hillary and her friends, and Jenny with a broken heart somewhere in this land, I go to sleep.

It's time to leave Miri. My goodbye text to Mr. Roland is still awaiting delivery—he will only receive it when he's back in town, where trees are ornaments for roads and the internet is life. I pray that he finds money to fix the roof and send kisses to the little angel who opened my eyes to the secret world of bees. Hope our paths cross again one day.

I regret nothing. The astrologer only predicted the arrival of many girls but did not specify when. I realize it's destined to happen only in this postenlightened life. With my friend Su by my side, I will soon find my girls. A smile runs through my lips and lights up my face. *But I have to remind Su that women in Catwoman costumes are poor choices.*

"You are excited to see your friend, Su. Aren't you?" Franklin asks. We are halfway to the airport.

I smile even more.

"Some friendships are priceless, Parker," Franklin says with his eyes fixed on the road. "You will cherish her memories when you are back in Little Lotus Pond. I'm sure Su will visit you."

"You're talking as though I'm going to live in that filthy enclave forever," I say.

He presents another eerie smile.

I rub my forehead, unable to say if he loves me or hates me. Don't get me wrong. I don't hate him, especially after that memorable date he set me up on. I just don't want to meet him again.

"You are a cool guy, Parker," he says, his face lighting up like the sunsets over the mother pond back home.

I straighten my back, bracing for the heavy rain that follows sunsets.

"A police officer showed up at my university yesterday, looking for me and my car."

"Police officer?"

My mind flashes a set of questions. *Is he being deported? Is he being arrested for cultivating marijuana?* He said he is a botanist.

"He was there to thank me for towing back a stolen Pajero. They identified my car from a CCTV image." He pulls out his cell phone from his pants pocket with one hand, unlocks it, and hands it over. "The police say those carjackers are habitual offenders. Check the photo album."

There are two spooky pictures of the Kembara, image grabs from some traffic signal. There is also a third picture of the towing truck I paid for with my hard-earned money. That explains how they tracked the car.

My lexicon hits empty. A gyre of remorse forms inside my cranium. One, my quest for enlightenment is not yet over; two, I can't believe how easily those carjackers tricked me into helping them; three, it's 2015, and Miri's CCTV cameras still can't click an Instagrammable picture of me.

Franklin parks the car and opens the boot for me. I retrieve my bag, and he walks me to the lobby. Before entering the foyer, I take a last look at the Kembara, with the cigarette packet stowed somewhere in the glove box.

I drop my bag and collect my boarding pass. He accompanies me to the first floor until the security queue. We hug and tell each other all the niceties civilized men say before parting ways.

"I hope to meet you soon in Little Lotus Pond, Parker," he says, taking two steps back.

I still don't want to meet him again, especially in Little Lotus Pond. But for formality's sake, I reply, "I hope so, too, Franklin."

He retreats two more steps and waves his arm. "Say hi to Isakki for me, will you?" He smiles, turns around, and walks away.

"Sure," I reply and turn around. The lady in front of me jingles her Pandora bangle and adjusts the multicolored scrunchie on her ponytail. I will not meet Isakki anymore. The only reason to return to that stupid enclave is to sell off my house and banana farms. My destiny is here in the East with Su, my friend. *Su and I are meeting Ketupat, and with the shaman's guidance, I shall optimize my quest, and there shall be no more futile pursuits!* My eyes follow the lady's ponytail swinging before me. What makes him think I will talk to Isakki, of all the people in Little Lotus Pond?

Wait, Isakki and Franklin! I never spoke about Isakki to him. How does he know her?

The turbo inside my heart ticks off, and blood gallops through my arteries. I jump out of the queue, say sorry to the gentleman who mutters something that's probably a cuss word, and run down the stairs. The gate ahead is obstructed by cameramen surrounding a man in a suit. I take a detour to the next one, where an extra-large family, uniformly dressed in yellow, is pulling their trolleys. I am late. Through the glass panes, I see Franklin's Kembara exiting the parking lot.

I sigh and stand still, watching it disappear.

Chapter 40

It's time for another Red Airlines flight. I want to save you the agony of flying with me on Red Airlines. But why should I suffer alone?

I sit in the narrow seat, throwing illusionary darts at Mr. Red Airlines Owner on the in-flight magazine cover. If only I could hypnotize him into boosting the legroom by two inches. Darn!

My co-passenger in the aisle seat has his fingers matted under his belly. This is the fifth time he catches my eye and smiles. I smile back, and he lifts his arm, abandoning his poor belly.

"You Bangla, *ka*?" he queries, as if he spotted a new star on the Hubble.

"Bangla?"

"Bangladeshi, *lah*."

"Oh . . . No, I'm Richard Parker."

"You? You, Richard Parker?" His eyes widen, and he giggles, shaking his belly.

"Unbelievable, right?" I laugh, too.

"You come here for citizenship, *ka*?"

I am about to snatch my next sign. But Su's free lecture on demographic engineering tames me.

I don't reply.

The tiniest glow on his face drains off. "In Sabah, they bring their religion people from Philippines and Indonesia. In West Malaysia, they bring Bangla. Bangla take our jobs. No good, *lah*."

My heart chakra activates, and I pour out some empathy. But he is in no mood to disbelieve that I'm his Bangladeshi. The last thing I want on this spiritual odyssey is to be sucked into some petty political stuff! I shut my eyes tight and count backward from ten thousand until I slip into a nap.

In the Balinese shack in my dream, Su and I sip rice wine with some super-hot chicks. I tip an extra hundred dollars and walk out with all the chicks, including the bar girl. Before boarding the van, I turn to wave at Su. Beside her is a bald white man fiddling with his gold-tipped walking stick. Su, too, deserves love!

I am about to send Su a flying kiss, but the air hostess taps on my shoulder. She prompts me to put my seat upright, as though it were generously reclining before. My watch reads 12:20 p.m. No matter how crappy their in-flight service is, you've got to give it to Red Airlines for their punctuality.

Another six hours before we fly to Bali. *Ketupat, please hone your foretelling skills!*

I collect my bags and sprint to the Arrival Hall at level two, our meeting point. A melodious voice pings the microphone for the third time that Mr. Shamsuddin Khan is to report to the immigration office. I recollect the Bollywood catalog to see if there's a superstar Shamsuddin Khan, but to no avail.

One day, I will also be a VIP like him, I tell myself.

I spot Su at the gate, tapping her finger on her smartphone. Between now and our rendezvous in a minute, she will have done business worth a hundred Malaysian ringgits. How fortunate I am to have the privilege of her friendship.

My eyes shift from their focal plane to five blue-uniformed men behind her. Su, flanked by men towering over her! I lift my cell phone to frame the moment. This shot will be my wild card for all our verbal duels from now on.

"Mr. Shamsuddin," I hear the name being shouted. This time, it's a hoarse male voice from behind me. The men behind Su leap forward in response to the call, while Su, being Su, is still busy with her phone.

The moment takes a golden turn. I'm seconds away from meeting Su and microseconds away from seeing Mr. Shamsuddin, the VIP everybody is looking for. In the book of Saint Richard Parker, this will be marked as a jackpot moment. I sacrifice my wild-card opportunity and turn around to see a gentleman in a navy-blue uniform with stars stuck to his epaulets.

He waves his hand. "Hello, Mr. Shamsuddin."

I'm confused now. I turn another half circle, only to bang my forehead straight into the insignia with the words *IMMIGRESEN MALAYSIA*.

"Sorry, sir." I rub my forehead and sidestep to make way for them. Instead, they stand to attention, confusing my already confused soul. A heavy arm drops on my shoulder.

"Hello, Mr. Shamsuddin. Welcome to Malaysia."

"Shamsuddin?" I scratch my head and look up at the six faces surrounding me.

"Yes, Mr. Shamsuddin, we have been awaiting your arrival." The officer puts his hand to his chest, bows, and continues. "Words can't express how privileged I am."

I see the sign. I'm glad that he recognizes how distinguished I am. But my name! Everything fits into the oracle except for my name. I unsee the sign.

"Sorry, Officer. I'm Richard Parker. Richard Parker from Little Lotus Pond. Perhaps there's some confusion here?"

"Oh yes, Richard Parker!" He shrugs his shoulders and chuckles. The other five follow suit as if they were given orders to laugh. "Shamsuddin, alias Saagar, alias Sumon. You have broken the S string to have an alias beginning with R. That's another first."

I rub my forehead, wondering what the first first is.

"Today is my first day at the helm of Project B, Mr. Shamsuddin. A blessed moment in the history of our country and my family."

I rub my forehead harder, hoping for some clarity.

"Let's go to my office, and I shall explain everything on the way."

"Sorry, sir. There has been a severe miscommunication here. I'm Richard Parker, and that is my friend waiting for me." I poke my hand in between two uniformed rib cages and open a valley to point at Su, who is still busy with her phone. "That's my friend, my dearest friend."

His eyes light up, followed by his cheekbones and mustache in sequence. That raises my confidence by a bar.

"Su . . . Su, Su!" I call out. She is coming over, and this confusion will end.

"Oh! No, Mr. Shamsuddin. Gentle, gentle." He pulls up his collar and looks around. "Not in public, please." Then he turns to the five men. "*Haiya*, this Mr. Shamsuddin, *ah*. Not even landed in Kuala Lumpur, o'ready naughty." They laugh in unison.

My sweat pores are back at work. Six faces, twelve eyes, they are all fixed on me. No truth would set me free. Then I remember my strength, my fabulous legs. They've always worked for me, from the temple courtyard of Thiruvananthapuram to the shop in Bandar Seri Begawan.

A strange glow kindles in my heart, something that only great sages can understand. I foresee events in time. In the next 0.1 seconds, I duck and leap forward, creating a glitch in the matrix. The eyes of the six men open wide and get stuck there, their mouths go round like onion rings, and their limbs remain glued to the floor. In another ten seconds, I'm before Su, pulling her arm. Thirty seconds later, we are in a taxi, speeding away to KLIA-1 for our next flight. In the next twenty-four hours, Mr. Officer is losing his job.

I look into the officer's eyes and smile. Poor soul, he can't see ahead like me. I duck and launch myself through the narrow space between the rib cages. The startled men give way, but they recompose fast and pounce on my bag. I skid and fall, followed by five heaps of muscles on top of me. The last ounce of air escapes from my lungs, and my soul dangles at my nose tip.

"Wait, wait. He's our guest, *lah*. Be gentle," I hear the officer say.

"Sorry, sir!"

They lift me to my feet, which drag like useless appendages. My soul sucks itself in through my nostrils and struggles in my lungs. I take multiple deep breaths to ease its pain.

"Take him—let's go," the officer commands, and I am rising in the air.

In the distance, I see the blurry image of Su stepping onto the road. I stretch my arm in her direction and yell her name, but my tongue recoils inside my dry mouth, and my voice dies a premature death.

"Not that way, *lah*. Mr. Shamsuddin so naughty. Might jump on that girl." The officer's voice resonates in the air.

The ceiling starts spinning over me.

Like the Filipino *balut*, I wake up curled inside an egg-shaped room with charts and posters blocking the cityscape beyond the glass walls. I touch my belly to take stock of my kidneys. No sutures yet.

Son, remember my lessons. Stay alert. Get yourself grounded and aware of your environment, I hear Bhagwan's feeble voice say.

I'm on a green velvet couch at the broad end of the egg. Before me is a glass coffee table with a miniature oil-palm tree. To the far right is a larger glass table with files arranged neatly next to a huge bouquet with the words *Congratulations on your first day*. I spot my bag on the floor, beneath the table.

I scan the posters—diagrams, milestones, a map of Bangladesh, and oily-faced men walking hand in hand in some street in Dhaka. As intended by the eggetarian architect, my gaze drifts toward the pointed end of the egg-shaped room. Through the space between the chart that screams *TARGET ONE MILLION VOTES* and another one that says *NEW EXPERIMENTS IN NATIONALISM*, I see a cylindrical skyscraper glowing in the afternoon sun. Some corner of my heart wishes that Su would appear on a parachute and rescue me.

"All units on alert. Mr. Shamsuddin is awake," a voice breaks on the speakers stuck on the Styrofoam ceiling.

I sit up on the couch. The tiptoeing of booted feet grows louder, and Mr. Officer appears before me.

"Allow me to apologize, Mr. Shamsuddin." He puts his arm to his chest and bows. This time, I notice the name *Ashraf* written on his name tag. "Our boys are not used to handling people gently," he continues.

I look at my watch: 3:05 p.m. If I can somehow wriggle out from this chicken hole, I can still catch the flight. I know Su is a woman of her word. She would have tracked my flight online. In her books, I'm relegated to a no-show. But what if she flies solo to Bali? After all, I know she has planned a vacation, and why would she throw it away for a guy who doesn't show up? Or maybe she will miss me and want to give it a last try. I won't know unless I hurry to the check-in counter at KLIA-1.

"I know what Mr. Shamsuddin is thinking." He rubs his hands as two young girls dressed in blue airline uniforms start spreading dishes on the coffee table: noodles, fried chicken, fruits, and carbonated drinks. The lady with extra-arched eyebrows flicks her straightened hair and winks at me.

"It's all for you." He points toward the food while the attendants stand with hands crossed across their holy chalices of life.

I stay put.

"Mr. Shamsuddin, do you want to live in our country?"

"Want? That's an understatement. How can I not want to be in a country with good food, lush green oil-palm plantations, and pretty girls? Besides . . ."

"Besides?" His eyes light up like the Northern Lights.

"It has been long foretold that my destiny is in the East," I say, then regret speaking.

"Yes, Mr. Shamsuddin." His face lights up. "Indeed, your destiny is here, and we are here to help you realize it."

He sits next to me and tilts his body to face me.

"Eh . . . no, Mr. Officer." I fish for the right words. "First, I'm not Shamsuddin. Second, my destiny includes the entire East, and third, my immediate destination is Bali with my dearest friend Su. Su and I have a flight to catch."

"Su Su in the flight?" He chuckles and tickles my rib bone. I wriggle awkwardly. "Mr. Shamsuddin very naughty."

"No, sir. Not Su Su. Just Su. My friend, Su."

"Hush, Mr. Shamsuddin." He slants his head, looks at me through one squinting eye, and says, "I know you like only one of the *susu*."

The two ladies behind him giggle with hands covering their mouths.

"Even if you like only one of that, it's still called *susu*. Left one or right one, or both, it's still *susu*."

I face-palm.

He gets serious. "I'm here to welcome you to become a Malaysian citizen, Mr. Shamsuddin. We offer you a passport with a new identity, a home to stay in, and a job to work at." Ashraf opens his arms. "This is a unique opportunity, Mr. Shamsuddin, an opportunity that repeats itself only once in three decades."

"Thank you, Officer. I'm touched by your kind offer, but I have to go. I am a global citizen and can't be tied to a country," I say, calculating the distance between me and my bag, readying for another sprint.

He scrunches his chin, gets up, and walks toward the skyscraper. My mind says there's some serious sermon coming in the next two minutes. I can live with that as long as he doesn't lock his arms behind him. Because I'm tired of seeing that. Not that he cares. He locks his arms behind him and speaks, his gaze fixed on the building. I watch his serious face reflected in the glass pane.

"This great country lives on nationalism, Mr. Shamsuddin."

I see his arms gripping each other as if this is Paula Hawkins's second novel.

"There was a time when nationalism was collapsing in our eastern states. And we were about to lose the support of the heathens there. That's when we launched Project M. My father was its first director. Thirty years ago, he brought our people from the southern Philippines and settled them in Sabah. Years later, my maternal uncle directed Project I. He brought our people from Indonesia and settled them down in Sandakan."

Like a haze, motifs with fern leaves and crosses appear and fade in my mind.

"My family legacy doesn't stop there, Mr. Shamsuddin." He takes a pause and continues. "My other uncle's nonprofit raises funds for the victims of pluralism in Mindanao and South Thailand. His son, my cousin, is soon starting a nonprofit for our people oppressed by secularism in Kashmir. Yes, Mr. Shamsuddin, you are talking to the youngest member of a great family." He raises his finger to make his point and then puts it back in the arm lock.

Charity! My mind flashes images of Black women and children enslaved by Boko Haram, as well as the Yazidis massacred by the ISIS. Euphoria replaces the gloom in my heart. This is not bad luck but the gods preparing ground for my Nobel Peace Prize! I snatch the opportunity and ask, "Do you also have plans to help the Black women and Yazidis affected by Boko Haram and ISIS?"

"Huh? Black women? Yazidis?" He turns around in slow motion and drops his jaw. "Those are petty issues, Mr. Shamsuddin. We are discussing some serious humanitarian issues here." He shakes his head in disbelief and points his thumb at the view behind him. "All these . . . all these developments wouldn't have happened if we had not reinforced nationalism in East Malaysia. Thanks to the work of great men, we continue to pump oil and gas. Today, Mr. Shamsuddin, my nation faces another crisis. Nationalism is fading, and we need another project to rejuvenate it. That's why we have conceived Project B—B for Bangla. You are the first lucky citizen, Mr. Shamsuddin. Please allow me to make my family proud again."

Project Bangla!

The turbidity in my head clears, and I am alert now. I can see the quicksand before me. This means that all those demographic engineering talks are not hearsay. Shite escalates fast! I need to get out now!

I look at my watch. It says 3:30 p.m.

"We welcome you to this promised land, Mr. Shamsuddin. You are free to work, free to do anything you want. You can also help us bring more Bangla from your *kampung*. But . . ."

"But?" My curiosity jabs the sticky milieu.

"Just don't hold hands in public, please." He points to the poster where two Bangladeshis have their hands locked. "I know you Bangla men love to hold hands. But it's not a cultural thing here, you see. People may stone you. Of course, you are free to hold hands in the privacy of your home."

He smiles, walks to the glass table, and picks up a file.

I face-palm again.

"Please, Mr. Shamsuddin." He looks at his watch. "I have ten more minutes before I meet our second VIP for the day. It's a good day. Ten new nationalists to add."

I pray to Lord Ayyappa and Lord Jesus to show me the way. My prayer is fast-tracked and gets a quick response. Of course, miracles happen only when gods and humans work together. In this case, my brilliant brain is what the gods tapped into.

"You have the profiles of those ten people there?" I point to the file in his hand.

"Yes. Yours is the lucky first."

"Can I look at them, please?"

He scratches his chin for a moment and then replies in the affirmative. "Please go ahead. You will be surprised to see your entire history here, Mr. Shamsuddin. We even have a picture of you picking your nose at Sadarghat." He grins.

I take it, turn to the first page, and look at the portrait stuck to a résumé. There are one hundred differences between him and me. For starters, I'm handsome; he is not. I have curly hair; his is wavy. I am Brown; he is dark. My eyes sparkle; his eyes burn. My beard is curly and handsome—fine, it could use a trim, but it's attractive—whereas his sticks out like a cranberry bush on a parched wasteland. I could say more, but I have a flight to catch.

I point to the photograph and explain all the differences.

He takes the file from me, scrutinizes the image, and scratches his head for two precious minutes. "No, Mr. Shamsuddin. Look at this. You two dark, hair rough, big eyes, beard same-same. Oh, the eyelashes, same-same. Don't get me wrong. You both very handsome. Girls, *ah* . . . they will really like you," he concludes.

"Girls!"

My face lights up a thousand watts as I remember Rachel and her confusion. I take the file from him, point at the image, and ask him again: "You think this is me?"

He looks at me. "Confirm, *lah!*"

I flip pages and stop at the profile of some dude named Satyajit. "How about this one?"

He looks at the image and then at me and scratches his head again. I turn the page again to another profile and then another. He is now scratching his head with both hands. "*Ya, lah*, everybody looks like you."

He drops onto the couch with his hands locked behind his head. An *uggh* and an *argh* escape through his Mussolini mustache.

His phone breaks the tension. When he finishes talking, he sighs and looks at me. "You're right. Mr. Shamsuddin has been found. He is on the way."

"Can I go now?" I jump, excited.

"Yes." He sighs and waves at the two damsels, who look more disappointed than him. I'm about to invite the ladies to join my voyage, but Ashraf interjects, "Please take the food away." They leave with the food.

I pick up my bag and prepare to hail a taxi. But Ashraf orders an officer to drop me at the airport. I am in awe of his manners.

They give me a free ride to KLIA-1, but that doesn't soften my three gripes: one, he has ruined the prospects of my immediate future with Su; two, he mistook me for a guy who in no way resembles me; three, he didn't allow me to taste that fried chicken.

But . . .

This is no time for regret.

I jump out as soon as we reach the airport and sprint to the check-in counter.

Chapter 41

My last chance to meet Su lies a few hundred meters away, inside this freezing airport.

I gather myself and run toward Lioness Air's check-in counter. This time, it is not the Red Airlines but its Indonesian equivalent. But Su is nowhere to be seen. Tears flow from my eyes and nose. I dab them with my handkerchief and inch forward in the queue.

Son, the best way to overcome grief is to accept reality, I hear Bhagwan's voice say.

I'm confused about what to grieve. That there's no Su in my future from here on out? Or worse, that the astrologer's predictions have gone wrong?

My jaw trembles, and a muffled whimper escapes through my handkerchief. *Men don't cry*. I remember Mom's words. I bite my lips and wipe my eyes and nose again.

A loud cry tears into the air, and I muffle my mouth. But it only gets louder. I realize it's not coming from me. My hazy vision sweeps around and homes in on a couple in a tight embrace, decanting tears onto each other's shoulders. A policewoman stands with folded hands, wondering if she should book them for their act of public indecency.

Another whimper bursts out from behind me, and I turn around to spot a bloke in his thirties struggling to suppress his tears. I look at the other faces around me, descrying the tears rolling down their grim cheeks. I turn my attention toward the two attendants below the LCD screen flashing *Lioness Air KUL-DPS, 18:30*. Their waxed arms move robotically on the touch screen while dried tears mar their Botoxed faces.

The best way to make a line appear shorter without touching it is to draw a longer line next to it. It works with grief, too. My calling is to empathize with the grievers. But the measly bit of evil that holds me back from total enlightenment relishes the scene. One would assume that travelers to Bali, the heaven on earth, would cry for joy. But in reality, every traveler is grieving some loss or another.

The ground staff, in her grim voice, reminds me I'm eligible for a visa on arrival for fifteen days. I thank Indonesia for keeping that fizz in the Indian passport.

The foyer now reeks of silence; the somber ambience stretches to the aircraft. Our tear glands have gone bone-dry. Even the mandatory safety announcements are dry. Perhaps the airline staff has never seen a flight full of passengers who have suffered misfortunes.

The bald white man in the seat next to me pulls out a rosary and recites the Hail Mary while his young Thai wife holds a picture of Lord Buddha in her open hands and mumbles some prayer. Strange is the world. Here I am, from a little-known village in India, now a frequent air traveler. I don't remember fearing takeoffs and landings. Trust me, imagining an aerophobic white guy isn't simple. It's strange. There's still so much in this world to learn!

It's time to open my eyes to the pit stop the gods have planned for me. But the image of Su in her soccer uniform dangles before my eyes; I mewl and lean over the fuselage.

The flight is at its predetermined altitude now, and I am in my fate. I wipe clean my itinerary slate. No more Nusa Penida for me—the island Su desired. Without her, Nusa Penida will be a painful ordeal. This means that once again, I must prepare to pursue the signs the gods reveal to me. *Should I really meet Ketupat, the celebrity shaman who guides every spiritual traveler?* I leave that to the gods, too.

A booming voice announces that food will be served shortly. The white-Thai couple refuses to accept the flight food. I follow suit. The service trolley returns to the stowaway, fully laden with food. Three gloomy hours later, our big bird touches the runway.

"Ladies and gentlemen, Lioness Air is proud to announce that today, we have landed on the runway," a beamy voice cracks the silence, and the aircraft erupts in joy.

Hallelujah!
Alhamdulillah!
Hey, Bhagwan!
Hooray!

Humanity rises in pluralism amid loud claps and cheers.

I shall pack enough Er Duo Bing for our flight. I want to eat those Chinese ear biscuits with you, I remember Su saying, and my mind jolts awake to her intention. She would have dished out flight-landing statistics the moment we took off and then munched into those biscuits while I struggled to hold the liquid inside my bladder. Evil lady!

The white giant gives me a fist bump. "Can you believe that? It's our lucky day."

My eyeballs run haywire while my brows crunch and my mouth sucks in some cold air.

"Have fun with the girls." He winks and turns his attention to his sweetheart for the first time since I saw them.

I open my ears and eyes moments after my mouth and scout for signs.

"Mommy, Ketupat?" a toddler looks up to his mom and asks before putting his binky back in his mouth.

The sign is here!

I hear Ketupat's name five more times before I reach the immigration counter.

Now that I have seen the sign, I must reinstate a major part of my preplanned itinerary, which is to meet Ketupat. With his advice, I am achieving enlightenment in no time.

I withdraw Indonesian rupiah from an ATM. The networked ATM doesn't display my bank balance. But I know I am left with 1,958 USD to find my destiny. I buy a local SIM card and walk to the tourism kiosk to gather leads that will kick-start my Bali adventures.

The signs tell me I will meet Ketupat. No writer visiting Bali returns without meeting him. I want to see his jaw drop as I walk into his house. The wooden betel box will then slip out of his aged hands, spilling the lime, betel leaves, betel nut, gambier, pestle, and knife. He will gaze into my eyes and foretell, *You'll be a great writer one day.*

I'm closer to the moment than ever before.

The lady at the tourism kiosk pulls down the lower end of her *kebaya* twice to tame her perky endowments before making Ubud a part of this epic novel. She promises me it's not on the beach and guarantees plenty of people around. I bite the lead because it offers the best departure from what Su had planned—a laid-back vacay on the beach with pork, beer, cigars, and hunks for her, girls for me. Seeing that I have taken her lead, she also suggests an accommodation—the Bali Heavens Homestay—and guarantees me its owner, Wayan, is a Balinese Hindu.

"Take the bluebird taxi, sir. No rip-off. When you reach"—she looks at her watch—"maybe twelve thirty at night, Wayan will receive you because I will inform him now." She offers me a glimpse of Indonesian hospitality.

I must leave a piece of me in her memory. "Are you from Ubud?" I ask.

"No. Me from Java," she replies and steps away to answer her ringing phone.

Inside the bluebird taxi, I repeat the question to the blue-shirt driver, and I hear the same response.

"Java so beautiful, sir," the driver, who introduces himself as Budianto, adds.

I rub my forehead, confused if it's a sign for me to visit Java instead. Then I remember that I'm already pursuing Ketupat, a bigger sign.

"Got headache? I give you a traditional Bali medicine." He digs into the glove box and fishes out a small bottle that reads *Minyak Sereh*.

I roll it on my palm and read the tiny words: Extracted from *asli* Cymbopogon winterianus. I read it again to see if cow urine, the omnipotent ingredient, is listed. I don't see it anywhere.

"Does this work?" I ask him, still rolling the bottle.

"Very good, sir. Bali medicine good. But Java medicine . . . very, very good."

I thank him and return the medicated oil, snubbing Bhagwan's quick advice that I might need it for imminent headaches. I hear Bhagwan grumbling. But ignore that, too.

Raindrops hit the windshield out of nowhere and disappear at the same speed.

"Wow, you very lucky, sir. Now not rainy season in Bali. But you come, and it rains. God's blessing." He points his open hand to the dark heavens and mumbles something in a language Saint Richard Parker is yet to learn.

I remind him about the steering wheel, which is exercising its free will, then close my eyes, sink into the seat, and take deep breaths.

Everything happens for a purpose in this world. I might have been through misfortunes, but destiny delayed is not destiny denied. Moksha, my moment of enlightenment, prowls in Ubud's paddy fields. The raindrops are just foretellers of that.

Thinking of destiny brings me to Tinder. I tap on the cellular data icon and open the app.

You have zero matches

It displays the familiar message as it zeroes in on my new pasture to present me the cards. I continue the Richard Parker mantra—always swipe right!

The bluebird turns into a narrow street lined with tiled houses, eateries, and shops. They are yet to sleep. I look at Budianto to convey that it wasn't wise of him to drive into a narrow street. There's just a tiny gap between our car and the motorbikes crawling by. But Budianto's bluebird glides through the maze and pulls up before the Bali Heavens Homestay.

The bluebird took a good two hours to journey the twenty-five-odd kilometers. In these two hours, I have begun to like Budianto a lot for three reasons: one, the manner in which he caresses his goatee reminds me of multiple Bollywood actors; two, the way he often thanked God tells me about his spiritual nature; three, his recognition of me being there as not a random event but something preplanned by gods.

Tears of happiness moisten my eyes, and before they trundle out, I whip out a Singapore ten-dollar note that has remained folded in my wallet. He thanks me with a cheerful *terima kasih*. The noble heart deserves more. I dig deeper into my wallet to locate the three Brunei dollars, but I cannot find them.

I wave my hand until the bluebird's taillamps are no longer visible.

"*Ohm Swastiastu*," I hear a heavenly voice say. Before I can raise my hands toward the heavens and shout in joy, Wayan, the owner of the homestay and the bass voice, appears. I greet him back with an *Ohm Swastiastu*, along with a namaste to highlight my Indianness. I have rehearsed this moment while in the car. Wayan is a Balinese Hindu, and I come from the land of ohm. It's natural for him to be excited about meeting an Indian. I have answers ready for all questions.

Wayan leads me through the doorway that's guarded by two granite angels and into the courtyard, which is protected like a precious pearl by the yellow-lit sandstone walls. I retrace his steps on the granite stones as the courtyard narrows into a corridor between villas. But he is yet to ask me questions. Perhaps he is tired.

He stops before the second row of villas and points to the stairs. "Your room is upstairs, sir. You have a VIP neighbor, a celebrity you don't want to miss while in Bali. You're about to have an amazing time."

Curiosity sprouts in me and grows into a banyan tree within seconds. My intuition boots up and displays fully clothed images of Julia Roberts for me. I lug my bag up the stairs behind Wayan. As we cross the first door, a strange perfume breaches my mustache and enters my nostrils. My olfactory lobes identify it as a new flavor, which is not surprising, as I haven't sniffed Julia Roberts before.

He pushes open the door, and I notice it has no locks. I focus my ears on Wayan as he gives me a sleepy overview of the resort. "Breakfast will be served on your balcony, and I can get you good prices on day tours if you want."

He leaves, closing the door behind him. I step into the washroom to take a leak. Minutes later, I open the door Wayan shut. I run my fingers through the ornamentation on the wooden door—flowers and gods etched into the wood. The tiniest shadows of them cast by the warm yellow lamp on the corridor paint a surreal image. I take a deep breath. *It's all real!* Here I am in the promised land, heaven on earth, right next to Julia Roberts. I don't want to sound like a pervert, but I must admit that my eyes refuse the 1:00 a.m. view before me and keep returning to the neighboring window. It's dark. Is she sleeping in the fetal position? Or on her back with an arm spread out, fingers forming a *mayura mudra*, the peacock sign?

Wayan said a VIP, which means she's all alone. A moist wind shakes the frangipani trees in the courtyard and whistles through the corridor. A bolt of lightning lights up the landscape for my sight; rains follow suit. I remember the words of Budiyanto, the driver, and raise my arms to the watery sky to thank Indra, the rain god, for the welcome party.

I sleep through the night like a baby, in the fetal position, just like Julia Roberts beyond the nine-inch brick wall, with the earworm singing its lullaby.

Pretty woman . . .

Chapter 42

My hopes of waking up to a chorus of Balinese birds come crashing down; a loud burst of thunder vibrates every atom on the tiled roof above me. I gather myself first, then my boxer shorts, which have slipped down to my knees, and walk to the window. I slide the curtain open, press my face to the glass, and stretch my vision to the courtyard. The lawn and the granite stone have all disappeared under muddy water. The resort is on a gradient, and there's no chance of flooding here. But the heavy downpour is just overwhelming for the tiny drains.

I get an idea of how my day will look—washed out.

Think of this, son. Julia's day is also washed out. In all probability, you both are holed up here. Son, that's your silver lining, shining right there before you.

Bhagwan makes perfect sense. They don't call him Bhagwan for nothing.

I might not walk down the street with the pretty woman, but I could be here, right opposite her, talking sweet nonsense all day long. A sudden rush of energy, or adrenaline, or whatever it is, pulls me away from the window and lands me in the terra-cotta-tiled washroom.

It's a perfect 8:00 a.m. when I step out into the corridor, all dressed up for the celebrity. The rain has cranked up its intensity, and I can barely see beyond the fence wall. I walk to the left, where the balcony extends to an outdoor dining space.

Wayan steps out from his home at the edge of the opposite villa under an enormous umbrella, holding a basket in his other hand. It's breakfast time.

I hear a latch being released.

It's springtime in my heart. Double rainbows appear inside dewdrops, white flowers open their petals from grass clumps, and ladybirds crawl to the sun-kissed side of the leaves.

I return to my door and stand in the corridor, pretending to enjoy the flooded view. A few more seconds for my celebrity to appear. My heart kicks below the apple of my throat. And my hairs stand erect on goose bumps.

Behind me, a few feet away, I hear the door creak.

I hold myself steady and let my peripheral vision run to the door. It remains shut.

I gush up some saliva to moisten my mouth and swivel my head. My puzzled glance drifts to the sandstone-colored wall and fixates on the half-open window. She is there, right there behind the curtains—the dream girl of millions, a few feet away from Richard Parker, the luckiest. I take a deep breath and try to divert my vision to the watery scene before me. The last thing I want now is to look like a Peeping Tom.

Thud.

Something pops out from the window, and I turn back to see two old flip-flops on the floor. One of them has been in the mouth of some dog or monkey. Two seconds later, the window opens farther, and a wrinkled foot hanging from blue-striped pajama pants appears. It rotates at the ankle like a periscope scanning for enemies in Bali floodwaters. Five rotations later, one-half of a wrinkled human appears in the window. The grand canyons on his cheeks and the hairless head tell me he has lived on this earth for a hundred years. He is so focused on getting himself out through the window that he doesn't notice me.

I curse myself for assuming Julia was here alone. Nobody ever told me she travels with her adventurous father.

He extends his leg to the floor and pulls up his other half as if he were tugging an elephant. A full three minutes later, he soft lands on the floor, raises his hand to the pouring heavens, and tries to say something. The poor guy can only spit out some *huh* and *fuh* sounds. The empath in me senses that something is stuck in his throat.

My heart chakra opens up and glows green. I step forward. "Is everything OK, sir?"

He takes ten seconds to turn on his feet and another three to lift his eyes toward mine. He tries speaking again, but his mouth doesn't cooperate.

"Can I offer you some warm water, sir?" I put my index fingers on my Adam's apple. "It could clear up your throat."

His eyes, which are not even close to Julia's almond eyes, dilate and squint and dilate again. "I was speaking Swedish."

"Oh . . . I'm sorry." I bite my tongue.

"Allen Allenson." He extends his leathery hand.

"Richard Parker," I reply, shaking it.

In the next ten minutes, we exchange mutual introductions and walk ten meters to the outdoor dining table. I ask him twice if he knows Julia Roberts.

"Is that a horse? Well, I only love elephants and monkeys," he says.

An ozone hole as big as the White House opens above my head. A hairless crow picks the dead ladybird from the edge of the burned grass blade in my heart.

I sigh, rub my forehead, and rephrase the question. "Are you here with your family?"

"Family? I'm happily single!" He shakes his head in slow motion, then explains that during his younger years, he was busy meeting the big shots of the history books, including Franco, Truman, Stalin, Kim Il-sung, and Mao Zedong.

I sigh again and do a quick reassessment of the scenario. My wilted heart opens to a new definition of celebrity: a hundred-year-old man who claims to have met some of the world's worst dictators and never uses the door to enter or exit a building.

Wayan serves toasted bread and eggs and English tea from the bamboo basket and trims off the crust for Allen.

I pick three reasons to trick my mind into believing it's still a glorious morning: one, a hundred-year-old soul is better than no human to talk to; two, I can take a hundred leaves out of his book; three, he doesn't have kids. This means the world doesn't have to deal with an Allen Allengrandson.

It's five in the afternoon, and we haven't seen the sun god yet. From lunch to tea, we have had our sore bums and souls stuck to the rattan chairs. Like Julia Roberts, my luck turns out to be nonexistent. Except for the frequent pee breaks, Allen Allenson talks nonstop, just like the pouring rain.

I wish I had packed a few books to save myself from the agony of listening to his adventures. But then, I had no books back home. I had given them away the day I turned into a businessman. What mattered to me was real-world knowledge—the know-how of how money flows from hand to hand. Now, I regret that moment—well, not so much, but a bit.

When Wayan serves his home-cooked lunch, Allen has concluded his story, or so I think. But soon after munching through *babi guling*, he resumes with, "Tis the sequel."

We finish the last sip of tea, and he smacks his lips, preparing to narrate the third part of his adventure. I try to wriggle out, using a bath as an excuse.

"Good. I will also leave, then. Got something important to do later in the night. Need to nap," he says. Then he double-stuns me. "It was nice listening to you, Oliver."

"Oliver?"

"Isn't that your name?"

Well, if I can be Kumar, why not Oliver? For a moment, I think of saying yes but then decide against misleading an old soul. So, I correct him after he leaves the table.

The warm shower does its part to cheer me up. At seven o'clock, I borrow an XXL-size umbrella from Wayan's wife and stroll down the lane. The rain has weakened into a drizzle, and I thank the rain gods for that. My night's mission is to hit the pub at the corner of the lane, the hub where foreigners socialize with the locals, according to Wayan.

I know he meant "local women."

Chapter 43

If I were to update Cousin Mercy on my location, I'd just have to send her a postcard of this pub, without even a caption. It is that Balinese!

Notes from the gamelan merge with those from the raindrops drumming on the tin roof to set up a welcoming symphony. I park my umbrella in the stand next to the polished wooden pillar that retains many characteristics of its erstwhile tree avatar. The tables under the warm yellow lights are all empty. Two men and a lady sit on the barstools, soaking in the violet neon lights from the bar counter. The guy and the lady are holding hands while the third wheel sips his drink, all removed from the world. The sexy bartender shaking the cocktail drifts her gaze beyond her customers and catches mine. We smile at each other. I rub my wet hands and catch a whiff of the alcohol-moist air mixture.

The third-wheel gentleman follows the gaze of the bartender and sees me.

"Hey." He waves, and I respond. This is what makes the white man special—his knack of connecting with anybody in a second.

I occupy the last barstool in the line, next to him. *Was it kept vacant, anticipating my arrival?* I smile and smile again.

"William." The gentleman extends his fist.

"Aussie William," the bartender says, giggling. A regular customer, I take note.

"Parker, Richard Parker." I extend my fist, and we fist bump. I order the fanciest-looking cocktail on the menu—the Bali Mary. The couple next to William is now rubbing their cheeks.

"My friends, Rose and Timothy," William says, pointing his free thumb at them, and then leans toward me to whisper. "Buckley's chance they would notice us even if lightning strikes us right now."

We laugh.

William and I exchange more information about ourselves. I don't skip the writer part.

He raises his glass toward his brown mustache and takes a deep sip. Then he nods his head twice and asks me, "So, when did you come out of the closet?"

"Closet?"

"Aren't you gay?"

I burn him with my laser eyes.

"Sorry, my bad. I just guessed you might be. Only gay men travel solo to Bali," he says and bows twice, imitating some Japanese geisha.

I forgive him and tell him I was supposed to be in Bali with a friend. "I'm not against gays, though. It's their life, their orientation. I'm just not one," I say, ending with the statutory declaration that every progressive man ought to make.

"How about you? Are you gay?" I ask.

"No, mate. My orientation is special." He winks.

A horse neighs in the street, and a shimmer of light beams through his boozy eyes. I wriggle on my bum. The images I have in my brain are those of men and women on horseback. I add a new one with an adult rating.

It's his life, Parker. Don't judge, Bhagwan reminds.

In a way, I have a special sexual orientation, too, which I am yet to figure out. So, Bhagwan is right. *Who am I to judge?*

"I have a special orientation, too," I blurt out.

His eyebrows rise and fall. *I have made my mark!*

I hear a bag of coins tumbling onto the floor, and I turn back, relieving my eyes from William. Four sisters dressed in white cackle around a table, their dresses wet in patches from the rain. Yet they look like nymphs out on an ethereal night.

I spot a cupid tattoo on the well-toned back of the lady facing away. Destiny should have been awaiting this moment. Because Cupid's fingers slip, and the arrow flies. The lady turns back and looks straight into my eyes. If George Bush were still the president, he would have hired her visual organs to rain missiles on oil-rich nations. The hairs on my arms stand up at right angles, and heat simmers in my belly.

I realize that my path to enlightenment is sexuality, and it is here.

The Balinese damsel whom destiny had prepared for me stands on her long legs, her semitransparent dress setting up her toned body for a sensory spectacle. Before I widen my eyes to soak in her approaching catwalk, I take a split second look at William. Once I leave with her, the poor guy will be back to his lone self!

I can now smell her perfume, which hovers in the erotic zone between durian and frangipani. I swallow half the saliva.

She stops at an arm's length before me and puts her hands on her hip. I look up to her face through the valley of happiness. A bushfire ignites in my belly and shoots up. I muster the strength to plant my warm feet on the earth. She cocks her head and winks, then turns sideways. Like a breeze, she then takes two steps forward to fit herself into the one-foot gap between William and me. My cheek is now against her metaphorical cheek, and I swallow the remaining saliva. My mouth is now 100 percent dry.

"Hey, handsome," I hear her say but can't lift my face to see her. *Who cares?*

"Would you like to join us?" I hear her ask. I pool in some saliva and wet my mouth to say yes.

But before I reply, I hear William say, "Sorry, ladies, I must decline this. You beauties have fun."

"There's more fun with you," she persuades.

A moment of silence later, I hear William again. "All right, let's go."

When I'm able to, I turn my head to see her leading William toward their table. All that remains around me is her tangy perfume.

William amalgamates into their huddle. Saint Lucifer now takes over Cupid's spot and turns my blood green. I turn to the bartender. She grins. I sigh.

The couple vacates their stools, leaving me on the front line of the moist, chill air. The bartender disappears, too. I finish the Bali Mary in the company of silence punctuated by the laughter from behind.

Turn me into a white guy in the next rebirth, Lord Ayyappa, I pray.

The bartender appears again to check if I want another one, and I ask for whiskey. Tonight, I will dump shots until I get drunk.

Halfway through the shot, I realize that the Bali Mary and whiskey are sworn enemies. I abort my mission and get up, holding my belly.

"Leaving so soon?"

It's William. I let my vision bypass him and glance to the empty tables behind.

"They left. Pests—I'm sick of them!" He shakes his head and takes the stool. "A coldie for me, please." He points at the bartender.

My blood returns to its normal state, except for the alcohol infusion. I sigh. "I thought you would leave with at least two of them," the cocktail in me says.

"No way. Not my taste," he says and then turns to the bartender.

I learn something new. White men can afford to have taste when it comes to girls.

Lord, let me be born as a white man in my next rebirth. I reiterate my prayer.

Stop blaming your birth, son, Bhagwan says, opening his quickie sermon and reminding me to take a leaf out of William's book. *Remember, your destiny has been foretold long ago. You just have to stand up and seize it.*

That makes perfect sense. If William can get four girls, I can get two. I spread open the notebook in my head and prepare to copy details from William's.

"Those women were pretty. I'm surprised you didn't like them." I set the bait.

He runs the bottom of his beer mug on the bar table to draw an imaginary circle. Then he looks at me and winks for the second time. "It's all about taste, mate."

I sense the return of Lucifer. I keep him at bay, telling myself I will be a man of taste from here on. But before that, I want to know how he finds his girls.

"Confused, mate?" he asks, reading my mind.

I nod. In one corner of my mind, the Balinese sun rises and shines its light on my ashram's roof. In the courtyard, my gorgeous female disciples, still wet from their shower, await my appearance.

"Mate." His voice thunderbolts me out of the dream. "You know what makes Balinese beauties bloody special?"

I wish I could tell him, but I haven't seen enough Balinese girls. But my ego saves me by fishing up some general truths. "Oh yes, they have awesome bosoms." I hide the fact that all boobs are exceptional.

"Just another furphy." He downs the beer in one go and slams the mug. "The best ones don't have them knockers at all, mate." He winks for the third time, sending my hand to my forehead, where it begins its work.

"Here, keep the change." He slides a few dollar bills toward the bartender and gets up. "You wanna go for a walk?"

I get the clue. Some trade secrets can't be revealed in public. I pay the bartender half a million rupiah, pick up my umbrella, and step out.

William awaits me at the roadside with a cigar smoking inside his cupped palm. I decide not to unfold the umbrella and join him as he begins strolling.

He is not the chatty William I had just met. Except for the smoke and the deep sighs, I hear nothing.

I break the silence. "We were talking about—"

"The special ones." He interrupts me, then continues, "You know what makes the Balinese special?"

I shake my head to signal that I don't know.

"A Balinese child is a holy being for one hundred and five days. During this period, her feet are not allowed to touch the earth." He takes another puff and blows the smoke into the drizzle. "To quote John Reader for you, an object of sublime innocence, blemished only by the means of its passage into the world."

I look at him with reverence for knowing so much about Balinese culture and for keeping the cigar alive in the drizzle.

A scooter honks as it passes by, and William hoots at the raincoat figure on it. A popular man in this part of the world! I look up into the drizzling rain and thank the gods for connecting us. I can't imagine how privileged I am.

I understand why the gods have brought me here. What was a hunch until a few moments ago solidifies now.

This is where I set up my ashram. This is where I live with my wife and girlfriends and disciples. My children will grow up as angels in this little heaven on earth. A hundred tiny hands hug my legs, and their cackles rise. The baby fever I haven't felt in a long time reappears. A teardrop forms on the edge of my eye and merges with a raindrop.

I look at William. The streetlight on the other side of the road casts his shadow over me. In my heart, the first sign of an unknown fear appears—if I talk to him a few minutes more, I might end up worshipping him.

He maintains his steady pace, ignoring the rain and the scooters and cars and, to some extent, me too. When the last puff is done, he stomps the stub and takes a deep, moist breath. I can hear the water droplets sucked through the diastema between his incisors.

He slides his wet hands into his pant pockets and looks at me. "I have slept with those angels, Parker."

Lightning strikes somewhere close, and when the microsecond of flash dies, the power dies along with it, smothering us in darkness. The clouds burst again, and it resumes pouring. I stand still, unable to move.

Did I hear that right?

"Parker, it's easy to befriend the families here. It's all about earning their trust, and once it's done, swish." He draws a swishing motion in the air, which I see despite the darkness. "That glorious feeling of cuddling with a little angel, that smell of innocence . . ."

He looks up in the rain, spreads his dark arms, and takes a deep whiff.

The umbrella slips from my arm and hits a puddle. My blood drains through the trembling arches of my feet. A twitch forms in my upper gut and knots a million cells. I hunch and drop to my knees. A cocktail of alcohol, enzymes, and acids storms out.

"Are you OK?" His voice pierces the jet streams of rain.

"Don't . . . don't come any closer!" I scream and puke again while my arms flail around to reach the umbrella. My fingers curl over the wet nylon, crushing its rib to the shaft. I slam it on the tarmac once, twice, thrice, and on the fourth time, it breaks. I end up slamming my knuckles on the gravel.

How could you? I look up in his direction. He is long gone. Two headlights curve in at the corner and shine into my eyes. I jump out of the road, straight into the drain. My leg hits the drain wall, and its sharp edge shaves my skin up to my hip.

Chapter 44

One hundred and twenty minutes later, I am back at the resort, staring into the mute eyes of the gate guardians. I have limped aimlessly in and out of the rain with a half-torn sandal on one foot and sat amid strangers smoking weird cigars on verandas. I don't even know if I have my cell phone in my pocket or if it is making bubbles in the drain.

One thing is clear now. Christ, Ayyappa, Buddha, and all the gods and goddesses have conspired over some high tea, ambrosia, or manna to set me up on this wild-goose chase. The signs they had shown me were all mere mirages. I don't have a third knee to bruise or a second heart to share my pain. I'm sure they are watching this game—the game they threw me into. They must have been high on drinks spiked by some disgruntled migrant worker!

The shop opposite Wayan's resort is lit by some battery light. The lady shopkeeper in her sarong trains her multitasking skills one last time before her day ends. Her hands are busy packing the pink flip-flops while her eyes are focused on the television box in the corner. The TV set is tiny enough to keep her battery from draining. I drag my sodden body toward her.

She veers her eyes off the TV and runs them from my head to my toes. The scanning ends on my sandal sole sticking out like a mad dog's tongue. She says nothing, retrieves a pair of flip-flops, hands them over to me, and continues multitasking. On another day, I would have been offended for being mistaken for a beggar. I can't accept her charity, either. Have you seen a tiger eating grass? I explain to her that I'm a tourist and have been wandering in the rain because I lost my way. She takes a few moments to come to terms with it. Maybe she has never seen a traveler like me.

"Sorry . . . I thought . . ." She fumbles for words.

"It's OK. I understand," I say, hiding my pain.

"Fif . . . Fifty thousand rupiah." She smiles, pointing reluctantly at the flip-flops in my hands.

I pay her, thank her again for her kindness, and bid adieu to my sandals before walking toward the only light alive in the resort.

It's pitch-dark outside Allen Allenson's room, and there's no sign of him. I stagger to my room and wash under the candlelight, using the lukewarm water the heater had saved for me.

Be thankful for the warm water, says Bhagwan.

I pay no heed.

I peel away the scab on my right knee and pat the fresh scab forming on my left leg. It hurts my skin but not my heart, for it has hit its threshold for the day.

William skulks in the dark, waiting for the candle to be smothered. He pounces over me, squeezing my lungs in their cage. I muster all my strength and kick him into the darkness. When he diminishes to a speck, the darkness gives way to light. Yellow crepuscular rays pierce the clouds on the western horizon and bathe the mountains in matching color. On the pond bund, I sit, rippling the golden water with pebble after pebble. Water waves rise and fall, rocking the lotus leaves like little coracles. Two kids, a boy and a girl, tussle over a coconut-leaf ball on the other side of the pond while an oblivious buffalo chews through the grass in the backdrop. The boy snatches the ball and throws it across the pond. It loses height and plunges into the water. The girl turns toward me, points at the sinking ball, and pleads, "Daddy, de baaall, please."

I snatch a breath and try to rise, but my bum weighs a thousand tons. A huge shadow looms over the pond, breaking the golden light. "Can I get you the ball, baby?" William's voice booms over and echoes from the mountains.

I spring out of bed, wet in sweat and panting for air. My ears are on fire. Hot tears roll over my cheeks and disappear below, along with my sleep.

I clutch my burning diaphragm and roll around as Bhagwan begins his monologue. This time it's about finding happiness despite all the odds.

You can have everything in the world and still be unhappy.

You can have the worst experience and still be happy.

It's all in your hands, son.

He makes sense. I try to focus on the bright side of the day. I imagine Bhagwan in a lotus pose and his serene turban, giving his early-morning sermons. But the sun god rises before him and shines light on the ninety-four Rolls-Royces behind him. My mind recoils, and any hope of finding happiness within me—and some sleep—slips away. Outside, the rain roars nonstop into the dawn.

When roosters call out to their beloveds, I drop my feet onto the cold, damp floor. The fluorescent arms of the clock Wayan got from some Chinese shop says 5:00 a.m. It will be a cold shower, but I must take it because I have set a mission for the day. I can't let nature beat me out. I wake my cell phone, and in its faint light, I light the candle.

After breakfast, I borrow another umbrella from Wayan's kind wife and walk across to the shop. The lady in the sarong isn't there, but a man who could be her husband or boss or a loan shark spots the pink flip-flops on my feet, greets me, and offers homemade breakfast. I inform him I just had mine and light up his disappointed face by inquiring about day-tour packages. He pulls out a folded pamphlet and hands it over.

"Choose the one that begins at the monkey temple, sir. The best one for the price. Will start at eight thirty from here."

I look at my watch—8:15. Looks perfect; maybe it's the Bali gods reaching out to me! I grab the sign, though a sour spot in my gut reminds me of all the signs that have bruised me before.

A white van arrives at eight forty, and I get ready for my next adventure.

A young man, around eighteen years old, with a Balinese cap, winds down the window and exchanges words with the shopkeeper before driving away. The shopkeeper informs me they are full. But before I slip back into the depressing mood, he offers me a taxi. Four hundred and fifty thousand rupiah, same itinerary. "One full car for you only, sir. I give you fifty thousand discount," he says.

I brush aside images of my anemic bank balance and say yes. He counts the five bills I hand him, returns me a fifty thousand bill, and makes a phone call.

A white taxi pulls up after thirty-five minutes. The driver offers me a big plastic bag to drop the umbrella in.

I introduce myself to him in simple terms. In return, he tells me his name. From now on, we will have to refer to him as Wayan II. I take note to keep on updating the Roman numerals as the list grows.

Wayan II gives me an overview of the trip. I release a few yawns, which he pretends not to notice. We are now driving north, and his discourse has moved on from volcanoes to Balinese spirituality.

I grab the sign and dice my question.

"Do you know where I can find Ketupat?"

His face brightens. "You like Ketupat? Me too, sir. So nice."

That's not a surprise because Ketupat is such a famous man. Count my words, his popularity will only grow once I publish my book.

"Will you take me to Ketupat?"

"My pleasure, sir. We first go to Tegalalang Rice Terrace, and then I bring you to shop to find Ketupat," he promises.

At Tegalalang, Wayan II walks me to the cafeteria that doubles as a view tower. It drizzles over the terrace fields. I tell him the view is gorgeous, hiding that I wouldn't even look toward paddy fields back home. What matters is that I'm going to meet my hero. I was hopeful of meeting him at his home. But as Wayan II says, if he is going to be in a shop, so be it. He matters and not the space. The drizzle halts by the time we finish our coffee.

Ten minutes after we leave the rice terrace, Wayan II pulls over before a *warung*, the traditional Indonesian eatery. My heart begins its familiar overpacing.

"I bring Ketupat for you," he says, insisting I stay in the car.

I'm unable to believe my luck. Ketupat coming down to meet me in the car! I don't want to sound boastful, but yes, I feel like royalty.

Wayan II returns alone. "Sorry, sir. Ketupat no more here. I take you to another shop where we can find Ketupat."

The optimist in me wakes up. If not in this shop, the next. I can travel a thousand miles to meet Ketupat and hear him foretell my writing odyssey.

We stop once more to look for him, but the plot repeats, building the suspense. Our next stop is at the sacred monkey forest. I wave my hand at the monkey smiling at me, and Wayan II reminds me that monkeys show teeth as a sign of threat.

I bow before Hyang Widhi, the Balinese Shiva, and seek his blessings. We return to the car, passing young women balancing multitier offerings on their heads. The smiles on their lips and the curves on their hips would make them an instant hit in Bollywood.

I am now armed with Lord Shiva's blessings. This will only make it easier for Ketupat to read my fate. The curly hairs on my arms stand up at right angles.

"Our next stop is Pura Ulun Danu Bratan. Very famous, sir. We get blessings from Goddess Danu, Brahma, Vishnu, and Shiva," Wayan says as his car gently bounces on our way out of the temple compound. "But we stop one more shop. Maybe, we find Ketupat there."

I smile, nodding my head.

We stop again before a shop that sells snacks and multicolored wooden phalluses. Wayan II interacts with the shopkeeper while I gawk at the oversize penises. When I find my Balinese girls, I will take them to these shops and watch them choose. Ones who pick the larger ones will have no place in my book. My readers don't deserve such toxicity.

"No luck here also, sir," I hear Wayan II say behind me.

"It's OK." I hide my disappointment.

"They bring good luck." He points at the phalluses, puncturing my Sherlock Holmes moment.

"Oh," I mull, swallowing the *So, it's not for sex* part of the sentence.

I buy a violet phallus with white and yellow dots and slip it into my shorts.

I doze off soon after getting into the car. When I wake up, my ears are blocked, and the taxi is pulling itself uphill. "Nice nap?" I hear Wayan II as though he is behind a glass door.

"You so lucky, sir, very beautiful view today." He points at the eleven-story main temple posing in the fog like an elegant Balinese lady wrapped in white. I step out of the car and take a deep breath. The chilly breeze toys with my mustache and numbs my nose. I slip my hands into my shorts pockets. No, I am not checking on the phalluses.

Wayan II stays back in the car, and I walk to the tiled-roof entrance and ticket complex. When I emerge on the other side, I'm lighter by thirty thousand rupiahs. I plant my steps carefully on the granite-topped earth, pursuing the arrow marks leading to divinity. I ignore the restaurant tempting me with its fried chicken and gelato. Just before the metaphorical split gate is a sign pointing toward the Buddhist stupa, a tumultuous past, and present-day religious harmony. With the tourists and devotees, I bow before Lord Buddha, who is draped below the waist in a gold and white cloth.

The lake surrounding the water goddess temple is full, creating an illusion of a floating temple. I realize why the gods sent the rain. I look up through the mist and thank them. A boat rowed by a lady in white tears through the fog as if she is returning from the heavens. I take another moist breath. The lady, the boat, and the temple make it a picture-perfect scene. I pull out my cell phone, wipe the water droplets off its lens, and snap twice.

There's a reason behind everything. Bhagwan appears.

I wish he didn't. Because I want to float alone in the surreal mist Goddess Dana casts on me. Around twenty meters away, a lady in a transparent poncho is posing for what looks like a honeymoon shot. A strong breeze from behind lifts and twirls her poncho, leaving her skirt floating in the air. She slouches her shoulders and struggles to stem the breach, striking a Marilyn Monroe moment. Her partner whistles, forgetting that it's a temple, and she blushes.

I would have stood there mystified were it not for my realization that it was Kama, the god of earthly pleasure, tempting me with forbidden lust. I take a deep breath, letting the cold air douse the fire in my underbelly.

It's time for Lord Brahma's blessings. Kama can wait until I find my girls. I turn around and walk to the entrance of the Black Lotus Temple courtyard, where a young white couple pleads before a guard. Moments away from them, I see them turning back, dejected.

"Nope, they won't let us in. Entry is only for people from the Pande caste," the man warns and follows the blonde girl like an obedient pup.

I smile because the clause does not apply to Indians. I walk straight to the entrance, making sure that I offer a smile to the poor guard.

"Sorry, sir, you cannot enter." The guard extends his arm and stops me.

I look down at his arm, which is pressing against my belly, and then into his eyes and smile again.

"I am an Indian."

"Good for you, sir. But you cannot go in." He kills half my smile.

I look into his dark-brown eyes. "Hinduism comes from India."

"Correct, sir. But I can't let you in."

The other half of my smile also disappears.

"Only Balinese Pande caste people can enter." He points to a red board near the entrance. Holy Place Forbidden to Enter, it reads.

A burst of fog emanates from my eyes and blends in with the ambience. The guard wraps his arm around my shoulder and turns me back, reminding me of the corpses pushed into the river Ganges. I totter back, wondering why people would visit Balinese temples if they can't enter the premises.

"Oh, my poor thing. Looks like somebody wasn't allowed into the temple." A voice catches me on my feet.

The thick accent appears familiar. I stop to look up. Mouth full of betel, white shirt tucked into gray, pleated pants that begin just below the diaphragm. It doesn't take much time to recognize him—Ranjit Sharma, the weasel I met at the Koh Pha-Ngan ashram. I can see that he is measuring me from head to toe, judging me every microsecond. "They don't let anybody other than Pande caste people in," I inform him.

"Of course they do. They only don't let in rice-bag converts in pink flip-flops, Mr. Richaaard Baaarker. Wait here and watch me speak to the guard," he says, smirking.

I stand there like another granite stone, watching him strut to the guard. But the guard stops him, exactly as he stopped me, and points at the board.

"Cannot go in, sir." His words swing in through the cold breeze.

"I am a Brahmin, Brahmin from India. We Brahmins can enter the sanctum sanctorum of any temple." Ranjit Sharma's voice fades as though he was disappearing behind the Himalayan horizons. My smile returns to my lips.

The wind changes direction, and I can't hear them anymore. Ranjit Sharma flings his arms in the air and points to the sky twice.

The guard stands his ground and nudges him away.

"They are not true Hindus. All bloody fakes," he says with a snort when he gets closer.

I shake my head, turn around, and walk to the parking lot. Karma is a guard.

The sky opens again like it wasn't happy with its act so far. I give up my idea to seek the blessings of Shiva and Vishnu and run to the car, regretting leaving the umbrella behind.

In the car, I apologize to Wayan II. "I'm sorry for muddying your precious car," I say.

"Don't worry, sir. It's just a machine," Wayan says, handing over a box of tissues.

I pluck a few tissues and place them between my bum and the seat. "You don't love your car?" I ask, wiping my face.

"I support public transport."

The rotten ideology strikes my face. I stop wiping. "So, you are a Communist?"

Wayan swivels his waist to look at me and then around. Looks like he wants to make sure nobody has heard me.

"In Indonesia, communism is banned. Calling someone Communist is best way to kill him."

"I'm sorry."

The car pulls forward, and ten minutes later, Wayan II breaks the uncomfortable pause. He explains why governments should prioritize public transport, focusing on people's mobility and not private cars. I resist the urge to repeat the question. But he continues to narrate the story of the great purge—Indonesia's genocide, where Suharto and the CIA jointly massacred over three hundred thousand people, branding them as Communists. He recollects the prominent Balinese figures who lost their lives, including his relatives, and how the purge opened the gates for Islamization and demographic shift in Bali. I have never heard such a thriller story before. The plot, the characters, and the narration are all flawless. Wayan II would win a duel with Stephen King or Susan Hill anytime. A fact the encyclopedia on "101 Great Genocides" will never mention this because it's a figment of Wayan II's imagination.

A good storyteller he is, says Bhagwan.

Aye, aye.

Bhagwan says the truth is a needle in a haystack. From my right, Wayan II bombards me with fake Communist stories wrapped in sympathy-evoking words, and from my heart, Bhagwan sermonizes on truth. I shut my eyes tight, bite my lips, and stay that way until the sleep goddess rescues me.

When Wayan II wakes me up at the parking lot of the Tanah Lot Temple, the first prayer I say is, "Oh, gods of Bali, please save me from Bhagwan." I omit Wayan II's name for two reasons: one, I need to reach the resort, and two, I hope he can still take me to Ketupat.

Wayan II picks up the damp yellow cloth and wipes the fogged windshield. Through the cleared streaks, I see a deserted parking lot drenched in the rain.

"Sea so rough, sir, cannot go to the temple." Wayan II points toward the rough sea that has swallowed the land bridge connecting the temple with the mainland. "Maybe you walk to the holy water cave and pray from distance, sir."

He makes sense.

Wayan II pulls the umbrella from the plastic bag and hands it over. "Be careful, sir, very windy."

I nod and step out, soaking in some rain before the umbrella unfolds, beginning the familiar sound of Balinese rain.

I walk down to the sea through puddles of water, crossing split gate after split gate, while my flip-flops splash muddy water all over my back. Spotting the cave isn't difficult; the Balinese have decent signboards everywhere, easy to follow. Except that the cave is equally inaccessible because it's right underneath the temple.

I close my eyes and pray to the sea god, the only one who knows why he has cut me off from the temple. The rain weakens, and the strong winds calm. It's like they were ordered to stand down.

Something in me tells me that this is the moment I get revealed, when the swelling sea retracts, leaving the path open—the moment when locals spot me and anoint me as their high priest.

The sign unravels.

It arrives as a salty breeze and caresses my beard before ballooning my T-shirt. I close my eyes and take a deep breath. "Lord, thy will be done." The breeze picks up speed, pushes me a few steps back, and snatches my umbrella. I narrow my eyes and watch my umbrella drift away in the gust. The salt in my eyes blinds me. I squat to resist the brute gust and let my tears and rain do their duty. Moments later, the wind weakens into a breeze again, and it stops raining over me, though I can hear it in the distance. I look up to thank the rain god, but I'm staring into the canopy of my umbrella.

"I believe this is yours, my son," says a voice.

Through my watery eyes, I see a lady in orange, with glasses and gray hair, holding my umbrella above my head.

"Yes, yes. Thanks, ma'am." I take the umbrella from her and hold it for both of us.

"You can call me Maa, or Mother. Mother Sheila."

She puts her hands together and makes the namaste sign.

"Namaste, Maa," I greet her with the umbrella handle sandwiched between my hands. Despite the rains, Maa Sheila is not wet, except for the tip of her orange sarong, where raindrops collect like beads. Her top is crisply dry, as if you can smell fresh linen. The jute bag on her shoulder bulges with the secrets to the other world, and her braids reveal years of solitary fasting in some dark cave, without food, sleep, or shower.

"Tell me, son, what do you seek?" Her warm hand rests on my shoulder.

I remember my mom and slip into a moment of silence. She lets a few moments slip by, like she is reading my thoughts, and repeats the question.

Never in the history of humankind has a traveler answered such a simple question with a thirty-minute essay. I tell her everything, not leaving anything out, not pausing for breath when the rain returns momentarily to compress us underneath the umbrella canopy. Her patience is flawless, like fresh milk, and the warmth of her arm is like hot tea on a misty morning in Little Lotus Pond.

When I'm done, she hugs me, strokes my upper back like a mother, and says, "What's yours will find you when the time comes. But you ought to be at the right spot, my son. This is a holy land, but it is not the space awaiting you."

My warm tears find their way onto her shoulders. She pats me one last time, relaxes her embrace, and slides her arms down my elbows. Then, she takes my hands and holds them like they were newborn infants. The rain stops as though the spell has broken.

"There's a five-day tantric retreat in Koh Pha-Ngan, beginning at sunrise the day after tomorrow. I see a ball of fire rising from the energy created by Shivas and Shaktis descending on the island, but only if you are there. For you, my son, are the chosen one for that space." She lets my arms go and reaches for her bag.

Tantra? Thailand? Again?

I bury my disappointment like any saint. "Are you sure, Maa? Perhaps there is a retreat in northern Vietnam, where the Hmong people live?"

"No, my son. Your sacred space awaits you in Koh Pha-Ngan." She waves her finger before me. "Here . . ." She retrieves a violet-colored ticket. "When you make the payment online, make sure you enter the promotion code 'Mother S.' You will get a ten percent discount."

I kneel and create an alms bowl with my arms.

She places the fluttering ticket in my arms. I clasp it before it flies off. She bows down, plants a warm kiss on my forehead, and walks away.

I look at the ticket. *One thousand one hundred euros*, it reads.

Don't leave Bali, Parker. This is the holy land, the land we came looking for. Bhagwan weaves his web of doubt in my mind.

But she looks genuine, Bhagwan.

A braid and orange clothes don't make her holy, my son.

But I felt her divine love, Bhagwan. Maa Sheila is a lamp.

His voice cracks, and I hear only a whirring noise, like a jammed radio signal. A minute later, I hear him again.

Son, she said she is Sheila?

Yes, Maa Sheila. Why?

You sure?

Yes. That's what she said.

Ah . . .

The signal breaks again and dies.

Bhagwan . . .

Bhagwan . . . You there?

I get no response. He has gone missing before, too. But seldom amid a conversation. I remember my prayers to get rid of him. Tears form in my eyes as thunder roars on the horizon. The temple lamps light up one after the other, followed by the streetlights.

I turn toward Maa Sheila. There she stands, fifty meters away, talking to herself, silhouetted against the cloudy evening sky. She's clutching her jute bag with one arm while the other frantically taps her sternum, panting as she speaks.

I pace toward her, and her words are now audible.

"Oh, Bhagwan, my sweet Krishna. Is this for real? Is it really you?"

Chapter 45

Wayan II is tired. I can tell from the gravitational pull on his facial muscles. Yet he keeps his promise, asking around for Ketupat, even when I suggest we give up. Ketupat, however, continues to be the elusive shaman, making me wonder if he has transmigrated into another human body, just as Bhagwan did.

Bhagwan, who has been with me since Thailand, belongs with Maa Sheila now. Between our pit stops, I close my eyes and try communicating with Bhagwan, but I only get a hollow sound, as if I'm breathing into an empty pot. Not even an echo bounces back to me.

We make one last pit stop for dinner. I order *ayam pelalah* and mixed rice. Wayan declines my dinner invitation, saying his wife is waiting for him. I chew the chicken, remembering that nobody expects me, neither here nor in Little Lotus Pond.

As our chariot turns onto the street where my temporary abode is, Wayan II looks back and says, "Sorry I couldn't find Ketupat for you."

He sounds genuine, the trademark of every *Urang Bali*. Their religion requires them to be honest and keep their promises. That's why you won't find a Balinese man or woman accused of theft.

"It's OK, Wayan, I understand. I shall always remember your kind help." I put my right hand on my chest in the classic Southeast Asian style.

"Maybe they will have at the shop now. You should check one last time," he suggests, and I concur.

It's time to part ways. He is not just my chauffeur, not anymore. A taxi driver in the morning but a trustable friend by the evening. Some corner of my mind says I will meet him again while another part overrules it. I pay him an extra fifty thousand rupiahs, and we exchange contact numbers.

Wayan II drives away, his taillamps waning into red dots at the far end of the street. The night sky opens to drizzle. I wait for a break among the steady streams of motorcycles and cross the street.

The lady who adorned my legs with pink flip-flops is back at the helm. She takes a split second to smile at me and then continues to serve her white guests at the round table. When she is done, she attends to me.

"The trip was good, sir?"

"Very much. I enjoyed it thoroughly. Wayan was really helpful."

"Nice to know, sir. He my brother."

"Wow," I exclaim. No wonder they exude similar warmth.

"All tourists like him."

I agree, though I would have preferred *traveler* rather than *tourist*. I want to inquire about Ketupat straightaway, but my wary mind advises me to wait for a sign. So, I point my finger at the black umbrellas hanging among the flip-flops and ask for one. I will have to return two umbrellas to Wayan I's wife.

She gets one for me and asks, with her eyes set on my feet, "You want pink one, sir? Got one in storeroom."

I cannot tell if she's trolling me or not. "I'm good with a black one. Thank you."

"You want to try some Balinese home-cooked dinner?"

"No . . . no . . . thanks. I just ate. Maybe tomorrow," I say, then add, "if I'm still here." My mind is searching for the right slot to ask for Ketupat.

"How about some snacks . . . maybe Ketupat?" she asks, like she could read the script running in my head.

Ketupat! She drops the sign just like that. My heart booms like a big bass drum. *But Ketupat and snacks?*

"Yes, yes. I can take some snacks." Blood rushes to my face. "You know Ketupat? I have been looking around for him since I landed in Bali."

She doesn't reply. Instead, she disappears behind the curtain.

After eluding me for a full day, the master magus is here right opposite my temporary home. Nervousness crawls up my legs. If Bhagwan was still around, he would have given some calming advice. I'm alone, all alone.

I divert my attention to the TV. *CNN News Update*, it flashes, accompanied by some jingling music. A lady with an '80s haircut, clad in a maroon midi, starts reading in Bahasa Indonesian. I try to catch a few familiar words but fail, no surprise.

"Here, sir. Got Ketupat for you."

The shopkeeper's voice caresses my ears. I turn back to see her holding tiny palm-leaf boxes. I slouch and extend my eyesight beyond her figure, but there's no one there. It never occurred to me he would have powers of invisibility.

"Ketupat, homemade, sir. You will love it," she says.

"Ketupat? Homemade?" I rub my forehead. *Ketupat is not a human?*

"Isn't Ketupat a famous person in Bali?" I ask.

She bursts into laughter. The two white men join her, too. I continue rubbing my forehead, wondering what went wrong.

"*Ketupat* no person, sir. *Ketupat* famous Indonesian snack. Very yummy."

Detailing its recipe, she quells the last coal in my heart. It could have been a straight entry into my buccal list, but my throat is jammed with disappointment. I pay her for the umbrella and the *ketupat*, thank her, and turn back.

"*Banjir* . . . *banjir* . . . your home, India," she calls from behind.

I don't understand what *banjir* means. But India, yes, the land I once called home. I turn toward the TV. *Eight feared dead in flash floods in South India*, an English banner runs below visuals of muddy floodwater. Some firefighters tug a lifeboat of women and children.

The scene shifts back and forth between multiple rescue scenes. Three firefighters are carrying an old man seated in his chair. He is drenched, but that doesn't stop me from recognizing him: Mohanan Panicker, the astrologer who predicted my destiny in the East. The man who foresees everything. I remember every word he said: *"To the east lies your destiny, your moksha, the enlightenment. Your luck line runs all the way to your wrist. You were born lucky; luck shall beckon you in every path you take, and you will make a lot of friends from across the seven seas and mountains. You will find answers to unanswered questions, eat food nobody else has eaten, and see things nobody else has seen."*

The scene replays faithfully in my head. Never will I forget his oracle that set me on a destiny hunt in the East. But . . . but . . . *Why couldn't he predict the flood?*

I rub my forehead and stare at the cemented floor, whirlpooling beneath my feet.

The street, the motorcycles, and the helmeted heads on them all spin at a constant speed. I plant my steps carefully and pull my spine up to level my sinking boat. The umbrellas and the *ketupat* weigh me down further; lugging myself upstairs turns into an ordeal.

Allen Allenson lounges on the balcony with a glass of liquor in his hand. I recall what my bald catechist taught me—*don't drink, or else you won't live long.*

"You look so tired," he says, taking a sip of the amber-colored liquid, shining with help from the tungsten lamp above.

A bit of that could drown my worries.

"The lights came back right in time," he says, following my gaze. Then adds, "Would you like to join me?"

I say nothing, but my feet drag me toward him as if he's the Parker magnet.

"Lakka, specially imported from Sweden." He pours some into an empty glass for me.

I notice there's another empty glass standing on the rattan coffee table.

"You will love this. Made from specially picked cloudberries."

My umbrella drops onto the floor, and I sink into the rattan chair opposite him. He is still holding the glass for me. I take it from him.

"Cheers to good company." He raises his glass.

"Cheers," I reply, skipping the good company part, and take my first-ever sip of lakka. Notes of honey and cinnamon play Ping-Pong underneath my tongue. And the lakka enters my buccal list.

Allen Allenson replaces the water in my blood with alcohol. He keeps talking; he keeps pouring. I keep drinking but forget to listen. My thoughts swirl around the failed oracle.

Despite the lakka, my thoughts are cogent because, one, the flood news spins me in a clockwise direction; two, the alcohol-infused spin is in the counterclockwise direction; three, they neutralize each other and clear my vision.

I have been conned! I have been conned by a fake astrologer.

Two teardrops preview in my eyes. I must preempt them from screening the doleful movie.

"Hey, handsome," a seductive voice jolts me, offering a sweet distraction.

My tears evaporate, and I raise my head to see a lady in a body-hugging floral midi. I'm unable to say if she is Balinese or Javanese, but that's not what matters now. What matters is that she calls for me, and she just called me "handsome." I'm the only good-looking man here, the other being an old spent force. Hope sprouts on the beds of my heart, fertilized with Swedish lakka.

If Bhagwan was here, he would have reminded me to show empathy. I imagine Allen drinking alone and take pity. Poor soul, I must find him the perfect company. And the centenarian will thank me for the rest of his life.

I sift through the wild cards in my mind and find the Singaporean mamasan who was to be Rachel's mother-in-law if the universe had not conspired against it. I look for the right words to introduce the topic, but the lady interrupts my thoughts.

"Hey, handsome," she repeats, with hands on her hips. Like a fashion show, she then turns to the left, then to the right, to showcase nature's splendor, which comes alive after dusk. "Am I pretty?"

I want to say yes, but Allen Allenson's voice beats me to it. "Of course, my babe. Absolutely gorgeous."

My head follows her as she glides from the veranda to Allen Allenson's lap while my brain is stuck like the tiny loop that appears before Microsoft Windows freezes on you.

"Hon, meet my new friend Oliver."

"Did you miss me, babe?" She wraps her hands around his wrinkly neck and asks, brushing her cheek against his.

"The day felt like a year waiting for you, honey."

He slides his hand up her back and pets her. "Honey, Oliver here—"

"I wanted to come in the morning, babe. But my freaking husband was stuck to his couch like stone."

"Glad that you got him off your sleeves."

"What sleeves? He not touch my shadow since I met you. His luck no more."

"That's my babe. By the way, Oliver here—"

"Ah . . . cannot wait to squeeze you like a teddy tonight," she says. "Let's go in. I can't wait no more." She releases her octopus grip around him, slides down to the floor, and pulls his arm with the right force, just enough to lift him without detaching his arm from his shoulder.

He waves at me and follows her like a lamb.

"See you tomorrow, Allen, and you, young lady." I stress the "young lady" part, hoping that will help her notice me, but the effort is in vain.

She holds the door open for Allen so that he can walk in like a king, so that he doesn't spend an hour pushing it open, so that he doesn't have to take the window route.

I sigh and sigh and sigh.

As Bhagwan would say, nobody is coming to rescue us. The last quarter of lakka left in the bottle catches my eye. I empty it into my gut. The flame of agony and frustration gets the fuel it wants.

I have been conned! I have been conned! I have been conned by a fake astrologer!

The lakka is now up to my neck; I must find my way to the bed before it climbs to my head.

I lean against the wall, inch to the door, and stagger to the bed. The voices next door grow louder and distinct.

Why doesn't he stand up, honey?

Wake up, little guy. You no happy to see me?

Wakie . . . wakiee

I hear her desperate voice.

I realize three things: one, the little guy is not rising; two, the little guy is not happy to see her; three, there was a little guy the whole time, and I didn't notice him.

When she failed to notice me, I was wondering if she was half-blind. I realize I am no better, either. How else could I miss the little guy—the fourth person who was there all the while?

Maa Sheila in an orange robe materializes before me.

Will you be there in time, Parker? Or will you let it go—the destiny you came looking for?

Awareness. Mindfulness. Meditation. She gifts me three words before fading into the dark horizon.

I drag myself out of the abyss, fish out the crumbled ticket, warm up my laptop, and key in the website address.

Welcome to the Open Heart, it says. As I prepare to pay, I remember it would make no sense if no flights were available. I pat myself for being mindful even when tipsy and look for tickets with Red Airlines for Sunday, June 14.

I reminisce about my luck with cheap air tickets. How could I miss this vital help from the gods? That infuses new enthusiasm in me. I buy flight tickets to

Bangkok and Koh Samui, along with a ferry ticket that includes land transport from the pier to the resort. I thank the gods for accomplishing the payments without floundering. Yes, I keyed in the promotional code that secured me a 10 percent discount and Maa Sheila a 10 percent commission.

I look at the time—1:04 a.m. Outside, it is raining. Next door, the young lady is still trying to wake up the little guy. The tenor and tone of her voice have withered. But her determination persists. As I slip into sleep, the question pops up again: *How did I miss the little guy who was there all the while?*

Chapter 46

Writing is a refuge. When the world betrays us, we authors find asylum in our literary realms. Our wordlandias are our revitalizing saunas. I massage my fingers, which ache from the continuous typing I've done through a rainy Friday and Saturday. The sun has set, but not in my world, as I am now even more determined. Before I leave Bali, I want to give one more try, my last try, to find the legendary shaman.

Wayan II calls me, offering to pick me up at seven on Sunday. He says I can make the 11:00 a.m. flight if we set out in the dawn. I ask him about Balinese shamans, careful not to mention anything that sounds like food. He agrees Bali has many wise men, but he can't say who is the legend among them. Even if he could, time is not on our side. I ponder for a moment and request him to pick me up at six, giving the gods an hour to take me to the diviner.

A voice in my heart says that I will find him in Denpasar. And I know for sure that this isn't Bhagwan speaking, as he has left me for cozy, warmer pastures. I imagine him sermonizing about valley orgasms, with Maa Sheila in the background playing the *tanpura* while his female disciples sway their heads, reminiscing about all the quickies they've had with him.

I make a deal with Wayan II. He stops wherever he wishes to, and I will ask around for the Balinese shaman.

I close my eyes and meditate. The trees, buildings, and paddy fields—my mind sees them all, though my eyes remain shut. I can even count the trees as we pass by—sixteen, seventeen, eighteen . . .

"Sir . . ." Wayan II taps my arm.

"Eh . . . yes . . . Are we at the airport?"

"No, we are entering Denpasar. You fell asleep."

"Eh, no . . . I was . . . I was in deep meditation."

Wayan II smiles. "Shall I keep driving?"

I wipe the stale saliva at the corner of my mouth, sit up, and peer out through the window. We are outside a café.

"Maybe you want a traditional Balinese breakfast. You know, breakfast that heals the body and mind?" Wayan II prods.

"Breakfast that heals." That's the sign. "Yes," I say, then alight. Wayan II has an adorable way of dropping hints. I also like that he stopped outside a café this time, instead of a traditional *warung*. The *warungs* were not helpful. Maybe the café will be.

The elderly man pours black tea for me and asks for my order. I pick egg and bread toast. He nods but doesn't turn away, as if he expects me to ask a question.

The sign, it's the sign! my mind screams. I don't hesitate because I can't afford to. This is my last chance.

"May I ask you something?"

"Yes, sir. Please." His face lights up.

"Do you know the legendary Balinese shaman?"

"Shaman?" He scratches his gray beard, which hangs from his chin like a funnel.

"Yes, the famous wise man who speaks the language of the gods." I put my hands together and raise them toward heaven. "One who can foresee things and tell you. One who—"

"Of course, I know one!" he exclaims.

The electrons in the outer orbits of my atoms get super excited. In my mind, I thank the gods for not betraying me.

"I shall tell your driver the route to his house. He will take you there," he says and steps out.

I sip the lukewarm tea, watching him talk to Wayan II, fully animated.

"Done, sir," he says when he is back.

"Thank you. Thank you so much. This is a big help to me."

"Welcome, sir. I hope you find whatever you are looking for."

I eat half the toast, as my tummy is half-filled with excitement. Here I am, moments before meeting the wise man who will foretell my rise as a writer. I close my eyes, take a deep breath, and give the fake Indian oracle an imaginary hug. I hold no grudges against him. His prophecy might be true or false; perhaps I will never know. What I know is that it has brought me closer to the legendary shaman.

Our car comes to a halt just outside a glossy green gate. I appreciate Wayan II's skill in parking, with barely a millimeter between his car and a white stone wall. This means that other cars and motorcycles can still pass by with an ample Balinese five millimeters to spare. Wayan II rolls down the window on the passenger side to take a good look. I rub my eyes to steady myself from the deep meditation.

"Sir, I think this one not right. Doesn't look like a shaman home."

"Is the location right, Wayan?" I ask.

"Yes."

"This is it, then. The signs don't lie."

He scratches his head. I open the door millimeters at a time to ensure that no motorcycles are harmed in the making of this epic novel and step out.

"But, sir . . ."

I hear Wayan II but ignore him and walk toward the gate.

I lift the gate from its chains, like every sage has done before, and give it a gentle push. It opens wide with a musical screech.

I step over the saddle and pause. Where the courtyard ends stands a white, stone-walled house with a tiled roof and a veranda. Two men sit before a round table and write something. Before them are glasses of black tea and a steel kettle. Not as much as I had imagined, but I can say that it's a home-run eatery. I stand still because I know that he who should know will know that I am here.

The door opens, and an elderly man steps out.

I smile.

He smiles.

I take slow steps to give him enough time to recognize the writer in me.

He smiles.

I smile.

I am now closer, close enough to smell the herbs boiling in his kitchen.

He smiles.

I smile.

I wait for his expression to change, the sign of recognition to glow in his eyes, and the pearls of prediction to flower on his lips. Time stands still, like everything around us is in a time freeze.

I get it. Destiny needs a nudge.

"Good morning. I am here looking for the shaman."

The smile on his face disappears. The two young men on the veranda stand up.

I remember the ethics classes I had attended, the brief passages on verbal hygiene. Drops of sweat appear on my chin and secretly roll down through my beard. I rephrase my sentence.

"Sorry, I . . . I am looking for the learned person."

The tension in his face relaxes. But the smile hasn't returned. He looks at the two young men and then at me.

Perhaps I haven't communicated enough. I append an explanation. "You know, the gentleman who does rituals?" I put my hands together as though I am holding an imaginary incense stick and pretend to pray. "You know, he who predicts the future . . ."

He looks at the two young men; they all exchange millions of glances.

"The Balinese learned man who makes herbal drinks."

"No Balinese herbal drink here." He raises his finger and pokes it on his chest. *"Mee, mee java . . . mee java!"*

I rub my forehead. He might not be a Balinese herbal drink lover. But *mee java* sounds good. I don't have enough time. But if he is going to make the prediction over delicious *mee java*, I should try. A spring of nectar opens underneath my tongue.

"*Mee java*. I would love to try it. But just a little noodle, please. Not much space." I rub my tummy and chuckle. A simple laugh is enough to loosen any tense situation, I know for sure.

"Stupid, *bodoh*," he says, his voice rising. His eyes are coal red now. "You no understand? Me no Balinese. Me *dari* Java. Means, me from Java. Bali no good. Bali full of voodoo. Voodoo no good. Go away."

Within a few sentences, he has gone from talking to shouting to screaming.

I begin sweating in my groin, remembering all my caustic experiences.

"I . . . I . . ."

"Stupid, *bodoh* . . . go away." He lunges forward, and in his hand shines the Javanese *kris*, the asymmetrical dagger.

My mouth is dry, and my tongue has sunk. But my mind appreciates the swiftness with which he pulled the dagger out of nowhere.

The two young men spring up and rein him in.

"Sir, you go away. He really kill you. Go, go!"

I retreat a few steps, and when they have reined him in, my mind repeats the familiar mantra.

Run, Parker, run.

I turn around and repeat the familiar drill. I have a flight to catch—and Shaktis to meet.

Chapter 47

My Thai SIM card gets another life in Koh Samui. And I complete my day's swipe meditation at the baggage carousel. Tinder chimes when I reach the daily limit.

> You have a match!
> Maya
> Age 29
> 16 km away

I decide to wait for a few minutes before messaging my only match.

My decision to book the tantric retreat in Koh Samui—and to purchase another last-minute flight ticket—was the right one. Maya's match only reaffirms it. I award a bonus point to myself for thinking clearly despite Allen Allenson's weird liquor.

Teleporting myself from the airport into the *songthaew* is smooth as the Koh Samui breeze, as my cells still remember the last trip. Being the first to board, I occupy the crew seat and busy myself on the phone, chatting with Maya.

Knock, knock.

I look up at the pale face within beastly dreadlocks peering from the other side of the window. I wind down the glass.

"Hey, bro. If you don't mind, could you please switch to the back? I prefer my *songthaew* seat in the front."

I admire his clean accent for a second, then reply, "What a coincidence, bro! I, too, prefer my *songthaew* seat in the front." I return to the goddess in my phone.

"Oh . . . eh . . . all right, bro. Enjoy your ride."

"Thanks, bro." I wind up the glass. I admire myself for being able to divide my tasks between my arms and perform them simultaneously. My left arm has just finished winding up the glass while my right arm is attending to Maya's texts. That's no ordinary feat!

I continue my heavenly discourse with Maya. Within a few minutes, I discover she's a skilled conversationalist. Three things I learn about her: one, she's a British citizen of Indian descent; two, like me, she's here for the tantra retreat; three, her match igniting the very moment I land in Pha-Ngan is not a coincidence. Maya is not just a match; she's also a sign foretelling my turning fortunes.

By the time my *songthaew* from Thong Sala reaches the resort, the sun is already on the horizon, flaunting its orange Thai silk cloak, and I'm snuggling in Maya's bosom in a parallel universe.

I'm here for the retreat, looking for my Shiva, she texts.

Your search is over. I am here, your Shiva. See you at the sacred space, I reply.

You have zero matches

Maya disappears.

I swallow my disappointment. It was bound to happen. Her name said it all—*Maya*, the illusion.

On the horizon, the orange mood of the sky is changing. It will take another twelve hours before I can see the same sea clothed in turquoise blue.

The check-in is easy because they already have my details. When the round-faced lady finishes flicking her hair for the third time, the printer coughs out a warm receipt.

"I shall call the bellboy, sir," she lies—it's a bell lady who escorts me to the second floor of the villa. My room is in the middle row. Another row of villas obstructs the ocean view. But because the resort is on a slope, I still see the horizon romancing the stars. It's Sunday evening, and the rock-music generation on the other side of Pha-Ngan has gone to sleep early to relieve the weekend fatigue.

The initiation ceremony is brief, with the organizers introducing the teachers and the program. There's a magical serenity broken only by the calm, rustic voice of the guru. If I could focus, I might even hear his dark beard swaying in the air.

> *Vakratunda mahakaya*
> *Suuryakotti samaprabha*
> *Nirvighnam kuru me deva*
> *Sarvakaaryessu sarvadaa*

The chief guru begins by invoking the blessings of Lord Ganesha, the obstacle remover. We sing and sway to the music that grows in strength, sending everybody into a trance, except me. I stand with my eyes closed—or half-closed if you were there to notice. Not that I don't try. Every time I shut my eyes, my mind tempts: *Parker! Open your eyes and look at the Shaktis around you. Remember, you are here for enlightenment through sexuality.*

We kiss the earth and honor her by raising our hands, facing the geographical north, then turn east to honor the air element, fire in the west, and water in the south.

"Look around; look into the eyes of every soul who has gathered here in this circle," the guru leads. "People of all sizes, shapes, colors, and genders! Yet the language of the eyes is the same. We don't need words to communicate in this sacred space," he says.

I spot Maya's face in the crowd and hook my mesmerizing eyes on her. I fire a dozen glances. But they all fall short. She avoids my gaze, and I move on as I'm supposed to. There are so many Shaktis in the tantric ocean, after all.

Man–woman, man–woman, my gaze sweeps the inner perimeter of the circular hall.

"In the tantric tradition, women are the Shaktis, and men are Shivas. Two powerful forces that complement each other," the guru continues.

How many of them will I get to kiss? I wonder, grazing the field for heads, necks, and bosoms, carefully skipping the Shivas.

We inhale together and exhale together with open jaws and an *ah* sound. Some make an opera-ish *ah*, some a shrieking *ah*. I, the great Richard Parker, make an *eh* sound that isn't audible, even when I contract the four major muscles in my belly and thrust the air up my windpipe.

The moment flows by. It's time to place our bare feet on Mother Earth and maunder around—our next step toward intimacy.

"Walk aimlessly and pause for ten seconds before the eyes you connect," the guru guides us. "Your inner eyes shall open to your twin flame. Let it go free; let it open and connect. How often have we judged someone to be unfriendly, only to find them so welcoming after a good chat? You are on the sacred tantric floor, where no prejudices shall block you from connecting."

My co-tantrics begin their random walk to bump into their treasure troves of love. My walk isn't aimless. I'm a man with a foretold destiny. I know my path. I know my destination. But Maya knows, too. She spots me and swerves.

I resume the maunder, halting before the eyes I come across, but I find no connection, no spark.

"Now, focus on the sacred spot between the eyes, the third eye," the guru continues.

I try the blonde Shakti in a peacock-colored sarong and a white top. She leans toward my ears, her warm breath awakening the soft hairs on the back of my neck. "Don't frown; relax," I hear her whisper.

It is a night of introductions. Eyes meet, shoulders rub, and souls hug. But it is not like what the guru said. There's a pattern in the connections. The six-and-half-foot-tall blonde connects with a man of her height; the prettiest of the Shaktis connects with the muscular, bare-chested Shiva. Perhaps the law of nature is in play. As for me, the fatigue of trying to connect with the empty space before me is steadily climbing up the barometer. I give up when my energy levels meet the floor.

I pick up my sandals, embrace the solitude, and trudge out. Behind me, the floor is transitioning into a cuddle space where hearts meet and bodies melt. I shake my head.

Four more days to go.

Day two, Monday, is better. I graduate from an *eh* sound to the *ah* sound when the svelte lady behind me plants her elbow into my rib. I maintain the sound thereafter.

We form groups to share our daily experiences.

"This is your sharing group, your family for the rest of your days in Pha-Ngan," says the guru.

The guidelines are simple: what we share in the group stays here. With the utmost glee, I volunteer to be the first person. I share how I got rid of the block in breathing, concealing the elbow part. My fellow tantrics share their mind-blowing experiences: the opening of the third eye, visions of their ancestors, tulips on sunflower trees, orange squash from wild berries, and crocodile cuddles in the oasis. I memorize every spoken word because stories are to be told.

Tuesday, day three, opens at dawn with *surya namaskar*. After a vegetarian breakfast, we meet at ten to listen to testimonies from a French-Italian couple in their forties. At eleven, we pair up at random and practice the art of communicating through energy vibes.

When the sun god is above the roof, every other soul has found their pairing, except me. I have been making progress—meeting more eyes and initiating chats. My mind wishes things could move faster, though. I comfort it with the hare and the tortoise fable.

I spot the blonde Shakti II eating alone and approach her with the customary namaste.

"I am Richard Parker from Little Lotus Pond."

"Namaste, Richard. I'm Glen. We all are from his lotus pond, aren't we?" She looks upward with open hands.

"No, no, I meant the name of my village is Little Lotus Pond," I say, laughing.

She smiles.

"It's hot today. Do you think it will rain?" I drop my pickup line.

"Maybe . . ." She gets up, pats off the dust from her yoga bottom, and leaves.

I learn something new—it takes two to tantra!

When the warm afternoon winds twist the thin white curtains, I count the newly formed cliques. There's so much chatter and laughter mixing with the smells of sweat. People sync into each other as though they have known each other for ages. Maya is floating on the other extreme, drifting from one white man to the other, while I fret in my niche.

"We transition into the intimate space this afternoon. But before we arrive in someone else's space, let's get intimate with ourselves." The guru escorts us to the classic meditative pose with our pointer fingers kissing the thumbs and eyes looking up to the roof. He shuts his eyes and sways his slender vegan body. The female tantrics next to him sway, too, followed by the floor, in perfect synchrony with each other, like meadows of Kans grass lilting with the wind.

> *I am the light of the soul*
> *I am beautiful*
> *I am bountiful*
> *I am bliss*
> *I am, I am . . .*

"This is the hymn we are singing this afternoon. As we chant 'I am, I am,' I want you all to place your right hand on your heart," he leads us.

I close my eyes, clutch the flesh on my chest, and tell myself not to waste another moment. I'm here now, and that's important. Without Maa Sheila, I would have been left dry, with no signs to follow. And I would have returned home with an empty soul and a broken heart. The thought of returning to that stinky bottom of India hammers a nail into my heart.

"I am, I am . . ." The guru's voice fills the room, and I repeat after him, mimicking the tenor of his voice.

> *I am, I am . . .*
> *I am the light of the soul*
> *I am beautiful*
> *I am bountiful*
> *I am bliss*
> *Maya maya*

When I hear "maya," my eyes flip open, and my inner self exhumes its obsession for Maya. I shake my head and hands to let go of the hunter's instinct and focus inward.

But, Maya . . . My mind is back on its hunting ritual again.

When the hymn ends, the guru pairs us randomly. I send him a virtual hug for rescuing me from my loner role.

"I want you to sit before each other with hands and eyes locked into each other's." He exudes that mesmerizing smile. "You will change partners every minute until your soul finds that special connection."

I look into many eyes but connect with none.

As the sunlight turns yellow and the breeze loses its warmth, ecstatic music resonates around us. People flow upward, their arms lifted and eyes half-closed as though an invisible force is pulling them toward the sky. Bodies swaying, arms stretched, feet barely touching the ground. The smell of sweat is everywhere, but the faces—they glow.

I'm still grounded, my bum anchored to the floor. Hip still, fingers numb, spine frozen, I paint a contrast to everyone else who has their wings spread. Not a soul notices me. Nobody sees the tears in my eyes. I stand up and walk out of the sacred space. Behind me, I can sense the souls transcending their earthly bodies and reaching out to the heavens.

Will I ever find a soul to connect with? No! It's clear—tantra is not for me.

I skip the evening session. I skip dinner. I skip sleep. Like a chapati, I lie flattened between the humid ambience and the heavy bed. I collect myself and sit up to gather my breath. It's 3:00 a.m. on my cell phone—exactly 3:00 a.m., not a second more, not a second less. I wipe off the sweat from my forehead with the tip of my blanket.

This can't be a random event. There must be a purpose, a reason, behind this.

It's a sign.

I set myself up in the lotus pose, close my eyes, and let myself slide through the tunnel. Maya is there in the tunnel; so are all the beautiful women I've met on this voyage. Their faces glow like neon signs in Kuala Lumpur's night markets.

I'm traveling fast. Visions flash by and brake before a dark face in the middle of the tunnel—a face that is indistinguishable from the darkness around. I choke and open my eyes. My tongue is parched, and I run to the table to grab a glass of water. I choke again while gulping the water but get some through. My breathing eases.

You don't need to sit in the lotus pose to meditate. You can meditate anywhere, anytime, in any pose. I remember Bhagwan's words. I sit on the chair and close my eyes. Never have I been able to focus so intently. The more I inhale–exhale, the clearer it becomes. I emerge out of the meditation knowing what to do—to come out of my cocoon, my self-doubts, my self-imposed barriers. There is so much energy in my veins, clarity in my head, and sweat on my skin.

It is not sexuality, but spirituality, my path!

I dash to the door, fling it open, and sprint down to the courtyard. The night is dark, the lamps are all off, and the moon is new. But my inner eye sees the path. I follow my feet, and my feet follow my soul.

I am running—I am, I am.

The force propelling me stops before an iron staircase fastened to the sides of a dark, brick-walled tower. I don't even remember noticing it before. Yet I am here before the tower. This is my calling. I know that this is the tower I am destined to enter—the tower where the guru meditates on new-moon nights. The tower of enlightenment!

I pull the rustic gate blocking the stairs. Its wings are chained together with a lock.

I am determined—I am, I am.

Locks and chains are to be broken. If not by me, then who? If not now, then when? I pull the lock and chain repeatedly, eyes fixed on the winding path and the quaint door hidden at the end—the door to my enlightenment.

Click. The lock releases.

I pull the gate with all my energy and slam it against the wall. A bright lamp lights up the ambience, followed by a loud whistle.

"Sir! What are you doing?" I hear a frantic voice approaching fast.

Nobody can stop me tonight! I grab the rails and sprint upward. But an arm restrains me at my waist, and the steel buttons of some thick uniform dig into my back. But I know I can't stop, for this is the new me. I struggle to free myself. More voices approach and join in the cacophony with the guy restraining me.

"You can't stop me from my mission. I'm going there. I know this is where the chief guru meditates on new-moon nights. This is the sign I have been waiting for. The universe is reaching out to me. Let me go!" I scream.

"Calm down, sir. We will get somebody for you to talk with. Suicide is not the answer." Words mixed with tobacco odor ring behind my neck.

"Suicide? I'm going up the tower to meditate. I know this is that special tower!" I scream again, tightening my grip on the handrail.

"Tower? What tower, sir? That's the water tank!"

"Water tank?" My grip loosens, and I am pulled away.

I collapse onto the pavement tiles with the smell of mud in my nostrils. The light in my eyes goes off.

When I rise, it is bright on this Wednesday morning. Bhagwan's dynamic music is seeping in from the meditation arena. I sit up and recollect the bad dream. My left cheek itches; I scratch it. Dried mud clinging to my beard falls off, telling me it wasn't a dream. A truckload of embarrassment weighs me down. The news must have spread all over. My fellow tantrics, how strange would they judge me? I don't have the stomach and intestines for it.

Hunger is a powerful motivator. After many failed attempts, I pull myself up and arrive at the breakfast corner. Of course, after a cold bath.

I have breakfast beside the pool in the company of the coconut tree. I'm too embarrassed to face the people in the dining area, but the wind brings fragments of their sound waves.

"Look at the floor. It's hard as a rock. In the US, they wouldn't have cleared the health and safety screening," someone says, steaming her anguish into the air, without the *ah* sound.

More words flow in, and I piece them together. I learn something new—the ecstatic music had sent many tantrics to the otherworldly dimension. Three had fractured their arms, and two banged their heads on the ground. One tantric went into a trance and tried to jump off the water tower—the humble Richard Parker.

The session starts, and incense and sandalwood aroma rise to fill the ambience. My inhibition has vanished, and I find the courage to appear in the sacred space. Like a child, I dance, eyes shut and hands reaching to the heavens. Someone hugs me to bring me down to Mother Earth. The music has stopped.

It's time for the sharing session, and my family welcomes me with open arms. I'm home. Rounds of confessions later, I discover that in their eyes, I am the chosen one who had transcended to the farthest point of the universe.

"I wish I could do that, too," the lady with brown curls and a nose stud says.

I put my hands together, close my eyes, and bow. "Namaste, sister."

It's the high priestess who leads the next session. "Time to connect more intimately," she says.

We are to walk around and sit down the moment we connect with another soul. I'm successful this time, as a Shakti comes looking for me. Mother Earth knows I wouldn't have gone looking for her. She is overweight by earthly standards, with a belly matching mine behind her semitransparent top. But she is pretty. We follow the instructions and meditate with our hands locked.

"Now, move closer and let your knees touch," the high priestess guides. We breathe together again and again until our cycles sync.

"Now, I call upon the Shivas to guide your precious Shaktis gently onto your laps without breaking eye connection or the rhythm of breathing," her voice echoes.

It isn't difficult. Like a gentle breeze that flows from the ocean to the sand dunes, she flows onto my lap, and I hold her by the small of her not-so-small back. Her beautiful eyes suck me in like the blue ocean while the spongy coconuts rub my chest, kindling the energy knot below my guts. We laugh, hug, breathe, pant, and sway to the music.

As we oscillate in a perfect rhythm, I discover myself in her. Looking into my image in someone else's eyes is a new experience. In my heart, I thank the beautiful eyes that spotted me and accepted me into their world. The more I reach for her soul, the more I connect with mine. I draw her closer and plunge my neck over her shoulder and sob. She holds me close, patting my back. I see heaven; I see me—the vulnerable me.

When the bell chimes, we say our namastes, thank each, other and move on. My soul is out of its cage, spreading wings to explore the newfound world of bliss and ecstasy. I connect with everyone the gods send my way, discovering the new me in them. The tall, the short, the French, the Russian, the blonde, the redhead—there are no barriers for the new me. My eyes see a new world, a brave new world that had always existed before me, but I could never see.

The evening is for water therapy, another session I have been looking forward to.

The session's guru is an elemental shaman who has learned the way of water. He asks us to partner up and take turns floating blindfolded. My partner is a short German lady, shorter than the short me.

She blindfolds me and ties the little floaters to my ankles. Her arms support my torso and help me float. Muffled voices ring from above as my ears go under the waterline. She sways me in the water to the left and right, like a cradle. When I am about to fall asleep, she drops my head into the water for a second and lifts me out again. I'm calm, for I know I'm in safe hands. She repeats it, each time varying the underwater interval. My body is under the water, but my soul flies to meet mermaids, squids, my parents, the mighty hills behind Little Lotus Pond. And the vision blurs. When it clears, I see two buffaloes. Behind them stands Isakki.

I look into her eyes, as I have never looked at her before.

It's my partner's turn. But she does not want to be blindfolded. So, we hug and part. She swims over to the edge of the pool and climbs out. I stand still with the waters waving at my chest. My partner is gone, but I am not alone. I smile.

The fourth night goes by.

Thursday, day five. We sing *bhajans* with the rising sun and listen to a fine talk on the various tantric schools of thought and practice. In the afternoon, I meet the guru in our private session. Every participant is entitled to one session with him. And it's now my turn.

"There's no light. I see only darkness—the darkest of the dark," I tell him. We are in the lotus pose, mirroring each other.

"Let's connect." He smiles and takes my hands. "Breathe with me. When you feel a gentle pressure on your hand, breathe in. Breathe out as the pressure eases."

We breathe.

"Ohm . . ." His hands resonate.

"Ohm . . ." My arms soak it up like a sponge.

"Ohm . . ." It is in my heart now.

I slide into the path of darkness again.

"Ohm . . ." The darkness loosens into a dusky tone, and the buffaloes appear again.

"Ohm . . ."

The timber in his arm mellows. Darkness fades, light returns, and the buffaloes disappear.

"Tell me what you saw." I sense a gentle tap on my arm.

I open my eyes to look into his warm eyes and begin speaking. He listens patiently, caressing his beard, and then hugs me. "You are blessed to see these visions."

But I wanted him to help me find the light, counsel me to let go of the darkness.

He sees through the mica of my mind and says, "Darkness is bliss; so is light. Together they make life tick on Earth. Light keeps us going, but it is the darkness that mothers us in her lap and recharges our souls. For without her, dawns will never be beautiful. Never will they be so energetic. The more we fight darkness, the more we tire."

"Come here." He points to his shoulder.

I lean forward as though someone is pushing me. He hugs me tightly and strokes my back. "Embrace her. Embrace her darkness, and when it dawns, you will be stronger."

I tremble in his arms. He continues until a fragile calmness beckons me. With a final tap, he releases me and looks into my eyes like a mother.

"Dark is beautiful, brother."

I put my hands together and thank him.

With his thumb, he draws a cross on my forehead. I know that would have been an ohm symbol had I been a Hindu.

"Like a feather, I let you go. To where you belong." He smiles.

I emerge out of the white circular hut. In the far-off view, the wavy sea melds into the blue sky above. I turn toward the young, sacred fig tree planted on a circular, brick-walled pedestal. It will be years before she matures into a tree. But even at around fifteen feet high, she casts a rich shade. I walk to her shade and take a seat beneath her. She drops a maroon leaf onto my lap, acknowledging my presence. I pick it up and place it on my palm. The needle tip points to the east, reminding me of the prophecy. A gentle breeze rubs in through my shoulder, and the leaf floats. It lifts, rotates, and settles with its tip pointing west. My mind draws an imaginary line from its tip across southern Thailand and Sri Lanka, ending at the southern tip of mainland India.

Why am I not rotating the leaf back toward the east? I find no answer.

I flip the leaf, and a ladybird crawls another millimeter along the midvein. She has been there all the while. A whistle pierces the canopy above, and I look up. Two tiny birds, one with blue upperparts and a red streak below and another in shiny olive green, chirp around a bunch of off-season figs—their treasure trove for today.

I am not alone. In fact, I have never been alone. I look around. There she is, on the white-painted bricks. I hear the rustle of leaves beneath her feet and the chiming of her anklet bells. I smell the magic potion in her hands, see her peering eyes, the fine hairs on her neckline, the sweat bead rolling down her sharp chin. I hear her whispering below my ears. *Parker, open your eyes and see the things you have never seen before.*

I shrug my shoulders and jump down.

Embrace her. Embrace her darkness, and when it dawns, you will be stronger. The guru's words ring in my ears. I flow down to the swimming pool, smiling at the couples passing by and relishing the frangipani in the air.

I spot the Shakti who opened my eyes and stretch out my arms. She hugs me tightly, and we sit by the pool under the coconut tree.

"Thank you for opening my eyes, my friend." I hold her arms in mine.

"Thanks to you, too. It was a divine experience." She flickers her eyes.

I open up and present my vulnerable self before her. "I thought I could never connect with someone like we did."

She presses my hands and looks into my eyes. "Me too! It was like magic. I felt like I was sitting before a handsome man with tattooed biceps. It was unbelievable. It wasn't you at all before me."

"Oh . . ." I sigh and withdraw my arms. "Thanks for opening my eyes."

We sit quietly for a while, and when we have parted, offering namaste, I walk to the outdoor shower. The stench of chlorine pinches my nostrils and leaves thousands of piercings there.

"Where are you from?" An unfamiliar voice beckons me.

I turn the shower knob and look up at the Shakti. She is white, too, like the previous one, but with a European face. I noticed her during the sessions before but never connected with her.

"India," I say as images of Little Lotus Pond appear in my mind.

"Oh, India! I was there last year, in Arambol. Amazing, you know?"

"Really? I'm glad to hear that," I say, dribbling water. It is welcoming to hear that after the episode about the muscular man with tattoos.

"The sessions were beautiful. So much happiness and sharing. There was marijuana, too. I totally enjoyed it."

I admire her speaking with hands on hips, with utter conviction, with the coconut trees and the blue-green sea behind her.

"But most of the ladies didn't enjoy it. I know. Sad, right? There were so many Indian men, you know? We rarely see that in tantric sessions. Yes, it was shocking, but I enjoyed it. I hope they limit the head count next time." She rolls her eyes.

I look at her forehead. The *pottu*, the Indian dot protecting her third eye, shines mismatched, like Captain America's shield in Spiderman's hands.

I skip sessions, walk to the beach, take a stroll, and sip pandan coconut.

It's evening, and time for the last session.

"Ohm Namah Shivaya." The guru's gentle voice reverberates around us. "Breathe into your chest and fill your chakra with love; now send it to the world," he guides.

I bring the energy into my arms and visualize it like a glowing ball. There are many people to send it to: Maya, who saw and unsaw me; the white goddess, for seeing the muscular tattooed man in me; the European face, who had to cope with the sight of so many Indian men in India; Maa Sheila, who led me to this gathering; the gurus, who are on one organic vegan meal a day throughout the retreat; the workers of the resort, for carrying me to my room after my tryst with the tower; and the housekeepers, who kept my room. Faces keep coming.

Send it, a voice whispers behind my ears.

I roll away the glowing ball, and it multiplies before floating away.

What do I have for the witch behind me? Do you want my life, Sorceress?

I look upward and continue breathing.

It's not me, Richard. Hear the frantic call of our mother pond? The breath behind my ears is warm now.

Two wiry arms slide under my arms and hug me around my waist. I don't look at them, for I know what color they are. I clutch the rough hands hardened by spade handles and buffalo harnesses.

Let your ego go, Richard. This is how the world is. Everyone chases love, but very few recognize it. Because to love unconditionally is the toughest task on earth. Learn to accept it.

But my calling is spirituality. Love and sexuality are distant dreams. They have only bogged me down.

Her arm glides up my face. Fingers run through my hair, kindling memories of my mother. Like a comet, silhouettes of unknown women who held me as a toddler flash before my eyes and disappear.

What have you been looking for, Ritchie? If you had closed your eyes and looked inward, you would have seen me; you would have seen us. We have always been inseparable, like night and day, light and dark, flowers and fruits, and spirituality and sexuality.

The hug tightens. I breathe deeper.

"Open your eyes, in your own time," the guru ushers.

Her hold slackens, and the whispers fade. The warmth disappears, and a dryness sets in. But I don't want to open my eyes. This happiness is new to me, like a fresh lotus bloom.

"Open your eyes, the world awaits you," the guru invites again.

I breathe deeply and unfold my eyelids.

The brightness of the space forces my gaze to the tiled floor. There's something special about the tiles. I trace their contours with my finger. Where the tiles meet, one has chipped, and a mason has reattached it. Nobody would notice it; it is that perfect. I shut my eyes and run my fingertip over the hairline crack.

I am the mason, and my hands ooze love for the tiles and the earth beneath.

I bow my head and kiss the earth.

Chapter 48

The retreat has ended. But Friday has an unofficial session—the sunrise *bhajans*. I sit in the last row and sing along.

The resort is reverting to its touristic avatar. Many have vacated their rooms. I eat with my sharing family members. We talk little, but an invisible string connects us all. After breakfast, we vow to remember each other in our meditations. I'm yet to spot my next sign. But my heart overflows with inexplicable happiness.

I walk to the sacred fig tree one last time and savor a deep breath in its shade.

Just a couple of hours to 12:00 p.m., my checkout time. And I have no place to go. Maybe my sign is hovering around. I approach the round-faced receptionist for location suggestions, hoping destiny speaks through her. But no sign comes through. What if there's no sign? I could still fly to Vietnam, Laos, Myanmar, or Cambodia—countries I haven't been to.

I return to my room and switch on my computer. By the time my laptop connects to Wi-Fi, my mind has zeroed in on Vietnam. Finding tickets and accommodations shouldn't be difficult, as I have had a lucky run with cheap air tickets so far. I log in to my bank account to take stock of the money left.

Nine thousand nine hundred and ninety-nine rupees, it screams, like I'm purchasing some running shoes on promotion.

I pull up my transaction history and learn something new: never buy a flight ticket when drunk.

It dawns on me in the middle of the day that the one-hundred-year-old man's liquor has done me in. I search for alternate tickets via Bangkok and Kuala Lumpur, but I find nothing within my budget. In the past, situations like this would see salt springs in my *kilikili*. But nothing happens. My armpit is still dry. I sit as calm as a stone, as clear as a brook, and as sharp as a knife.

My cell phone coos. Last night, just before going to sleep, I changed my ringtone to a bird call.

I swipe for the message. It's Cousin Mercy.

Hey Richard, things all right on your end?

Yes, but stuck as a wedge, though.

She rings me in return and listens to snippets of my odyssey. "I wish I could meet some indigenous people," I end. I don't hint about the Hmong people, though my heart projects images of them in the blue hills.

"I'll get you tickets, Richard."

My jaw drops. "To where?"

"Surprise! I assure you that you'll meet plenty of indigenous people. Check your mail in an hour, OK?"

"Aye, aye, ma'am," I salute.

Fifty-six minutes later, her email arrives with the subject *Re: USM–KUL–MAA*.

I disregard my cautioning mind and open the e-tickets with a pot full of enthusiasm.

E-ticket for Mr. Parker, Richard from Koh Samui (USM) 19 Jun to Chennai (MAA) 19 Jun via Kuala Lumpur (KUL), it says.

Somewhere in the garden, two pigeons coo happily. I cross my arms behind my head, close my eyes, and breathe with an *ah* sound.

Chapter 49

Cousin Mercy's email ends my adventures in the East, puts a full stop to my novel, and brings me to Kuala Lumpur International Airport.

I am on my way back to India. But I'm not ready for Little Lotus Pond yet. Kannan, my classmate from my journalism days, has permitted me to use his Chennai apartment until July 30. He uses it as a writing area, but he is touring until July 29. I'll sleep on his couch for the next one and a half months with book-loaded shelves for company.

I have traveled through airports alone before, too. But something has changed this time. No matter how hard I try, I can't shrug off the feeling that someone else is with me. I try not to worry about it and keep my mind occupied with my draft.

I add the final touches to my book. Writers plan their climax early in the writing stages. I, too, had imagined a climax for my epic novel—a happy-ending one where I achieve enlightenment and settle down with my lady, or ladies, and child, or children, and many disciples. But none of it has materialized, and in the actual climax, I sit confused under the fig tree.

Sigh.

Maybe it's nature's way of keeping the split gate open for a sequel.

—*The End*—

I send it to Oxtail Publishing. In my email, I specify that this is an unedited draft and add that I'm excited to meet them soon.

I shut down my laptop and secure it inside my bag. An Indian family is pushing a trolley with a forty-four-inch LED television box. Electronics are cheaper in

Malaysia, I remember. Next to me, a gentleman in his Armani suit checks his watch for the umpteenth time.

I pull out my cell phone and insert my Malaysian SIM card, which has another ten days' validity. I tap on the data button and go to Instagram.

>Su the carlady follows you

I smile and scroll through her profile. As expected, it's all about classic cars. I open Tinder.

>You have zero matches.

I go to my profile and hit the "Delete Account" button. It prompts me to choose a reason to go. I click on the "Something is broken" option.

>Your account has been deleted
>We are sad to see you go

My mission has ended in a way that I had never expected. Penning the events in the *songthaews*, ferry, and airports has helped me numb the mysterious emotion in my throat. There's nothing that stops me from looking back to reflect or ruminate, whichever way you want to look at it. But my mind doesn't cooperate, as though it has lost the knack.

Tinder was another unsuccessful attempt. But it led me to Su, and I will always be thankful for that. In my head, Su is focusing her microscopic vision on car paint, telling her mohawk-headed assistant, "*Haiya*, you, *ah*, can see this scratch or not?"

I smile.

There's still an hour more before my flight to Chennai. I log in to Amazon India on my phone. Amazon's algorithm absorbs my keywords and fishes me John Roosa's *Pretext for Mass Murder* for 2,179 rupees. I key in the address of Kannan's studio apartment for shipment. I also mark *Tamils and the Haunting of Justice: History and Recognition in Malaysia's Plantations* by Andrew C. Willford for future purchase, as I have only 6,100 rupees left in my account.

The local expenses in Koh Samui, including airport transfers and food, were bearable at 1,720 rupees. Another forty-two days of instant-noodle life in Chennai and a train fare to Nagercoil, and I will be the synonym of *bankrupt*. But then, Susheela's husband, Thankamoni, will have the banana lessee fee ready. Broke but not broke. Su would be flabbergasted by my business acumen.

WhatsApp coos. I swipe up the banner and tap on the app. It's Mariyam. She calls me.

Mariyam expresses sympathy for Jenny and inquires about my travel plans. I tell her bits and pieces and finish by saying, "For the rest, you'll have to wait for the book."

I hear her giggling at the other end of the spectrum. "That's smart, Parker. You know what?" She pauses. "I like you, Parker. You one hell of a smart, witty, well-educated, liberal, and open-minded guy. Aren't you, man?"

"Well . . . err . . ." I fumble. In my heart, new shoots sprout, but my rational spade stomps them out. *Stay grounded, Richard Parker,* I tell myself.

"You're the man I have been looking for, Parker. I want a liberal, open-minded man who will accept my culture, my religion, and our ways of life and settle down here." She continues, explaining why she doesn't like men from her community because they are all close-minded. "All my cousins have found liberal men, Parker. You wouldn't believe how much these men have transformed. They don't have an iota of their old culture in them. From how they dress to their food, they changed everything for love. Oh, Parker, isn't that unconditional love?"

"Oh yes, yes. It is," I reply and rub my forehead.

She wants an open-minded man who will give up his religion and culture and accept hers. I try to find meaning in such open-mindedness. But my overworked head refuses to process the information.

"Parker, you there?" Mariyam checks.

I switch off my cell phone and replace the SIM card with my Indian one. It won't work in Little Lotus Pond but will serve its purpose in Chennai.

The gentleman in the Armani suit is still there in the seat beside me.

"I am Colonel Joshi," he initiates, catching my gaze.

"Richard Parker." I extend my hand. He takes his hand off his black briefcase and shakes my hand firmly.

I noticed him the very moment he sat next to me. His Armani suit reminded me of Mr. Sajeev, my former chairman—the only other person I have seen in an Armani.

"That's a nice Armani."

"It's our supreme leader's initiative—that all diplomats should wear Armani. He is a man of great taste, you see," he starts, introducing himself as a diplomat returning from Vietnam.

"Must be damn expensive."

"Doesn't cost a penny to the exchequer. It's all sponsored by industry partners."

I remember our supreme leader's million-dollar suit. Gifted by some industrialist, it had his name monogrammed in gold. Since I set out on this mission, I haven't thought of him even once. That's a surprise because while in India, he was smiling from everywhere—on the billboards at fuel stations, government offices, hospitals, and even food packets dropped during floods.

"I'm glad to work for such a visionary." He puts his arm on his chest. "He resuscitated our Look East Policy. Thanks to him, we will soon be a major force in Southeast Asia," he says, glancing at his watch. "Our supreme leader is so particular about auspicious and inauspicious times. Since he took over, there has been a great cultural awakening among the bureaucrats."

Politics is of little interest to me. Even in the good old times when I was floating in cow urine, I stayed away from political talk. I'm surprised I haven't yet yawned.

"They have ripped off our collective wisdom. Look at astrology—it has been our forte for centuries. The previous governments killed it. Our supreme leader wants to revitalize the science, but very few elders know it anymore. It's a mad run against time to document the knowledge before we lose it forever." He shakes his head in the Indian way.

"I know a learned person in southern Kerala who is an expert astrologer." I offer him the address of Mohanan Panicker. "You might want to wait for a while, though, as his house is under unforeseen floodwaters now."

He thanks me and notes it down on his cell phone. When the screen locks, he draws my attention to its live wallpaper. It is a video loop of the supreme leader, photographing a peacock that is a few feet away with a 200 mm telephoto lens. "Our hero. Isn't he mesmerizing?"

"Hmm . . ."

He runs his hand on the leather of his briefcase for a while and resumes with a question. "I presume you are based in Malaysia?"

"No, no. I'm in transit." I shake my head. "Returning from Thailand. I have been traveling through Southeast Asia for the last few months."

"Wow. That's so great. I bet people are so happy to know that you are Indian?"

"Well . . . kind of," I mumble.

"It's all because of the master diplomacy of our supreme leader. We have been spending billions of dollars in Southeast Asia, and it's all bound to reinforce our standing."

"May I know what projects we are doing, sir?" I ask. In my mind, images of universities and hospitals and schools and scholarships flash by.

"We are helping in the restoration of Angkor Wat in Cambodia. We will soon launch an archeological project at the Cham temple complex, Vietnam, and also some conservatory projects for the Hindu temples of Indonesia." He looks at his watch again and continues. "In another five years, we will have restored India's glory."

The term *keling* flashes before my eyes.

"These people have forgotten their Hindu ancestry. India is rising, and we will awaken people to their true history." He pumps his fist and thuds it on the briefcase. "Can you believe we ruled the entire Southeast Asia once upon a time? Isn't that a matter of pride for all of us?"

I stand up, clutch the harness of my daypack, look at him, and smile. "India was once conquered by Alexander the Great, then by the Mughals, and later by the British. I'm sure the Greeks, Arabs, and British are also proud of it, sir."

Part IV

The Return to Little Lotus Pond

Chapter 50

Bus number 1½ lugs herself out of yet another puddle, rustling and creaking. A lone wiper hangs on her windshield like a broken arm, clearing the remaining drops of rain that have followed us from Nagercoil since noon. She faithfully sticks to the hairpin bend of the road to avoid nosediving into the market ground beyond the roadside shrubs. As a kid, it was fun to flock to the buses that dug their worn-out tires into the soggy end of the ground, ignoring the passengers emerging with bruises on their foreheads and grocery bags in their hands. It's not fun when you're the passenger.

My hands and clothing smell like lignin. Forty-two days of life among books with little human contact was another never before experience. I've read John Roosa's *Pretext for Mass Murder* twice, skimmed through volumes of *Socialist Register*, and also fell in love with Fictions. Sue Monk Kidd's *The Secret Life of Bees* shall remain my all-time favorite for the story it tells, and also for the metaphorical value the title holds for me. Days went past like a wink, and it's time to go home.

I count the neem trees jutting out from the roadside bushes—six more to go before the market ground, and the banyan trees at the far end of the road are visible.

I count six . . . five . . . and the water-filled market ground is already visible beyond the trees denuded by the rain. My count ends at four; the last three trees lie uprooted, with their crowns submerged in the temporary lake. I have seen the ground flooded only once before in my life, as the networking lotus ponds kept the floodwaters to themselves.

The bus tilts left and steadies herself. I run my eyes over the kids boating on banana trunks. The bus swallows another two hundred meters of wet tarmac, curves rightward at the banyan tree, and screeches to a halt.

"Little Lotus Pond, anybody?" the conductor shouts, and I rise from my seat and pick up my duffel bag.

"Lazy fellas of Little Lotus Pond. Always taking their sweet time to alight," I hear the conductor murmur as I step down, pulling my bag.

I had dreamed of a grandiose homecoming. Vinyl boards would welcome Saint Richard Parker from his successful quest in the East, thanking him for making the village proud. All that is vaporware today.

The bus kicks some mud slurry and grunts away. A mongrel lifts his head, barks twice, and curls back to his afternoon nap. Underneath the banyan tree, heads turn in my direction, spot me, and begin concocting stories.

I look at the footpath to my left that I usually take to avoid the main street. It appears the same as the day I walked out, pulling my luggage. I skip it this time and take the main street. I walk past the three shops and stop before the saffron-colored, rammed-earth *nizhal thangal*. Two familiar faces squat on the temple veranda, engaged in another animated discussion, caressing their gray beards. The third face, Murugan, is missing. Gurusaamy, who is facing the wall, raises his arm, signaling the chief servant to stop talking. And as if his inner eye sees me, he turns around and looks straight at me. He stretches out his arm in my direction and laughs like a baby. "I see you, my son."

Son! How nice it is to hear that again. I drop my bag and hop onto the veranda. He pulls me down like a thirsty elephant and hugs me.

"I knew . . . I knew you would come for us," I hear him cackle as his arms stroke my back. I take deep breaths and hug him back.

"I'm back . . . I'm back," I say as images of my parents appear and vanish in my closed eyes.

"Isakki said you were on your way back."

We part, and I squat before him with my mouth wide open. "Isakki? How does she know?"

Gurusaamy laughs. I realize that I'm looking at one of the happiest humans on earth, capable of laughing even when he hardly has any teeth left.

"There's nothing she doesn't know, Ritchie."

The chief servant steps down from the veranda and picks up my bag. I watch him wipe the mud with the end of his saffron-colored dhoti as though it's his baby; he hauls it over and returns to his squatting position to look at us. I smile at him for the first time in my life. He smiles back, raising the white flame-shaped mark on his forehead, but says nothing.

"When was the last time you looked in the mirror, my son?" Gurusaamy asks.

"Every day, Saamy."

He laughs. "I doubt that. The chief servant has a mirror inside." He points to the entrance of the *nizhal thangal*. "Take a look at yourself there."

For the last forty-two years on this planet, I've protected my shadow from falling on the floor of this obscure temple, and here's a man I place on an equal pedestal as my dad asking me to break the norm.

"Come, my son." The chief servant takes my arm.

I float in the direction of his pull.

Chapter 51

A mélange of odors squeezed out of sandalwood, incense, and Nerium flowers cloaks me as I struggle to adjust to the natural light—or the lack of it. The chief servant retreats after leaving me. Like a feather, his feet grace the earth behind me, moving farther and farther away, fading back into the exit.

I plod toward the open door of the sanctum sanctorum, adorned by two human-size brass oil lamps on both sides. The smell of freshly burned wicks tells me that today's rituals have passed and prayers have been said. I look at the chair wrapped in red silk and the mirror behind it with hardly any light to reflect.

I inhale, listening to the cycles of my breath, grounding myself in the sacred space that has always been near, yet far from reach. I hear my breath fill the tiniest air sacs of my lungs, bartering aromatic yin for yang. I feel my heart pumping within its sanctum sanctorum. I sense a lightness in my forehead—the only part of me faintly visible in the mirror now. I plant the balls of my bare feet firmly on the terra-cotta floor and rise to present more of myself to the mirror.

A face that I can hardly discern from the surrounding darkness appears in the mirror—a face that is dark, as dark as Isakki, as dark as her buffaloes. A face that left this little village for greener pastures, only to become another *kallu, kumar, ooran, keling,* and *bumbay.* Tears ooze from my eyes, and a fur ball stuffs my airway. The tendons of my legs ache, and the heels of my feet relax back on the floor.

I swallow some moments to center myself. When I'm at ease, I take a deep breath and let it out.

Ohhhhhmmmmm.

Chapter 52

Both wise men are on the veranda. Like life-size idols, they sit in utter silence with their eyes fixed on the entrance. In my head, I contrast it with the animated faces I saw before I went in.

I look at their blank faces, expecting them to ask about my experience. Instead, Gurusaamy says, "It's a full-moon night, my son. The moon will be at the helm, awaiting you."

I stand perplexed, wondering why he would bring up an unrelated topic now.

"Speaking of your home, son, Susheela cleaned it every week, even though her husband was battling death."

"Battling death? He was healthy when I left."

"He took a fall from the palmyra palm."

The scene reenacts itself in my head like I was there witnessing it. A shock wave rises from my belly and shoots upward. Thankamoni has fallen from the palm—the man who was always a part of my home.

"How is he now?"

"He is with Isakki. The doctors sent him back, as he was paralyzed below the neck. Isakki was at Kudankulam with the fisherfolk, protesting the nuclear plant. Luckily for Thankamoni, she got back in time, before his pulse dropped to zero."

"That's good, Saamy. But . . . but . . . I think we should take him to another hospital and not rely on magic."

"Magic?" Gurusaamy gives me a mysterious look. "It's her fingers, Ritchie! Her fingers—that girl is Lord Ayyappa's gift to Little Lotus Pond. They breathe life into the hardest stone. She can find any nerve in the human body, even in the darkest of nights, and trigger it. It's just a matter of time before Thankamoni's spine springs back to life!" He wipes the tears from his eyes, as if Thankamoni is his son or brother.

I squat before them, fishing for words.

"Ritchie, misfortune doesn't come alone," he says, his voice dropping.

I look at him, wondering what else awaits me.

"The rains leveled the banana crops."

I remember the faces of Susheela's kids. *Have they been eating? Who feeds them?*

"Murugan has been helping her to claim compensation from the government."

"So nice of him. But why Murugan? He is not an elected representative, Saamy."

"He is a Communist, Ritchie. In India, only a Communist can get things done without bribes. No bureaucrat wants to see a picketer with a red flag in his office. He has been filing petitions, but chances look bleak." Gurusaamy takes my arms and cradles them like a little bunny. "I assured Susheela that my Ritchie is wealthy enough to write off the loan."

"I understand, Saamy," I mutter. A few months ago, I would have pulled out the contract where the couple affixed their thumbprints.

"No worries, Saamy. Thankamoni's health is more important now."

"I want—" A loud honk interrupts Gurusaamy's sentence. A mini-lorry carrying steel rods zips past through the narrow street at unusual speed, followed by three white SUVs.

"Hmm." Gurusaamy sighs. *"For the Lord, your God is he that goeth with you, to fight for you against your enemies, to save you."*

I look at the chief servant. He shuts his eyes and nods in agreement.

I turn toward Gurusaamy. "I'm . . . I'm lost here."

"Little Lotus Pond is getting its base transceiver station, Ritchie."

"Why now? Why do they remember us all of a sudden?"

"They want to unleash Facebook and WhatsApp's perception-manipulation algorithms on us. A divided land is easy to conquer, you see."

I rub my forehead.

"Troubles flock together, Ritchie. The Minerals Department found lithium deposits in the pegmatites behind Isakki's home. Little Lotus Pond is getting a renewable energy plant—and a township. They want to bring their people from North India and settle them here. Our village will soon be another testing laboratory for their fascistic agendas."

I recollect my recent lessons on demographic engineering and majority versus minority games.

"The Brotherhood's nonprofits, including the Kendram, have received foreign funding to campaign for renewable energy. Back in 1980, the Kendram received funding for biogas plants. Two years later, our district witnessed the first and bloodiest communal riots." He draws imaginary circles on the floor with his fingertip and continues. "They visit homes on the pretext of installing a biogas plant, campaign for the sacredness of the cow, and then promote hatred between communities. And the benefit is reaped by their political wing to install poor leaders, like the supreme leader, who destabilize India. This benefits the American, Israeli, and Chinese masters who fund the Brotherhood through proxy nonprofits." Gurusaamy heaves a sigh and pauses, eyes fixed on me.

It is clear that since the 1980s, the modus operandi of the Brotherhood has remained the same. I remember the Brotherhood's nonprofits campaigning for national security and cow-based organic farming in the Christian tribal-dominated Northeast India. Wherever they set up camp, communities ended up hating each other. Today, the entire northeast is another vote bank for the supreme leader's party.

"Later in the 1990s, the Kendram received massive foreign funding for renewable energy," Gurusaamy continues. "They used the money to campaign for the nuclear plant, vilifying the protesting Christian fisherfolk as foreign agents. The renewable energy funding is back again, Ritchie. And they have picked up Father Cornelius as the villain. For the average Brotherhood sympathizer, a Catholic priest protesting a development project fits the narrative."

"But is he alone, Saamy? What are others doing?"

"Of course, Ritchie. We will stand up. But they are good spin doctors. They will brand Christians as foreign-funded rice-bag converts, journalists supporting us will be presstitutes, and protesting liberal Hindus will be anti-nationals. It's an old game, tried and tested in Germany by the man they venerate every morning."

Gurusaamy is right. The journey ahead will be long and arduous.

Chapter 53

The shadows grow longer as the sunlight turns warmer. The hills at the end of the main street revel in their day's dose of evening glory, flaunting necklaces of rivulets. Soon, red, yellow, and green dragonflies will re-create aerial dances above the little ponds. When they droop their wings and tuck under the comfort of sleepy leaves, winged termites will rise from the foothills, pursued by the anteaters of the underworld. Some will escape to mob our lights.

I'm passing by Khader Bhai's abandoned, green-colored house. Khader Bhai was a famous Sufi elder, and when he was alive, this house was always busy. It has been three years since the only Muslim man in the village passed away. Yet, his home is tidy and alive because the villagers tend to it, hoping that his son and daughter, now living in Saudi Arabia, will return someday. The fluorescent tube before the next house in line comes alive—the place where widow Shanta lives. I hang my head and double my pace when a voice pulls me.

"Brother Ritchie!"

I pause for a second, wondering if I should pretend not to hear it. Then I decide against it and turn toward the veranda of the house.

Shanta's face is visible above the half-closed door. Her face lights up when she notices I have indeed stopped. She swings open the lower half of the door, runs across the veranda, hops down like a kid, and stops before me.

"It has been a long time since I saw you. I heard you have been traveling. It's so nice to have you back. Come in." She takes the duffel bag from my arm without even asking if I want to.

I know not what she implies and look around to see if anybody is watching us.

A bicycle rider passes by, raising his arm to acknowledge us. I wave back, though I don't remember seeing him before. In the opposite house, next to the sleeping flour mill, the deaf and blind grandma leaning against the veranda pillar is busy extracting the last drop of heavenly pleasure out of the betel in her mouth. On the power lines overhead, a bunch of crows rant about the cuckoos they reared last season, vowing to be careful next time. Life goes on as usual in the Little Lotus Pond way.

"Someone will be jumping for joy tonight," she says.

I rub my forehead, wondering if I should meet this person or not.

I slide off my flip-flops and climb the steps. Shanta is already inside. I cross the veranda and pause at the doorstep, below the picture of Christ with his open heart. At the lower end of the framed print is a passport-size photograph of a man whom I assume is her deceased husband.

Rubber wheels squeak inside, like she's pulling a washing machine or cupboard. I step into the living room, where a television coexists with books and rattan furniture. A pink-laced portiere partitions the living room from the inner spaces. I take a whiff of aged lignin and some weird medicinal oil lingering in the damp air. The squeaking grows from the other side of the portiere. The curtain splits into two, and Shanta rolls in an elderly woman in a wheelchair. Her right arm is wobbling in the air while the left hangs lifeless.

"Take me closer, Shanta. I want to touch my son." Her voice trembles.

My feet refuse to move, and my tongue has retreated into the hollow of my throat. I stand still. Shanta pushes the wheelchair closer, and the smell of the medicated oil is now stronger.

Her trembling hand latches on to mine. "The last time I held this arm, it was just like a banana flower. So gentle and pure. Just three months old, and it was my last day as your mom's midwife. I used to tell your mother, this is the hand that will take you around the world," she sobs. "And then . . . then we left the village. When I returned as a widow with a widowed daughter, your parents were gone." She wipes the tears with her shaking hand. "I've asked Shanta many times to bring you home at least once. She says you're always lost in thought and hardly notice anybody, even if they bump straight into you."

I only pretended to listen to my mom whenever she spoke of the midwife and babysitters who took care of me as a toddler. I don't remember any of them. The thought that I wasn't aware of her existence until today stings me. She narrates her fond memories of my parents; the tragic story of her husband, who died soon after gifting her a precious daughter; and her son-in-law, who did not return from the antinuclear agitation at Koodankulam. Everybody knew that the Brotherhood eliminated him, but there was no evidence to pin it on them.

Shanta excuses herself and disappears inside.

"I suffered a stroke, and allopathy could only restore my speech and one arm. Thanks to God and the guardian angels, I am breathing. As the Gita says, 'If thou wilt not fight this righteous war, then having abandoned thine own duty and fame, thou shalt incur sin.' We all have our own battles to fight, my son."

I look at the Catholic before me quoting the Bhagavad Gita and recollect the Hindu Gurusaamy quoting the Bible a while ago. With wet eyes, I realize how precious this little village of mine is.

I place my hand on her hanging arm. "Allow me to take you to Thiruvananthapuram, *amma*. I will get you the best possible treatment." I know I'm broke, but I don't know where I got the courage to utter those words.

She takes my arm in her other trembling hand and kisses it. "Your words sound like honey, my son. But I get the best treatment I can. Isakki and Father Cornelius take turns giving me my physiotherapy sessions. All these years, they have never missed a session. Running all-day physiotherapy camps for bedridden patients is so tiring for Father. He might return late in the night like a wrung towel, but Father always drops by to attend to me every Wednesday. As for that wild horse, Isakki, she appears in front of me even before I finish thinking of her. I'm glad we made the right decision to return to this place. When I go, I will be at peace knowing that no harm will befall my daughter."

A spring in my head uncoils, shattering the glass in my head. Sweat beads form on my forehead as the village I had known before spins like a crystal top to unravel its truer self. I learn something new—Father Cornelius is a physiotherapist. Thus the visits in and out of Shanta's house.

Shanta serves tea. Guilt and remorse stop me from looking at her face. My heart wishes to run home as soon as possible.

Shanta must have sensed the whirlpool in me. She changes the topic, asking me about my voyage. I take a few moments to switch thoughts and reconstruct the frame in my head. Then, I dramatize it to make it as funny as I can.

"This is so interesting, brother. It's an exciting story to tell."

"Oh yes, a story without a story." I laugh.

"Call it whatever you want, brother. I'm reserving a copy. Let's ask Isakki to translate it into Tamil. We will make sure that every soul in this village reads it."

"You think this is a winning story, sister?"

"You're always a winner for this village, brother. If someone from Little Lotus Pond does something worthy, it's our tradition to support them with all our might. Folks will bicker as usual for the sake of it, but when the time comes, they will rise as scaffolding, piecing together all the little bamboo sticks."

Her words put the guilt back in my throat where it was moments ago.

I thank her. We talk for a while more before I excuse myself, promising to visit them often.

"It's dark, my son. There won't be any light in the east after the main street," Shanta's mom worries.

"Don't worry, *amma*. Ritchie knows every stone and every blade of grass in this village. Besides . . . besides, tonight is the fifteenth of *Adi* month, July thirty-first in the English calendar." She smiles and looks at me. "It's a full-moon night. There will be moonlight in the east."

"Thank God," says her mom.

I rub my weary forehead and pick up my duffel bag.

Chapter 54

Where the tarmac lit by human-made light ends, the moonlight begins.

My duffel's wheels tear the silence with their grinding, reminding me how faithful they have been to me. I haven't taken this route to my home in a long time. The vegetation on this side is sparse and dry, unlike the lush green on my usual footpath. As Shanta said, moonlight finds its way through the gaps to take me home—the home I desperately yearned to leave.

The footpath curves right, and my home's roof ridge is visible through the coconut fronds. A streak of happiness lights up in my heart. I know it's just a building, but I hear its frantic call, reaching out to me like a mother cow that has lost its calf. Is this what differentiates a home from a house—the life in the former, the soul breathed in by my grandparents, my parents, and me? She's as lively as when I left her.

Susheela's face appears before me. I don't remember asking her to take care of the house. Would she—

Wrrrrrr.

A rustle beyond the hibiscus-lined hedge derails my thoughts.

I stop and look in that direction. The sound stops, and silence follows. But I sense life, the eerie feeling of being watched from a distance, the intuition of faint heartbeats. Anonymous! I'm surprised the dog is still alive. I wait awhile more, but it is all quiet. Somewhere in the west, a night heron croaks in pursuit of the merrymaking frogs.

I reach the door and flick the switch next to it. The fluorescent tube overhead blinks twice and hums to life. The first winged termite appears out of nowhere, hits the light, and falls on the porch. I open the side zipper of my daypack, retrieve the key, and push it into the keyhole. It squeals as the levers struggle to part ways; Susheela always uses the rear door. I remove the flip-flops and arrange them carefully next to the entrance. I push open the door, swing it shut behind me, and switch on the lights.

Gurusaamy only gave a glimpse of what Susheela has done. Everything looks better than before. I press my right foot on the terra-cotta tiles and drag it. It squeaks—she must have washed it recently. I expected a musty smell, plenty of dust, and a night full of cockroaches. How did Susheela muster the courage to do it? That meek lady who speaks little and only nods at my instructions!

I close my eyes, take a deep breath, and put myself in her shoes. A struggling wife whose husband is battling for his life, housekeeping for a guy who will be back only to collect his lessee fee, one who may not even notice that she has been keeping the house.

I unpack the remains of my voyage. The dancing shoes enter the shoe rack, the jumping spider on the table, clothes on their hangers, laptop on the writing table. I switch on the Wi-Fi router and walk to the backyard. The pail on the well and the aluminum bucket on the floor remain inverted. The wire mesh is neatly tucked around the well. I count five dry leaves trapped on the net. If not for Susheela, the mesh would have given up on the weight of the debris from the jackfruit tree. I open the wire mesh and drop the pail in. The coir rope whirrs as it uncoils, and the pail splashes against the water, the ripples gleaming in the moonlight. I draw the warm water and take a bath.

Getting back into the house, I lock the rear door from the inside and open all the windows. Cool air from the mountains rushes in from the east through the netting and exits through the windows on the west, toward the three seas. I turn on my computer, log in to my publisher's account, and check my earnings report—it remains at eleven dollars and forty-five cents.

I walk to the living room and look at the clock; 11:30 p.m., its pendulum swings. I sink into the couch, stretch my legs over the coffee table, and shut my eyes, rehashing the day's happenings. I'm not tired, even after fourteen hours on the train from Chennai and one hour on the bumpy bus. That's new to me.

I count all the things about Little Lotus Pond I learned today and ask myself if I really had to wander around when I didn't know my own village very well. What did I achieve in the East? All I did was eat, pray, and run.

My cell phone buzzes. I pick it up.

You have one notification, says Instagram.

I click the app icon.

Su the carlady likes your post.

I smile as the picture of a lone lady with an unlit cigar in hand, tracking the rise and fall of stocks, screens in my mind.

Not all was bad. I learned a lot about this world and a lot more about myself. If Bhagwan was here, he would have said that it's not for the world to love you but for you to love it without expectations. I shouldn't expect to be accepted and loved everywhere I go. There are people like Su, and there are people like Chandini. Why blame other countries when I'm called *kallu* in my country? I should invest in counting my blessings.

A-ooooooo!

Anonymous rips into the silence with his howl. It's been a while, but his wail is not something I can forget. I unlatch the door and step out. The howling ceases, and the routine drama plays out. At the corner of the courtyard, where the hibiscus hedge makes way for the footpath, he sits, as usual, with his shiny coat and menacing eyes, gazing at me. I know he's waiting for me to bend down and pick up the imaginary stone so that he can run before it hits him.

I cross my arms across my chest and stand looking at him. He stares at me for a while, drops his head, and stretches forward, confused by the change of routine. We stay still for a while. All we hear is the wind whooshing through the leaves.

He is more stubborn than I thought. I sit down on the steps, and he raises his ears, anticipating the imaginary stone again. When that doesn't happen, he drops his ears and settles into the sphinx position.

I snap my fingers. "Come over," I call. He sits on his butt and yawns twice.

"Come here." I snap my fingers again.

He yawns once more and advances toward me, wagging his tail. I expect him to walk straight to me. Instead, he sidesteps me and darts into the house. I spring to my feet and follow his yelp into the kitchen. There he is, on the kitchen floor, snuffling and whimpering.

He reminds me how much my mom was fond of stray pups. Dad liked dogs, too, but he never permitted them inside the house. They had worked out an understanding—Mom could bring pups in, but once they grew up, they were only allowed in the backyard.

I inch toward Anonymous. He is still sniffing the air around him.

I sit beside him and rub underneath his neck. "Mom's not here, buddy. She left us long back." He smells amazingly fresh for an old street dog. Isakki must have been taking good care of him. He whines for a while more, hangs his head, and walks to the door. I follow him to the front door. He stops in the middle of the courtyard as if he has forgotten something.

Ding, dong . . . The clock strikes twelve.

The wind from the east shakes the coconut fronds and whistles away. When the fronds settle, a faint humming fills the air. Anonymous raises his ears, wags his tail, and woofs. The humming intensifies and transitions into a song. I tease out the words as they rise and fall with the flow of the wind, and I string them together.

> Flowers of the jungle are
> Tiny, dull, and rare
> But
> Know ye not, my dear?
> They know no fear

Woof . . . woof . . . He looks at me, wagging his tail. I step down to the courtyard. He takes a few more steps, stops at the footpath, and turns back to look at me again. I take a few more steps, and he does the same, too, to maintain the lead. I follow him through the moonlit path toward the junction next to the Indian coral tree, where it splits in two.

The words in the air are clearer now.

> Flowers of the garden are
> Flashy, fragrant, and fair
> But
> Yearn ye not, my bairn
> They live at the mercy of man

He stops under the coral tree and looks around for me with his tongue hanging out. When he spots me, he woofs one last time, turns toward the path forking left, and darts away.

I halt. There's no wind, no breeze, no air. Wet red flowers on the leafless coral tree sleep under the lemony moonlight. Somewhere in a puddle, a frog croaks for his mate. Two flying foxes brush past my head, and I bow down instinctively.

I look at the path to my right. I know what lies ahead, should I take it. It will lead me through the main street to the market ground. A right turn will loop me back home. I'll wake up in the morning, bathe in the pond, read my newspapers, eat, nap, write, sleep, and repeat. I look at the path running eastward, into which Anonymous disappeared. I know that beyond the tiny-leaved gooseberry trees lies a cottage by the side of a little pond, where a dark sorceress sings happily with her buffaloes and dogs and birds and spirits. But I know not what awaits me.

I look toward my right one more time and then turn left and walk to the east, where my destiny lies.

My journey has just begun.

Acknowledgements

I owe some masala chai to these extraordinary souls:

To you, the beautiful human in you, who, like everybody else on this planet, is on an everyday struggle to love and be loved. I hope you find the love, happiness, and enlightenment you have been looking for, in you, in your backyard, in your wretched little neighborhood.

My editors at WritersServices and Kirkus Reviews, for shaping Richard Parker into the darling saint he has become.

Estella, for translating my imagination into a beautiful cover and modelling Richard Parker after me. The perils of being a handsome Brown man—sigh!

Matt McAvoy, for the ruthless critique of my drafts. Man, you sting like a hornet, you know?

MY and her friend (without benefit), for the timely help in refining my Singlish, the mellifluous language of *atas* Singaporeans. *Ger*, your friend's Singlish *ah*, so *shiok*!

Wichita, for dialing up the Ting in my Tinglish, and Enrico for curling the "r" in my Filipino English. I wish the signs had also taken Richard Parker to the Hmong people. My wish to acknowledge a Nguyen, Tran, Le, Pham, or Hoang for support with Vietnamese English remains an unfulfilled dream!

Cee, for the lovely kisses on that full-moon night, and *oso* for civilizing my Manglish.

Su . . . Su, I know you are putting out a contract on my head soon. I want to opt for a superhot Latino hitwoman. Can or not?

Love
Merlin Franco

About the author

Merlin Franco is an Indian-born academic with a PhD in Ethnobiology. He currently lives in Borneo with his imaginary girlfriend and a gang of feral monkeys. Merlin's hobbies include staring at the ceiling, stroking his greying beard, and running away from stray dogs.

Printed in Great Britain
by Amazon